Baby Bye

P.S. Divine

In the ghetto, men are only born after death.
　　　　　　　—Dwight Mannschein

CHAPTER 1

IT WAS A DELIGHT TO DIE that way. To be struck by a sudden deathblow—an accusation—freeing her breath from a prison of lies and unchaining her lonely heart from the shackles of uncertainty. Yes, a life without him meant death, but death was the price paid for peace, nonetheless. The torment of being ignored proved to be much worse than the verbal abuse she was currently incurring. Sure, he was wrong. All that he accused her of just then. Dead wrong. Well, at least partly wrong. But his allegations, while fatally wounding the person she'd become, had brought her closer to the reality of who he was. A child. A grown ass child. And he was definitely acting like one at the moment, screaming and cursing.

With only half the truth uncovered, Lola knew it was only a matter of time before her secret would be discovered. She may have lost love, but she was no longer willing to lose herself. And for that reason alone, her heart hadn't stopped battering her ribcage since the battle began. The pain she felt that showery November evening—his words—was nothing in comparison to the suffering she'd endured in silence for the last couple of years—trying to be somebody she wasn't. For him. And now he was willing to give it all up. Give her up. Let his family fall to the wayside. All for a half-truth. All because he couldn't see the whole truth.

His charges of wrongdoing exploded through her thoughts in a seething blast, scorching her sanity with every syllable. She'd grown tired of his tongue-tied tantrum, her remorse ripped apart by that awful sound. Hearing one last scream of his utterly unintelligible fury echoing through their two-bedroom Brooklyn apartment, she finally opened her mouth—dread knotting in her gut—and yelled back, "Shut—the—fuck—up! God! I swear I hate you, Shine! I hate you! I wish you were dead!"

Every word resounded into a shrieking assault on his ears, casting his thoughts into suspension while his emotions ignited a flame of unsettled feelings deep down in his gut. Not trusting himself to respond, he suddenly stiffened, blinking his bloodshot eyes hard to hold back his tears. *Be a man Shine*, he commanded himself. *Don't let her break you! Be a man!*

From their red, full grain leather sofa, Lola watched him—with growing regret—as he paced back and forth in their living room turning over her words in his mind. From the second he walked out their front door last night and left her crying on the couch, she hadn't had one comforting moment. All she could think about was Shine. The way he made her feel when he was mad at her, when he wouldn't touch her, when he would touch her, when he made love to her, when he simply looked at her.

But now all she could see was a pulse of anger beneath his pale brown, amber-like flesh. There were moments when she even thought that she saw horns growing out of his thick soft-curled hair. And yet with all the rage she saw in him, the muscles sloping down to his shoulders reminded her of how pleasant it felt to wrap her arms around his neck and hang in his embrace, limp as a rag doll, her feet dangling an inch off the floor, staring up into his handsome face. He was beastly beautiful, but it was those eyes. *Those eyes*, she thought, *those eyes*. It was those steel green eyes—filled with passion for everything he loved and was willing to fight for—that weakened her; that made her stay and face his wrath.

A strange sense of sympathy betrayed her rage. She despised the way her heart twisted from just looking at him. After five years of being with him, she despised having her heart do anything. But to have it feel, and feel so strongly, so passionately, pleasantly terrified her so much that she sat stock-still and offered him no apology.

"You hate me?" Shine asked, those dilated, green eyes narrowing with sudden contempt. "How the hell can you hate me? After I've taken care of you for all these years. Paid all the bills! All while you were laying up in here with another dude!" His face lit up with a smirk of anger. "How can you hate me? You're the slut of this relationship!

Not me! You're the one that's out there hoeing!"

A vicious scowl contorted her oval dark, cherry-oak face. "Watch your damn mouth!" she hissed as she brushed a storm of inky curls from her forehead, the short strands looking like silk. "You will not disrespect me like that in front of my son!"

"In front of your son? He's our son! And besides, Trayvon is not even awake. He's still in the back sleep—"

"Yes, I said my son, because the last time I checked, he had my last name and not yours," interrupted Lola.

"What are you talking about? I begged you to give him my name, but you wouldn't—"

"If you wanted his last name to be Mannschein, and not Bye, you should've made me your wife! So, until you marry me, do not call me out of my name anywhere near or around *my*—" her eyes shot forth a scorching bolt of rage, "—*son!* I do not disrespect you in front of him. So, do not disrespect me! Period!"

"Yeah right! You don't disrespect me in front of him? Oh, really?" he asked, pent-up frustration etching lines in his forehead. "What? You just go outside of our household and do it in front of others? Or do you not call that disrespect? I mean, c'mon, of all people—you did this with Badrick, knowing all that has gone down between us and them!" Shine shook his head and cast his eyes to the ground.

Suddenly the living room wall vibrated with three loud thuds. The couple went silent, listening to see if more would follow. It came from the apartment next door, and they were quite familiar with the sound. It was Old Lady Wellington banging on their thin apartment wall with a broom, telling them to lower the noise. She did that every time they argued. The couple just stared at each other, knowing better than to complain. She was their landlord.

"You're crazy," Lola whispered. "I told you already. I haven't even spoken to Badrick since I met you. That was years ago. And nothing even happened between us back then."

"But he *was* claiming you."

"We were barely dating. Had I not come to the neighborhood to see him, I would have never met you. And we would have not had Trayvon. So, you need to get over it."

"Oh what, so now I'm supposed to thank that nigga?"

"God! You're so insecure!" she screamed in a whisper. "I'm not messing around. I don't even know why you would believe that."

Fire ran through him, spiraling at her words. His muscles knotted, and his teeth clenched. "You don't know why I would believe that? Um, let's see. Maybe because yesterday when I came home there was a goddamn half-torn condom wrapper under the covers. On my side of the bed!"

Lola swallowed hard and thirstily, as if she couldn't get enough saliva, and her eyes fluttered with equal abandon. Guilt surged through her, yet his past actions and each disrespectful word he uttered justified her in what she had done. Her thoughts ran from her, carrying her back to every insult she had endured. Her vivid mind pictured all the times she'd been left at home alone to care for their child while he ran the streets doing God knows what to God knows who. She was filled, full, with all the memories of him returning to the apartment after spending nights away and not saying a word to her. All the while wondering what she'd done wrong to warrant his neglect. She could only imagine why he avoided her each night.

At least, on this Thursday evening he spoke to her, saying more to her than he had done for the years past, accusing her of cheating, calling her out of her name, telling her how disgusted he was with her, threatening to take their son and leave her. But she wouldn't let it go on any longer. No. The complaining and the blaming would not continue. There would be an end to it now.

"Look, I have told you a hundred times already, and I am going to say it again for the last time. I do not know where that came from. It's not mines."

"Well, it ain't mine!" he screamed.

"Shine, you're making a mistake. I don't know why you would think I would waste my time dealing with Badrick." She lowered her eyes. "I wouldn't do that. I wouldn't mess with someone you were beefing with."

His eyebrows arched. "What? So, you would sleep with someone I was friends with?"

"C'mon Shine, grow up," she huffed.

"First of all, I know it was Badrick because someone I trust told me they saw him walking up out of our building yesterday, right before I got home. And the only other person that lives in this building other than us is Ms. Wellington. So, what?" He puckered his lips in disbelief.

"You're telling me a drug dealer was here to see our eighty-year old landlord?"

"I don't know who he was here to see. I don't know if he was even here at all. I mean, when did this so-called person decide to tell you that they saw Badrick? Before or after you stormed out of the apartment last night?"

"Obviously after. Or I would've stepped to you about him then instead of bouncing." A frown appeared on his face as he paused and inhaled deeply. "After I found that condom, I left because I was about to flip out on and do something stupid."

"And you don't think you're doing something stupid now by running out of here and stepping to Badrick over this?" Lola's neck swayed with the force of emotion which she sought to hold back.

"Oh," his chest rose, "I'm going to do more than just step to him."

"Yeah, like what?" She rolled her eyes. "You're going to go and risk your life over a misunderstanding?"

"He's risking his life! Not me!"

"Don't be stupid. You know who his uncle is. You'd be risking our lives also. We can't afford any problems with Chinnah."

At the mention of Chinnah, the room became deathly still. The quiet noise of the night crept in through their closed second floor window; the barking dogs, the tires screeching through the driving rain, the sewer beneath the street gurgling with polluted water. Shine felt the muscles twitch in his face, concern pulling at his mouth. A vein throbbed along his temple, his fists clenched, his jaws tight and his teeth chattering. He fought for words to say, but his thoughts were fragmented by fear.

Before his eyes could give away his uneasiness, his lips crept open and he spoke with a menacing intensity but not volume. "Man, ain't no one scared of Chinnah! Or his Gully Gods. I'm Damu!"

Lola sighed and rolled her eyes. "And so is Malik—I mean Gorilla Leek. And he is an actual murderer. And even he knows better than to mess with Chinnah. Even after what Chinnah did to his family, he still knows his lane." She paused to let out another sigh. "I mean Shine, you might have a bunch of little teenagers scared of you because of that little time you did on Rikers—but you are not a killer like Chinnah."

Gritting his teeth because he knew she was right; his eyes fell to the thick pile of beige carpet beneath his red and black Jordans. He noticed the wool was worn, showing the string over the space that led from the couch to the front door. He bit off a curse beneath his breath, realizing that nothing remained intact forever. There was a time when his woman believed him to be the toughest man that she'd ever known. But then she grew to love him.

An almost somber look washed over his face as he fixed his eyes on her again, their green depths no longer icy, but fiery. "You don't know what I am! Or what I could be when it comes to this family! I would hurt Chinnah in a one on one."

"In a one on one?" Lola burst out laughing with such lightheartedness that it enraged him. "What the hell do you think this is? I am not even from New York and I know better than to think like that," she said.

"What? You don't think I would damage that skinny-ass coconut? Look at him compared to me."

He raised his eyebrow and pulled up his red V-neck t-shirt, showing off the taut muscles in his abdomen and chest. He hadn't been with her all those years without knowing exactly what his body did to her. He watched as her tongue momentarily flickered out to wet her lips. The shapely beauty of his biceps bound beneath the cotton fabric of his shirt shot a thunderbolt of warmth between her thighs. She crossed her legs, her scarlet nightgown riding up her thick thighs showing off her polished red toe nails and the deep crease in her crotch.

"Seriously Shine?" Her voice became breathy and husky, but she didn't look as inviting as she sounded. "All you have is muscles and pride. He has money and power. Messing with him could put our whole family in danger. He would kill us all. You. Me. And Trayvon."

"Well, you should've thought about that before you went and jumped in bed with his nephew!"

"Look, I'm not going back and forth over this. I didn't—"

"Mommy, daddy" A child's voice came from their son's bedroom—a little boy's voice sounding through quiet words. There was no mistaking the innocent charm of that tone. "You guys fight?"

Lola and Shine turned toward the bedroom door with surprised looks on their faces to see their three-year-old son, Trayvon standing in the open doorway. His little brown face was puffy and sweaty, his eyes half closed. He blinked, coughed, and then wiped his mouth.

"Why you guys yelling? You don't like each other no more?" asked the little boy who'd just awoken from one nightmare to face another.

"No, baby boy. Mommy and daddy—uh—we're not fighting," Lola answered, as she shot Shine a cursing glance that was more of a motherly command to speak up.

He immediately took notice and knew he would have to lay his grievances aside. "Yeah little man. We were just talking about you. That's all."

Trayvon's eyes went wide with worry. "Why? You mad at me?"

"Huh? No. Why would you say that?" asked Shine.

"Cause mommy said not to put toys in couch for clean time."

The little boy ran into the living and over to the couch where his mother was sitting. He tossed one of the cushions off and ran a careful, tiny hand along the edge. His forehead creased in concentration as he combed the furniture with his fingers, searching for something.

Shine stood perfectly silent, watching, thinking how to make things right between them for the sake of their son. Although he and Lola were perfectly different in their own flawed ways, they both had one thing in common—genuine love for their son. Shine had not encountered many positive male role models in his life, so he wanted Trayvon to see with his own eyes what a father truly was. He had never claimed to be a great dad but tried to be better than the dad he never had. Through good times and bad, he would be in his son's life. And in his mind, that made him a super dad.

If history was anything to judge by, Shine knew he would have to always be there to protect his boy from the inevitable suffering of growing up in the Nineties section of Brooklyn, New York. With deception, danger, and death lurking around every corner in that narcotic mecca of sweat-shop store fronts, he would have to prey on the predators to keep his young safe. He didn't care about anyone else, not really. As though mastering some strong emotion, he stared deeply at his son for a moment.

Trayvon began glancing about the couch with a sort of innocently searching look. Then the boy smiled. "I got it!" he shouted.

At last, his hand came out of the couch holding a small, black plastic cap gun. "I put it in toy box now mommy. So, you guys don't be mad anymore. K?"

"It's ok, Trayvon. You can leave it in the couch for now," Lola insisted with a yawn, not bothering to conceal her weariness. "Mommy wasn't mad at you. Mommy was mad at daddy for acting like an asshole."

Shine's lip curled in disgust. "Weren't you just beefing about me disrespecting you in front of our son? But now you want to say some dumb shit like that," he hissed through his teeth as he snatched his beige fatigue jacket from the red Badcock loveseat adjacent to the couch.

He turned over the cushion of the recliner and picked up a Ruger P-89 9mm semi-automatic pistol then stomped toward the front door of the apartment.

"Daddy, where you go?" asked a wide-eyed Trayvon.

"Daddy just need to get out of here for a sec. To take care of someone trying to hurt our family," answered Shine, stopping just short of the door to shove the gun into his pants. He threw his arms into his jacket, looked over his shoulder, and said, "All I do I do for you. Love you lil' man."

There was an army marching in Lola's eyes. "So, what? You're going to just run out of here like you did last night when you didn't like what was being said? Huh? We are not finished discussing this."

Shine quickly turned his head toward her with a baffled look. "I am not leaving because of what was said. I'm leaving because of what was done."

At the mention of leaving, Lola leaned back into the couch a little bit. She didn't like that word. *Leaving.* The idea of another man abandoning her brought her breath in short gasps. In a panic, her emotions jumped ahead of her common sense, taking his words to mean he was saying his final goodbye. She watched him as he palmed the doorknob, his movements quick and certain. A flash of guilt ricocheted through her skull and she wasn't sure if she wanted to shove him out the door or drag him back to the couch.

She considered saying sorry, but not because she was sorry. If an apology would stop him from running out into the streets and committing suicide—by approaching Badrick and bringing down the wrath of Chinnah upon their family—then she would offer him one.

She jumped to her feet just as he opened the door and walked out. "Shine!" she screamed out. "Please don't go and do something stupid. I'm sorry. Let's talk about this. Please don't leave!"

Lola ran after him, jerking the door open before it closed and stepping out into the hallway of the apartment building, calling his government name, "Dwight Mann——"

She snapped her lips shut, biting the bottom one from the inside when she saw two teenagers standing at the far end of the hall rolling dice. The older of the two was wearing camouflage fatigue pants and a red hoodie underneath a red ski-vest. The teens stopped keenly as Shine neared them, staring. The oldest kid who was holding the dice held out his free hand, but Shine ignored it.

The other boy spoke up. "What up, Shine?"

"What up, Lil' John John?" Shine replied, stopping to give the younger of the two a fist bump.

"I guess you're upset with my grandmother for selling the building and all," stated John John.

"What?" Shine had no idea of what the teen was talking about.

"All the yelling you and your girlfriend were just doing," John John pointed out. "You were arguing about the rent going up, right?"

"No," answered Shine.

"No?"

"No."

"Oh."

Shine's eyebrow went up. "Did you just say that your grandmother was raising the rent on us?"

"Yeah, well, not her. She's selling the building and we're moving to a house on Long Island. The new owners are the ones talking about raising the rent. Grandma wasn't with that and wouldn't sell to them at first." The boy shrugged his shoulders. "But then she started worrying about me getting into too much trouble around here. So, she called them up last week and said she would do it. She said she was going to tell you."

"Word? Shit."

"Yeah, I really don't want to move, because all of my friends are here. But, I am happy that I can finally live on the bottom floor now without worrying about stray bullets coming through our window or walls. You know?" John John gave a nervous grin. "That's the only reason she has us living up here on the second floor next to you now. To keep me safe—she says—from violent accidents."

"Well, that's good. You need to stay safe. And you need to stay away from violence," Shine eyed John John's friend with hostility. "You're too smart to be hanging around negativity."

"Yeah, I guess. I just—"

"Ask him," the friend interrupted, nudging John John with his elbow. "Ask him now, man. Forget all that other talk. You said you would ask him when you saw him."

Shine stared at the two teens with scornful curiosity. "Ask me what?"

"Na, you ask him, Ant," John John suggested to his friend Anthony. .

Ant didn't hesitate. "We were wondering if you could Blood us in, so we could work for you. So, we can start making some doe like you."

Shine snickered. "Bring you home? To be Blood for doe? Ha! Get the fuck out of here!" He shifted his eyes and glowered at John John. "Didn't you just say your grandmoms was selling off this building to get you away from the bullshit around here? You're about to be up in Long Island with straight bank. What do you need to hustle for?"

Anthony answered for his friend, "Yo, Blood, we trying to get Baby Love just like you. I'm saying, I'm only seventeen but I got a seed and a wifey to take care of just like you."

"Little nigga watch your mouth!" snarled Shine. "Flamin' and speaking in codes don't make you no Blood. False flaggin' will have niggas eating your food real quick out here. You feel me?"

Anthony frowned then said, "I'm saying Shine. We bout that life too. Ask John John, I be—"

"John John ain't about nothing! So, I ain't asking him nothing!" Shine spewed out spit with each word. "I've known him since he was a baby. He ain't ready for no real banging. Ms. Wellington ain't having that."

"Trust, fam," Anthony said with a menacing grin. "We can hold our own. I'm saying, I stays with the platinum on me!"

The thug raised his hooded sweatshirt, revealing a Desert Eagle .44 Magnum tucked into his fatigues.

Ice blasted from Shine's pupils. He turned to John John and asked, "How old are you?"

"Fourteen," John John answered, his eyes darting to the floor.

"Feel me, son—don't follow behind this kid if you want to make it to twenty-one. Cause if you stay running with this dude, you'll soon be dead or in jail with him."

"Man, please. I ain't no kid," Anthony hissed heavily. "You think I'm scared to do a bid or taste dirt? Let a nigga test my gangsta! Anybody can get it. Even you."

"Little dude, I'm eight years older than you, so I'm going to take that as a joke. Plus, I got more important business to take care of right now. Grown man business." Shine laughed. It was a bitter and hostile laugh. "Besides, with the rate you're going, someone's going to test your gangsta one day for sure. And you'll get what you're asking for."

The teen crossed his arms and stood defiant with chin in the air, red eyes ablaze, facing Shine. "And what? You don't think someone's gonna test your gangsta soon too? You ain't invincible, you know. You or anyone who rocks out with you can get a hot one," Ant's eyes fell on Lola who was still watching from the doorway of their apartment, "at any time."

"Chill Ant," pleaded John John as he jumped in front of his friend and placed one hand on his chest. He turned to Shine. "Yo, he's bugging. We respect you and yours. You know? We just wanna roll like you, that's all."

The look of contempt that Shine cast upon the seventeen-year old was not lost on the boys. "Yeah well, rolling with a friend like him, ain't rolling like me," he said as he smirked and slowly walked toward the staircase.

John John glanced at Lola as if to apologize. But his gaze went unnoticed. Her eyes remained on her man until he disappeared down the stairs, wanting to chase after him and beg him to come back. She knew he was about to go and do something foolish that would change their lives forever. But as always, she had to stay home and tend to their son. So, she slipped her head back inside, closed the door, and prayed for his safe return.

CHAPTER 2

"BLOOD SHE'S A SNAKE!"

"Dog calm down. We don't need that right now."

"I can't believe she's dealing with that dude!"

"It happens dog. Let's focus."

"That's easy for you to say, Leek" Shine said, almost yelling at his best friend, as he sat behind the steering wheel of his black Ford Expedition. "Dina's faithful to you and the kids. Meanwhile, my shorty just said, forget our whole family."

"Blood, you can't say that. Lo does a lot for you and Trayvon. She's the one who's always home with him, waiting on you and holding it down. Besides you don't know for sure if she was sleeping with him."

"What?" Shine shot his friend a stern glance. "Whose side are you on, son?" He looked outside the tinted windows into the pitch-black night of the dead street, then stared at his hand, willing it to let go of the pistol he held so he could turn around and go home. His eyes fell on his partner who sat in the passenger seat checking the load in his .44 Remington Magnum magazine.

Gorilla Leek, bald and clad in dark skin and even darker tattoos on his face, slapped the magazine back in the pistol grip of his gun, then glanced at his friend and said, "Look dog, if I knew it was going to affect you like this, I would've never told you about seeing that cat coming out your crib. But you're my brother, so it's no doubt that you had to know. And as you can see, I'm obviously on your side or I wouldn't be here right now getting ready to do this."

Shine's head fell back on the leather car seat. He could feel his emotions thudding painfully beneath his chest as he replayed the plan his best friend had quickly laid out after learning Lola had been unfaithful.

"Yeah son, but I don't know if this is even the right way to handle this," Shine said, almost apologetically. "I mean, I could step to this dude on my own and shoot him the fair. We ain't got to do this. This could cause a war."

"Dog, this here—what he did to you—is war. Ya heard? You think that yardie cat just ran back up on Lola after all of these years of ignoring her. Na, he did that to get at us. Ya heard? Both of us!" Gorilla Leek was excited, and he was clearly not in the mood to argue his point.

"Yeah, but—"

"But nothing! How long has Chinnah been trying to get us to sale Minimart? Huh?"

"For a while now."

"Facts! First, he tries to get us to cut him in on what we were moving, talking about this is his neighborhood. We say no, and he don't say a damn thing to us for mad years. Left us alone and everything." Gorilla Leek rubbed his chin. "Then all of a sudden, out of the blue, he sends his son to offer us straight cash for our store. They want to buy our property? Really? Dog, Chinnah's plotting on something. And his nephew laying up with your baby mama is all a part of his scheme. Ya heard?"

"I know. I know. But what we're about to do will take it to the next level."

"What level do you want to take it to? Look, I hate to say it, but bitches come, and bitches go. That's why we don't put no trust in them. Most chics will sleep with your homeboy in a heartbeat, let alone your enemy. That's on my word!" declared Gorilla Leek. "So, you can't sit around trying to cuff these hoes. I've been telling you that since we were in high school. And you can't let it hurt you. But if you want to hurt Badrick back, you don't take his woman or his manhood by beating his ass. You take his doe!"

"Yeah, I understand that, but . . ." Shine said, reluctance edging his voice, "it's Chinnah's money, not Badrick's."

"Yeah, but out of all Chinnah's stash spots, he put Badrick in charge of this one." He motioned with his head at the house they were parked across the street from. "So, running up in there will have Chinnah at his nephew's neck. It'll be a come-up for us, and you won't have to even put a finger on that dude. You and I both know what Chinnah will do to him once he finds out he lost all of that coke? Family or no family."

"I'm more worried about what he will do to us, once he finds out that we were the ones who robbed him."

"He won't. That's why we brought those masks. And that's why I'm rocking all black fatigues and I ain't flamin' tonight."

"And you're sure they have ten bricks up in there?"

"Facts. They had a shipment come in today. Ten bricks. And they're bagging it up tonight."

"And you know this how?" quizzed Shine.

"I got word from White Mike."

Shine's head jerked back, and his eyebrows rose in surprise. "The Latin King O.G. who owns the store on Pitkin?"

"Yeah."

"But don't he work for Chinnah?"

"Na. He doesn't work for Chinnah. He works with Chinnah. He cops his coke from the old man."

"And you trust him?"

"I do. Because he told me that Chinnah not only sells to him, but he be taking a big cut of what he makes every month. And he's tired of it. He's getting ready to sell his store and get out of the game." Gorilla Leek grinned wickedly. "So, kicking in the door to this crib won't affect him at all. All we have to do is hit him off with a brick for giving us the inside scoop."

"Really? So, what's the inside scoop? What are we looking at when we run up in there? Is Badrick going to be in there?" The questions came out of Shine's mouth in a flurry.

"Yeah, he will. He'll be bagging it up—you know—getting it ready to be dropped off at different spots. And it will only be one other person up in there with him."

"We're only looking at two people?"

"Exactly dog. We're gonna go up in there, lay them down on their faces, snatch the work up then be out in less than five minutes."

"What if them cats don't want to lay down and decide to go out guns blazing?"

Gorilla Leek could see worry filling his friend's eyes. In the past, he'd always made Shine aware of his murderous forays against their enemies, but he would never ask him to participate. He knew his best friend was willing to rep Blood, but was not prepared to shed blood. And although Shine had been convicted in the past on charges of assault with a deadly weapon, he had never committed a murder.

"Dog, if them dudes try to put up a fight, we'll give them what they ask for. Ya heard? This is our time to come up, and this is how we're gonna do it!" demanded Gorilla Leek. "Trust me, Chinnah, won't be around for too much longer, anyway. He's an old man and his time is limited. Ain't nothing to be scared about."

Gorilla Leek intentionally aimed his words at the bullseye of his friend's ego, watching as they pierced through the jittery mists in which his thoughts were wandering. As he saw Shine's eyes zero in on the stash house, he could tell the cogs were moving in his partner's head and he knew he had said the right thing.

"Scared?" Shine whispered. "Son, I ain't scared. I just want to make sure we do this right."

"Then let's do it right! But sitting here in this car talking about it ain't gonna get it done at all. We need to make a move now while there's only two of them in there. Ya heard? We all in together, right?"

Shine swallowed down his nerves, trying to hide his edginess, then unlocked the doors and said, "Yeah."

Both men burst out of the vehicle, slamming the doors behind them, and made their way across a wet 91st Street. Before stepping onto the curb, Shine looked around the block then—seeing no movement— he pulled back the slide of his pistol, putting a round in the chamber. Forcing his heart-rate to steady and his breath to calm, he continued toward the house. The two men tiptoed up the porch steps, the tattered stair treads slightly creaking beneath their weight. Stopping in front of the door, they both reached into their coat pockets, pulled out ski masks, and slid them over their face.

Gorilla Leek crept over to the large front window. The curtains were drawn, but he could see the dark shadow of a man moving about. He pressed close to the glass, trying to peer through the tiny chink at the curtains' center. A light from a television set flickered off the walls, bathing the entire room in a shaded glow. But other than the one obscure figure, he didn't see any activity.

Shine moved carefully along the porch to check the side of the house. As he walked, the pace of his breath quickened with the anticipation of what might happen. He glanced over the side of the porch. His eyes slowly scanned the driveway as they had once scanned the block for the police when he was into petty corner-hustling. But there was no movement. No signs of life. It appeared that the neighborhood was deserted. With his hand tightly gripping his pistol, he turned around just in time to see Gorilla Leek unlocking the door with a key.

"What the hell, son," he whispered. "Is that a key?"

"Yeah," Gorilla Leek whispered back.

"Where'd you get that from?"

"We can talk about that later. Let's hurry up and get this over with." Gorilla Leek reached out his hand and grasped the doorknob.

"Wait!" Shine shouted in another whisper. "How many people did you see in there?"

"Two."

"Two? You sure?"

"Yeah."

"You see Badrick?"

"Yeah," answered Gorilla Leek, his growing agitation evident in his tone. "Now let's do this."

He turned the knob swiftly and, with one foot, kicked the door open, rushing into the living room. He caught a glance of denim-clad legs and booted feet running toward the back of the house. Gorilla Leek aimed at the fleeing man and let off several savage shots—he had ammo to burn and he couldn't risk letting the man make it to a weapon. The bullets tore into his target's lower legs, ripping flesh and shattering bone. The man's pants oozed red as he fell forward onto his face, clutching his leg and writhing in pain.

Fearful of being left alone outside, Shine quickly followed his partner into the house, stopping at the staircase facing the front entrance. He watched as Gorilla Leek held his weapon at the ready and slowly walked toward the wounded man on the ground.

"What the hell man!" Shine yelled. "We were supposed to be in and out. No shooting."

Gorilla Leek glanced over his shoulder. "He was running for his gun."

Shine let out a sigh. "Well, did you at least get both of them?"

"Na. I think Badrick ran upstairs. Go check. I'll keep my eye on our little belly dancer here," Gorilla Leek said as he cut the T.V. off.

Shine gaped at the staircase, studying it. He grasped the wooden post and rested his foot on the first step. He gave his friend a wry look then carefully trotted up the stairs. Pausing on the last step, he inhaled a shaky breath, then swung right into the narrow hallway to face a partially open door. For a spilt second, he considered turning around and leaving. He could run out the house and wait in the car for his partner. Then his stubborn streak kicked in. Gorilla Leek was his best friend and Blood brother. He couldn't leave him. That would make him a punk. Besides, Badrick had to pay for what he'd done, and that was the reason he was there in the first place.

Shine pushed the door open, listened for movement then leaned to look inside. The cramped dark room was filled with shipping boxes to either side of the door, mostly unmarked. He entered with a hushed and cautious footstep, passing over the carpet and moving in the direction where he thought the bed to be. Still listening with every sense on soundless alert, he reached into his pocket and pulled out his phone. The small light, bright and clear, was sufficient enough to enable him to see that the room was empty. Then he heard a sudden noise in the hallway—maybe downstairs—a heavy thump, and then a clatter. Then two gunshots.

Startled, Shine dropped his phone, and it clanged against the metal bed rail before being muffled by the carpet. He froze, listening intently for more sounds of danger. There was silence for a second, then a shuffling noise, as if someone was trying to find their way around the bottom floor. The tapping continued, like bone clacking against the wooden walkway, but then it was accompanied by a clicking sound, then a terrible thumping. Terror-stricken, he turned around and went still.

"Yo, Leek!" he called out.

There was no answer.

"Blood are—are you good?"

He waited a few moments, but there was still no answer. Something must be wrong.

He stepped out of the room as quickly as his body would allow him to. He looked to the left then to the right. Nothing. No one. His only exit out of the house, the staircase, ended a couple of feet from the front door. All he had to do was run. Instead, he crept along the dimly lit hall then kneeled down and peered through the banister. Only half of the door was visible from that position, so he stood up and staggered down the staircase. The T-shirt beneath his fatigue jacket clung to his back, damp with sweat as he stopped on the bottom step, looking around. Gorilla Leek was nowhere in sight.

I hope this nigga didn't leave me, he thought to himself. But Shine knew better than that. Gorilla Leek had always been there to back him up during beef. He had been Shine's best friend since the first day he moved to the Nineties to live with his grandmother. And when both his grandmother and mother had passed, Gorilla Leek became the only family he had left until Trayvon was born. So, he knew his friend wouldn't leave him, and he couldn't leave his friend. They had come there together, and they would leave together.

Shine turned to the left and walked through the living room into the kitchen area, his eyes searching for his partner. He saw something that startled him. There lay a man before him sprawled out on the linoleum floor, face down, arms spread like Christ on the cross. Beneath his skull, blood stained the ground like a devil-red, hellish halo. He wasn't the person Gorilla Leek shot when they first entered the house. This guy was wearing sandals.

Glancing about, Shine noticed a door that led to the basement. It was ajar. Unsure of what to expect, he slowly proceeded toward it. In his mind, sudden death was everywhere waiting, a teasing gloom that hid out of sight until the right moment. And right at that moment—just when that thought came to mind—he caught a glimpse out of the corner of his eye of a shadow charging across the kitchen toward him. The figure stiff-armed him from the side, slamming into him, and knocking him off balance for a second. They both fell into the wall. Shine gasped from the pain of the impact. With his consciousness flickering and his hand still gripping the pistol, he instinctively squeezed the trigger, getting off a single round. The shadowy figure fell backwards against the refrigerator and slid to the ground.

The sound of the gunshot rang in Shine's ears as he slowly looked around the room, dazed and expecting another ambush. Seeing no one, he shut his eyes tightly for a moment before blinking them rapidly against the sight of the body on the floor. It was Badrick.

With long dreadlocks draping down over his greyish-brown face, and blood-soaked legs stretched out in front of him, the Jamaican looked like a ghoulish man-sized rag doll. His eyes were open, but he made no sound. He just sat there, his hand looking like a candy-apple clutching his crimson-soaked abdomen. Shine carefully approached him and prodded the man with his foot, evoking a faint groan in response. Every nerve in his body screamed for him to run out the house, but Shine remained motionless, the hand gripping the gun shaking uncontrollably. He took another step forward, raising his pistol over the puzzled and moaning man.

Staring down at Badrick and with his voice cracking, he said, "Look at me, yo. This is what happens when you mess with what's mine!"

Lifting his head, Badrick drew a deep breath that came up from his boots, and stared up into Shine's scared, nervous eyes. He held his shooter's gaze for agonizing seconds then, lowering his eyes, his throat constricted as he uttered, "Mi kno yuh. Mi kno yuh voice. Mi kno yuh eyes."

Shine's gaze fell to his feet in fear. He took a step back.

Badrick's face winced, probably from pain, then he let out a purring chuckle. "Fos, yuh tek di uhman mi did trying to deal wid. Now yuh here to tek mi life?"

"Shut up!" Shine nervously yelled, his face a portrait of unhappiness and tears beneath the ski mask. "You ruined my family!"

"Wah yuh chat bout?"

"You've been sleeping with my wifey, yo!"

A look of surprised washed across Badrick's face. "Ave yuh gaan mad? Mi nuh care bout shi. Mi ave nuff girls who look twice as gud as shi! Mi neva fuck yuh girlfriend, bowy. But now—now—mi might just haffi tek di pussy from shi, afta wah happen here. Seen?"

Shine glanced to the ground once again. But this time in anger. Then something caught his attention. He noticed that Badrick's jeans were in tatters. There was blood, a sticky, scarlet stream flowing beneath his calves down to his boots. The injured man had suffered gunshot wounds to both of his legs, but Shine had only squeezed his trigger once. Then it suddenly came to him that Badrick was the person who his best friend was shooting at when they first entered the house. The wounded Jamaican's stomach had been torn apart by the bullet from Shine's 9mm. But his bloodied legs—that was the work of Gorilla

Leek's .44 Magnum.

Suddenly, the basement door flew open and crashed against the wall with a loud *clack-thunk* of the doorknob driving into the plaster. Shine jumped at the noise then spun around to see his friend standing in the doorway, a black trash bag slung over his shoulder.

"Was that you who let that shot off, dog?" Gorilla Leek asked as he approached, nodding his head at Badrick. "Oh snap. That dude is still alive?"

"You sent me upstairs looking for him because you said you didn't get him." There was worry in Shine's eyes but a scowl on his lips.

"I didn't know it was him at first until the other dread came running out and I had to blast him also. Shoot, I thought Badrick was dead because he had stopped moving and was just lying there—slick as nigga. So, I grabbed a trash-bag from off the table, headed down into the basement, and loaded it up with the work."

Shine's eyebrows knotted, and he rounded his mouth as he asked, "You got the bricks?"

"Yep."

"All ten?"

"Na."

"No?"

"Na, there were only six wrapped up. Did you see anything upstairs?"

"There were some boxes in the room I was in. But that was it."

"Did you check inside of them?"

"No. I came back down here after I heard the shots go off."

"The rest must be up in there then. I'll go and double check. You need to finish ole boy off while I do that."

"Finish him off?" Shine's tone echoed the flash of fear in his eyes. "Let's just be out. Cops will be here soon. And what you got in that bag is enough for us to be good."

"Na dog, we came here to get at this dude for what he did to you. The cat is already halfway dead. You need to finish him before the cops come and question him."

"But we didn't come here to kill him."

"Yeah, well it's too late now. Dog, you can't live this lifestyle and never get blood on your hands."

"Yeah, Shine," Badrick giggled a little then quickly screwed up his face in pain. "Yuh cyaa be fraid foreva."

Shock turned Gorilla Leek's face toward the dying dread. "You know his name?"

Badrick grunted out a laugh. "Yeah, mi kno fi him name. Mi kno fi him gyal. Mi kno fi him pickney. An mi kno fi him address." He snickered and wheezed at the same time, his chest constricting as if his soul was being sucked in by a black hole of eternal pain.

"What the hell, dog?" Gorilla Leek turned his attention to Shine. "You told him your name?"

"No, he just knew somehow."

"Really? He just somehow knew?" Gorilla Leek walked closer to Badrick then kicked his damaged legs. The dread let out a grunt of pain. "What else you know, Rasta?" he asked.

With a grimace of discomfort and wild eyes, the Jamaican uttered, "Guh suck yuh granny!"

Gorilla Leek smiled a terrible mirthless grin, then turned to Shine. "You know what? This is your food, dog. You need to handle it now!"

Shine looked past his partner at Badrick, and said, "Son, I can't."

"What are talking about? You can't? You better! This dude just threatened your family. If anything, you gotta do this to protect your son."

Gorilla Leek's words echoed around in Shine's head. Badrick knew who he was, and if the Jamaican lived to tell Chinnah who robbed him, the Gully Gods might come after his family. And he couldn't let that happen. On the other hand, if Chinnah found out that he had something to do with the murder of his nephew, he would definitely come after his family. He quickly weighed his options though the correct choice was clear. If he didn't pull the trigger now, he might not get a second chance. And he figured he stood a much better chance of protecting his family with Badrick out of the picture. Not to mention, this was the man who slept with his woman.

Then, without warning, the confusion in his mind grew into a wide-eyed, blinding torment. At that moment, the insecure, little boy deep inside began to imagine Lola in bed with the Jamaican on top of her. He could hear her moans. He could see her face tighten as she began to orgasm. He thought about her calling out his name—*Baaadrrrick.* Shine tried, but he couldn't separate her betrayal from the terror of the moment. The anger in him was unlike anything he'd experienced since the emotional outbreaks of his childhood. A tornado of hate and love spun his thoughts around in his skull, shredding his compassion into pieces and ripping apart his rationality. Jealousy and the uncertainty of love made the rage in him spill over. And then, with a sudden movement, Shine leveled his gun at Badrick, and fired without thinking.

It was a blur of movement, but enough to make Gorilla Leek duck out of the way as his friend fired several rounds into the dread's body. The bullets tore into Badrick's head, chest, and hands, bursting out in a grisly shred of bloody bone and burned flesh, taking off fingers, and leaving behind a mangled heap. Shine kept squeezing the trigger until he exhausted the magazine, slicing the Jamaican's skin and clothes into red ribbons of blood. The last shot he fired had dumped the corpse hard on the floor, sending it off to sleep on the wet and warm, dark rose blossoming beneath it.

Shine stared at the dead body, fearfully fascinated. He had only gone through with it because he was afraid of ending up like Badrick. He had no desire to be a killer. Not for anything in this world, and he wished he could take it back. But the consequences he now faced would never let him take it back. And he would one day have to pay for the life he took. He wanted to go home to Lola and fold himself into her arms, and never leave her again. He wanted to feel forgiven and loved. Because at that instance, he felt nothing. He had no feeling from the neck down. His nerves had gone numb. Then, suddenly, he felt something. He felt Gorilla Leek's hand tugging at his arm.

"Blood, we gotta be out, now!" Gorilla Leek screamed.

"What did I just do?" asked a stunned Shine.

"It doesn't matter. Do you hear that?"

Sirens sounded in the distance, growing louder, and drawing near. In shock, Shine looked at Gorilla Leek, seeming to snap out of his trance. "I'm going to have to pay for this."

"Yeah, maybe one day you will. But not tonight. Let's bounce!" Gorilla Leek commanded as he pulled his friend out of the house. "Give me your keys. You ain't in the right state of mind to be driving right now. Especially with all of this work we gonna have up in the car."

Shine went into his pocket as they jogged down the steps and came back out with the key to the Ford. Gorilla Leek snatched it from his grip and shoved him into the passenger side of the car. He quickly jumped into the driver's seat, and sped off down the desolate street, the dimly lit neighborhood slipping to the rear of them.

Shine sat silent for the entire ride home. There was almost no sound, except for the steady purr of the engine and the low swooshing noise of the tires breaking the rainfall. The flush of images inside his mind made him shudder. Like a bad horror movie, he replayed the awful event over and over again—especially that moment before he pulled the trigger when Badrick had said his name.

Why did you say my name? he thought as he struggled to drive the memories out of his brain each time they returned to haunt him. *Why did you say my name?*

Along the way, and in between his memories of the murder, Shine thought about the felonious quantity of drugs they had in the vehicle. It appeared they were driving around aimlessly, and he was concerned about getting stopped by the police. He considered asking Gorilla Leek where they were headed, until they pulled in front of his building and he had his answer.

Gorilla Leek put the car in park then faced his friend. "Dog, I was afraid we were gonna get pulled over. How the hell you drive around like this? I had to fight to keep the car steady the whole time. It kept tugging to the side."

"I've been meaning to get a wheel alignment," replied Shine, his voice lacking emotion.

Gorilla Leek could see the battle in his friend's eyes. "Look Blood, I know your mind's still going through it because of what you just did. It was like that for me the first time also." He swallowed hard against the lump large in his throat before continuing. "So, until you get yourself together, I'm gonna hold on to the bricks at my place. You know, just until we find a spot to stash it. I'll drop your whip off at Minimart in the morning, since you have to be there to open up. You have enough going on right now. So, I got this. Cool?"

Shine hesitantly tore his eyes away from the windshield and turned his head to look at his best friend. "You think we're going to go to jail for this?"

"Huh?" Gorilla Leek furrowed his brow, stroking his carefully trimmed goatee. "Na. Blood, I read somewhere that like only one out of every ten murderers gets caught. So, we good."

Shine's upper lip curled in a snarl of disbelief, "Yeah, right. I'm sure the number has to be much higher than that, with all the niggas we know who got bagged for a hommie."

"Na, dog. I'm telling you it's true. Look at me. Have I ever been locked for returning a cat?"

"Na. As far as I know, you've only done time for drugs and dumb shit like stabbing Cutty for calling you by your government."

"Right. And I've returned how many crabs?"

"A lot."

"Exactly. They don't go after murderers as much as they go after dealers. They follow the money, not the blood." Gorilla Leek gave him a flat look then said soberly, "And as far as Cutty calling me by my government, I got caught because it was a heat of the moment type thang. I warned that Yardie about that. The only person who could call me Malik was my mother and she's not around anymore."

When Gorilla Leek's face went grim, Shine was sorry he mentioned the Cutty incident. Although his childhood friend's given name was Malik Moore, everyone outside of his parents called him Gorilla Leek—except for Dina, the woman he loved. And Shine was the only person allowed to make that mistake in some instances, because he'd known him for such a long time.

They had met just before Gorilla Leek's parents were murdered so horribly—being locked in a building full of suffocating smoke and burning to death. The sole arsonist of that night's tragedy was Chinnah. And Gorilla Leek had never forgotten what he'd done. He carried his parents ghosts around with him each night he wandered into the streets to deal, steal, and kill. After their funeral, he promised himself he would never suffer the fate of a victim. Being incarcerated, stabbed, shot, or even set on fire was one thing, but to each day die the lingering death of a coward was abominable. That is why the consequences of his sins didn't keep him up at night. And nightmares were beside the point, as most of his memories had faded into burning visions of revenge. He would one day kill Chinnah—without bringing harm to his wife and children. And then, he would finally satisfy his bloodlust and calm the savage beast that had been brutally beating out his brains for so long.

Gorilla Leek seemed upset at the moment, ready to murder more— which made Shine want to change the subject. What he had asked his friend about going to jail—that question, that fear of getting caught—had come unexpectedly, and he wanted to consider it at length, alone, in his own home, before speaking about it again.

Shine narrowed his eyes and shook his head. "You're right. They don't go after murderers like that, and we didn't leave any witnesses or evidence so we're good," He forced a grin to surface. "You know me. I just need to cover all the angles. You feel me?"

Gorilla Leek grinned. "Yeah, I do. As long as neither of us talks, we'll be fine. But what you do need to do is get rid of that ratchet. Ya heard? That pistol is the only thing that can link you to the murder. I'm tossing mines tonight. Shit, I have new XD9 I've been wanting to break in. You want me to toss yours?"

"No."

"Na?"

"No, I'll take care of it in the morning after you drop my whip off at Minimart. Like you said, this is the only thing that can link me to what happened at that house. So, I won't feel comfortable taking my eyes off of it until I get rid of it myself." Shine raised his chin slightly. "Can't risk you driving around and get pulled over with a bunch of coke in the car. Then they find my gun also? Na, I'm good. I got this."

"Yeah. I guess."

"I think it's best," replied Shine. "And I probably need to go on and get out of here before them roscoes roll up on us for sitting in this car looking all suspicious. I ain't trying to get arrested so soon after getting away with what we just did."

"Aight you scary-ass nigga." Gorilla Leek let out stifled laugh. "Go on and get upstairs to that beautiful girl of yours."

Shine slid out of the passenger's seat, circled the car and climbed the steps to his building. Just as he was about to walk through the front door, Gorilla Leek wound down the window and called out to him.

"A'yo dog!"

Shine looked over his shoulder. "What up?"

"Make sure you get rid of that burner."

"Red," Shine replied, letting his partner know that he understood.

"Aight. Peace Almighty!" Gorilla Leek hollered from the car as it pulled off, moving at a screeching speed down the street.

Shine walked into the building and up the stairs to his second-floor apartment. He unlocked the door, stepped inside and quietly eased it shut behind him.

"Shine is that you?" Lola yelled from their bedroom.

"Uh, yeah."

Without saying another word, he tiptoed over to the sofa, and quickly shoved his pistol under the cushion where Trayvon's cap gun had been. Lola would soon find out about Badrick's fate, and if she saw Shine walking into the apartment with his gun out—the night of the murder—she would become suspicious of his involvement. He was too fearful of letting anyone else know about what he had done. The less people who knew, the better. His family would remain unharmed and he would never see the inside of a prison.

"Are you coming to bed now?" Lola asked, again yelling out from the bedroom.

"Yeah. I'm coming now."

"Good, because we need to talk. I don't like us arguing over a misunderstanding. I do love you."

Shine say nothing in return. Arguing with her was the least of his worries. He glanced around. For a second, the apartment seemed as if it was about to swamp him. The large red bandanna spread out and hanging seemingly across the bare wall. The living room full of red Studio Décor pictures frames—of his son, his mother, and even Lola. The red loveseat. The red sofa. The Redwood Burl coffee table. Suddenly, he pictured the entire bloody scene he had just fled.

A sense of panic gripped him. He was revisiting his childhood in one instant and he was seeing the murder he committed the next. He wondered if the sound of the bullets screaming off the barrel of his gun and punching through flesh and wood woke the neighbors. What if someone saw them running out of the house and wrote down his license plate? What if someone took pictures of them? What if they left a witness hiding in the house and didn't know it. Shine tried to think of a single mistake he might have made, and just as he began to make his way into the bedroom, he came up with one.

"Oh shit!" he screamed aloud. "I don't have my phone!"

CHAPTER 3

AT FIRST GLANCE, it looked like the smoking aftermath of a disastrous raid on a terrorist safe house—the dirty, tiled walls peppered with crimson splotches that ran down to the floor, the cordite stench of hell, the shredded kitchen window curtains, the crumpled corpse riddled with bullets lying in front of the refrigerator, and the fleshly ghost of a street-soldier whose skull was cracked wetly open on top of a floor littered with shell casings. The initial glimpse of the room convinced Detective Buckminster Brown that not only had something terrible taken place, but that someone had entered the home with the intention of robbing the inhabitants.

The thirty-something year old detective mopped his leather-shiny, dark sapphire forehead with a handkerchief, his bulging brown eyes searching the crime scene in front of him. The jaw beneath the blue-black shadow of his beard as razor sharp as the creases in the black dress slacks that fell over his polished, black shoes. Wearing a dark-grey blazer over a white Egyptian cotton shirt, Brown was dressed a bit more formal than the other officers searching Chinnah's house.

"What do you make of this?" he asked with a sweeping glance that took in the two detectives standing behind him.

"Well, the neighbor in Three Twenty-Four reported the shots about an hour ago," dryly replied the grey-haired and unshaven Archibald O'Reilly. His tall body rigid, the lines in his freckled face deep. Thick arms folded across his chest, taking in the back of his colleague's head, he continued, "She said she saw two men jump into a black SUV that was parked in front of the house. We were the first to arrive on the scene. However, with the two bodies on the floor here, and with you being on the homicide squad, I'd have to assume you're going to be leading this investigation. So, you should be the one answering that question."

"Well, this is your area. And your boys were supposed to be on watch, right?" Brown turned to face the older man. "I mean, correct me if I am wrong O'Reilly. But, you were investigating Orville Linton Lee-Chin, a.k.a. Chinnah, right? And this is his house, correct?"

The Irishman didn't take kindly to Brown's subtle recrimination. "Wrong. The house doesn't belong to Chinnah. He was only leasing it. And he doesn't live here."

"Of course, he doesn't live here detective. It's a drug house! I think every half-ass intelligent mind here knows that." Brown turned back toward the body on the floor.

O'Reilly found himself nervous and then hostile because of the detective's sarcastic remark, particularly because he—*a nigger*—did it in front of the other white detective standing there.

Phillip Cardillo, the sandy-haired rookie working his first case and assigned to accompany Brown, just stared at his two superiors. He had hoped to get to know O'Reilly more intimately than he could through talking on the job. And O'Reilly desired to do the same. The Irishman wanted to know how a Harvard grad—who had come from an upper-middleclass Italian family—could be willing to leave his beautiful wife and newborn daughter for nights on end to investigate the death of niggers. What kind of man would forgo a high-paying and highly successful corporate career in preference for the low-paying and highly demanding job of a zookeeper to these animals? He had to regret his decision, and probably could use the extra money O'Reilly was thinking about offering him in the near future. But the Irishman had to get to know the young detective first. He had to know if he could trust him. Because, at that moment, the Italian was too close to Brown.

O'Reilly's eyes fell on the young rookie. He gave a cruel grin then asked sarcastically, "So, Cardillo. What about you? Was your half-ass mind aware of the fact that Chinnah didn't live here? And if he doesn't live here, why would any of us be able to answer the question of what took place here?" His belly shook with a chuckle. "I mean, you're new and I'm in the Narcotics Borough. It seems our little homo-dic Brown over there needs some help and may be a little too proud to ask for it."

O'Reilly shook his head. "Douchebag."

Detective Cardillo just stared back at his senior, not knowing what to say. Either he thought O'Reilly would be offended or he wasn't going to respect his opinion, being so young and so new to the job. An uncomfortable silence stretched between the two detectives. Then Cardillo broke it by saying softly, "Well, maybe he's asking you because this is a known drug house and there aren't any narcotics here. So, the killing may likely be a drug-related robbery."

"I see Brown has you trained well," O'Reilly muttered.

"Well, Brown had me interview the witness when we arrived," Cardillo replied, seemingly unaware of O'Reilly's sarcasm. "And our guys are still searching around outside where the two men had their car reportedly parked. I'm told that the geek who did the initial walk-through has worked hundreds of cases like this and that she can usually determine the make and model of a vehicle by just looking at the tracks. And so far, she believes that the tread pattern of the tire tracks found in front of the house belong to a Ford SUV. They just need to check the database to be sure."

O'Reilly decided to be blunt. He took great pleasure in doing that. "Look around Cardillo, there's no need to go overboard with this investigation. The guys who died here today are scumbags. Not even worthy of a proper burial let alone a thorough investigation. They are not like you and I," the Irishman pointed out. "Brown has a different motive for getting caught up in these kinds of investigations. Heed my warning lad, don't let him pull you into his bullshit. You don't want to go down that Brer Rabbit Hole."

Cardillo's forehead wrinkled in confusion and his nose crinkled with disgust. "I'm not sure I know what you mean, O'Reilly. Brown seems to be a good and honest detective, which is what I aspire to be."

O'Reilly gave a chuckle that quickly became a somber, wheezing, smoker's cough that he immediately gobbled back. "An honest detective? You must be absolutely fluthered? Eh? You can't be that naïve, boy," he said in between gulps of air. "Sure, Brown can read, write, and think as swiftly as some of us, but that's unnatural for him—as is being honest. He only excels at what he does because he emulates us and lives according to the standards that your people and my people have set over the years of being in this country. Just look around in this house. His people don't have any standards of their own."

He paused to see if the rookie understood, or at least sympathized, with what he was attempting to convey. Cardillo glanced around to see two uniformed Caucasian officers crouching near one of the bodies and taking selfies. He turned back to the Irishman and appeared reluctant to agree. And O'Reilly noticed it a second before he continued speaking.

"Look, you can see it in Africa, where they kill each other wholesale, some of them becoming killers before they turn six years old. Just check out what they are doing to themselves over there. Sheesh, just look at what they do to themselves over here. I see it every day on the job." O'Reilly shook his head. "So, for the sake of peace, it is a must that they follow our customs and, as such, because of the natural relationship between teacher and student, they should find themselves being humble as often as they can. Which is something that proves difficult for Buck Brown over there."

Cardillo was feeling conflicted. This wasn't what he signed up for. O'Reilly's words were making him uncomfortable—like all of a sudden Detective Brown was one of the bad guys. He thought back to the monkey suit joke he had made when he first met Brown. He only said it because he had thought it odd that he had bothered to dress so formal. Was that racist? He had not thought it to be so. After all, he liked a lot of Black people. He grew up idolizing Michael Jordan and listening to Michael Jackson. How could he be a racist? No, he wasn't. But O'Reilly was. And O'Reilly had automatically perceived him to be one also. Cardillo felt guilt then shame. There was also anger and defensiveness as he stared solemnly at the Irishman. He prepared to speak in defense of the Black detective, but Brown's deep, commanding voice stopped him.

"O'Reilly," Brown called out, still facing the kitchen. "If you're done trying to recruit my partner with your racial rhetoric, would you mind searching the top floor for any trace evidence we may have missed?"

There was a sneer to O'Reilly's lips, and subtle anger. Coolly confident, he grinned and said, "Sure. Don't eat the head off me. I'll do your job for you."

Cardillo watched as the Irishman headed up the staircase, cursing under his breath. When the detective was no longer in view, the rookie wandered off toward the open basement door.

The faint sounds of crackling walkie-talkies, the clicking of cameras, glass crunching underfoot, and a dozen or so chattering cops moving about downstairs followed O'Reilly as he crossed the upstairs hall to an open bedroom door. He blew a bitter breath through his nostrils when something about two feet into the room captured his attention. He walked over, crouching beside the bed, and stared down at it.

A cell phone.

"Christ! Them fellas sure made a right bags of this," O'Reilly muttered as he picked it up and shoved it into his jacket. "I swear, niggers must be thick as a plank."

He quickly fished his own phone out of his pants pocket and sighing, dialed a number. Someone picked up on the second ring, and O'Reilly didn't hesitate to speak. "Aye, I'm at the stash house on 91st Street. There was an incident here tonight, and we have a bit of a problem. You need to put Chinnah on the phone right now."

♠　♠　♠

"OH SHINE!" STARK NAKED with her skin a sweaty silk, Lola let out a long moan, the sound of her own desire heightening her pleasure. "Harder, baby, fuck me harder!"

Wetness slicked her center as Shine clasped his hand on the back of her neck, holding her face-down across their bed and pushing himself inside her. The pillowy cushion smothered her, the soft-feathered fabric forming to her face, choking off her air each time he savagely slammed his hips into her upraised ass. With a pace bordering on berserk, his pulsating stroke tamed the animalistic throbbing deep inside her. Feeling his other hand gripping and spreading her creamy, firm cheek, she lifted her head in delight, and screamed, "Yes, daddy! Yes!"

Blood throbbed in her ears and her breathing came in ragged pants that were ripped from her lungs. She glanced over one shoulder at her man and saw his hard lust brimming from his open mouth. One long thrust after another, his brown manhood spread the swollen, slippery lips of her vagina. Suddenly a gush of sizzling, sticky wetness spurted out of her and onto him. Her eyes rolled to the back of her head as the feeling overwhelmed her, and she let out a helpless, high-pitched cry.

She whimpered as she came, heavy, wrenching whimpers that vibrated from deep inside where her muscles convulsed.

Shine looked down at his greasy, thick and tense penis as it prodded her wet flesh, then slapped her ass and smiled. Her creamy pussy quivered and clenched hard around him. To give him access to power in deeper, she spread her legs wider, and commanded, "Don't stop!"

Swiftly, he reached between her legs with one dexterous hand, and rubbed his fingers on her clit. Her vagina vibrated wonderfully tight against his cock, his powerful shift into her drenched folds sending her body collapsing to the bed and shaking beneath him. Softly, his fingers glided across the back of her neck, cold when they curled around and clutched her throat. His other hand slipped under her arm and gripped her shoulder. He pulled her to him and held her in place while continuing to passionately plunge his penis into her bone-weary body, digging and digging, as if he was trying to bury himself in her womb— like a baby yearning to be back in the belly of his mother. Knowing she would, like always, tug at the sheets to crawl away from the dick after she came down from her orgasm, Shine held her tightly. He listened with pride as her vagina sobbed and pleaded for mercy.

Squish. Squash. Squish.

"Damn girl, your pussy is so warm, so—mmm—so tight— mmm—so wet—so—"

Knock. Knock.

A light rap sounded against the other side of their bedroom door interrupting their fun, and Trayvon called in a loud whisper, "Mommy, daddy?"

Shine stopped suddenly, and Lola flinched visibly. He abruptly broke away from her and rose from the bed. "Tray give daddy a second. Hold on."

Lola bit off a curse as she watched his muscular, tattooed flesh and prominent, brown buttocks strut away from her. Sucking in a shaken gulp of breath, she whispered, "Goddammit, I thought he was asleep on the couch. He had fell back out after I got up and made him breakfast. What time is it?"

As Shine neared the door, he spotted his boxers by his feet, leaned forward and snatched them up. He yanked them on then glanced at the clock on his nightstand, 11:26 a.m.

"Damn," he moaned. "I was supposed to be at Minimart over an hour ago. I don't know why I let you talk me into laying back down with you after I took my shower."

He knew he should have left the house hours ago, but he had been occupied with thoughts of what happened the night before and was in no rush to see sunlight. It was as if, during the day, someone would see him for who he was. Not to mention, the flashbacks of the murder had made him horny for some reason, so his woman's naked body was a welcomed distraction and a good reason to stay home.

Lola's mouth curved almost into a smile, her lower lip full and sensuous as she said, "That's not my fault. And besides, it can't be nowhere near midday. We got up around nine." She looked over at the clock, and her eyes went wide. "Oh snap! You're right! It's late. It is 11:26! You got to go, now!"

"Huh? Now you're rushing me to leave?" Shine asked, with a puzzled look on his face.

"As much as I want you to stay at home right now, you can't afford to let those incompetent knuckleheads open up Minimart without you there. Even though it's a drug spot, it's still a business. And a business that could one day help you to leave that lifestyle alone."

Knock. Knock.

"Daddy are you going to open the door?" Trayvon yelled from the hall.

Shine turned the knob and cracked the door open enough to peer out into the hallway. "Hey little man. What's up?"

Trayvon looked up at his father through half-closed eyes, and begged, "Daddy, daddy. Can I watch Disney Channel?"

Shine stretched a little, then yawned a great, big yawn before answering his son. "Yeah, little man. Go ahead and cut the T.V. on while daddy gets prepared to go to work. Ok?"

"Ok!" replied Trayvon, unable to hide the excitement in his voice. The little boy pulled the door shut, spun on his heels and disappeared down the hall.

As Shine stood staring at the closed door, he thought about Lola and Trayvon and about Chinnah and the police, about Gorilla Leek and his family, and about himself and the murder he committed. He thought about the countless sons and daughters who were born only to die after spending such a short life striving to survive in the savage slums of the

Nineties. He thought about a life without violence, without fear, without poverty and tragedy. A life without loss. That was what he had wished to provide for his son. He'd almost convinced himself to believe that it was a good deed to blast what remained of life out of that violent killer who had threatened his family. But then, as the flames of rage began to burn low, the embers of regret ignited a new fire in his wilderness of confusion—he needed to leave the gang life.

Yeah, he thought, *I can't do this anymore. I have to think about my son. I should be attending parent-teacher conferences, playing catch in the park without looking over my shoulder, and teaching him about the birds and the bees. Not hanging out in the streets committing murder and breaking the law. Trayvon deserves more than that. More than what this neighborhood could offer him.* Shine had decided at that moment that he should put Badrick's death out of his thoughts and just move forward. That he should also leave the gang and leave New York. That is was time for a change—for his son.

Before he could turn around to share his thoughts with Lola, he felt a tug on his boxers from behind. He glanced down to see Lola's hand, with a shiny clear glob of Vaseline, delving beneath the waistband of his shorts, fingertips dancing over his dick. He drew in a deep breath, trying to calm the excitement tingling into the tip of his blood-throbbing penis as she raked her nails up and down his length.

"Ahhh." A strangled groan escaped his lips, the friction in his boxers causing him to rest his palms against the door.

"Damn ma keep it slow—Uhh."

She guided her free hand into the back of his shorts to cuddle his testicles, while the other continued stroking.

"I know you didn't get to get off because of Tray's little interruption," she said, voice breathy and low. "And I can't have my man stepping out into those streets all stressed out and backed up. You can leave this house upset, but you will never walk out wanting another bitch."

"But I don't have time to—"

"Shshsh, this won't take long."

She was right. It took little effort to arouse him, as he could feel the head of his manhood beginning to swell and explode.

His waist jerked, and he warned in a husky voice, "Mmm, girl, I'm about to—"

BLAAAAM!

A thunderous, pulsing roar echoed beyond their bedroom door, startling Shine. He jumped back, heart in his throat, and turned to Lola who stood there in awe, mouth open, staring back at him.

"What the hell was that? Was that a gunshot? Was that in here?" Lola frantically asked.

"I think it was a gunshot. But it sounded like it came from next door."

"Are you sure? I feel like it came from our living room," Lola said, her heart beating so hard beneath her chest that it felt like it was trying to break free of her flesh.

Her last words suddenly struck cold on Shine's thoughts. His fearful curiosity died out abruptly. And in his restless mind a voice, not unlike his, screamed out, *Trayvon!* Panic-stricken, he leaped onto the bed, pulled an old rusty .38 revolver from under the pillow, then he dashed out of the bedroom. Lola stood motionless, confused, and terrified. Suddenly a piercing scream sliced through the air, the wail rebounding off the living room walls, and splitting her eardrums.

"Nooooooo!"

It was Shine.

Dread filled Lola. She was struck with a sense that time was against her. Without thinking, she bolted down the corridor of their apartment, all the while her mind screaming at her to run faster. The bathroom and hallway closet were a blur as she passed them at an incredible speed. She immediately noticed that the front door to their apartment was slightly open. However, once she made it to the living room, she was abruptly startled. Stopping dead in her tracks, her eyes wide in shock, she looked to the right. The sofa cushions had been removed and set aside on the carpet. And next to them was the rusty revolver and Shine.

He was sitting on the floor, legs crossed, Indian style, weeping with his back to her. Lola could see a little foot dangling from the edge of his torso. And beneath it, a puddle of blood soaking into the carpet. There was blood on Shine's elbow. There was blood on the side of his boxers. The couch was slick with blood. Lola quickly shot a glance over Shine's shoulders.

He was clutching a lifeless Trayvon. Seeing her standing there, he made a weak gesture to pass their son to her just as he began shouting uncontrollably, "I can't—please! Lil' man, no! Please! This can't be.

Please. Please!"

Lola's face grew bloodless, and a fierce shaking racked through her body as she wrapped her arms tightly around herself.

"Naw, uh—uh. No—That's not my baby!" She began trembling violently, rocking on her heels, her hands clenched on each of her shoulders. "Shine? What is that? That's not my baby! Right?"

Lola's screams brought Shine crashing back to the surface of reality, and he stood to his feet sobbing. He tried to lift Trayvon's body from the floor, but the corpse barely moved and held close to the ground as though stuck with glue. Feeling the last of his confusion and sorrow wither away, he released his son, and watched him collapse lifelessly to the carpet, half of his scalp hanging to his cheek by a strip of crimson-soggy skin. Blood rained down out the wound when the body thudded to the floor, forming a scarlet hoodie around the boy's head.

Lost in a roar of anguish, the sound of Lola's screams rose until she could only feel and not hear the cries shredding her throat. She kept crying and crying and crying. Long, loud, terrible cries that clawed at her sanity. Her knees buckled, and she sunk to the carpet—through the carpet, even—but Shine reached under her shoulders, and yanked her back to her feet. Overcome by the nearness of the grim sight, she tore free and looked high up toward the ceiling trying, impossibly, to wipe away the nightmare from her eyes.

"This can't be! This is not real! No! No! This is not real! This is not fair!" she shouted to the heavens.

She desperately needed for God to feel sorry for what he had just done to her. And she was certain it was a 'he', because no woman would be cruel enough to murder a mother's baby. She sucked in a breath and flicked a quick nervous glance down at the couch. Through the blinking blur of her tearful eyes she saw Shine's Ruger laying on the sofa frame where the cushions had been. All time stopped at that moment. She could hear the commotion of Shine pacing back and forth. He was screaming. She couldn't make out what he was saying. Then his frantic voice burst through her fog of grief as he shouted, "He accidentally shot himself with my gun! My gun!"

Then suddenly, time resumed. Lola snapped her eyes up at Shine. She looked baffled. "What—what—what do you mean—your gun?"

Shine's eyes turned from the ground to Lola as he struggled for words. "I hid my gun in the couch last night. In the same place he hid his cap gun. He must've picked it up, not knowing and—I'm sorry, I'm—"

"Your gun? It was your fault? No. No. That's a joke, right? You killed our son?"

"My gun—"

"He's got to come back to us, Shine," Lola cut him off bitterly. "Please try to wake him up. He has to come back. Call the ambulance. They can save him. Please, Shine, call someone!"

The emptiness around her seemed to swell as she abruptly dashed into the bedroom, snapped up her mobile phone from the nightstand, and dialed 1-1-9. Heart pounding, skin hot, and hands shaking, she was too frightened and hysterical to notice her mistake.

She spoke into the phone. "Hello. Hello? Is anyone there? Hello? Is anyone going to answer?"

Shine could hear her yelling from the bedroom but couldn't make out her words. He was too busy searching the carpet with his watery eyes for the spent shells. He didn't see any. *Must have fallen under the couch*, he thought. He looked around the living room wildly, noticing for the first time that the front door was slightly cracked open. He ran toward it— tears flooding his face, shaking with every step he took—and pushed it closed. Although it was a Friday morning and he knew that Old Lady Wellington wouldn't be home for some time, he didn't want to risk the chance of someone walking by their apartment and looking inside.

"Shine, no one is answering. No one cares," Lola's voice came from behind him.

He turned around to see her standing in their living room, clutching a phone. He immediately approached her then snatched it from her hand. "Baby girl, we can't call anyone."

He shuddered at the bare thought of what he had done with the gun the night before. Badrick was dead—and he watched him die—he couldn't believe it at first, but he was now a murderer. And the same weapon that Trayvon had accidently shot himself with was the only thing that could connect him to that crime. He couldn't report his son's death. He wasn't sure what to do.

"Give me my phone! Our son needs help!" Lola screamed.

"I can't." His eyes fell to the ground. "We will both be arrested."

"I don't care! We have to save him!"

She reached for her phone, but he pulled it back. Every inch of her trembled—her hands, her legs, her shoulders, even her teeth. Suddenly, she leaped at him, scratching and punching, out of control. She pulled his hair, kicked him, and gouged a long slash across his cheek with her nails but couldn't wrest the mobile phone from him. She was a windstorm of rage and sorrow, but within seconds Shine had seized her wrist and wrenched her arm over, turning her around and slamming her back against his chest. Her body quaked with her sobs as he held her.

Pressing his lips against her ears, he whispered, "Lo, please. Calm down and listen baby girl. He's—he's already de–de—we can't save him," His gaze roamed the length of his son's body. "God has taken him."

"God? God? Where is he? Huh?" Her eyes darted left and right in a panic. "Trayvon needs him now! Where is he? Why can't you find him for us?"

His eyes shifted toward the ceiling. "I wish I knew where he was baby girl, but right now, he's not with us. Right now, he's a mystery. The only thing for certain at the moment is that we cannot call 9-1-1." He sighed heavily. "We can't report this. We would both go to jail. Wherever God is, I would rather he be the one to know about this than the police."

He spun her around in his embrace and held her until he felt her shoulders slump.

"We have to keep this between us," he said. "Do you understand?"

There was silence for a moment, then Lola answered, "Yes—I guess."

Holding her tightly with one arm, Shine used his other hand to dial Gorilla Leek's number. It seemed to take an eternity to ring. Terror skyrocketed with each second that passed as he waited for his best friend to pick up. Fighting to control his emotions, he felt his heart rate increase. He was afraid that his grief might suffocate him and kill him where he stood. For a moment he fantasized about retrieving his revolver from the floor and ending his life right then and there. Then suddenly, he felt a sticky wetness warming his legs. He looked down and clenched his eyes in disgust when he saw his underwear. It was soiled with his sperm.

CHAPTER 4

THE CRISP LIGHT of the midday sun cast sinister shadows across the trash-littered concrete as it glinted off the windows of a two-story brick building. The old, red store-front with an apartment above stood there on the corner of Rockaway Parkway and Rutland Road, an icon symbolizing prosperity in the Nineties section of Brooklyn. Like a landmark, sort of like a creation of Nimrod, the building towered above everything else. Above crushed crack vials, faded soda cans, wrinkled fast food wrappers, empty cellophane bags. Above the kind of things passersby, too fearful of stopping, pitched out the windows of moving cars. The kind of things that hinted at the undying death surrounding the *Free Market*—a grocery store that stood as the ring leader of the neighborhood's circus of poverty.

The basement floor of the *Free Market* was a smoke-filled, unfinished room serving as a makeshift conference space for the members of the Gully Gods. As an organization they've never had a graver, a more serious matter called to their attention than the reason for which they were assembled there that afternoon. Someone had murdered the nephew of their leader, Chinnah.

Those present sat around a table exchanging nervous glances among themselves as their boss paced back and forth hurling abuses at them. "Wah di bloodclot! Yuh nuh doing yuh jobs out there! None of yuh! Cuz eff yuh did doing yuh jobs, dem likkle thieves wouldn't ave had di balls to duh wah dem did!"

Beyond the curtain of long, grey dreadlocks that hid him from the world, Chinnah's beige wrinkled face was scored with lines of subdued rage. The almond-shaped eyes he inherited from his Chinese father like black ice, dark and cold. His hands clenched into a fist.

"Yuh lose yuh respect. Yuh lose mi respect!"

His roar rumbled through the entire room, bouncing off the eardrums of the four men present. They were trapped in a cement cage with a maddened beast, surrounded by walls that were neither plastered nor painted, with bare bricks jutting out through layers of peeling posters and faded advertisements. It felt like the room was closing in on them, all the chairs were getting smaller, and Chinnah was growing larger and soaring over them.

Yellowman sat on the edge of his seat with startling snow-white deadlocks dangling untended in his multi-colored eyes, his albino-pale skin seeming even paler against the dim light of the basement. Much like a chameleon, each eye appeared to move on its own, with the blue one following Chinnah as he walked, and the green one staring straight ahead at the man who sat silently across from him. Cutty, a dark skinny Jamaican of perhaps forty-something years and bald like an 8-ball, was clearly desperately afraid. And while Yellowman knew that wasn't his problem—he was only responsible for collecting the extortion payments from the local business owners, whereas Cutty oversaw the entire drug distribution in the Nineties—he recognized that an angry Chinnah was still an unpredictable Chinnah. Anybody could get it.

"Pauley!" Chinnah's tone harsh and dripping with enough acid to eat through the sleek bullet-proof vest that the three-hundred-pound ape of an enforcer wore underneath his army-green high neck pullover.

"Yea, sah," replied Pauley, a man who Chinnah always kept by his side because of his willingness to use violence unhesitatingly.

"We kno who did dis an mi wa dem dead! Dem entire fambly mi wa dead!" Chinnah commanded the enforcer.

"Yea, sah. Mi already pan it." Pauley shifted in his chair and adjusted his bulletproof vest, the outline of which was clearly visible beneath his sweater. "Mi ave O'Reilly running dem aliases through di system as wi speak. Dem ave both been arrest before, suh it nuh fi be haad to track dem dung. Plus, O'Reilly ave one of dem phones, suh wi should soon ave dem addresses."

"One of dem names Gorilla Leek," interjected Cutty, "him di one mi had an issue wid a couple of years ago. Di one who stabbed me. Mi had mi eyes pan him since him come home from prison. But yuh tell mi nuh fi touch di bowy cuz it wud mess up bizniz."

"Yea, mi kno di bowy. Mi memba him parents," replied Chinnah. "Mi kno him well."

"Weel, now mi cya deal wid dis pussyhole," The words rushed out of Cutty's mouth breathlessly. He was eager to seize the opportunity to make things right. "Yuh cya truss mi fi get back wah him stole from wi."

Chinnah's eyes darkened at his words. "Yuh wa mi to truss you? Truss you?" He strutted over to the head of the table and slammed his fist down, making the domino pieces and empty beer bottles resting on it rattle with an unnerving clatter. "Mi trust yuh to mek sure sup'm like dis wud neva happen! Yuh kno how much funds dem tief from mi?"

Cutty swallowed hard and looked down at his hands, gathering himself to speak. "Mi kno how fi get it back," he said, still staring at his hands. "Copper say fi him crew si dem all di time. At di club. Pan di kaanah. Inna di park. Mi cya use di soldias dat him ave anda him to—"

"Copper? Crips? No! Yuh wi nuh duh dat. Dis a nuh mi son's problem to deal wid. It yours!"

Copper's sand-brown sleek jawline tightened at the mention of his name. Thoughtfully, he rubbed the stubble that shaded his chin and lowered his eyelids like a person sheltering a secret. He was the fourth man present at the meeting and Chinnah's only son. At the age of twenty-four, he was at the head of a gang that was slowly growing to dominate and displace all of the criminal organizations in the Nineties, the G-Stone Crips. He tilted the brim of his navy-blue Yankee fitted baseball cap then spoke with a thick American accent.

"Pops. All day I diss all slobs. You know that. My locs can take care of it. And I know where that slob, Gorilla Leek stays. I have his address. I can send my—"

"No," interrupted Chinnah. "Mi naah guh to involve yuh or yuh gang."

His son's decision to join the gang as a teen was a choice Chinnah had not only supported but long urged. He was disappointed that his own lieutenants' bungling of the drug trade in the Nineties—their failure to plan for the sudden appearance of the new, violent youth gangs, their refusal even now to change their plan of action or so much as acknowledge the rise of a more violent and feared group—was putting all that he had built at risk. At least with his son as one of the heads of the gangs in his neighborhood, he could ensure that the Gully Gods established direct links with the young petty dealers on the corners. And this meant that he could be assured of a steady distribution of his drugs throughout the Nineties without resorting to extortion or violence.

Chinnah would never involve himself in senseless, nonprofitable gangbanging. It would bring too much unwanted attention to the activities of his organization. And he would never rely on the Crips to commit a murder for him. He didn't want his operation sabotaged by the unprofessional recklessness of ignorant American teenage thugs. So, he kept them at a distance and he let his son, who wanted to dress like them and speak like them, deal with them. However, because of this, he didn't trust Copper to run his organization.

"But pops," Copper said. "I be seeing their soldiers all the time at Tilden Ballroom, partying. We could take out some of the other slobs they run with to send them a message."

"No," Chinnah barked. "Mi nuh wa fi start a gang war. Dat a wah dem deh devils wa. It a mi fault mi sey. Mi should ave let Cutty tek care of di bowy a lang time ago. Him stabbed Cutty, an since den, him tink dat Cutty weak. Him tink dat him cya rob Cutty. Suh, no. Yuh nah handle dis mi son. Cutty wi. Give him di man's address. Let him alone clean up dis mess."

"But Pops—"

"No!" In one sudden movement, Chinnah reached down and pulled a machete from the ground then brought it crashing down on top of the table, sending the domino pieces scattering again. "Mi word final!"

"Understood sir." Copper swallowed hard and looked away.

Chinnah turned his attention to Pauley. "Pauley, dem mash up mi yaad. Suh, mi wa yuh to mash up dem store," he ordered. "Mek sure it neva opens fi bizniz again. Seen?"

"Yeah man," Pauley answered without hesitation. "Yuh wa mi fi get Arab involved?"

Copper bit his lip and rolled his eyes as if he couldn't believe Pauley had mentioned that name out loud. Arab. No one inside or outside that basement was more frightening and more dangerous than Arab, a man whose keen intelligence delivered sharp, severe punishment on their enemies. A man loyal only to himself. A man feared by everyone in the Gully Gods, including Chinnah. Copper could think of a number of different reasons why involving Arab would qualify as insane. It was overkill. He could easily handle Shine and Gorilla Leek himself. His father's lack of trust in the Crips, in his own son, bothered him. He was over twenty years of age and was still being treated like a baby. When his father looked at him, he saw a pitiful, childlike savage, half boy, half wild thug, totally incompetent to cope with all the sordid details of running a criminal organization. Was he as stupid as his father made him out to be? No. He didn't believe himself to be, and his father would soon realize how intelligent he actually was.

"No, Pauley," Chinnah's voice echoed through the basement, interrupting Copper's thoughts. "Wi nuh need fi call pan Arab. Mi truss dat yuh cya tek care of it yuhself. Seen?"

"Yeah, man," Pauley replied. "Yuh nuh ave any reason to worry. Mi wi tek care of it. Mi a guh—"

There was a sudden loud shriek from above, and the group of men were struck silent. Then a monstrous thud shook the ceiling, louder, much louder than the scream. Copper looked up, his head pounding with a sudden surge of adrenaline. He got heavily to his feet, darted for staircase, and ran up the steps. He could hear someone moving around upstairs, so he quickened his pace, and flung the door open.

He pushed past the two burly men standing guard outside the basement door. He moved quickly down the canned food aisle to find Lennox, the storekeeper, severely pistol-whipping a teen's skull into a bloody mass. For a moment, he observed his father's trusted store manager strike the boy's crimson-covered face mercilessly, blow after blow. The kid was cowered in the corner trying to deflect them with his forearms and by moving his head. Unwilling to watch anymore of the brutal beating, Copper screamed at the storekeeper to stop. The man ignored him.

He then shot a quick glance toward the entrance to the store, not managing to hide a flicker of concern as he glared at the person who had accompanied him to his father's meeting. Jigga Blue. Earlier, Copper had ordered him to stand with his hand on his pistol in front of the entrance to the store where he could watch everyone who came in.

"Yo, Jigga, what's the deal with this?" Copper asked.

Before Jigga Blue could respond, Lennox stopped beating the boy and with his breath huffing out hard, said, "Mi catch dis blackheart man trying fi tief an Heineken from di refrigerata. Suh, mi tell Jigga Blue, ta lakk off di doa, suh mi cud teach dis tegareg a les—"

"Wha gwan?" Chinnah's voice cut him short. "Yuh say him try to steal from mi?"

Copper turned around to see his father standing in the basement doorway, gripping his faithful machete. Chinnah began whistling as he strolled over to the whimpering thief. Lennox grabbed the injured man under his arms and dragged him up against the wall of the store. Staring at a sea of hostile faces, the boy felt an icy wave of terror rush over him.

Chinnah approached him waving the machete in his right hand, with his crew behind him. "Place fi him hand pan di counta ova there suh," he said to Lennox.

With a grimace of terrible expectation, the boy began pleading, "Please, don't, sir—Please, I'll pay for—no—I'll pay double–Please–I'm sorry!"

Lennox and Pauley lugged the thief over to the deli counter and pinned his hands down next to the meat-slicing machine. The teen tried to wiggle free, but his wrist was held down firmly. He felt weak. Pathetic. Pauley slapped him across his face, and a sudden silver flash momentarily blinded him. Lennox forced the boy's skull to the counter, sending his senses spinning near the brink of consciousness. A gruff, calm voice whispered in his ear, and hot, marijuana breath fell on his cheek.

"Yuh know wah dem deh Arabs duh inna dem country wen dem catch a tief?" Chinnah asked, before chuckling. "No, there wi nuh be any mercy fi yuh. Suh, tap all a dat bloodclot crying!"

Without uttering another word, he swung the machete into an arc. The blade caught the sunlight that had crept through the front poster-covered window, carving the store into shattered shadows as it came down again and again, hacking through the boy's wrist. His hand spasmed with a spurt of crimson and he let out a bone-chilling scream. It was a gruesome spectacle to watch Chinnah do such a thing— swinging a dull machete down on a boy begging for mercy—while humming Bob Marley's "Song of Freedom", completely unaffected by the horror he was inflicting.

Before the blade had raked its way completely through the bone, the boy passed out, his hand dangling from a grisly bloody flap of skin, largely unattached from the rest of his arm. The unconscious teen slumped to the floor.

The leader of the Gully Gods flung the blood-smeared blade to the ground, turned on his heels and headed back to the basement. "Throw fi him ass out inna di back an clean up di counta," he said to no one in particular. "Oh, an let off di Heineken to di mon."

Before Chinnah disappeared beyond the basement door, he whispered, "Mo'time."

Copper's eyes darted over the men gathering around the bleeding teen. "Don't look at me for help. I'm bout to go light up a blunt and be out." He motioned for Jigga Blue to follow him, then he hurried down the stairs behind his father.

♠   ♠   ♠

KOLD FIRE, AN OLIVE-SKINNED Puerto Rican, stood behind the front counter of Minimart, counting out Sour Power straws from a plastic bucket into a brown paper bag for a little six-year-old boy. He was taking the candies out one by one with a pair of plastic tongs when two teenage girls entered the store giggling. They were about sixteen or seventeen, judging by the curves of their bodies and their young faces. Their dresses were so short that almost every step they took provoked a flash of their red panties. They idled in front of the magazine rack for a moment, and though he took no apparent notice of them, he watched them closely. He knew there were only two kinds of customers who came into the store after 3 p.m.—school kids purchasing candy and adults buying cocaine. And the two girls who had just entered Minimart were neither. If they were there for the candy they would've made their way directly to the front counter. And since they didn't make a beeline straight for the refrigerator section at the back of the store, he knew they weren't looking to cop coke.

He wondered what the young girls were saying—their gestures were as cryptic to him as the Crips' gang signs. Their voices were lively and occasionally they burst out laughing. With no one to help him assist the customers that were entering, he couldn't get a good listen.

"Yo, Venom, come up here!" Kold Fire yelled out while handing the young boy his change.

"Thank you, Kold Fire," the boy said as he turned around to exit the store.

"One," replied Kold Fire.

"One," the boy answered without looking over his shoulder as he passed the girls and walked out of the store.

Kold Fire's eyes fell on the young females. "Can I help ya'll?"

With a soft giggle, one of the girls grasped the other's arm and yanked her forward, their high heels clicking as they neared the counter.

"This here is my friend, Lilith. She thinks you're cute," said the girl, holding her friend by the elbow.

The second teen blushed prettily. Then her eyes fell to the ground, her long lashes laying gently on her glowing cheeks, as she forced her mouth open to speak, "Hey."

Before she could get any other words out, Venom came running out from the back of the store. "What's poppin', Blood?"

Turning his eyes away from the girls to face Venom, Kold Fire replied, "Yo, I'm about to head up to Shine's crib. He should've been here by now with the reup. I need you to hold the fort down while K-Bang handles the back."

"No problem, dog," Venom replied, staring wantonly at the young girls as he walked behind the counter. "Who they?"

"Who cares?" said Kold Fire. "I need you to focus on the business at hand. Take a count of the doe so we know how much came in this morning. I should be back with more work before you run out."

"Aight," answered Venom.

Lilith interpreted Kold Fire's lack of attention toward her as a sign that he was too busy to talk. He was seemingly unconcerned about the way her breasts were lolling freely under the red bodycon bandage dress that flattered her figure. She looked at her friend and motioned for her to turn around. The two walked away without saying a word, slamming the store's door behind them.

Kold Fire stepped out from behind the counter and walked toward the front of the store. "Four eyes nigga!" he commanded in their coded language as he opened the door.

Venom was, busy counting money from the cash register and

didn't hear his friend.

Kold Fire flicked a glance over his shoulder, mildly troubled by the lack of response and asked, "Gangsta Dim?"

Venom's head popped up and he replied, "Half Glass."

"Aight then, Peace Blood!"

"Peace, Blood!" echoed Venom.

"Washington DC!" were the last words that left Kold Fire's lips as the door closed behind him and he stepped onto the sidewalk of Rutland Road.

Lilith and her friend stood talking outside the store. When she saw Kold Fire come out, she grudgingly moved out of the way to let him pass, still upset for being ignored by him.

Hissing through her teeth as she watched him get into his car and pull off, Lilith waved her hand and said, "He ain't that cute anyway. Just a Spanish speaking Negro with good hair."

Out of nowhere, a black sedan with tinted windows came to a screeching halt only a few feet in front of the girls. A back door opened, and all they saw was a leathered-gloved hand gripping a Ruger AR556, and they froze in disbelief. The rifle jerked like a big dick exploding from an orgasm and before the girls could open their mouths, slugs went soaring at and past them, perforating their chests, heads, and legs. One girl's body shook and rattled in a twerking dance of death before falling to the ground in convulsions. While she lay there barely gasping—her mouth sucking at the air like a fish out of water—Pauley eased out of the car clutching a Mossberg 590 pump-action shotgun and instantly bucked a shocked Lilith off her feet, catapulting her and her tattered bandage dress backward through Minimart's glass window. Blood exploded out of her, misting the air around her shredded body.

The two men sent scores of bullets through the store, smashing through glass, shredding wood, tearing apart old cereal boxes, and ripping flesh open. Pauley stopped firing and pulled a grenade from his jacket pocket, yanked the pin free, and sent it flying through what was left of Minimart's shattered window. He pushed his companion into the back seat and got in after him. The driver shifted the car into gear and peeled out of the parking space, letting his excitement squeal the tires. A firestorm erupted behind their vehicle, shaking the pavement and exploding in flickering bursts of orange and yellow. The luminous blaze whipped out through the window panes like a ripple in a pond with flames rushing into the air, curling out and up toward the roof of the store. There was no chance of anyone inside of Minimart surviving.

♠ ♠ ♠

"GODDAMMIT!" HOLLERED DINA, her fat helpless hand hanging at the wrist, tugging a red laundry cart and the other holding a plastic shopping bag. "Stop running ahead of me! It's getting dark out here, and I don't have my glasses."

Her three children were up and down Rutland Road, playing tag.

"Gemma, Jamel, and Tracy! You better stop when you get to the house! You hear me? And you better not open the door up with those keys—Jamel!"

Eight-year-old Jamel led the way up the steps as his younger siblings followed him into their building and out of their mother's sight.

"Raaas, I'm gonna kill these kids," she complained out loud. "They're gonna give me grey hair before I reach twenty-five."

With half-moon hips jutting out her jeans in a sassy Bajan strut, she struggled to pull the cart up the stairs, her breath laboring in her lungs. "Jamel, come and help mommy!"

There was no response.

"I'm gonna tear his little butt up. They never treat Malik like this."

She pushed through the front door into the building's hallway. Her breath escaped on a ragged sigh when she realized the door to her apartment was left open.

"I told 'em not to go in. Boy, they're gonna get it."

Suddenly, an ear-splitting shriek of the most horrid and blood-curdling intensity came from the apartment. The unexpected, horrifying sound reverberated off her eardrums and jolted her heart.

"Mommmmy!"

It was Gemma.

Soon after, a bright silver flash lit up the interior of the apartment, followed by a loud thunderous boom that crackled through the air, vibrating the building.

"Oh my god!"

Releasing the cart and the bag, and slipping through the door to her apartment, the terrified mother leaped into action like a cheetah chasing a prey she could smell but could not yet see. The hallway appeared longer than usual. As she approached the bedroom, she observed the door. It had been kicked open.

"What the?" she yelled out.

A tall, bald and dark figure startled her as he stumbled out of the room and jostled her to the side, clutching his stomach. Staggering, he reached out his free hand to brace himself against a wooden panel before crumpling to the floor, his palm leaving a trail of crimson smeared across the wall. Dina stood frozen in fear.

CHAPTER 5

SHINE SAT LOW in the passenger seat of Gorilla Leek's Yukon, staring coldly off into the night, his face almost invisible beneath the red Yankees cap pulled over his eyes. A burst of lightning ripped through the dark underbelly of the clouds, snarling, as rain pounded against the windshield. Waiting in the parked vehicle on Rochester Avenue, across the street from Lincoln Terrace Park, he turned over the incident in his mind.

The glow of the traffic light ahead danced in the rain as it blinked from yellow to red, taunting him. Suddenly stricken with a dizzying flashback warped with blood, he shut his eyes tightly and tried to think about something pleasant. Hazy images, of the grisly scene he had to clean up earlier that day, kept surfacing in his mind. Before moving the body, he sent Lola to her friend's house to stay the night. And he reminded her of the prison time they could face if she violated their vow of secrecy. After she left, he couldn't help but wonder if she was being harassed by the same mixed feelings of pain, anger, guilt, and anguish that were tormenting him. Trayvon's death mauled the deepest parts of him and there was no hiding that.

"What the hell am I doing?" he whispered to himself, shaking his head. *I'm burying my son in the middle of a park. How am I going to explain his absence? How am I going to get used to his absence?* He slammed his fist against the dashboard. "Shit, lil man—shit!"

Tears flooded his pain-filled eyes. "I'm so sorry. Please forgive me. God, I'm sorry." Removing a red bandana from his fatigue jacket, he wiped away his grief. "God, I messed up."

He considered turning himself in as a punishment for his mistake.

"Turn myself in? Na, I can't do that, but I promise you, lil' man, I'll make it up to you some way," he whispered aloud.

As moonlight fought its way through the swaying branches of the trees surrounding the park, it cast a wavering shadow over a dark figure nearing the car. Wearing a black nylon flight jacket, with a black hood tightly drawn over his face, Gorilla Leek opened the door to the vehicle and settled into the driver's seat. He eyed his best friend with remorse.

"You aight, Blood?"

"Yeah," Shine answered. "Is everything handled?"

"No doubt," Gorilla Leek inhaled deeply, and let out a long sigh. "I buried him on Dead Man Hill."

"What about the burner?"

"Handled it. I buried your ratchet on the other side of the park by Buffalo Avenue."

"Good, good," Shine tried hard to appear unmoved by the tragic circumstances he faced, "You're always there for me son. I would've done it myself, but—"

"Look Blood, say no more. I'm your dog for life. You the only brother and family I have." Gorilla Leek paused then scanned his companion up and down. "All I care about is whether you're good or not. Ya heard?"

A perplexed expression crossed Shine's face. He forced a smile to surface. "I won't know how good I am until I find out if them roscoes found my phone. For all I know they could have a warrant out for me now."

Gorilla Leek suppressed his frown to a mere smirk then replied, "Check it dog, if the scramz ain't ran up on you yet about it, then that means they ain't found nothing. So, just be easy."

"Yeah, I guess you're right. But what if one of Chinnah's peoples found it?"

"Stop letting your thoughts run wild dog. Look," Gorilla Leek reached inside his coat, pulled out a Springfield XD9 9mm pistol, and handed it to Shine, "you probably could use this, seeing how I just buried your other joint. So, if Chinnah comes after you, well—you know—you handle yours."

Shine took the weapon. "But what about you? Whatchoo holding?"

"I never threw my ratchet away. I still got it on me." Gorilla Leek raised his eyebrow. "Don't worry bout me? Are *you* good to roll?

"Yeah man, we got BI to handle, whether I like it or not."

"Aight, so where to?"

"We need to hook up with Kold Fire and find out exactly what happened at Minimart today. It's best not to go over there 'cause it'll be crawling with pigs. This will set us back like crazy." Shine shook his head. "Not to mention the heat it will bring on us if my phone turns up. It's a lot to have to deal with right now, son."

Gorilla Leek sighed and rolled his head to the side, meeting Shine's solemn gaze. Suddenly, the shrill sound of a cell phone ringing cut through the air of awkwardness. They both fumbled through their pockets, muttering incoherently.

"It's mine," declared Gorilla Leek. He touched the screen on his phone. "Peace!"

Shine watched as his friend's expression transformed from glowering to a malicious smile.

For several endless seconds, Gorilla Leek's eyes narrowed with rage. His jaw dropped, and the veins in his throat stood out as he shouted into the phone, "Aight, I'm on my way. Peace!"

Removing the phone from his ear, he clasped the steering wheel with both hands and swept a glance around the outside of the car. His eyes searched the area in front of him slowly, inch by inch, but the driving rain was making everything a blur.

Shine eyed his partner with the most earnest attention. "Is everything good?"

Gorilla Leek responded without hesitation, "Make sure there's no pigs behind us. I'm about to bust a eweey. Need to make a quick change of plans."

"Where to?"

"My crib."

"What's up? What happened?" Shine nervously inquired.

Gorilla Leek braced the wheel. "Things just got worst. Fasten your seatbelt. I'm 'bout to push this baby!"

The tires spun on the pavement and smoke billowed from the rear of the SUV, filling the evening air as they burst their way into traffic. Cars honked and screeched to a halt as the vehicle snaked into a U-turn and peeled off down the hill of Rochester Avenue.

Upon arriving at his apartment building, Gorilla Leek noticed the opened front door and immediately got out of the vehicle, running up the steps two at a time. Shine cautiously followed behind.

"Where is he?" Gorilla Leek barked as he swung open the door to the apartment.

Dina and the children came scrambling out of the kitchen.

"Daddy!" excitedly yelled the three young ones as they wrapped their tiny arms around their father's legs.

Dina sluggishly trotted toward them with her head to the ground. Her light brown skin was deathly pale, eyes still revealing the shock of what she just witnessed.

Jamel tilted his head up to catch his father's eyes and flashed a smile that showed very white teeth. "Daddy, I just shot him with your gun." He pointed to a bleak shape, covered in a pale green bed linen sodden with blood.

Gorilla Leek glanced down at the lifeless figure and grimaced. Shine removed the covering from the face which was frozen into a look of surprise. Dead eyes bulged as they stared sightlessly toward the ceiling.

"It's Cutty, Chinnah's coke boy," revealed Shine.

Gorilla Leek embraced Dina. "You aight?"

She said nothing.

"What happened?" he asked her.

Jamel spoke up for his mother. "Me, Gemma, and Tracy came into the house. We saw the man in the kitchen looking under the sink, so we ran into you and mommy's room and locked the door. I remembered where I saw you put your gun, so I climbed up on the chair, looked in the closet, and got it." There was a flash of triumph in his wide brown eyes. "I didn't forget how you showed me to use it. You said I have to protect mommy and my sisters, remember?"

"Indeed," Gorilla Leek gave his son a reassuring smile, yet the smile appeared strained, the worry in his eyes visibly apparent, "now finish telling daddy what happened."

Jamel nodded then continued, "So, I pulled the top of it back. That's when the man kicked the door open and Gemma screamed. I got scared, and squeezed the trigger, like you showed me. And the man ran out of the room."

The little boy's chest gently rose again then fell as he released a sigh of accomplishment.

"Are you still scared?" Gorilla Leek asked, hearing his son's voice tremble.

"Nope. I protected, mommy and my sister."

Joy and fear mingled at his son's unexpected declaration, making Gorilla Leek uneasy. He stooped low and peered into Jamel's eyes with a searching look.

"Check this Jamel, never ever tell anyone what happened today. You have to keep this a secret. Make sure your sisters never say anything ever about this. Ya heard?"

"Yes sir." Jamel swallowed hard and looked to his father with worrisome eyes. "Daddy, did I do a bad thing?"

Taking a deep breath, Gorilla Leek rubbed his son's head with both hands. "Are mommy and your sisters okay?"

Jamel's brows raised, he quickly nodded, "Yes."

Gorilla Leek stood erect and stared blankly at the lifeless corpse of Cutty. A reluctant smile tugged at his lips. "Well then, you were not wrong."

He brought his attention to Shine, who was talking into his cell phone.

"Yo, Kold Fire, check it. I need you to round up Bloody Papers, Sinnin' Blood, Redrum, and Flames. Tell them to meet me over at Gorilla Leek's kingdom in one hour. One hour, you feel me?" A little muscle on the side of his neck moved up and down. "Don't make me wait. Got a cleanup for y'all to take care of. Alright? Peace Almighty."

He stuck his phone into his pocket, walked over to the body and nudged it with his foot. "Dumb ass. Because you went and got taken out by a kid," he inhaled deeply and let out a long sigh, "this war definitely has to go down now."

Suddenly, nothing else seemed important. Agonizing over his son's death seemed a waste of time in view of what was to come. Now—perhaps—a war with Chinnah was inevitable, even necessary. He was obviously coming for them, and in desperation they would now have to strike back. He shot a glance at Gorilla Leek. Then, feeling an abrupt jealous wave settle over him as he watched his partner console his loved ones, Shine thought to himself, *Leek's lucky. No matter what happens, at least he still has his family.* At that very moment, a growing sense of vulnerability descended upon him.

♠   ♠   ♠

"IS SHE STILL ASLEEP BACK THERE?" Ferlisha looked up from Desiree's tattered couch where she was reclining idly, shoes off, sausage fingers leafing through a magazine.

"Yeah, that chick is pretty much out of it." Desiree snapped her head toward the bedroom door and slid down the arm of the couch until she collapsed onto the cushion next to her friend. She stretched out her long legs to the floor, her feet petite and perfectly shaped. "She came over here really shaken up."

"I would be too if that happened to me. I mean, she probably feels like dying right now. That was her only son," Ferlisha pointed out.

"That's why when she got here, I told her to go in the room and lie down. She looked exhausted like she had too much on her mind to deal with."

"Yeah, that has to be painful for Shine too. I mean, your only child accidentally killing himself with your gun. That would mess me up if it happened to me." Ferlisha shook her head with a slight wobble. "I mean, really, that was kind of his fault. That's why I don't believe in keeping guns in the house."

"And that's why your ass is a damn square. Hell, they need to keep some sort of protection in there, with all the stuff he's into," Desiree countered.

The conversation was abruptly cut short by the cordless phone ringing. Desiree reached past Ferlisha's chest and retrieved it from the base.

"Hello?"

She listened keenly into the receiver before replying.

"Oh, what up? Na, she's asleep in the back. What do you want me to tell her?"

Desiree fell silent as the caller spoke.

"Hmm? Coming over where? Why? What popped off?" She shrugged her shoulders with a heavy sigh. "I guess so. What about Shine? He ain't doing too good, you know—with the Trayvon thang and all."

Ferlisha sat up, her weed-burned lips curving upward, blatant interest flaring in her narrow red-eyed gaze as she examined Desiree. Wondering who was on the other end of the conversation, she listened as her friend spoke freely about Lola's personal business. She thought to herself, *who else knows about Trayvon?* Then it hit her; there was only one person who, aware of the incident, would have a need to call Desiree's house at that moment. It was Lola's sweetheart, her secret lover, her bedroom buddy.

"Ok, got it. I'll tell Lo you called, and you can—Uh, hold on." Desiree removed the phone from her ear and peered down at the screen to view the number of an incoming call. She positioned it back to her face and said, "Give me a sec. I got someone calling on the other line. Hold on." After pressing the flash button on the receiver, she spoke into the phone. "Hello? Who this?"

Suddenly, a hoarse, bitter voice, croaky with sleep, came from behind the two friends. "You'll tell me who called?"

Startled, both girls turned to find Lola lingering in the middle of the doorway. Her face looked tired and her hair was disheveled as she stood barefoot with both hands hanging limply at her sides. When she spoke, the words came slowly and unwillingly.

"Who was that?" she asked, rubbing the fatigue from her eyes.

"Your dude," Desiree briskly answered, ignoring the person on the phone. "Hold on," she uttered into the receiver before pressing the mute button.

"Shine? What did he say?" Lola's voice was breathy with excitement.

"Na, not Shine. Your other dude," Desiree replied.

The grieving mother's eyelids drooped as she leisurely moved toward the couch. "Is he still on the phone?" she asked flatly.

Noticing the sudden change in her friend's demeanor, Desiree became a bit concerned. "You sure you wanna speak to him? I mean, you seem heartbroken now that you know it's not Shine."

"Heartbroken? No. I just want to know what's going on with Trayvon. What they did with my son?" Lola rubbed her cheeks and blinked tears from her eyes. "As far as I'm concerned, Shine is the reason this happened, and he barely seems affected by this."

Desiree attempted to be motherly, but sounded less than sympathetic when she said, "Lo girl, you know he's hurting too. He's a dude. He has a different way of dealing with it. He's probably scared to death and at the same time depressed as hell."

Lola frowned, wondering why her friend was defending Shine.

"Whatever. He didn't care about us before this, and I'm sure he doesn't care now. This will probably be a reason for him to leave. I mean, we were on shaky grounds already." Tears pricked her eyes once more. "I wouldn't be surprised if he was out there tricking on some other bitch."

Beneath half-lowered lids, Desiree secretly smiled as her mouth flinched in response, "Yeah well, if you get tired of him, I'll be more than happy to take care of him for you."

Lola stabbed a finger at Desiree, stopping just short of poking her in the eye. "Bitch, watch yourself."

"I'm just keeping it real, girl." Desiree choked back a laugh. "Besides, it ain't like you're faithful to Shine anyway. Why are you worried about who he deals with, if he's still paying your bills?"

Lola gritted her teeth as she reflected on Desiree's comment. Something in her friend's eyes had warnings hammering in her brain. And rightfully so. Seldom had Desiree ever been so attracted to a man as she was to her home-girl's baby daddy. She believed he needed a street-smart chic by his side and who better than a Brooklyn-born and Brownsville-raised woman such as herself. Bitterly jealous of Lola's pampered bourgeois Georgia upbringing, she did not believe a naïve little country girl deserved the love of a handsome smooth-talking hustler like Shine.

Recognizing her friend's hidden desire to possess her man, Lola shuddered in disgust. Her eyes shot forwarded with an empty look before uttering, "This is really not the moment to be saying something like that. Besides, like I said mad times before, I love both of them. Now pass me the phone."

Desiree brought the phone up to her ear, and without addressing the person on hold, clicked over to the other line. She listened into the receiver then tossed it on to the couch.

"He hung up," she stated nonchalantly, watching closely for her friend's response.

Lola's breath hissed between her clenched teeth.

Desiree ignored her and said bluntly, "Look, I know one thing, you better at least figure out who's the one if it doesn't come."

"Bitch, that's my business," Lola's voice hummed with the force of her emotion. "And it better not get outside of this apartment."

"Yeah, 'cause we know it'll be a wrap if Shine finds out and Mr. Lover-man already think he's the one." With a grim smile of satisfaction, Desiree folded her arms across her chest and leaned back against the couch. "I don't know why you told him when you're not even sure if it is true or not yet. You said dude was ready to leave his fam and all. That nigga must be crazy open."

"Sheesh, men are dogs!" added Ferlisha.

Desiree nodded in agreement. "Girl, you only got a couple of months before everything is out in the open. I hope you—"

Lola's friend was interrupted by the doorbell. Rising from the couch warily, Desiree crossed the room and stuck her head out of the window.

"What's going on, girl?" She shouted into the street below. "Damn, that was fast. Y'all must've been around the corner. Hold on, let me get the keys."

She snatched up the keys from a small card table which served as a dining table, returned to the window, and dropped them to the street. The keys went sailing down at Dina, landing at her feet. Little Jamel scrabbled weakly across the cold, wet pavement and seized them. Turning away from the window, Desiree found Lola staring directly at her.

"That's Dina," she said. "Something happened at their crib, so Gorilla Leek sent her over here."

Lola's lips tightened with a look of alarm and hopelessness. "You didn't tell her, did you?"

"Girl, no. What you told us stay with us," Desiree assured her. "Both things!"

"What do you think happened?" wondered Ferlisha as she twisted up some weed in a rolling paper between her long, willowy fingers.

Desiree shrugged her shoulders. "I don't know Leesh, but she didn't seem like herself. She sounded down."

"You think Malik said something?" Lola sank into one of the single-padded grey folding chairs that surrounded the card table.

Confusion washed over Desiree's face. "About what?"

"Whatever he knows!" Lola nervously shouted.

The sound of a key rattling in the door drew the ladies' attention. The lock gave way with a loud *clack* and Dina entered with her three children. The kids stripped themselves of their wet coats and untidily piled them in a corner near the entrance. They plopped down on a cushion-less loveseat, the springs squeaking tiredly. Dina sat at the table with Lola.

"Where's Trayvon?" asked Gemma, the second oldest of the siblings.

A silence pressed against Desiree and Ferlisha. They fixed their gaze on Lola whose nerves were already tingling with agony.

Tears welled in Lola's eyes. Her bottom lip trembled, and her voice quivered as she blurted out the words, "He—he's—Trayvon's not here!"

She abruptly rose up from the chair and brushed her hands across the table, sending a Heineken beer bottle crashing to the ground. Shattered shards of green glass skidded across the discolored, dull-looking hardwood floor. Lola stormed out of the room and locked herself in the bathroom. Her reaction thoroughly surprised Dina who swept her eyes downward to conceal her shock.

Desiree spoke up, "She and Shine are going through something."

Noticing Ferlisha inclining her head to light up the weed, Dina called out to her children, "Jamel, Gemma, and Tracy, go to the back and play."

Without a word, the children quickly disappeared into the bedroom and shut the door. Cupping the marijuana cigarette carefully, Ferlisha took a long satisfying drag then coughed until she wheezed. Saliva ran out the corner of her mouth, wetting the paper as she attempted to take another pull. It came apart between her fingers and trails of marijuana threaded across her hand. Desiree took notice then plucked the unraveled joint from her friend's grip. She licked the edge of the wrap, smoothed it down, and twirled up the ends.

After taking a long slow pull, she opened her mouth to speak and a wisp of smoke came out. "So, what happened over there, Dina?"

Dina let out a short weary sigh. "Chinnah is what happened."

Desiree and Ferlisha scrunched their faces, displaying shock as their eyes settled on their friend. There was a long, deadly pause. Everyone in the room knew that Chinnah's territorial rivalries had contributed to the increasing violence in the Nineties over the years. That every business in the area, whether legal or illegal, paid him a percentage of their earnings. He was infamous for threatening to enforce his green or red rule. That is, either green you pay, or in red you will lay. And shortly after Shine and Gorilla Leek purchased Minimart, he had painstakingly sought to extort them. But they refused his offer. And though it meant death in most cases, Chinnah did nothing. Times had changed, and with the advent of gangs in the area, the Jamaican elder recognized that attempting to extort members of the Bloods would prove difficult and likely lead to a war. A war he wanted to avoid.

For the past two decades the fifty-eight-year-old drug-lord went unchallenged, the neighborhood remained quiet and the police did not interfere with his operation as long as he paid them. He had grown so accustomed to being respected that he found Shine and Gorilla Leek's defiance difficult to bear at first. However, since they ran a small-time enterprise compared to his organization, Chinnah figured that the police attention the bloodshed would bring would not be worth it. Failing to realize that the duo was the beating heart of a rapidly changing neighborhood, the leader of the Gully Gods regarded their business venture as harmless and turned his attention away from them.

But now, after murdering his nephew and walking off with his drugs, Shine and Gorilla Leek had provoked Chinnah to unleash a war. And this was exactly what Gorilla Leek desired. From the time he was a boy, he would lay in bed at night thinking about killing the man responsible for his parents' death. It wasn't too long after their demise that his heart had hardened, his despair turning into a blind thirst for blood. He yearned to witness the end of the man who blighted his life and robbed him of a family. And now, with both Badrick and Cutty dead, he might finally get what he had been looking forward to all these years.

CHAPTER 6

BLOOD SPLASHED OUT OF THE TUB and onto the ivory tile covering the bathroom floor.

"Aarggh!" Sinnin Blood gripped the crimson-soaked saw and violently raked it back and forth over what was left of Cutty's mutilated, swollen corpse. Furious were the strokes he dealt as the saw teeth growled against the bone. Several times the blade got stuck and he had to yank it with both hands to free it. The left arm was almost completely severed at the shoulder.

Releasing the saw in frustration, he snatched the arm straight up into the air and stomped his foot down onto the armpit. Pulling and tugging on the limb, his effort made a sickening sound.

Splush. Splash. Splat.

"I know this is your first time doing this, but damn son, you can move a little quicker," ordered Redrum who, leaning on a blue 55-gallon oil drum near the doorway, was growing impatient with his companion.

Sinnin Blood stopped struggling and fixed his gaze upon his partner who had just interrupted him. Still holding the arm up, he pointed to drum. "What's that?"

"Sulfuric acid. It's for the body parts," answered Redrum. "After you dump 'em in there, it'll take about two days to dissolve. And then—Bam!" He snapped his finger for emphasis. "Just like that, there will be no trace of Cutty left on this planet."

Gulping to swallow saliva, with his Adam's apple bobbing up and down, Sinnin Blood nervously asked, "We have to stay here for two days? What if po-po comes through? Can't we be out after we dump him in the acid?"

"Na, you scary-ass nigga, we don't have to stay here for two days. But we ain't bouncing til we clean that tub up and reglaze it," Redrum regarded him with a cold and ghostly eye and his lips lengthened in a smirk. "Not to mention, we have to come back here later anyway with Dina, so she can get pack some clothes. So, stop worry about being in such a hurry and get your job done. Ya smell me?"

Awkward footsteps echoing off the hallway's hardwood abruptly ended their conversation. It was Kold Fire. He approached the entrance of the bathroom without a whisper of sound and calmly surveyed the scene as Sinnin Blood continued hacking away. He usually tried to steer clear of the cleanup process. He could stomach murder, but not chopping up or burning bodies. Normally, he would remain in the background, breathing through his mouth to avoid the stench of melting flesh and hair. As a highly respected Blood, the young Puerto Rican would order his soldiers to do all the dirty work of cleaning. However, this time it was taking longer than usual, and the scent of blood was beginning to fill the air.

"Yo! This is making me sick!" Kold Fire's sudden outburst startled the other members of his gang. "Can y'all move faster? I was supposed to pick up that pack from Shine since ten. Y'all got me running mad late!"

"Blood, I'm trying to get this shit done as fast as I can," Sinnin Blood informed him. Looking up from the tub, he asked without hesitation, "Whose work is this anyway?"

Knowing the answer but not wanting to give it, Kold Fire shouted with scathing sarcasm, "Oh, a nigga got questions like he five-O now! Man, dead all that yappin' and worry about what you supposed to be doing. I'm not trying to be here all night! I can't take the smell!"

Sinnin Blood looked away and shook his head as Kold Fire pivoted on his heels and bopped toward the front of the apartment.

Jogging to catch up, Redrum called out from behind him, "Yo, Blood, hold up!"

Kold Fire glanced solemnly over his shoulders. "What?"

"Is it true we're going to war with Chinnah?" the young soldier asked, a bit out of breath.

Disgusted, Kold Fire curled his lip and let out a venomous snorting hiss, "Man, just focus on what we need to take care of now. You're worrying about the wrong thing. Besides, we won't be doing anything if the scramz decide to show up here and we haven't gotten all of this cleaned up." He turned and confronted his soldier sternly, staring him in the face. "Why are you out here anyway, dog? You should be helping Sin, not quizzing me. So, bounce, yo!"

With a faint sheen of sweat gleaming on his forehead, Redrum nervously nodded and returned to the bathroom.

As Kold Fire proceeded to exit the apartment he took out his cell phone, tapped the screen a couple of times, and whispered, "What up, Shine? They're almost finished. Right now, we . . ."

♠ ♠ ♠

SHINE STOOD IN HIS LIVING room, holding the phone tightly to his ear while he listened to Redrum give him the details of the cleanup.

"Word. By the time you get here, I'll have that pack for you to give to the young cat. So, make sure you dudes move fast," Shine instructed into the phone. "About to cook it up now. It's light work so it won't take long."

After uttering a few more words, he hung up on Kold Fire without giving him a chance to say goodbye. He inhaled a quick breath. He didn't want his soldier's pointless questions and he didn't want his concerns. The living death of his own memories troubled him enough. Staring at the carpet, Shine pondered his situation until his attention was drawn from his thoughts. He noticed a blood-stained cloth sticking out from the bottom of the sofa. It was a baby wipe.

He bent over to retrieve it, but it was stuck on some part of the furniture. With fast and urgent fingers, he fumbled with it until a strip of the fabric tore loose in his hands. The sight of the half-torn baby wipe, stained with his son's dried blood, caused a swift wave of guilt to wash over him. The bereaved father was overcome with a mixed feeling of sorrow and anger. A single tear clung to his lower eyelid before gently falling onto the tattered cloth. He wiped his eye then jammed the baby wipe into his pocket.

Scraping the soles of his Jordans onto the rug, he strolled sluggishly into the kitchen and glanced at the microwave's clock. It read 10:28 p.m. In sullen silence he rummaged through the cabinet beneath the kitchen sink and retrieved a folded black trash bag. Unfolding it, he removed a medium-sized Ziploc bag packed with cocaine and opened it.

His free hand dove into the sink. In the cold dishwater his fingers trailed across the metal bottom to find a teaspoon. Thank God the water was clean. He pulled it out and rubbed it dry on his red Polo sweater. With steady hands, he stuck the spoon in the Ziploc bag— scooping up as much powder as it could hold—and brought it straight to his nose then sniffed sharply with the force of a Kirby vacuum cleaner.

A loud snorting sound cut through the air as he tilted his head back and started blinking and pinching his nose. After tossing the spoon into the sink he stuck his hand inside the cabinet once more. There was a clattering metallic noise as he struck a large pot and it slid off a smaller one. He pulled the small pot out and placed it on the stove. At a zombie's pace, he dragged himself lazily over to the refrigerator, like a ghastly skeleton with the bones falling apart, his feet sliding along.

The dust on the top of the fridge was thick but when he ran his fingers over it, the brush of ceramic against his skin made him ignore the filth. He found what he was looking for. His hand came down with a large white dinner plate. There was a small electronic scale, a razor blade, a half-cut straw, a box of baking soda, and a measuring cup on it. Carefully, he placed the dish onto the counter next to the stove, taking off the scale and baking soda.

A hiccup of air escaped his lips as the bitterness of the cocaine tingled in the back of his throat and drained from his sinuses. He turned on the scale and spread the Ziploc bag evenly on top of it. The number 28 appeared in red on the front of the screen. Holding the measuring cup under the faucet, he ran water in it until it measured three-fourths. He poured the water into the pot and turned the stove on medium high.

There was a quick zip as Shine tore a paper towel from the roll that hung beneath the upper cabinets. Removing the razor and straw first, he covered the plate with the napkin. After measuring the baking soda with the teaspoon, he then dumped it into the water followed by the cocaine from the Ziploc bag. The mixture began bubbling.

The young *Chef de Narcotic Cuisine* tossed the razor blade and straw back on the plate. With an equally deft motion of his hand—the grace of his movements very much like those of a *Food Network* star—he yanked a butter knife from the dish rack and stuck it into the pot while the mixture cooked. Gently pressing the blade on the surface of the water to flatten the bubbles, he watched the cocaine harden. He spooned the substance from the saucepan onto the paper towel to drain. He placed the dish in the freezer, then leaned against the refrigerator, wearied.

Pale moonlight streamed in through the window over the sink as the fridge hummed its usual late-night symphony. Besides the clattering of raindrops against the window pane, an eerie silence filled the rest of the apartment. All the nightmares that had ever plagued a father loomed in Shine's mind. He couldn't get the image of his son out of his head; Trayvon's vacant eyes staring at nothing, his curly hair thick with blood, the cold lifeless look. A wave of nausea swept over him and a creeping feeling of urgency heightened his misery. He thought about the situation brewing with Chinnah and considered his options. *Is a war necessary?* It would only place him in deeper trouble. Besides, he couldn't focus on another enemy before he faced the one within himself. He needed to decide. The right decision.

A cold, bottomless emptiness settled inside of him. It would prove difficult hiding his son's death from relatives and friends. He drew a deep breath and felt his stomach churn as he exhaled. Struggling to withstand the crippling burden of guilt bubbling in him, he pondered going to the cops and explaining what happened to Trayvon. Yet, the thought of spending the rest of his life in a small cell seemed bleak. For a moment, leaving the state appeared to be the best solution. Then, without warning, it hit him like a knife piercing his heart.

Someone will eventually question Trayvon's disappearance. I can't hide it forever.

If his son's absence aroused suspicions, police would eventually get involved. And since he did not report it, he would likely be viewed as a suspect. The truth will surface sooner or later. He pondered over the possible consequences of not going to the police. No matter how much he overthought it, he kept coming up with the same answer.

Shaking his head, he took a deep breath to calm his nerves then made his way into the bathroom. He pulled out a lighter, grabbed a blunt from off the sink, lit it and inhaled slowly. He mulled the smoke around in his mouth before letting it fill his lungs. It relaxed him as it filtered out through his nose. He took three more short and quick pulls from the blunt then smothered the fiery tip into the sink. The effects of the weed took over and a shiver of warmth moved through him.

Suddenly, his heart gave a nasty jump and a dizzying sensation overcame him. He wobbled for a few seconds as paranoia, guided by the mixture of weed and cocaine, raced through his mind. Realizing what he had to do, he swung around on his heels and headed toward the living room. Grabbing his jacket from the love seat, he bolted out of his apartment, barely closing the door behind him. As he hustled down the staircase, taking three steps at once, he whipped out his cell phone and began dialing 9-1-1. He was in such a hurry he had forgotten about the cocaine in his freezer.

♠   ♠   ♠

BLACK CLOUDS ROLLED OVER the midnight skyline as ice-cold rain slammed down in a blinding torrent onto Snyder Ave, pounding the roof of the Sixty-seventh Precinct. The wind shrieked and wailed around the building, vibrating the window while the late Friday night showers pelted the glass like bullets. Inside, the precinct was a circus of activity. A burly, red-faced desk sergeant with a short crew cut busily fielded hundreds of calls, scanners crackled, imploring cries from suspects sounded over the whir of printers, detectives diligently pecked away at computer keyboards, and civilians argued with officers while filing police reports.

The ceiling lights burned with an unforgiving fluorescence, casting a glare on Detective Cardillo's reading glasses as he held a Twinkie up to the bare-bulb examining it. He lifted his glasses and curiously peered over its rim, studying the sponge cake. Letting out a deep sigh, he tossed the snack whole into his mouth. He brought his attention to Brown, who was busy yelling into the phone.

"Yes, Yes! You have said that three times already! You were able to determine from the impression pattern left at the scene, that the outer edge of the tire was a bit worn. So, what? How does that help me?" Brown cast his eyes to the ground, shook his head in disgust and listened into the phone. Then lifting his head and grinning like a madman he excitedly replied, "Oh, ok. Well why didn't you just say that at first? Instead of all of the technical mumbo jumbo, you could have simply gotten to the point. Ok, so I understand now. We are looking for a Ford Expedition with a bad wheel alignment."

Seeing his partner was obviously too engrossed in his investigation to entertain a conversation, Cardillo turned away. He caught sight of Detective Howard Seidman approaching his desk, his belly bulging and one chubby white hand holding a bottle of water.

"Hey, Seidman, you're a part of the Special Investigations Division, so you must be one of the smarter ones around here. How do you suppose they get the cream into this thing?" Cardillo inquired, his words faintly muffled with a mouth full of cake. Slightly smirking, he opened his lips just wide enough to reveal the white and yellow mush that covered his tongue.

Seidman could see the detective's jaw working to make enough saliva to swallow the junk food. He eyed him with disgust and shook his head, strands of his thin greying hair sliding over his forehead. Running his finger through his thick mustache, he looked as though he was about to say something profound. Instead he squinted his eyes at the rookie and asked, "What the hell did that used to be?"

"A Twinkie!" Cardillo exclaimed, surprised at his ignorance of junk food.

"Whatever." Seidman rolled his eyes and waved Cardillo off. "Look, I have a missing child case to attend to. The vic's father has been sitting at my desk for about an hour. So, I don't have time for your 'did the chicken or the egg come first' theories. Some of us here are real detectives."

Cardillo's blank stare immediately fell on Seidman as he walked away. "Yeah, you're a real dick all right."

Seidman heard Cardillo's comment but ignored it. He continued past the brightly lit, bar-free holding cell area. Closed in by shatterproof glass, the sullen eyes of dope fiends, male prostitutes, alcoholics, thieves, and murderers watched him with furtive, disdainful curiosity. Wondering who would be the next person called out of the cell, their gaze followed the detective's movement until he disappeared from view.

As Seidman approached his desk, he realized he forgot to get the M&M's the gentleman requested. He started to turn around and go back, but quickly dismissed the thought. Certain the young man would prefer to have his son in front of him than a pack of candy, Seidman hurried on until he neared the area where the grieving father was seated.

"Here you go," Seidman handed the water to him. "The machine was out of M&M's."

Shine glanced over his right shoulder to reach for the bottle. "Thanks."

Seidman shuffled to his chair, and gingerly eased into it. Twitching in his seat and frowning uncertainly, the detective rummaged through a stack of papers. Without looking up, he dully stated, "It doesn't appear we have much to go on to conduct a thorough investigation. However, we will look into it. I strongly advise you to contact us if you can remember anything else regarding your son's disappearance." He brought his eyes up, searched Shine's face, and with a slightly interested tone of voice asked, "You are sure you have no reason to suspect he's been kidnapped? I mean, that neighborhood is dangerous. I'm certain there are several people you could point a finger at. You know—to point us in some direction."

Shine began shifting in his seat trying to get comfortable, "No, not that I can think of. I mean, one minute he was in the front room watching TV, and the next, he was gone."

"Well, we are going to need to speak with the mother, and I can send officers by your apartment to examine the place for any evidence of foul play. Just in case." Detective Seidman rose from his chair and extended his hand across the desk.

Shine stood and received the detective's handshake, his eyes brimming with unshed tears. His voice was rough with emotion as he spoke, "Please, sir, please find my boy."

Lacking concern in his expression, Seidman responded in an even tone, "We will do our best. Usually, the precinct wouldn't hand off a case like this to me until after a couple of weeks had gone by and they were unsuccessful in finding your son. But I noticed you when you first walked in and, overhearing your situation, I thought you could use all the help you could get right now." Seidman sighed slowly before continuing. "We don't need to wait around for this situation to get worse for any of us. Anyways, for now, please go home and await our call. We will be in contact with you soon."

The detective's response troubled Shine. He wasn't certain if Seidman believed his story, wondering if he had given himself away by talking too much. He stared unseeingly past the cop as he quickly replayed the entire conversation in his head. Positive he had not said anything to make the detective suspicious, he allowed his gaze to drift around the precinct. He eyed the crowded holding cell, his heart aching at the silent message it presented.

"May I ask you something sir?" Shine's lips twisted into a crooked line of anguish, his face fixed somewhere between a smile and a frown.

"Sure," said Seidman.

"How long have you been a cop?"

"Uh. About thirty years or so. But it's like I've always been a cop. It runs deep in my blood." Seidman let out a low, ponderous chuckle. "My father was a cop his whole life—well, up until he retired and invested his savings in real estate. And before that, his father was a cop. So, it's all I've ever known. Why do you ask?"

"Because," an overwhelming sadness welled up inside Shine as he tightened his throat muscles to contain his emotions. Rubbing his eyes to squeeze the tears back inside, he choked out the words, "Because I need to know that the right person will be searching for my son. I need to know that he's in good hands. That he will be alright."

It pained him to utter those words: *I need to know that he's in good hands.*

"You will soon find out that you came to the right person. I will help you get through this. Whatever happened to your son, I will make sure that finding a suspect won't be a burden for you." Seidman furrowed his brow and squinted his eyes. "Look, I'm sure you have important business to attend to, so go home and let me take care of this."

"Yeah, ok." Shine hung his head low, slowly pivoted, and started back toward the entrance of the precinct. "I'll wait to hear from you detective," he said without looking back.

Suddenly, remembering he hadn't given the man his personal contact information, Seidman called out to the grieving young father. "Hey…sir???"

Racked with guilt, Shine couldn't hear much over the thoughts dancing in his head. He kept walking.

"Cardillo!" Seidman yelled out to the detective, noticing that the young man was headed toward his desk.

The Italian rookie gave Seidman a surly look as he glanced up from the conversation he was having with a female officer about Twinkies. "Yes?"

"Stop that gentleman in the red cap for me," demanded Seidman.

Seeing the young man approaching, Cardillo stepped forward blocking his path, and extended his hand. "Um, excuse me, sir. You can't leave just yet."

Shine halted his steps. His eyes narrowed at the detective's words. *They didn't believe me. They know what happened.* Still high, paranoia immediately set in. He considered bolting past the officer and running out of the precinct. Instead, he received his handshake.

"Sorry for the abrupt stop. My name is Detective Cardillo. I am sure you would like to leave this place as soon as possible. However, it appears there is one more thing Detective Seidman would like to speak to you about." Both men turned their attention to Seidman who was fumbling around his desk.

Seidman felt the two staring at him but wouldn't meet their gaze as he clumsily searched his workspace.

"Cardillo, do you have a card at your desk with the station's main number on it?" Seidman asked while tossing paper and folders to the side.

"Sure," answered Cardillo. As he scanned the pile of paperwork covering his desk, his attention was drawn to Shine who was searching through his jeans. He glanced at the young man's face and noted his scar.

"No need for the card. I might have a pen and a piece of paper to write it down on," Shine said with his fingers tucked inside his pockets.

He wanted to leave the precinct as quickly as possible. As he removed his hand from his pants revealing a red ink pen, he unintentionally brought out a piece of cloth with it. Stained with dried blood, it dangled from his right pocket. Cardillo couldn't help but see it. His eyes scanned Shine's body, looking for additional injuries.

He decided to be blunt. "Sir, are you still bleeding?"

Shine seemed thrown off by the question.

"Huh?"

Detective Cardillo pointed to his pocket. "You have a bloody tissue hanging from your pocket, and the scratch on your face looks recent."

Hearing the discussion between the two, Detective Brown looked up from his desk. He turned his attention away from his phone conversation and watched as the young man nervously looked down at the baby wipe hanging from his pocket. Shine tried to think of an explanation, but his mind was troubled, his heart thumped dreadfully. He opened his mouth but said nothing. He feigned surprise at Cardillo's remark then finally blurted out the first thing that came into his head.

"I thought I threw that away. Besides the scrape, I had a really bad nosebleed." A sheepish smile tugged at Shine's lips as he tucked the baby wipe deeper into his pants. "I was in a small fender bender yesterday."

Brown gazed at him with a raised eyebrow and a smirk on his face. He then shoved his hand inside his blazer and retrieved his wallet. After opening it up and pulling out a card, the detective removed the receiver from his ear then motioned to his partner.

"Here, I have a card for the young man," offered Brown.

Cardillo paid him no attention. His mind was too busy racing, weighing Shine's words. Something wasn't right about the young man's answer, but he couldn't put his finger on it. His intuition bothered him, but his thoughts came to a halt when he caught sight of Brown's hand holding out the card in front of his face.

"You can give him this. The station's main number is on it. He can just ask for Seidman," stated the senior detective.

Cardillo calmly reached for the card then handed it off. Shine accepted it. Without uttering another word, he nodded then spun on his heels and continued toward the exit.

Cardillo glared at the young man as he walked away. "You're welcome!" he exclaimed sarcastically.

Without facing the detective, Shine threw his hand up into the air and waved him off.

Cardillo turned to Brown. "Ungrateful son of a bitch."

A vague, half grin appeared beneath Brown's furrowed brow as he eyed his partner and shrugged. "Umm. I don't know about that. His case hasn't been solved yet, so I wouldn't say he was ungrateful. Suspicious maybe, but not ungrateful."

Cardillo stared at Brown, scrutinizing him closely, as if he was trying to read his mind. "I don't understand."

Brown smiled at the rookie's ignorance. "According to what Seidman said earlier, this is the father of a missing child, right?"

Cardillo nodded his head, hoping Brown would skip the dramatics and get to the point.

"For someone who doesn't know where his child is, he seemed to be in a hurry to leave."

Cardillo again nodded.

Brown continued, "What was in his pocket?"

Cardillo raised his eyebrow. "Are you referring to the tissue?"

Still smiling, Brown corrected him. "It wasn't a tissue. It was a baby wipe."

"Okay?" Cardillo didn't understand where his partner was going with his questions.

Seeing the younger officer was having a hard time following him, Brown decided to stop beating around the bush. "This man came in and reported a missing child, yet he also had a baby wipe hanging from his pants that was covered in blood. A baby wipe!" He tilted his head forward and widened his eyes. "When you questioned him, he seemed startled by your observation and took a second before he answered you."

Cardillo's eyebrow went up, a hint of astonishment in his expression. "You know, I could sense something but wasn't sure. He is hiding something, isn't he?"

"Not sure. Not our case."

"Hey, guys!" Seidman yelled out, while nearing the two. "Did you give that gentleman a card?"

Both men nodded.

"Well, there was no need to rush him off. He can't go anywhere," said Seidman to his two colleagues.

They eyed the detective keenly, trying to understand him. Seidman held up a set of keys.

"He forgot his car keys. They were sitting on my desk. One of you guys mind running this out there to him." Seidman shot an apologetic grin at the men. "I have a couple of important calls to make."

Without hesitation Brown snatched the keys from the officer's grasp and headed outside.

Seidman let his eyes fall on Cardillo. "He's in a helpful mood today, I see."

"No, he's just playing detective again," replied Cardillo. "He's part bloodhound and part human."

Both men laughed.

Brown's pace was quick. As he stepped through the doors of the precinct, he ran into Shine, who was on his way back inside. The detective held the keys up.

"You forgot something?"

Shine took the keys, a look of barely suppressed relief on his face. "Yeah, I was just coming back in there for those."

Brown offered a grin that was more of a faint sneer. "You weren't going to get too far."

"Who are you telling? I damn sure wasn't about to walk back to Rutland Road."

"Rutland Road, really?" Brown wondered if he knew about the killings that recently occurred on and near that street. In his investigation of the deaths at Minimart he weighed the possibility that it was somehow connected to the murders at Chinnah's house.

"Yeah, I'm from the Nineties," Shine mentioned.

"Really? And you get away with walking up and down Rutland Road with all of that red on?" Brown nodded toward the Red Yankees baseball cap that sat on top of the young man's head. "The Nineties is Crip central over there. Stone Cold Crips at that."

Detecting an undercurrent of suspicion in the older man's voice, Shine fell quiet.

The men stood in silence for an uncomfortable amount of time facing each other. Brown's smirk was unsettling. Shine tried to appear relaxed, but the detective could see the nervous darting of his eyes. Staring wide-eyed, Brown followed his gaze.

Shine decided to end the awkwardness of the moment. "Yeah, I don't know about all of that." He glanced at his watch. "Look, I have to go. I have some business to attend to."

Saying nothing, the detective continued smiling. A rumble of thunder sounded in the distance. The awkward gangsta didn't bother to extend his hand. Welcoming the cold and unpleasant rain, his boots splashed through the dark puddles as he stepped off the sidewalk and bopped toward his SUV.

Detective Brown caught sight of Shine's vehicle and tilted his head to the side. *A Ford Expedition*, he thought. *What are the odds?* He approached the car and immediately noticed the uneven tread wear on the tires, an indication of poor wheel alignment. As he neared the vehicle it roared to life and inched out of the parking space, veering off to side before straightening up and speeding down the street. Brown took a mental note of the license plate. *ALA 1964*. He turned and hurried back into the precinct. With his curiosity concerning the missing child heightened, he needed to discuss the case with Detective Seidman.

CHAPTER 7

NOISE ENGULFED LOLA on all sides, battering her eardrums. The sound of carts squeaking along the corridor, the loud paging system blaring overhead, doors opening and closing, telephones ringing, and infants crying. She paced furiously back and forth in the emergency room of Brookdale Hospital, fists clenched, and head hung low. Her dark face was pale and tight with tension, her eyes sleep starved. Clearly exhausted, Lola decided to take a seat. Her legs trembled as she settled into the chair and clutched the armrests.

The soft glow of the linoleum floors caught her attention and her eyes followed the multi-colored lines that crisscrossed along the hallway. With a low frustrated growl, she buried her face into her clammy palms. Pain throbbed in her temples. Lifting her head to blink the tears out of her eyes, she took a long, wobbling breath—a breath filled with the sickening odor of unwashed, damp bodies and antiseptic solution. Her foot swung back and forth under the chair while she sat clicking her nails against the metal armrest. The sight of mothers cradling screaming babies tormented the young woman. Barely twenty-four hours had passed since Trayvon's death.

Earlier that morning, she had awakened with a strange taste in her mouth and tightness in her throat, shivering with fear. There was a profound sense of aloneness lodged deep in her being. Drenched in sweat and her heart hammering, she rose out of bed nauseous, with a feeling of hopelessness and grief brought on by the memories of the previous day. After witnessing her vomit several times at breakfast before fainting, Desiree finally convinced her friend to go to the hospital.

Now, with a stabbing headache and her nausea barely in check, Lola sat in the emergency room fighting off a wave of overwhelming, stomach wrenching panic. She took a slow, deep breath trying to push the thoughts of her deceased child out of her mind. Her head spun, replaying scenes from her childhood in Georgia. That didn't help. It only depressed her more. The memories set off a violent fluttering in her belly. She felt terribly vulnerable.

What happened to me? I have changed.

She wondered whether she was to blame for Trayvon's death.

No, it was Shine's gun, so it was his fault.

She wanted desperately to remove the stain of guilt from her conscience. Not the guilt she felt because of her son's death. But the guilt she felt for wanting to abandon Shine at a time like this and run to her other lover. That feeling of guilt clawed at her heart and made her cringe.

Lola sighed, knowing she was being naïve. It was a foolish idea, because her lover not only had a family, but was in a relationship with one of her closest friends. Her disloyalty to Shine hardly troubled her as much as the thought of betraying a friend. The deception bothered her. She felt as if she was concealing some secret part of herself and imagined the consequences of being exposed. Suddenly the tension of her nerves gave way, making her skin crawl. Teeth chattering, she shrank into the chair just as Desiree came strutting into the waiting area clutching an opened can of ginger ale.

She approached Lola. "They ain't seen you yet?" she yelled out.

Lola shook her head and reached for the can. Desiree handed it over. Lola's companion cast a wistful glance around the emergency room then heaved a long-suffering sigh.

"Girl, how long is this going to take? You need to make some noise up in this piece or you'll never be seen. That's the problem with you country chicks. Y'all too passive," Desiree scolded in a loud whisper of frustration.

Ignoring her friend, Lola drew a deep breath then threw a disheartening glance at the can in her hand. She shook it and mumbled in silence. A frown of disappointment dragged on her face. With her anger spilling over, she strained her neck to look up at Desiree.

"You drank from this?"

Desiree gave a weak, apologetic smile. "Just a little. I haven't had a ginger ale in a while, and besides, I paid for it."

Lola leered at her friend, ice in her eyes. "Desiree, I'm the one who's sick."

A hint of embarrassment flashed across Desiree's face and she quickly glanced down at the floor. "Yeah, you right. You've been through a lot this week. I shouldn't be so selfish. I'll go get you another one."

Suddenly, Lola winced as a ripple of pain shot through her. Dropping the can, she bent over and clutched her stomach, her face twisting into a grimace of agony. She gritted her teeth to hide her distress then in a faint voice uttered, "Forget the soda. It's alright. I'm good."

Desiree's eyes swept Lola quizzically, "You sure you aight?"

"Uh—huh," Lola murmured.

The sound of heels clicking on the linoleum tiles caught the girls' attention, interrupting their thoughts. Then there was the *swoosh* of the hospital doors sweeping against the floor just as a soft voice reached them.

"Bye—Lola?"

"Lola Bye," the nurse repeated in a soothing tone. "Lola Bye."

Lola felt her gut unclench a little. Her gaze wandered across the dull beige hospital walls surrounding her. The sight was depressing. It reminded her of the prison visitation room she sat in as a teenager when she first met her father.

"Lola Bye?" the nurse's voice floated through the air once more.

Desiree gently touched Lola's knee. "Girl, I know what you're thinking and why you are hesitating to go in there, but you need to get up now before she decides to call the next person. We've been here for mad long now. Come on, mommy."

Lola growled a muffled reply, her eyes widening as she cast a look in the direction of the young olive-skinned hospital attendant. The nurse's blue contacts peered back at her from behind the bangs of a platinum-blonde wig. Desiree put an arm around her friend and helped her out of her chair. With terrifying slowness, Lola inched along the corridor towards the double doors being held open for her. Stopping just short of the nurse, she stood and pondered over her dilemma until a sense of dread swept over her. A thousand regrets harassed her mind.

"Why me?" she admonished herself out loud, snapping back to reality. Whipping her head around to give Desiree a fierce look over her shoulder, Lola abruptly blurted out, "This shit can't be happening to me." She then followed the nurse beyond the doors.

♠ ♠ ♠

WISPY CLOUDS DOTTED the pale blue sky, dimming the late fall sunlight. A cold wetness clung to the midday air, threatening drizzle, as a light damp breeze stirred the few trees in the Brownsville neighborhood. The B14 bus belched out black fumes at the many shoppers who hurried up and down Pitkin Avenue. Bargaining more than purchasing, they mingled with countless teenagers thronging the pavement in a noisy, chaotic melee, selling stolen merchandise and narcotics. The noise of the Saturday traffic was deafening, while the A train rumbled beneath the street with a muffled roar. Occasionally, random burst of obscenities or sirens from police cars could be heard over the salsa music that thumped from corner store speakers.

A little bit of sunlight found its way through the gloomy atmosphere and glinted dully off the side window of a dark blue sedan. It was parked at the corner of the block, the driver visible only as a silhouette behind the tint. His face was half hidden by a long, bushy black beard. Dressed in a dusty dark coat, the stern-looking young man sat, peering unkindly through his sunglasses at the many empty-faced, mindless zombies wandering, block after block, in an unself-conscious daze. Lightly puffing on a Newport, there was something alarming in his calmness. Almost deathly still, only allowing his eyes to move, he searched the area around him. Filled with a sudden intense feeling of disgust at the people he watched, he thought, *America a wicked country.*

He started to turn on his stereo when he saw a familiar face stroll past his car. From his rearview mirror he observed the man as he approached an aging and seemingly dilapidated apartment building that sat between a clothing store and a bodega. The lone driver had patiently waited for this moment. Now he could make his move.

After strutting past the sedan, Gorilla Leek glanced over his shoulder as if aware he was being watched. For a moment it appeared as if he looked directly into the vehicle. Donning a black hoodie cinched tight around his face, he continued slowly along the sidewalk to Mama Young's apartment building. Before entering, he scanned the area around him, his eyes darting from one spot to another. Though he knew the building was almost completely abandoned, he wasn't sure if he was making the right decision.

The only tenant, Mama Young kept herself isolated inside her first-floor apartment eating sardines and peanut-butter-and-jelly sandwiches. Bitter over her declining health, the elderly lady seldom ventured out of her hole. That was the reason Gorilla Leek chose her building. Anywhere else would have meant death for him. His face was too well-known, and he didn't want to be seen.

Slowly, he entered the building. It reeked with moldy floor tiles and old painted walls. The lights were out. Shadows danced near an illuminated crack at the bottom of a door at the end of the hall. As he closed the door behind him, the hinges creaked and a gust of cold air crept in. He immediately reeled at the sickly stench of urine and cigarette smoke that slammed into his nostrils. The odor along with the frigid rain from the morning left the hallway feeling like a damp cave. He peered cautiously ahead of him, waiting for his eyes to become accustomed to the dim light seeping through a drawn window curtain. Moving silently, he stopped at the foot of the staircase, pressed close to the wall, and waited. Deafened by a mysterious roar of silence, Gorilla Leek tensed, removed his hoodie, and looked up into the darkness at the top of the stairs.

He didn't hear the door open behind him but felt the chilling breeze that blew past the bearded man who had just entered through it. With the stealth of a leopard hunting beneath the sub-Saharan night sky, the bearded man eased quietly toward him, gun drawn. He cocked his weapon slowly as to not make a sound and leveled it toward the back of his prey's head.

Just as the would-be assassin set off to close the distance between himself and his target, the freezing wind ripped against the back of Gorilla Leek's neck, drawing his attention and making him shiver. He spun around. His breathed quickened and his heart dropped. Looking into the barrel of a Colt Double Eagle, inches from his face, the Blood gang leader stood completely still and cursed himself. There was no time to pull out his .44 or answer his ringing cell phone. He got caught slipping.

♠   ♠   ♠

SHINE HUNG UP THE PHONE, wondering why his best friend had not answered his calls. That was unlike him, unless he was with a woman. *Yeah, he's probably with a chick.* A faint grin touched the corner of his lips as he continued strolling leisurely down Fulton Avenue, stopping and looking in several store windows. The shrill whining of an ambulance filled the afternoon air, reminding him of Lola's wailing after she discovered Trayvon's body. The memory unsettled his stomach. Lost in a myriad of conflicting thoughts and emotions, he walked for several minutes until he came to a pizza shop. He paused to ponder over all the painful circumstances of his own situation. It was both his lifestyle and his gun that led to his son's death and the war with Chinnah.

For a second, he contemplated telling his best friend about his visit to the precinct, but then he decided against it. He was half-convinced Gorilla Leek would panic once he learned the police would soon be snooping around. Lately, his partner had been especially concerned about the cops investigating Minimart. And Shine knew that telling him about the sit-down with Detective Seidman would only add to his paranoia and possibly drive him to a ridiculous extreme. His mind racing, he stood, staring blankly at the door to the pizza shop considering his next move.

The annoying noise of the Downtown Brooklyn traffic brought him back to the present moment and he felt his stomach growl, reminding him that he had not eaten all day. Initially, he ventured into that part of Brooklyn to buy a new pair of sneakers, hoping it would clear his head. But now he decided to give in to his appetite and forgo shopping.

He entered the pizza shop, approached the counter and glanced up at the menu. Flashes of his son's corpse suddenly flooded his mind and if he was alone, he would have allowed the tears to fall. Details in the store blurred in front of his blinking eyes as a vision of Trayvon's wet and bloody scalp swam before him. His surroundings went strangely out of focus. Only the dim ghostly image of his son's mutilated face remained. With a gaping hole blossoming like a giant rose and crimson strings of blood running down his cheeks, the boy struggled to part his lips and lift his tongue as his head twitched.

A long guttural sound came out of the phantom child's mouth. "Yooouuuu—yooouuuuuu . . ."

The cloudy, wraithlike illusion of the boy began to fade, and his voice took on the sound of a much older Italian man.

"You! You! Aye, you," a husky, red-faced gentleman bellowed across the counter, startling Shine out of his momentary daydream.

The sight of the store owner's apron spattered with tomato sauce and flour greeted him. Shine looked up. Dark eyes met his gaze.

"You! Sir! Are you ordering something?" the owner impatiently asked.

Shine said nothing and examined the menu.

The man grew impatient. "Listen buddy, move to the side. I don't have all day. There are other customers behind you."

Shine exhaled through gritted teeth, furrowed his brow, and with a look of cold fury in his green eyes, cast a hateful glance at the man.

"Yo, you better watch how you yappin, motherfucka!" Shine hardened his stare. "Fuck who's behind me. You better worry about who's in front of you! Ain't nobody beefing but you! Open your mouth up like that again, and I'll cut the shit wide-open!"

A stillness gathered in the air as the store fell silent. The man blinked nervously, a slight smile lifted the corner of his trembling lips. His eyes darted uncomfortably around the restaurant to avoid looking at Shine. Just as he considered apologizing, his gaze fell on a customer sitting alone at a table in the back of the shop talking on a cell phone. With long, coal-black dreadlocks trailing over his wiry shoulders in uneven clumps, the young man sat, staring at the back of Shine's head in a tense and uncertain way. This caught the store owner's attention. Fear twisted his gut at the cold, ghastly calmness on the stranger's face.

Following the wandering eyes of the owner, Shine glanced over his shoulder. Seeing nothing to concern him, he returned his gaze toward the counter. A warm smile playing on his lips, he spoke clear and sharp, cutting through the dense silence with a simple question. "Now, may I have one cheese slice?" The fierceness of his stare still conveying his anger, Shine added, "Please!"

The Italian gentleman brought his attention back to the irate customer in front of him, nodded his head and winced as he swallowed involuntarily. He found his mouth dry and sticky.

"Yes, s-s-s-sir, one slice it is. W-w-would you like th-th-that warm or h-h-hot?" he stuttered in a still, small voice.

Shine's smile faded into a grimace. The taut lines of his face told the man how angry he was. "The hell you think?"

The owner moistened his lips nervously with a dry tongue. "I'm— I'm not sure, sir. I wouldn't—"

"Nigga, I want it hot!"

At that moment, the man's face was a mask of fear and anger. The sting of being labeled a nigger roused conflicting emotions in him that distorted his features. He recalled a similar experience from his childhood when someone once referred to him by that vile slur. However, it wasn't a nigga who called him a nigger back then.

Arriving to this country in his youth, he endured belittling comments from other whites about his ethnicity. The focus of relentless harassment, he was told by an older American male that all Sicilians came from the Moors who were black, making him a nigger and not a white man. More hurtful words followed before the young Italian was brutally beaten into unconsciousness by the man and his friends.

Now, reliving that hellish moment, his face was hard with restrained emotion, his hands clenched at his sides. His mind came back to the present and he met Shine's angry glare with a smoldering intensity of his own. A tense silence hung between them. The Italian stood rigid as the other customers in the store held their breath, silently watching the drama unfold.

After a moment of contemplation, the owner calmly nodded then spoke icily in a tone taut with emotion. "No problem, sir. Hot it is."

He hacked a slice from the 18-inch pie and slid it into the open oven. Business being slow that afternoon, he considered the customers he would lose if he engaged in a verbal tussle, let alone a fight. Resisting the overwhelming urge to curse, his mouth twitched into a reluctant grin. There was a fierce rage beneath his relaxed countenance. It was deep and dark, boiling inside him, demanding action. With a smug turn of his lips, he eyed Shine coldly, clenched his fists, and asked, "Will that be all, sir?"

Shine slammed a twenty-dollar bill onto the counter, turned on his heels, and proceeded to exit the store. Without looking back, he yelled, "I'll return in a sec. Make sure my change is right!"

A wistful sigh escaped the owner's lips. Relieved that the young man left without incident, he relaxed his fists. Then, allowing his gaze to drift around the shop, he noticed the dreadlock stranger moving quickly to follow behind Shine as he walked out the door.

The stalker kept his distance as he watched his prey cross Fulton Street and stop in front of a sneaker store. Immersed in thought and completely oblivious to the predator's presence, Shine stood motionless looking at the window display. The stalker gazed about—examining his environment—then discreetly unzipped his jacket, reached inside, and removed a small .380 pistol. The gun held down tight against his leg, he crept forward slowly.

Kam had been following Shine closely ever since he left his apartment that morning. He drove behind his prey, patiently waiting for him to pull over and get out so he could get a clear shot. Taking notice of the vehicle trailing him, Shine regarded the car suspiciously when it parked a few feet behind him. However, with his current problems demanding attention, he dismissed the rumblings of his intuition and proceeded to walk down Fulton Street, unaware of the man shadowing him. Kam was on Shine's heels when he entered the pizza shop. To avoid being seen, he went straight to the back of the store, sat down, and dialed Pauley. Clearly upset that their enemy was still breathing, Pauley instructed his soldier to quickly carry out the task.

Unwilling to disappoint his boss, Kam rushed out behind his target, shuffling through the customers until he reached the sidewalk. Gun in hand, he was ready now. He raised his weapon in preparation, his index finger on the trigger. *One shot to di head an den waak away* is what he thought as he crossed the street. He moved swiftly, eyes keeping watch over his surroundings for unexpected movement. As he neared Shine, he snuck a peek at his watch. It read 12:41. His other hand fully extended toward his target, he abruptly froze. His gaze caught sight of another familiar face. Squinting to refocus his vision, he blinked against the sunlight that peeked from behind a thinning grey cloud. There was a young woman walking toward Shine, and Kam recognized her.

Her caramel complexion gleamed like a reflection on sunlit water. With her shoulders gracefully thrown back, she strutted proudly down the sidewalk, weaving in and out of the oncoming crowd. The young beauty's large brown eyes, passionate with love and dread, stood out among the several hardened stares of the Brooklyn natives. Her face wreath in a smile of bliss, she appeared to be deep in thought as she strolled elegantly on long shapely legs, taking small steps. Not paying attention, Shine slowly stepped back from the store window into her path. The two collided, causing her to drop the books she held in her hands.

Kam stepped onto the curb and positioned himself a few feet away from them, next to a street lamp. To avoid suspicion, he retrieved his cell phone and pretended to dial. Under his anxious gaze, Shine scrambled to pick up the young lady's books.

"Damn!" she angrily exclaimed. "You need to watch where you are going, brother."

A bit embarrassed, Shine replied, "Pardon self ma." He handed her the books. "Uh, I was kind of in my own world."

The lady detected the grief flooding through his words. She watched him with interest. He covered his face with mock calmness, but his eyes betrayed him. She looked straight through his hardened exterior without blinking. The man was in deep mourning, his torn emotions evident. Pain hollowed his eyes. The story of a tormenting sorrow was written across his face and it touched her. The tone of his voice tugging at her heart, she was now curious about the man in front of her.

"It's all right," Her voice softened as her anger turned to concern. "I can see you have a lot on your mind. Are you good?"

Touched by her discernment and warmed by her concern for his feelings, Shine stared at her in fascination and nodded.

She continued, "Whatever it is, know that life will present you with more of the same, but life will never burden you with more than you can handle. So, if you are going through a lot, then it says much about your character. You are a strong person. You can get through it . . ."

The sternness in his expression suddenly lessened. He felt his resolve soften. She impressed him. As he listened to her, curiosity and desire nibbled at him. His mind was blown. No one ever spoke to him in such a manner before. Watching her face, Shine traced the lines of her heart-shaped lips with his eyes. Her words were weighed and delivered very cautiously. She sent his head whirling. He had never met a woman like her.

Kam's eyes narrowed, the corners of his mouth turned down just a little. Anticipation almost consumed him as he watched the two interact. He couldn't wait any longer, but the woman's presence discouraged him from firing his weapon. The lady would surely recognize him and possibly identify him to the cops. Realizing there was nothing he could do now, a slight bitterness consumed him. He decided it would be best to get away from them as quickly as possible. Thinking madly of a way to leave the area unnoticed, he spotted a cab approaching and he flagged it down. The cab stopped. *Dis a probably di fastest way back to di car,* he thought as he eased into the backseat.

He glanced at his phone. He needed to call Pauley, but the battery was dead. Now he was worried. There was no way to reach his boss. Probably a good thing, because he could only imagine how that call would go over. The cab pulled out into the middle of the street and merged into the line of cars going toward the Brooklyn Bridge. Kam stared stonily out the back window, feeling in his blood the eager throbbing of the car's engine. Catching a fleeting image of the back of Shine's head, he bit his lip and swore savagely under his breath, "Yuh time limited, yankee."

Suddenly, a flash of paranoia swept over Shine. It was the strangest sensation. Like someone was watching him. Call it a premonition, but he knew he was being followed. That awful feeling begged him to turn around just in time to see a cab pulling into traffic. But the vehicle was too far away to make out the driver or the passenger. Once the car was out of view, he took in a deep, steady breath, inhaling the cool, damp air. It did nothing to soothe the edginess inside him. He was sure he was losing his sanity. *I'm bugging out. I can't stay in this city anymore,* he thought.

"Are you okay?" The lady asked, her soft words dragging him from his thoughts. "You seem very troubled. You know, conscious is a killer."

Shine's head titled slightly as he surveyed her through heavy lidded eyes. She was beautiful. A red, black, and green knitted scarf, tied as a headband, allowed her waist-length dreadlocks to flow down her back. The straight black skirt she wore covered her ankles, but it outlined, revealingly, the lines of her flesh-padded hips. Her black leather jacket was half-unzipped, catching Shine's attention, as his eyes fell on the ankh chain nestled between her breasts. Desire pulsed through his body. The young woman's long eyelashes fluttered when she spoke, her voice barely audible with a slight accent.

Shine snapped out of his hypnotic gaze. "I'm good, ma. Are you?"

"Indeed. I'm at peace, King." she said, her accent pleasingly melodic.

"Where are you from?"

"Flatbush," she answered.

"Na, I'm talking about your family. Your background."

She let out a deep sigh. "I don't really see my family like that. I am kind of alone out here in New York."

"Where do you call home? I mean—you know—before you came here."

"The earth is my home brother," she replied, not giving a straight answer and slightly frustrating Shine.

He decided to ask once more, but this time in a very blunt manner, "Ok, well—what island is your family from?"

"My family is," she declared with a tinge of pride, "Jamaican."

Fearful she had spoken too loudly, she looked around. As she turned her head, her hair brushed Shine's nose, and he found himself taking a deep breath. Her locks gave off a maddeningly sweet scent that awakened his senses. Every nook and cranny of the block they stood on was fouled with garbage. Horrible was the stench of discarded food left to rot and raw sewage that roiled out of open gutters. Yet her sweet, delicious odor blotted out the gagging stink.

"I could kind of tell. You know, with your accent and all. A lot of people in my neighborhood are Yardie," he explained.

A smile flickered across her face then disappeared. "Really? Where are you from?" It was her turn to ask questions.

He stuck out his chest and proudly lifted his chin, "The Nineties. Over by Rutland Road."

She held his gaze and smiled once more, batting her eyes flirtatiously, her lashes touching the top of her high cheekbones. "Oh yeah? I'm very familiar with that area. Probably too familiar. And what is your name? Because you are asking me all types of questions and you haven't even introduced yourself."

The corner of his lips turned up.

"Shine," he said, eyes scanning the area around him. "And your name?"

"Eden."

Glancing across the street, Shine saw a stout elderly man entering the pizza shop. It was then that he suddenly remembered he had ordered a slice. Being anxious to meet up with Gorilla Leek, he decided to cut the conversation short and get his food. But there was no way he was going to let this beauty get away from him. He thought she was probably the most interesting woman he'd ever met. When his eyes fell upon her, the rest of the world receded; his war with Chinnah seemed unimportant, the consequences of his son's death too distant to be concerned with. The woman in front of him was a diversion during this tumultuous time of his life. She was alluring. And he was not strong enough to resist the invitation of her sensuous eyes. Much as he resented leaving without getting to know her better, he had little choice but to do so.

"Well Eden, won't you give me a way to contact you?" he asked.

"May I ask why?" While she wanted to explore the mystery surrounding him, she refused to appear over anxious.

"Because you're fine as hell and I'm attracted to you." He shrugged, completely unapologetic about his words.

Eden looked down to her feet, feeling magnificently female. Although she was usually cold to the attention of most men, she blushed and that charmed him. Leisurely she slid her gaze back up until her eyes climbed over the stubble covering his elegant face. He carried his sins in his eyes, so she wasn't sure if giving out her number was a good idea. She knew nothing about him, except to realize he attracted her strongly in a physical sense. She was captivated by his glorious green eyes. He was handsome, even with a scar marring his face. The lines on his forehead, she could tell, were from a life filled with frustration. His expression was impassive, yet his stare, so intense and so passionate.

Eden involuntarily darted a glance at his crotch, noticing the obvious bulge pressing against the front of his jeans. She couldn't tear her eyes away. He caught her looking and gave her a wry grin.

He raised his eyebrow, mischief tilting his lips, and in a voice barely above a whisper, he said, "And it appears that you're attracted to me too. Right?"

Eden's cheeks grew hot in embarrassment, her attempt at a small smile bordered on apologetic. She quickly composed herself and managed to stammer, "Aren't you just confident. And yes, you are very attractive brother. But, sorry, I don't give out my number to random strangers." Squaring her shoulders, she forced a small grin. "Everything in our universe happens for a reason. So, if there is a deeper purpose for us meeting here today, we will run into each other again."

He wasn't used to being given the brush-off. It made him burn for her even more. He was sorely tempted to ask if he could spend time with her later that evening, but not wanting to risk offending her, he held back. Deep inside, Shine wanted more from her than a fling that would end once the police investigation of his son's disappearance heightened the drama surrounding his life. So, he decided not to pursue her any further.

"Really? That's the nicest rejection I've ever heard in my life." He held a lighthearted curl at his lips. "Well, I guess there's no need to keep bothering you. I'll let you get back to where you were going." The disappointment was evident in his tone.

"Indeed. I need to head home to brush off my poor books."

They both laughed.

Eden looked down at her watch then stared at him teasingly. "Bye brother. If we meet again, then it was meant to be," she said before walking away. Without glancing back, she spoke aloud, "Take some time out for yourself to clear your head."

A surge of lust swept through Shine as he watched her stride away down the sidewalk, hips swaying provocatively and her body bouncing in rhythm with her steps. He could see the shape of her ass moving beneath the fabric. The remarkable slenderness of her waistline revealed her delicacy. He wanted to call out to her to come back, but he hesitated too long. She was halfway down the block. At her approach, the crowd of shoppers cramming the street parted. And just like that, she disappeared into the sea of faces.

Coldness hung thick in the air, making him shiver and jolting him out of his trance. Suddenly reminded of the warm food that awaited him, he crossed the street and entered the pizza shop. He hadn't eaten since yesterday.

Upon seeing Shine, the store owner smiled jovially then slid the bagged pizza slice and his change across the counter. "Here you go, sir. If it is not hot enough, I can put it back into the oven." He nervously awaited the young man's reply.

"It's okay my dude. I'll take it whichever way I get it. I'm starving like hell," Shine responded pleasantly, without the least trace of rancor in his voice.

The blank look on the owner's face showed he was confused by the sudden change of attitude. Yet, it was a relief that the tension between them was gone. And sensing that Shine was a dangerous man, he wanted very much to keep it that way. So, in an attempt to get on his customer's good side, the Italian decided to tell the young gangster that he was being followed.

"Did you know that guy with the long dreadlocks?" The owner didn't wait for a reply. "He rushed in here right behind you and sat down in the back corner there without buying anything. He couldn't keep his eyes off of you. He just sat there talking on the phone and staring at you. And when you left he left right behind you, still speaking on the phone." He paused and scratched his palms over his grey beard, taking a deep breath.

"Really?" was all Shine could say.

"By the way he was checking you out, I would say that whoever he was talking to, they were having a conversation about you. When he walked past my counter I tried to listen to what he was saying but couldn't make out his words because he was speaking in that Jamaican language."

Shine smirked at the thought of the owner calling it *that Jamaican language.*

The Italian swallowed nervously, uncertain whether or not it was his place to say something about the gun he saw in the stalker's hand. He chose to leave that part out, not knowing how the person in front of him would react.

He continued, "The guy posted up outside by the street lamp and watched you while you were flirting with that pretty little lady."

And in that moment, it hit Shine that he wasn't being paranoid earlier. Only one person would have sent a Jamaican to follow him. He remained calm, not wanting to show his surprise, and flashed the store owner the most charming smile before inquiring pleasantly, "Where did he go?"

"He got in a cab."

"Which way did the cab go?"

"Toward Court Street."

Without saying a word, Shine swung abruptly on his heels and stormed out of the shop, leaving his pizza and money on the counter.

The store owner let his eyes linger on the closing door, wondering if telling the young man about the stalker was a mistake that would come back to haunt him. Many thoughts ran through his head, giving his face a look of fearful anticipation as he greeted his next customer.

CHAPTER 8

"**C**UZ OF YUH BREDREN'S** mistakes, mi boss considering a change of plans."

Gorilla Leek stared blankly at the bearded man who was speaking to him. A slight shudder of rage swept through him. Apprehension made his shoulders tighten as he glanced down at the cocked pistol the man held close to his side. Although the weapon was no longer pointed at him, the safety was still off. A snarl escaped Gorilla Leek's lips and his fingers curled into a fist.

"A change of plans? Man, where's your boss?" Gorilla Leek snorted in disgust. "He was supposed to be here to get the bricks off of me himself. I'm only speaking with him."

"But mi nuh si nuhting inna yuh hand. Yuh come here wid nuttin."

"You think I'm stupid enough to walk in here with them, before knowing what you cats were up to? They're in my whip." Gorilla Leek rubbed the back of his hand hastily across his mouth. "When I see your boss face to face I will give them to him myself. I'm not handing them over to no stranger."

The man's eyes smoldered with mischief as a cocky grin lifted one side of his mouth. "Stranga? Mi? Ney! Let mi introduce miself."

He offered his hand, but Gorilla Leek refused to shake it.

"I'm Six, my nigga," No longer speaking in a deep Jamaican dialect, the bearded stranger uttered his words with a contrived Brooklyn accent. "Now I'm no stranger," he hissed through stiff, smiling teeth.

Gorilla Leek grew furious. "Man fuck you. Tell him to get his ass down here or I'm out!" he declared in an emotion thick voice.

Six stared at Gorilla Leek long and hard without uttering a word, his face expressing no emotion. Yet his burning gaze failed to make the Blood gang member cower. With calmness breathing through, the man finally opened his mouth and said, "He don't really trust you like that."

"You think I trust him?" Gorilla Leek blatantly glowered down at Six's gun, "Or you!"

"Understand this. You need to settle down, first and foremost. Ya'namean? He don't like when things get messy and out of hand. And your boy's situation is putting all of our plans in jeopardy."

"All that got handled. And Badrick got handled. But your boss ain't holding up his part. We were supposed to meet face to face." Gorilla Leek raised an eyebrow. "He also promised to introduce me to the connect. But he ain't here. On the real, it seems like your boss doesn't care if things get messy."

Six clamped his teeth and said through them, "Ain't nothing messy on our end."

"Yeah? Then why was Cutty up in my crib looking for the coke? How did he get my address?"

"That wasn't our fault. And my boss damn sure didn't plan it out that way. But look at the bright side—your family's alive and Cutty's dead. It was going to happen sooner or later anyway. Right?" Six asked with a hint of irritation in his voice. "So why are you complaining? You said you were ready for all this to go down asap, but it seems like now you're worried about whose gonna come after you."

"Worried? Dog, I ain't worried! I just need a heads up when someone is trying to get at me. That is, if we're supposed to be playing on the same side!" Gorilla Leek's nostrils were flaring, and his voice close to cracking with anxiety. "I'm about this paper and your boss should be too. And we only got one cat standing in our way right now. So, the only thing I'm worried about is when we're taking him off of here! I've been ready for the next step!"

"Settle down son, all that screaming ain't necessary. We came to you because we knew you had no problem putting in that work. And we knew you were about that doe." Six cocked his head to the side like a cat eyeing a mouse. "We all want the same thing. But we're new to this relationship here, so I don't think any of us are free of doubts or concerns."

Gorilla Leek scrunched up his eyes to get a better view of the young Jamaican's face through the dimmed light. Six wore the expression of a man who knew a confrontation was at hand and was ready to see it through. And Gorilla Leek was very much the same, but he wasn't going to allow his temper to blow the deal. The muscles in his jaw tightened as he fought to keep the anger out of his voice.

"Look, what went down with my boy ain't gonna affect us. And your boss should be able to see that. So, I hope he ain't talking about changing the plans because he's leery about whether I can be trusted or not." Gorilla Leek clenched his teeth and hissed. "What? Because I'm going behind my dude's back? Trust dog, I'm all in. This means more to me than anything. All we gotta do is keep to the plan that was first laid out. Get him to come down to the store and," he looked Six in the eye and sharpened his tone again, "I will do the rest."

"Listen fam, we don't care what you do behind your boy's back, obviously. You were the one who wanted to get him involved. We didn't need him down with this. That's why we came to you and asked you, and not him, to rob the house to set all of this off," Six pointed out.

"So?"

"So, the plan to get your boy onboard had holes in it from the beginning. And we still put our trust in you." Six glanced up and down the dim hallway. "My boss and the connect ain't down here because your boy made some crucial mistakes. And if either of them was seen with any of you, that would be the end of all our plans."

Six's hardened stare seemed to go right through the man in front of him. Gorilla Leek wanted to say something to show he wasn't bothered by it. Instead he relaxed his muscles and swallowed the disrespectful words that danced at the edge of his lips. He struggled to soften his tone.

"Son, I got the coke. Didn't I? So, don't worry about my boy. I got that. What your boss needs to do now is introduce me to the connect and pick those bricks up, so he can make the next move."

"Yeah but—"

"But nothing. There's no need for the plans to change. Everything the connect told your boss is right and exact. With this war we're going to set off, we will all make crazy doe." Gorilla Leek paused, wanting to choose his next words with caution. He studied Six's blank expression, wishing he could read his mind. He continued carefully, aware that the Jamaican's finger remained curled around the trigger. "I'm saying, there's a reason your boss came to me. And what? Because we had some unexpected setbacks, he thinking 'bout switching things up?"

Six's face darkened as if he was cursing Gorilla Leek under his breath. "It's not that anyone is switching things up. But after your homeboy's phone turned up, everyone had to fall back and reassess things. Even the connect."

A naïve frown washed over Gorilla Leek's face. "Reassess? What the hell does that mean?"

Six shook his head. "You know what? You just said, not too long ago, that you weren't gonna talk to strangers," he remarked, his voice heavy with sarcasm. "You're doing a whole lot of talking now. I only came here to pick up the coke. But you ain't got it, so you're wasting my time."

Gorilla Leek held back his fury, his eyes narrowing. "Word. I got you, son. Promise. But you're right. We are talking too much. If your boss wants them bricks, he needs to speak to me face to face." He cast an obvious glance at the pistol in Six's hand. "And you need to put that away. You ain't scaring no one."

A smirk graced Six's face. He said nothing, just gave a wink. He tucked his gun into the back waist of his pants and retrieved a cell phone from his coat. Turning his back slightly, he dialed a number and waited patiently for the ringing to begin. Gorilla Leek noticed the Blue rag hanging from his back pocket and spat silently in disgust.

Six gave him a furtive look over his shoulder, uncomfortable having his enemy where he could not keep watch on his movements. He began speaking into the phone. "Eeh, di bowy bring di wuk but him say him ongle wa fi chat wid yuh. Or him naah guh through wid it." He waited for the person on the other line to respond. Gorilla Leek could hear profane screaming coming through the phone.

"Alright, alright. Mi wi let him kno," replied the young Jamaican before hanging up.

He turned to face his company and regarded him with disdain. "He said he'll meet up with you tonight at the store. Bring the bricks. And the coke connect will be there also. He'll hit you up later to let you know the time."

Frustration etched lines on Gorilla Leek's face. "You mean to tell me, with all that screaming, that's all he said? So, what? I came out here for nothing?"

He brushed past the man, stormed down the hallway, and pushed furiously at the door. Without looking back, he yelled, "Tell that cat I won't be waiting long for his call. If I don't hear from him, I'm looking for a buyer and he won't get none of this back! I'm out of here."

"Eh man!"

Hearing Six call out behind him, Gorilla Leek turned around and held the door open with his foot, a spark of anger lighting in the darkness of his eyes. "What?"

"Di next time wi meet," Six said crisply, his urban accent disappearing. "Mek sure yuh kip yuh eyes open. Eff mi did here to kill yuh todeh, yuh wudda ave been dead already."

Gorilla Leek sucked his teeth in annoyance. "Nigga, please." He turned on his heels and exited the hallway, allowing the slam of the door to demonstrate his irritation. Six just stood there, his face twisted into a frown and his eyes darkened with a cold hard seething rage that vibrated through his entire body.

♠   ♠   ♠

"I KNEW IT!" DESIREE YELLED out triumphantly as she and Lola walked down 95th Street. "I told you-you were pregnant."

Sickened by her friend's obvious gloating, Lola stopped dead in her tracks and started to shake. She raised a trembling finger to her lips as her eyes begged Desiree to be quiet. "Girl, can you hush before someone on the block hears you?"

The streetlights began to flicker and the illumination in the sky was moderately becoming purple as night began to set in. A car passed by, throbbing with loud music, rattling Lola's nerves. Her thoughts being momentarily interrupted—she couldn't make out the words of the song but felt the visceral thump of the bass line—she noticed a group of children playing football in the street. She watched as they scurried to get out of the vehicle's way. Just seeing them having fun, made her anguish seem unbearable. Her heart sank with the thought that Trayvon would never be able to run up and down that block with his friends.

A rush of frigid air swept over her, reminding her of the coldness she felt when she last held him. Pain clutched at her heart. She needed to seek the solace of her apartment, so no one could see her suffer.

Hoping no one heard Desiree, she cast a hasty look around.

"Look, I never said it wasn't possible. So, I don't need your ratchet insensitive-ass throwing it in my face. Having you praying for it to be true was enough to deal with as it . . ." Lola hurled her words at Desiree in a thick Georgia accent, gaining satisfaction each time her friend winced. "Plus, I did not want to make it a reality by speaking on it. Words are powerful. You know? But you kept wanting to bring it up."

"Yeah, well, silence must be powerful also because you're still pregnant. You knew you were. You were just in denial." Desiree replied sharply, in a matter-of-fact tone. "And since you told dude, you must think it's his or you would have been told Shine."

"I would've told Sh—"

"Wait," Desiree cut her off. "Is that why you decided to come back to yawls apartment? To tell Shine?"

Lola rolled her eyes at her friend and sucked her teeth in disgust before turning away and proceeding toward the entrance of her building. She searched the faces of the many people hanging out on the sidewalk before continuing her conversation.

"No. I came back to the apartment because Shine asked me to meet him here this evening. He said he needed to talk about something that happened with the cops last night," she uttered in a whisper, rolling her eyes in obvious frustration. "And no, I don't plan to tell him anything about the pregnancy right now. Because, with everything that happened to Trayvon, I have more to lose if it is not his."

Desiree's eyes widened a fraction at the mention of the deceased child. A twinge of sympathy pinched her heart. Not the same feeling of empathy one has for a loved one in trouble but the sad, helpless reaction of a person watching a little puppy suffer. Remorse tinged with guilt. For a brief moment she wondered, if faced with the same circumstances, whether she would have been able to hold up as well as Lola had. Just as quickly as the thought entered her head, she dismissed it. Deep down she knew she would never experience what Lola just went through. A past horrifying incident had left her barren, unable to have children of her own. And not once did anyone ever consider how badly it hurt her to be around their children. Now—having listened to her friend grieve over her son's death after discovering that she's again pregnant—Desiree felt the sickness of misery creeping over her own heart. She decided to change the subject.

"I feel you girl. And with him thinking you been dealing with Badrick, it's probably best not to add to Shine's problems," Desiree suggested.

"Yeah, well, that already got out of hand from what I was told."

"What do you mean?"

"Well for one . . ." Lola deluged her friend with a flood of words until they stopped in front of her building. "And I think that he needs to let it go, the beef, the hustling, everything. Just walk away." Lola glanced around. "It's going to cause too many problems—serious problems. I know the root of all this drama is money, but I would much rather a deadbeat baby-daddy than a dead baby-daddy."

Desiree met her friend's eyes, not knowing what to say. Not really knowing who she was talking about. "Yeah, I guess."

"Umm, excuse me, ladies." A short, pudgy Caucasian gentleman with a rounded cherub face suddenly appeared out of the shadowy gap between two parked cars.

He stepped onto the sidewalk and into the pale light of the street lamp. The girls regarded him with solemn looks. Waves of suspicion and distrust washed over them. He seemed too old to be threatening, his thinning black hair greying on the sides. He had a neatly trimmed salt and pepper mustache and his chin was freshly shaven. The man seemed to have eaten well over the years, wearing a dark blue suit that desperately needed to be let out in certain places.

Another fellow followed closely behind him, accompanied by two cops in uniforms. Desiree instantly recognized his face as he walked alongside the police officers. Though clearly a Blackman, he was spectacularly out of place in their urban environment. Tall, clean-cut, wearing a finely tailored charcoal suit beneath a black woolen overcoat, and black Oxford shoes, his appearance gave him a distinguished presence as far removed as possible from the common nigger in the Nineties. Desiree watched him closely, trying to gauge his reason for being there. *I know him. He's a homo dick*, she thought to herself.

The portly white man, taking notice of Desiree's troubled look, flashed a practiced smile as he reached into his pocket and yielded his badge. "I apologize for interrupting your conversation. My name is Detective Howard Seidman. And this here is Detective Buck Brown," Seidman said, nodding toward his colleague. "We were looking for Ms.

Lola Bye."

Seeing the look of pained surprise that suddenly appeared on her face, Seidman eyed Lola intently. A wry note entered his voice. "Well, someone loves hearing the sound of their name. Don't they? I take it you must be Lola. Correct?"

Desiree didn't give her friend a chance to answer. "Why you asking? What she do?"

Seidman smiled inwardly. *The first thing they think when they see us is that they're in trouble,* he thought to himself. *Everyone in this forsaken neighborhood is into something. It's just a matter of whether they slip up and get themselves caught or not. And they wonder why we come into their neighborhood suspecting everyone. It's the same reason we had to burn those civilian homes back in Panama when we were trying to get Noriega out.*

Like many veterans, Seidman took pride in his military service. Always he kept a warrior's creed of courage. But his soldier's sense of duty was deepened over the years as he watched his old neighborhood become a hood overrun with unemployable black migrants from the South with a less achieving culture. The Nineties section of Brooklyn, once a peaceful Jewish community held together by a common sense of its history and a strong desire to preserve ethnic traditions, was now a battlefield where black teenage gangs roamed the littered streets wreaking havoc.

This gave Seidman a new sense of purpose after having retired from the marines a decorated combat veteran. In the beginning, he tried to tell himself that the locals wanted him there to protect the neighborhood—that they understood how crime increased their cost of living while lowering their quality of life, and that they were fighting on the same side against the same enemy. But he knew it was only wishful thinking on his part to believe that they would see beyond their obvious differences and help him clean the neighborhood up.

"She is in no trouble," mentioned Seidman before turning to Lola. "Well, at least not with us. We just need to speak with Ms. Bye concerning her child."

Desiree unconsciously took a step back, the movement not going unnoticed by the detective. Lola had confided everything to her and now police were involved. Not just police, but a homicide detective. Her eyes shifted toward Lola, begging her to say or do something. Seidman saw the internal battle Desiree was waging, deciding whether to reveal what she knew. He could sense that there might be more to the story than what he got from the father.

Lola's heart began pounding a dull thud that she could feel in her temple. She stood frozen, wondering if they knew about Trayvon. *Could they know? How? Do they think I did it? Should I say I'm sorry?* A million thoughts began racing through her head all at once. She cast her eyes to the ground and contemplated running.

"It appears Detective Seidman is right. You must be the mother of Trayvon Bye, I presume?" Detective Brown asked, his voice deep. He extended his hand to Lola. "Please ma'am, at least tell me if I'm correct."

His tone, becoming almost hypnotic, penetrated her fear, calming her. She inhaled deeply and regained control over herself, ignoring his gesture. The panic dimmed in her eyes. She lifted her chin and nodded.

"Yes, I'm Lola," she said softly.

Brown smiled then continued. "We spoke to your boyfriend—"

"My boyfriend?" Lola's heart began to crash against her chest and fear took control again. There was a rushing in her ears as the pulse of her blood thumped against her skull. She felt dizzy. *How could Shine go to the cops after telling me not to*, she wondered. *Or—did the cops go to him?* Guilt ripped through her soul as she thought about her son. The memory of the horror still fresh in her head, her thoughts sped up until they spilled out a torrent of images. She breathed deeply, trying to make her mind a blank and then, with some effort, blurted out, "It wasn't my fault!" The words were out of her mouth before she realized what she said.

Detective Brown gave her a raised eyebrow.

Before he could respond, Seidman interrupted. "No, ma'am, it is not your fault. We try our best to keep our eyes on our children and to prevent any harm from coming to them." Seeing he had her attention and knowing the reason for her outburst, he continued, "It's not enough that we have to protect them from bullies, drugs, and so forth. But possibly kidnappers also?"

Lola's eyes widened slightly at the mention of kidnappers. She started to reply when the sudden honking of a car horn startled her. Seidman appeared unmoved by the noise. He kept his focus locked on the missing child's mother.

"Can you think of anyone who might want to hurt your family?"

The Jewish detective narrowed his eyes. "Anyone who may have access to your apartment?"

Lola did not reply. She didn't like the direction the conversation was heading, wondering why the detective mentioned kidnappers. *What in the hell did Shine tell them?* she thought to herself as all eyes remained glued to her.

Seidman tried another question. "Anyone you suspect? Anyone you may have problems with?"

Lola remained silent, thinking things over until the other detective grew impatient and decided to speak.

"What about Chinnah?" A twitch of irritation and anger played across Brown's features as he fixed his eyes on Lola with suspicion. Concern pinched her soft mouth then vanished in a quick, nervous smile. *Yeah*, he thought, *she knows Chinnah.* "Do you think Chinnah might've had something to do with this?"

Seidman frowned at his companion. *I knew he had his own agenda for coming along.* He regarded Brown as a decent, hardworking cop. But he felt the detective would at times go overboard on whatever case he was working. Once he had his mind set on someone being a suspect, he would relentlessly badger them through a barrage of repeated interruptions without giving them time to think, let alone explain themselves. He would search for answers where there were only questions. Often Brown was told that his tactics were too abrasive. And now here he was preparing to bully a victim.

Seidman sighed aloud and shook his head in a gesture approaching despair. "Uh, Brown don't you think—"

"Not now Seidman," Brown interrupted. He shook his finger at Lola. "Does your boyfriend have any dealings with Chinnah?"

Again, Seidman shook his head then he grimaced with embarrassment. Knowing his colleague's history, he was half-ashamed of his behavior. Over the years, Seidman had watched as the horror of the unsolved murder of Brown's son had steadily wore at his nerves. He became increasingly consumed by his job, losing himself in his cases and eventually losing his wife. His badge and his gun were all he had. And solving murder cases occasionally brought him back from the madness he suffered.

Looking into Buck Brown's eyes, Lola wondered if she had seen an emotion deeper than anger—like sorrow. But when it passed, only curiosity was left behind. *Why would he ask me about Chinnah when he is supposed to be investigating Trayvon's disappearance?* she silently asked herself, trying to read the detective's expression. Incessant questions bounced back and forth within her head along with the constant thud of her now thunderous headache. Seidman inched forward to interject a comment to remind his peer what they were there for and to keep him on task. But Lola's tongue was much faster than his.

"You're asking me about Chinnah, really?" The words shot out of her mouth like a cannonball. "I live in this neighborhood. Who doesn't know who Chinnah is?" Her eyes swept across the officers' faces with careful scrutiny as if she was waiting for one of them to confess to a crime. The disappointment was evident in her tone. "I mean—you guys are the cops. Wouldn't you know more about him than I would?"

Detective Brown regarded Lola for a moment without saying a word, his eyebrows raised. His silence made Desiree uncomfortable, her nerves shattering like glass. She stared at him, this officer whose face blazed with madness, eyes dark and condescending, focusing on her friend. She was aware that Brown was watching both of them closely, a strange glare in his eyes, as if he suspected they were hiding something. She knew who he was but didn't know his angle. So, she decided to ask.

"Why would a homicide detective, looking for Chinnah, be assigned to a missing child's case?" inquired Desiree.

There was a cruel twist of Detective Brown's mouth beneath his mustache. He was not surprised the young lady had recognized him. A little over ten years ago, her father had walked in on one of his friends violating her. During the attempt to stop the savage he was stabbed several times and left to bleed out in front of his eleven-year-old daughter. The detective assigned to the case was Brown, and Desiree was his primary witness. Over the years he would run into her while patrolling the neighborhood, and troubled by how young she was, he couldn't help but think of himself as her guardian angel as he would sit in his car and watch her. Consumed by shame and seething with inward fury, she eventually grew into a woman whose heart had become corrupted by lust and brutality. Soon Brown was unable to recognize her from the countless snakes that slithered through Brooklyn's ghetto garden. So, he eventually gave up on her. And now, years later, here she was somehow involved in a missing child case.

Refusing to answer Desiree, Brown brought his attention back to Lola. "Ma'am, unfortunately, Chinnah is involved with much of the crime plaguing this neighborhood. And he is no stranger to kidnapping."

Uncomfortable with where the conversation was going, Seidman decided to intervene. "It's not to say we suspect Chinnah of having anything to do with your situation, but we just need to check every angle possible."

Lola caught on to the reason behind Desiree questioning Brown. She wanted to see if the cops were suspecting her of foul play. However, given that Seidman's voice bordered on apologetic, the grieving mother knew that the cops didn't know anything. Her breathing slowed, and her body relaxed slightly. Now she was curious to know why the officers were interested in Chinnah.

"So, as my friend just asked, how is a homicide detective going to help find my child?" Lola asked.

She realized that if she didn't handle the next few exchanges of conversation carefully, both detectives would become suspicious of her. So, she decided to retreat into the sanctuary of feigned ignorance.

"I mean, you think Chinnah, the biggest murderer in this neighborhood, has something to do with Trayvon being missing? Why would he do that? Why would he want Trayvon?" She caught Brown's stare and batted her eyes, giving him her most guileless expression before asking in a detached manner, "Are you guys going to get my son back from him?"

Brown clumsily answered her, "Um, well. No. We are not saying Chinnah has your son. We don't know that he's involved."

At that point Seidman interjected, "We are definitely not implying that ma'am. To narrow things down, we have to know the environments you frequent, and we have to considered everyone in those environments." He decided to redirect the focus of their questions since Lola's responses weren't yielding any useful information. "Speaking of environments, where do you work ma'am? What do you do for a living?"

Lola quickly replied, "I take care of my son," She raised her chin up defiantly into the passing wind, the cold breeze washing against her face. "And his father takes care of us."

Brown gave off a condescending smirk, suspicion lurking large on his face. His brief encounter with the father is what originally heightened his curiosity and prompted him to accompany Seidman to interview the mother. He couldn't shake the feeling that somehow the missing child had something to do with his own case. He now had more questions than before. The detective needed to know more about Shine.

"What does he do for a living?" Brown asked.

"He has his own business." Lola grinned sheepishly.

She had always felt a secret sense of pride whenever she mentioned her man was a business owner. For that, her friends admired her. Yet they were silently envious of her lifestyle. Most of them would trade places with her if they could. Her life was simple. All she had to do every day was tend to her son and shop. The thought brought a lump into her throat. *All I had to do was take care of my son.* Along with the whispered warning of the wind, the wavering shadows of the trees seemed sinister that night. Lola suddenly became saddened, more so than she'd ever been in her life. She could sense that things were getting ready to change for the worst.

In his soothing, deep voice, Detective Brown continued his questioning. "What kind of business does your boyfriend own?"

Still deep in her own thoughts, Lola didn't hear the detective.

Desiree answered for her. "He owns a bodega."

Brown's police instincts went on alert. "A bodega? Really? Where is this bodega located?"

Desiree didn't hesitate to answer, "It's the Mini-mart on Rutland Road."

With his eyes darting back and forth from Lola to Desiree, Brown searched their faces. "Rutland! Where?" There was eagerness in his voice this time.

His words struck Lola's ears and danced through her like a jolt of lightning, violently tearing her apart from her thoughts. Brown's eyes lit up with excitement and Lola took notice. A wide grin ran across his face. He gave a dry, humorless chuckle, one that struck fear in her heart. "Please don't tell me it's the one on the corner of 93rd Street. Is it?"

Lola grew uncomfortable with Brown's questions. "Why are you asking about his store?"

There was no time for her to ask questions, Brown wanted to get straight to the point. "Rutland Road and 93rd Street?"

Desiree once again spoke up for her friend, "Yes, it is. It's the Minimart right on that corner."

Lola shot her a sharp look and cursed under her breath, "Bitch."

Seidman now understood the reasoning behind his companion's questions, and it made him nervous. The last thing he needed was Brown's nose snooping around this case.

Brown had all the information he needed from Lola at the moment. Her son's disappearance seemed to be connected to the murders that recently occurred at Minimart. Suddenly, a flashing thought humored him; the two ladies did not appear to be aware of the store's current state—that it lay in ruins and was now the scene of a murder investigation. Gone was the business Lola was so proud of. Only traces of unsparing destruction remained.

When Brown first began his investigation of the explosion at Minimart, he interviewed the person he thought to be the owner, an elderly Puerto Rican man named Jesus Israel. During their conversation, he had a hunch that Jesus' story had more holes in it than the bodies sprawled out on the sidewalk leading to the store. Brown realized that he was only a front man for the real owner. And the real owner was unknown to the police until now. Not only was Shine connected to Mini-mart, but he also owned a Ford Expedition. The same make and model of the vehicle determined to be present at one of the murder scenes he was investigating.

Somehow this kid has gotten himself into some deep trouble with the Gully Gods, thought Brown.

It had fallen on him to break the news of Minimart's fate without alarming the ladies. And though he was humored by their ignorance of what happened, he didn't look forward to the bitter task.

Gazing at Lola, Brown mentioned, "93rd Street. Really? You probably don't want to hear this right now, considering your circumstance, but your boyfriend's business was just blown to pieces by a hand grenade."

Astonishment had forced Lola's mouth wide open. "What?"

An expression of total surprise covered the ladies' faces.

Taking notice of their reaction, Brown continued, "Those who didn't perish in the explosion went down in a hail of bullets without ever knowing what was happening. Several people were killed."

"No. No. You are joking, right?" Shock leaped from Lola's eyes as they darted between the two detectives.

"It seems your boyfriend has made some really bad enemies." His mood suddenly darkening, Brown looked sternly into Lola's gaze. "Hell, someone must be very upset with him, seeing how they blew up his store. I guess it is a matter of luck he wasn't there when it happened. Did he mention it to you?"

What look like fear flickered briefly in Lola's eyes. She knew there was something brewing between Chinnah and her man, and that it was only a matter of time before it boiled over. But she didn't expect it to go this far. Now she was standing in front of a detective, being warned in rather vague terms that her life might be in danger.

Brown stared at her. He could sense she was hiding something. As he thought of how to get the truth out of her, his mind kept going back to the baby wipe he saw in her boyfriend's pocket. There was something he was missing. Maybe the answers were to be sought inside of the couple's residence.

"I'm guessing this is your first-time hearing about Minimart." He massaged his chin and raised his eyebrow. "If we can continue this conversation inside, I would be more than happy to tell you everything I know about the incident."

With a worrisome voice, Lola asked, "What? My apartment?"

Seidman stepped forward, sensing it was his turn to speak. "Yes, ma'am, we need to let the officers who accompanied us conduct a thorough search of the apartment to see if there is any indication of foul play. We need to see the place your son was last seen." He surveyed the street about him. "And seeing how it is getting late, the sooner the better. Agreed?"

Lola looked utterly terror stricken, her gaze shifting from the detectives to the uniformed officers. "Uh. Okay. I guess that's fine."

The situation was getting too complicated for Desiree, and she feared the police would soon be swarming all over her friend like flies at a dumpster. How much longer could Lola lie to them? Should she be keeping Lola at a distance? Desiree dragged her hands down her face, momentarily stretching her eyes and cheeks into a mask of despair. She didn't see any reason to stay around and get involved. She decided to cut her visit short.

"Aw girl, I just remembered I have to be ghost. You know I want to hold you down, but I'm supposed to meet someone in like thirty minutes. It's real important so I gotta be out. Ok?" Inwardly she winced as she spoke the next words, "Look, I'm sure they will find Trayvon."

Lola could see she was lying about needing to leave. But she also knew that this wasn't Desiree's problem. Besides, it would be easier to deal with the detectives without her there. She figured she would let her friend off the hook. "Yeah, I understand girl. I will call you later tonight."

Feeling guilty for abandoning her friend, Desiree asked hesitantly, "You sure you're straight, mommy?"

Lola shuddered at the word *mommy*. "Yes, I'm good."

Desiree wasted no time on further conversation. She pivoted on her heels and made her way past the two detectives not saying a word to them. Without looking back, she shouted, "Definitely hit me later, after you get rid of those two dicks!"

Brown raised his hand and gestured toward the entrance of Lola's building. "Please, ma'am, after you."

Lola led the men inside.

CHAPTER 9

"YOU GOING TO THE PARTY TONIGHT?"** Shine was too deeply engrossed in his own gloomy thoughts to heed his best friend.

"The party at Tilden Ballroom? You going, or not?" Gorilla Leek asked in a tone of petty anger as he sat halfway down a park bench next to his partner.

His question brought his companion rudely back to his senses. Already troubled by the idea of the police getting involved, Shine had a flickering thought of leaving the state. Staring off into the darkness of the night, he lifted a bottle of Crown Royal up to his mouth, clamped his teeth around the top, and twisted violently. The top gave way between his lips. He spit it out into his free hand then threw his head back and began sucking at the bottle. After quenching his thirst, he sat gazing at the trees that surrounded them, trying to make out the shadows. The dark, slender trunks sprouting branches in all directions, and the thin veil of leaves. He thought he saw something move. It was nothing.

Distant sounds of voices along with the clattering of footsteps and car engines echoed up from the streets flanking Lincoln Terrace Park. The noise blended with the shrilling of the wind through the bushes and tree branches, each gust blowing past the empty basketball court they sat in like the deep roar of a rough ocean wave breaking on an open beach.

"This dude," Gorilla Leek said aloud to himself, clearly upset by his friend's unresponsiveness. "Blood, are you going to the party or not?"

Sensing his frustration, Shine decided to answer, "The Party?

Dunno."

"Whatchoo mean, you don't know? You need to be there."

"Why?"

"We can't look like we're afraid to show our faces after what happened at Minimart."

"And?"

"And, someone has to keep an eye on our soldiers while they grindin'. Dog, you know how much money we gonna make up in there tonight? One of us gotta show up early and provide a presence."

"So, why don't you go?" Shine solemnly asked.

"I gotta go up to White Mike's tonight to hit him off with that brick for putting us on to Chinnah's spot. So, I won't get there until late." He gave the bereaved father a look tinged in sympathy. "Plus, the party will take your mind off your situation."

He might be right, Shine thought. *I do need to do something to get this shit off my head.*

"Alright, alright, man, I'll go," he answered without looking at Gorilla Leek. "I have to meet Lola at the apartment first, then I'll head out there."

"Cool son. You driving alone?"

"Na, I'll probably pick up Kold Fire in my whip, then let him drive me there. I'm really not in the mood to be getting behind a steering wheel for too long."

"That's what's up."

With his attention suddenly broken from his growing sense of unease, Shine watched as his friend fumbled through his pockets before pulling out a thin strip of aluminum foil.

"This is the stuff we snatched from Chinnah. That is, after we stepped on it," said Gorilla Leek.

Shine passed his bottle to his partner and reached for the foil. He opened it up. It contained a little over a gram of cocaine. His eyes opened wide and he searched the area around him for any lifeforms. Sliding two fingers into his pocket, he pulled out his car key and scooped up a small mountain of cocaine.

Gorilla Leek leaned back, a smirk plastered to his lips as he watched his friend bring the key up to his nostril and, holding the other closed with a finger, sniff deeply. A scorching sandstorm blasted up Shine's nose and dripped from his sinuses. It tickled the back of his throat. His fingers trembled, the blood in his eyes throbbed in rhythm with his heart. He felt his nose go cold then numb.

"Damn! This is some good stuff!" Shine excitedly announced, licking his lips and jabbing a finger at the foil in his palm. The drug began to massage his doubts and fears about his current predicament into confirmation that all would be well. "Dog, this is going to bring in mad doe. We'll have cats lining up for blocks to cop this."

It was impossible to hide the grin of satisfaction that overtook Gorilla Leek's mind and mouth, yet he was careful not to give away the true intent of his smile as he replied, "Yeah, I know. It's that good. We hit the jackpot on this one. Imagine how much bread we gonna make."

His own misery no longer occupying his mind, Shine's thoughts were now turning towards the money they could make. "This is ten times better than the work we're moving."

Gorilla Leek nodded his head in agreement. "Indeed so, it is."

"Well," Shine, lowered his eyes momentarily, then quickly regained eye contact. His tone was icy. "We need to find out who Chinnah's connect is before we take him off."

"Word is bond, Blood!" Gorilla Leek rose to his feet, took a sip from the bottle then placed it on the ground in front of them. "Now we're talking. If we snatch up his connect and work something out with him, we'll get paid like a crazy once Chinnah is out of the picture and we're one of the only ones left with this type of product. I'm saying, that shit is that good, right?"

Shine knew what his partner was saying was true and he was prepared to grasp whatever opportunity presented itself to improve his situation. The money they stood to gain could help him eventually leave the state and get away from it all. The hustling, the murders, the gang-banging, the police, everything. Yes, this money would set him right. So, he had to stay around long enough to see this Chinnah thing through. As well, he didn't want to be regarded as a punk or a deserter for walking away after starting the war. But once Chinnah was dead and enough money was made, he would disappear. He had grown tired of Brooklyn. He wanted to start life over.

Taking notice of the big fat "gotcha" grin on his best friend's face, Shine decided to keep his plans of leaving to himself. Remaining silent about the concerns that nagged his mind, he didn't reply to Gorilla Leek's last comments. Instead, he placed the foil down on the seat of the bench, went into his pockets and pulled out a roll of money, a wad a little bigger than his fist. He peeled the first bill from the stack and shoved the rest back into his jeans. Folding one end of a one-hundred-dollar bill, he started rolling it up until it looked like a thin straw. With shaky fingers, he picked the aluminum foil up then brought his rolled bill down to the cocaine and vacuumed it up into his nostrils once again.

The burn was a painful pleasure, the powder dripping down to the back of his throat. He gagged from the taste and potency. Numbness quickly set in on the tip of his tongue as it involuntarily clamped to the roof of his mouth. With a wild look in his eyes, his head darted from side to side. His grin almost splitting his face.

"Goddamn! Yeah, you're right. We can definitely make mad cream from this." Shine balled the empty foil up and tossed it over his shoulder. "This is a huge come up, son. Where did you stash the bricks?"

"I got it put up in Daffney's crib."

Shine stared into his partner's eyes in astonishment. "At Daffney's? What about Bolo? You know he ain't letting just anyone bring work up into Rutland Plaza. I mean now we're fucking with Chinnah and Bo—"

"We're good, Blood," Gorilla Leek assured.

"How so?"

"Daffney don't even stay up in the Plaza anymore. She bounced to Harlem a while ago. She has a brownstone up there, but she's currently staying out in Queens with her boyfriend."

"So—"

"So, since the apartment is empty, she is letting us use it to stash the work. We can cut it up and bag it there."

"Say word?"

"Word." Gorilla Leek smiled. "And I take it, you're feeling the product. Right?"

Shine did not respond. Instead, he licked his lips in anticipation of the big payoff. Gorilla Leek too remained silent, gloating over his friend's inability to stay sober for more than a few hours. He thought it ironic that he was addicted to cocaine. Gorilla Leek himself, while violent, hot-blooded, and reckless, would never go near the stuff unless he was selling it. He regarded cocaine users as fiends, as customers. To him, they were one step away from smoking crack. Seizing the Crown

Royal from the ground, he took another sip, swallowing as he searched Shine's face for an answer to his last question.

"Well, it's definitely on point," Shine finally said.

"Right on," replied Gorilla Leek. "We could knock off onions for six bills a pop. So, we shouldn't have a hard time getting rid of the work. We got it for free, so we can afford to cut the price."

"So, we're not chopping any of it up into eight balls or quarters? Just ounces and up?" Shine scratched his chin, squinting reflectively. "I mean, we have some fools acting like they can't even afford to spend twenty-five dollars for a gram, let alone trying to sell them ounces."

"Blood, we're used to breaking down big eights and quarter keys. We're sitting on six bricks. We can think bigger now. We can be the ones supplying cats instead of begging broke fiends to buy that little ass weight." Making a face that might have been a reluctant smile, Gorilla Leek sighed then continued, "I'm saying, dog…we can still sell a gram to a nigga. Or if cats want to cop an eight ball or whatever, we can still do that. But we need to start focusing on getting away from that hand to hand shit."

"Yeah but we don't have a spot to sell it from. I'm saying, I feel you on stepping up our game and thinking bigger. But either way, we still need a place that can handle the traffic."

"Check it dog, I got that covered," Gorilla Leek gave his friend a look like they were sharing a secret. "You know how I was telling you that White Mike wants out of the game?" He paused to take another swig.

Shine nodded his head. "Yeah, and?"

"Well, tonight he wants to discuss letting us use his store to move our product, now that we don't have Mini—"

"I thought you said he was selling off his store." Shine interrupted, not concealing the awe on his face.

"He is. To a commercial real estate company."

"And?"

"And, as a part of the agreement he has with them, he has to find someone for them to lease it out to right away. And he got them to agree to lease it to me."

"They agreed to lease it to *you*? Really?"

"You know what I mean, Blood." Gorilla Leek detected the sarcasm in his tone and gave him a dull smile. "They agreed to lease it to *us*. So now, we not only have a new spot, but we will be getting White Mike's customers also. And you know he moves mad work out of there as it is. That's really one of the reasons I'm meeting him tonight, to discuss all of this and seal the deal between us."

The mentioning of a deal troubled Shine. He didn't trust his partner to negotiate behind his back.

Shine let out a long steady breath. "This all sounds good. But the customers we will be getting from him are used to Chinnah's product. That quality is mad different from what we usually cop. And we only have six bricks of it left, minus what you're taking to White Mike tonight. We still need the hook-up with the old man's connect if we—"

"Don't worry about that," Gorilla Leek interrupted. "I didn't want to tell you this until I knew it was a sure thing, but I'm also getting the hook up on that connect tonight."

"How?"

A sly, devilish smile appeared on Gorilla Leek's face. "White Mike knows him, and he is introducing us at the store."

"Without me there?"

"Yeah, I mean you do trust me to work all of this out right?"

Shine rolled his eyes before giving a reluctant nod. "Yeah I guess. But I still can't imagine White Mike being brave enough to go behind Chinnah's back."

"He doesn't have any reason to be afraid of Chinnah anymore. He knows that the old man is on his way out." Gorilla Leek's lip curled into a sinister sneer. After a moment he peered cautiously around the basketball court to make sure they were alone. Barely able to suppress a chuckle, he brought his eyes back to Shine and spoke low, "You should've seen his face when I told him about what we did to Cutty?"

Shine's eyes lit up in anger. "We didn't do anything to Cutty! We weren't even there."

Gorilla Leek's mouth slowly crept up on one side, reluctantly amused by his partner's frustration. Silently he thought, *it's too late to be pissed. There ain't anything you can do about it now but roll with it*. He laughed bitterly to himself before uttering, "You're right, we weren't there, so what? You scared Chinnah's gonna get at us?"

"First of all, I ain't afraid of no one!" Shine snarled so fierce that spit flew out of his mouth.

Gorilla Leek smiled. "If you say so."

"It's just stupid to run around trying to get props off a murder you didn't commit. No one even knows son is dead yet, so why advertise it? You know?" Shine paused, realizing he was becoming emotional. Lowering his voice, he continued, "Look, you already know I'm not feeling the idea of having a war with Chinnah. But once he sent Cutty to your house, I knew it was a matter of time before he sent someone to mine."

"No doubt," Gorilla Leek remarked.

"Badrick was his nephew and apparently, he now knows that one of us killed him. So, whether I want a war with Chinnah or not, it's going to go down." Shine shook his head and his forehead furrowed. "It's going to get red hot and the scramz will be sniffing around the hood soon. You feel me? So, putting that out there that we had something to do with returning Cutty could get our asses locked up quick fast."

Gorilla Leek just nodded as if he couldn't care less. "I wasn't trying to get a rep off of that body. I was taking the blame away from Jamel. I'm saying my dude, I'm not going to have that old Jamaican fool putting a hit out on my son for Cutty's death."

Shine eyes narrowed. "He already put out a hit on you and your family. That's why Cutty ran up in your house and didn't wait to catch you in the streets."

"Yeah, and now the fool's dead," Gorilla Leek growled out.

"Yeah, but not by your bullet. In fact, you ain't even kill Badrick or anyone Chinnah cared about." Shine couldn't hide the frustration in his tone and Gorilla Leek took notice.

"Dog, Chinnah cares more about his money than anything or anyone else, and as it stands, we both took that from him. He's looking to get some get-back right now. So, we have to move quick and get at him before he gets at us!" Gorilla Leek shouted, his voice radiating authority. "We don't have time to worry about what he knows. Once he is gone and we have his connect, we can start making some real doe. And none of that will matter. Let's focus on what we need to do and not what was done!"

Shine managed to respond casually, "Sounds like you've had all of this worked out for a minute now."

"What can I say dog? I plan quickly. Listen, White Mike is already down with all of this, and I'm taking care of securing the connect tonight also. By the time we meet up at the party, everything will be good."

Shine stared at his best friend, a muscle twitching in his jaw as he silently weighed his words. He gave a narrow, enigmatic smile. "You mean the party you keep pushing me to go to while you're out handling this meeting?"

"Yeah. You don't need to be at the meeting. You have enough on your plate already. Besides, when they meet with me, they are meeting with you. We are one," declared Gorilla Leek.

Shine considered his partner's remarks, turning the situation over in his mind. "So, after this meeting between you and White Mike, how soon before we get to set up shop in his store—to begin moving the work?"

"Tomorrow."

Shine let out an exaggerated sigh, his eyes beset with doubt and worry. "Tomorrow? Are we ready for that?"

He wasn't really concerned with whether they were ready or not but was more annoyed than anything simply because his partner planned all of this without him. Awaiting a reply, he fell silent and stared off into the darkness thinking to himself. *When did son have time to set all of this up, with everything that's been going on?*

"Yeah, we'll be ready to go tomorrow. We have the product already." Gorilla Leek sucked his bottom lip in between his teeth, released it then added, "Tonight's meeting is just to make sure we are all on the same page. That's why he is introducing us to Chinnah's connect at the store. So that nothing stops after we knock off them six bricks."

"You mean introducing you," A look somewhere between suspicion and curiosity washed over Shine's face. "It seems like all of this is going down without me. I guess you didn't think mentioning this first was—"

"Of course, it's going down without you," shaking his head up and down, Gorilla Leek cut his friend off. "Look at everything that has happened to you recently. I'm doing you a favor. Check it . . ." His voice sunk to a confidential murmur.

Shine listened, his suspicion gradually turning into admiration. At one point he held up a hand. "Yo, feel me, son. I'm hearing you and all, but still—let me know when something major like this is going down.

Four eyes are better than two my nigga."

"Indeed, dog. Just trying to reduce your stress. That's all."

"Word, but—"

"Yo, Shine! Is that you?" Their conversation was cut short by the sudden, familiar voice of a female piercing the darkness at full volume. The men fell silent.

Again, she yelled out, "Yo Shine!"

Both men remained still, searching the dark with their eyes, trying to make out the voice they heard.

As Shine's eyes adjusted, a gauzy outline began to appear. The figure slowly approached them, her tangled weave straggling dark shadows over her face. It was as if she appeared out of nowhere. She stopped just short of them. There was a scrape then a crackling sound, and her lips, nose, and eyes emerged from the darkness in a small pool of match light.

It was Desiree.

Cupping her hand around a match to protect it from the wind, she brought it up to a blunt dangling from her mouth and lit it. The flame danced in the wind as it burned down to the tip of her thumb and index finger. She shook the match out and flicked it to the ground. Only the red glow of the blunt remained, accentuating a set of full moist lips.

Desiree looked Shine directly in the eye as she parted her mouth to speak, "I've been running up and down the hood looking for you."

Shine stared at her while she paused to take another pull from the blunt.

"Why?" he asked nonchalantly.

"Me and Lo got approached by these two detectives today, asking about Trayvon," she quickly answered.

The two friends looked at each other, their eyes darting this way and that. Shine grew worried, his face clouding. And Desiree took notice.

"I already know what happened. Lo told me." Her words hung in the air as she waited to see how he would respond.

A bit stunned by her comment, he lowered his head and bit his lip. He didn't know how much she actually knew but by her behavior he figured she knew too much. She seemed all too anxious to discuss it with him, but his mind was elsewhere at the moment. And she could tell.

"Can I talk to you for a sec?" Desiree asked, frustrated by his calm lack of response.

Gorilla Leek eyed her with suspicion.

"You're talking to me now," Shine answered sarcastically.

She rolled her eyes, flared her nostrils, and let out a deep breath, clearly gathering her patience. "Look, those dicks went up in your crib with Lo. And like I said, I know what happened. So how long do you think it will be before someone else finds out?"

Gorilla Leek interrupted. "Dog, you gonna yap to this shorty? You know how big her mouth is."

Desiree shot a baleful glance in his direction then threw her head back and began to laugh. Her shrieking cackle echoed through the basketball court silencing the stillness. After a few seconds of continued laughter, she regained her composure and gave Gorilla Leek another stern look. "Yeah, maybe you're right, Leek. Maybe I do gotta big mouth. But you and I both know that you don't want your man to see how big it really is."

Gorilla Leek swallowed nervously then looked at his friend, whose eyes had gone fiercely cold. Shine just stood there frozen in unsure emotion. Uncertain of how to respond to her words, he stared at her rudely, his twisted lips proclaiming his disgust. A moment of silence engulfed them.

Out of nowhere, a brisk wind blew roughly, fluttering paper and trash across the basketball court, chilling Desiree's flesh. Her hands trembled, and her fingertips became cold just as gunshots erupted in the distance. Her nerves jumped beneath her skin and she dropped the blunt into a puddle of water at her feet. It sizzled into silence.

"Goddammit." She carefully picked it up and put it in her pocket.

Turning toward Shine, who watched in silence, she spoke quickly to hide her embarrassment, "Like I was saying, I know what happened. So, we need to talk asap."

Gorilla Leek snorted. "Nothing happened. Whatchoo talking bout?"

Desiree sucked her teeth and waved her hand dismissively, "Nigga please. I'm not speaking to your trifling ass. This between me and Shine."

Shine spoke up. "Like my man said, nothing happened."

She huffed out an impatient sigh. "Shine, I'm dead ass. I know what went down. I have proof that it happened. So, trust me, we need to speak," she cut her eyes at Gorilla Leek, "and we need to speak alone."

Shine would have bet she hadn't any proof. Still, he would hear her out and then decide what to do. "Yeah, alright, we can talk." He turned his face toward his partner for approval. "Leek, you mind?"

Gorilla Leek shrugged his shoulders with some indifference and spoke, "It's whatever my nigga. I gotta go handle that business before I hit the club tonight anyway." He snatched up the bottle of Crown Royal and took a swift inspection of its contents. "And I will be taking the rest of this with me."

Shine nodded.

"I'll link up with you after I get everything straight with the connect. I'm out. Peace!" Gorilla Leek shouted as he proceeded to walk away.

He bopped toward a large hole that had been cut in the fence near the south end of the park. He squeezed through it as so many others had done before him and took a few steps forward. He approached a large gate, lifted himself up to the top of it then disappeared from view, having jumped to the sidewalk several feet below.

Shine brought his attention to Desiree. "So, what's up?"

Desiree glared at him for a moment before opening her mouth. "I know how Trayvon died."

Shine ran his tongue over his teeth as the muscles of his face worked hard to conceal his concern. He offered a smile, but it appeared more like a nervous smirk. "What, because Lola told you some bullshit? Shorty please. I don't know what you're up to but it's not going to work."

The irritable look on her face was not lost on him and he grinned broadly at her. He watched as an eyebrow slowly crept skyward and a snarl formed on her lips. Her face then became contorted and her eyes narrowed to barely open slits. With one hand on her hip, she pointed a finger in his face.

"That ain't all. I know what you did the night before with the same gun that killed him."

Shine's smile faded into a thin line that showed no emotion. *How could she know about Badrick when I never told Lola?* He could feel his thoughts moving across the surface of his brain. *She has to be bluffing. But what if she's not. The only person who knew about what went down was Leek.* He thought about it for a few seconds more and then concluded, *Leek must be in bed with this bitch.*

"Who told you whatever it is you think you know?" he asked.

Desiree smiled. She knew she had him. "Don't worry about that. Just worry about what I need in order to keep my mouth shut."

A self-pitying lump came into Shine's throat. He swallowed it away and stared at Desiree while a cold deadly anger surged through him, settling like ice in the pit of his gut. He envisioned himself pulling out his gun and pressing it against her temple. But his hands refused. And before he could muster up the strength to budge, the skies opened up. The rain came in a sudden and blinding torrent, soaking them instantly.

Squinting against the raindrops, Desiree spun around toward the entrance located at the west end of the park. Her wet weave whipped across her face. "Can we finish talking about this in a dry place? Where did you park?"

Shine nodded and without uttering a word he motioned for her to follow him. Lightly jogging along a stone path, they quietly passed through the playground and exited the park. They came upon his SUV, breathing heavily, rain hitting them, rolling down their faces and off of their clothes. When he opened the door, she slid her weary body onto the passenger seat. He entered the driver's side and put the key in the ignition. The Ford roared to life. It was freezing in the vehicle, so Shine reached forward to turn up the heating.

"It'll warm up in a sec. So, what's up? What are you talking? What do you want?" he asked.

The smell of the exhaust leaked through the car's heater. Desiree turned up her nose. "Uh, you need to get that checked out."

"Never mind that. Go ahead and say what you have to say."

Batting her eyes, she said, "Well, seeing I know enough to get you locked up, there are a couple of things I—"

"First of all, you don't know anything to get me locked up," he interrupted. "All you got is hearsay. So, you better not be going around starting any rumors! You feel me! You don't have proof of anything!" he hissed, sounding as angry as he looked.

That garnered a mischievous smile from her. "Proof? What, like the body and the gun buried right here in Lincoln Terrace Park?"

Shine's heart raced along with his thoughts. *Why would Leek tell this bitch anything?* He wanted to call his partner and tell him to come back to the park, so they could sort this out. Instead, he glowered at Desiree, suspicion in every line of his face. He had gone completely still, allowing only his mouth to move. "So again, what do you want?"

She stared at him, wondering at his calmness, searching for fear. She didn't know what his reaction would be because she hadn't thought about it. Shine watched as she studied him for a moment. She crossed her leg and began tapping her foot. The glint in her eye was roguish.

"Well?" He was growing impatient.

She licked her lips and looked down at his crotch. "What do I want? Hmm." Her breath quickened as she dragged her eyes away from the impressive ridge in his pants to look at his face. *Is this nigga hard?* she wondered before opening her mouth to speak, "Well, from the looks of what you got going on down there, it seems we might want the same thing. You know?"

"Na, I don't know."

"Mmm, I want to know what that dick feels like," she said, a slow, sardonic smile shaping her mouth. "I want you to fuck the fuck out of me."

"What are you talking about? I ain't got time for the bullshit." He thought she was joking until he saw the heat in her eyes. "Are you serious?"

Desiree slid her hand down his thigh and cupped the bulge between his legs. "Yeah I'm dead serious. I want this inside of me. You have a problem with that?"

If he had any sense of decency left, he would've cursed her out and sent her on her way. But he couldn't. Her hand on his dick felt so good. There was little he could do to resist her. And a quickie might give him the time he needed to think things through. Once he spoke to Gorilla Leek, they could decide what to do with her. But for now, what on earth was he supposed to say? My girl is your best friend so yes, I have a problem with that. No. That wouldn't work. She had her mind set on what she wanted. What she desired at the moment he would provide or suffer the consequences. At least, that is what he told himself. Secretly, there was a part of him that wanted revenge on the woman who cheated on him. And what better way than this? With her best friend.

"Are you sure this is what you want? Seeing how cool you and Lola are?" he asked.

Responding with the abandonment of a woman who wouldn't be denied, she answered, "Mmm, Shine. The last time I checked, Lola ain't got a dick. Especially not one this big. So, she can't give me what you can. And you will give it to me."

Almost urgently, her hand was busy with his belt buckle and zipper. Within seconds she was inside of his pants gripping his erection firmly. Looking at him through hooded eyes, she stroked him slowly. His dick jumped in her hand as he pressed it deeper into her grasp. She leaned over, pulled it out of his pants and took him into her mouth. Shine arched his hips toward her as she lifted her long lashes, gazing upward, with her lips around his manhood. She watched him intently, reveling in the lust darkening his eyes.

Her warm tongue snaked out to lick around the head of his thick muscle. As his lips parted on a groan, he tangled his hand in her hair, and started grinding on her face. Desiree sucked slowly, enjoying the weight of his cock throbbing against her tongue. Her hand slid from her mouth to the base of his shaft, squeezing firmly while she relaxed her throat, taking him as deep as she could. Moaning around Shine's thickness, her pussy pulsed, contracting deep inside. Suddenly she stopped sucking and glanced toward the back seat.

"There's more room back there," she said, her voice low, her warm breath teasing him as she hovered above the head of his dick.

She climbed into the back and he followed, his pants at his ankles. He laid her down on the seat and began tearing at her jeans, ripping the buttons, as he guided them down her hips. Pressing his erection against her pussy, he pulled at the fabric of her panties violently until the band keeping them around the waist tore. Quivers of anticipation shuddered through her. A shallow cry escaped from her throat. He snatched the torn material out from under her and threw it to the floor. With a moan he ran a thick finger through her dripping pussy before pulling what was left of her panties to the side and slipping inside her with a powerful thrust of his hips.

Tight with the first stroke, her muscles quickly relaxed, welcoming the brute force pulsing within her. He plunged deep into her, and she clenched her pussy tight around his dick, wanting to keep it inside her forever. Closing her eyes, she gave way to his violent invasion, her fat ass bouncing about. With legs squeezing his waist, she encouraged him in farther. Her eyes shot open as the sensation of being impaled by his stiffness shook her whole body. Feeling his testicles slapping against the lips of her cunt, she met each of his thrusts, bucking her hips up to him and moaning every time he filled her up. As he stroked, her clit hardened so that it rubbed up against his shaft. She raised her ass off the seat and pushed her pelvic towards him. His big dick pulling at her pussy lips and tugging at her clit, she finally had Lola's man and it felt good.

The wind had picked up and slammed the rain roughly against the window, rocking the SUV slightly. Shine, a bit startled, stopped moving and looked up but couldn't see anything on the outside of the car. The windows were foggy with the heat of their breathing. Out of nowhere, headlights oozed through the steamy glass as a vehicle pulled up behind them. Then a swirl of red and blue lights appeared in his rearview. Through the rain, the glow from the police car was blurry and took on an almost hallucinatory feel, shining and strobing, looming out of the dense mist tinting the car windows. Shine abruptly pulled his dick out of Desiree and brought his pants up to his waist.

"Oh shit. It's the scramz," In one swift motion he hopped back into the driver's seat. He adjusted his rearview and spoke to Desiree's reflection. "Put your clothes on and stay down."

The officer got out of the patrol car with his hand on his holster, and strolled up to the driver's window, oblivious to the young lady in the back seat. Beaming a flashlight in Shine's face he tapped on the glass. Shine wound it down and a blast of wind and rain came rushing in.

"Good evening sir," said the officer in a muffled voice. "I need you to move this vehicle. You can't park here."

Feeling relieved that the cop only wanted him to move his SUV, yet ashamed at feeling so relieved, Shine humbly replied, "Yes, sir. I will most certainly do that right this minute."

The officer said nothing further but walked back to his car and got in. He didn't appear to be too fond of the rain.

"So, what now?" Desiree asked while easing very carefully out of the back seat.

Shine threw the Ford in drive. "We ain't done. I ain't know your pussy was that juicy. I'm going to find another spot to park and we're going to finish this." With his attention still on the police car behind him, he slowly guided his vehicle out into the rain-soaked road and drove into the night.

CHAPTER 10

LOLA SAT ON HER COUCH staring blankly into the darkness of her unlit apartment. Ghostly images of her dead son danced behind her eyes. An eerie and lonely silence hung in the air broken only by the clatter of rain hammering the roof. However, with the faint rays of moonlight filtering in through the curtains and casting shadows around the room, she felt everything but alone. She sighed deeply, inhaling the very damp and cold air. Several clouds moved over the moon, blocking its light and the blackness of the sky spilled like ink into the chilly, gloom of the living room. She shivered.

No matter how hard she attempted to think away the past few hours, she couldn't. The chaos in her mind threatened to drive her mad. Thoughts ricocheted in her skull, tearing apart her mask of self-control. She sobbed and cursed half a dozen times, replaying the conversation over and over in her head, worrying about what she might have inadvertently let slip. Detective Brown's questions had been unnerving, and she had the impression that he saw right through her guilt and lies. She just hoped she didn't contradict anything Shine had told them.

Lola wanted to light up the blunt dangling between her two fingers, but she was concerned that the police might return at any moment. *What if they only left to get a warrant?* Her emotions varied every few minutes. She wasn't ready to be locked away in a cell.

Shame overwhelmed her as she thought of her past. In all those bitter years between then and now she had made several bad decisions which often brought unexpected consequences. But nothing like this.

What would her life have been like if she had an abortion and stayed in college? If she had heeded her mother and stayed away from northern black rednecks like Shine, she wouldn't be experiencing this nightmare. The thoughts came flooding in; thoughts of her childhood, her life in Georgia, school, cheerleading, her first kiss. But those memories didn't belong to her. They belonged to someone else, someone she once knew long ago. It was as though she had become a different person. She didn't feel like herself anymore. This stranger was concealing the death of her child.

Then it hit her.

I didn't do this. I didn't commit any murder. That gun didn't even belong to me. It was Shine's gun that killed Trayvon. If I hide this, I will get in trouble.

Over the last few days she refused to acknowledge the role she played in concealing her son's death. She sank into a numbing depression and found it difficult to face reality. But learning that she was pregnant actually perked her up a little. Helped her to sometimes forget. The baby could be a sign from God. Maybe this was His way of telling her to leave Shine and start all over? Perhaps she might do well if given another chance in life—one with more favorable odds. Lola drew in a ragged breath and laid her free hand on her belly.

She had no right to think of herself, indulge in self-pity or waste energy complaining about her circumstances. She had to decide what was best for her unborn child. Whether the pregnancy was a blessing or not, she would see to it that her baby would not be born in anyone's prison. Besides, what kind of madness required a pregnant woman to worry about protecting a man who caused the death of her first child? Sure, she loved him, but did she love him enough to risk her freedom and her unborn child's future?

She knew what she had to do. Some sense of relief washed over her but only momentarily. Glancing down at the blunt she was holding, she thought, *hmm, might as well. I deserve it. If the police come back right now, they will be more interested in what's coming from my lips than what's in between them.*

Suddenly, there was the sound of keys at the front door, the top lock tumbling over and over again. Lola tensed, waiting for the door of the apartment to burst open, but it remained shut. There was a loud thump on the other side of it, a loud hard thumping sound. Realizing her room was a lot darker than it had been a minute ago, she began trembling. Something was scraping against the door and she thought she heard a low murmuring.

Her eyes were just beginning to adjust to the darkness again when all three locks rotated in sequence from top to bottom. She watched the door edge open slowly and a slight shaft of light penetrated the dark room. A cold stab of fear shot through her when a dark silhouette, too wide to be Shine, appeared in the doorway. Dim light from the hallway showered over the figure. Thinking back to what Detective Brown had said to her, one piece of the conversation came to mind—because of the war between Chinnah and her man, her life was now in danger.

Shutting her eyes tightly, anticipating violence, she shuddered at the sound of the door closing and the heavy deliberate footsteps moving toward her. Her heart pounded painfully against her chest. Light-headed with panic, a wave of nausea bubbled through her stomach. She squinted her eyes open just a thread to see the intruder. But darkness danced along the edges of her vision. He was almost on top of her. His features barely recognizable in the eternal night of the living room. Then without warning, light flooded the apartment.

Shine stood near the lamp, facing Lola, a box under one arm and two shopping bags under the other. He dumped his load of packages on the floor, then staggered over and collapsed beside her.

"I went downtown earlier today, to cop us a couple of things."

"Ugh! Shine, you scared the hell out of me!" Lola rolled her eyes and sighed in frustration. "You can't be doing that. With those bags you were carrying, and this apartment being dark, I didn't know who you were. You could've said something to let me know it was you."

"I could see from the outside there weren't any lights on, so I didn't think you was up in here. I was trying to sneak in and put the stuff I bought you on the bed before you came back. You know, to surprise you."

"You can't shop away your guilt," she replied in her painfully truthful manner.

He let out a long, heavy sigh. "Whatever. Did the scramz come by here?"

"Yeah," she responded in a soft husky emotional tone, "they said you came to them and reported Trayvon missing."

Taking notice of the blunt in her hand, he asked, "Are you going to light that?"

"Don't have a lighter," she answered flatly.

Shine fished a lighter out of his pants pocket and passed it to her. She raised her hand, clapping the blunt to her lips, then lit it, taking a long drag. The smoke slowly curled out of her mouth and hung frozen in the air. He watched her, not knowing what to say. It was the first time they'd been alone since that horrific morning. And though she was silent, he knew she blamed him for what happened. Of course, he was aware of how she felt because he blamed himself. He wanted to hold her in his arms, tell her how sorry he was and grieve with her over the child they'd lost. He was willing to promise her anything just to wipe the sadness from her eyes. But he couldn't. Someone had to be strong.

The apartment was deathly still as they sat on the couch next to each other. An uncomfortable silence stretched between them while Shine pondered what to say next. Finally, his anxiety and anticipation overwhelmed him.

"So, what did they say?"

Lola took two quick pulls on the blunt then held it out to him. "What did who say?"

He took it and inhaled the weed smoke. "The scramz. When they came here. What did they say?"

Her head fell back against the couch. "They said you reported Trayvon missing and that it might have something to do with a kidnapping." She rolled her head on the cushion to look directly at him, accusation and pain in her eyes. "Why didn't you tell me you were going to go to the cops?"

Shine found himself ensnared by her gaze, returning her raging, impassioned stare with his own apologetic one. "That's why I asked you to come back to the apartment. I wanted to talk to you about that before they did." He paused and took another hit of the blunt, before continuing, "I had to go to them. It was a spur of the moment type thing. I wasn't thinking about calling you first. I mean what if someone would have questioned Trayvon's absence and went to the police. They would've been wondering why I didn't come to them right away."

Lola sat upright and leaned forward. "Yeah, but how was I supposed to know what to say to them."

"I'm sure you did fine."

"Shine, are you insane? You left a plate of coke in the freezer and they came inside our home. Had I not gone to get some water for one of the detectives, I wouldn't have seen it . . ." Her words were pouring out in rapid, bitter, blaring bursts as her neck swayed from side to side like a cobra. "They said they were going to start checking all of the front rooms first, so I had to quickly sneak it out of the fridge and carry to our bedroom."

"Did you hide it?"

"No, I didn't have a chance to. As I soon as I stepped into the bedroom, the other detective—the white one, Seidman—called for me to come back into the living room. Said he had a question about something. So, I quickly threw the plate on the dresser then shut the door."

"And they never saw you?" he asked in a throaty whisper, trying not to sound too unconcerned and insensitive and knowing that he was failing miserably.

"I sure as hell thought that Seidman guy saw me. And he was the only one who searched our bedroom, but he never mentioned the cocaine."

Shine inhaled deeply, rolling his shoulders back. "I'm sorry I didn't warn you ahead of time," he said as he exhaled.

"You're never upfront with me. It's like you try to hide everything. I mean, why didn't you tell me about what had happened at Minimart?"

The question caught him off guard. *How the hell did she know that? Goddamn cops.* A few stammering words came to his lips. "I—I was going to—I mean—you know—I wanted to keep you away—you know—from all that—" He paused for an uneasy moment as he nervously took another pull from the blunt.

The look on her face indicated that she was not buying the bullshit he was trying to sell. She was clearly upset. But more than anything, she was tired. Not physically tired, but tired of trying to keep her dysfunctional family together. Tired of being left in the dark, tired of being ordered to stay at home with her son. Tired of being told what was best for her. Most of all, she was tired of hoping. How could she ever hope to have a complete family once again? Hope had ruined her. Wasting hope on Black men always seemed to end up in disappointment. First it was her father, and now it was Shine. She swore to herself that he would be the last Blackman to ever let her down.

Shine's a destructive influence, she told herself. She was deserving of better. The drugs, the crime, the verbal abuse, that lifestyle was something she had grown accustomed to as it was now almost a daily routine. Yet all the while, she was slipping further and further into insanity. Her mother, aware of what she was going through, never seemed to understand why she'd put up with all that she had. While Lola knew that the emotional pain of verbal violence and the loneliness suffocating her soul wouldn't heal quickly, she had to at least try to have as normal a family life as possible, for the sake of her son. Her baby would never know the feeling of being abandoned by his father. But now, some three years after becoming a mother, she no longer had her son.

She decided to ignore her man's skittish behavior and get on with what would most certainly be devastating for him to hear. "Well, they brought other cops here to investigate the apartment." She paused to let him take in the information. "They found a torn baby wipe with blood on it under the couch, next to the spot on the carpet where,"— she glanced at the ground and swallowed heavily— "Trayvon died."

With her chin to her chest, she continued, "They noticed that there was a big bleach stain there. Said they were going to come back to conduct a more thorough search. I heard the detective tell one of the cops that they will come back and spray the carpet with lemon oil or something or another to check for blood. I tried calling you because I didn't know what to do or say to them."

"Lemon oil? You are such a square. I think you mean Luminol." He let out a slight chuckle, trying to lighten the air between them.

Lola, however, wasn't amused. "Shine, this is serious. They said they might need to take samples of the carpet. And they told me to have you call them as soon as you came home."

"Call them? For what?" A surge of worrying, unpleasant thoughts were beginning to flood his mind. *What if that baby wipe can prove Trayvon died here? What if they found more evidence of his death in the apartment that they're not telling Lola?*

He imagined living the rest of his life behind bars. Now that the thrill of the streets had faded, he could sense the prison walls starting to close in on him.

Stupid-ass nigga.

That's what he was. *Another ignorant ass street nigga.*

Should have packed up his family and left Brooklyn years ago.

Should have gotten out of the game when Lola was pregnant with Trayvon. If he had done that, his son would still be here. If only he could go back and unravel all the mistakes he had made. Mistakes that cost him dearly, mistakes like keeping a gun in his home and letting his son see where it was hidden.

He got to thinking that maybe he should have reported Trayvon's death as a murder instead. All he would've needed to do was get rid of the gun. Then it suddenly hit him: *The gun is the only thing that could connect me to Trayvon's death and those murders. And that bitch Desiree might lead the cops right to it. I got to get that gun back and throw it away somewhere far from the neighborhood.*

He didn't realize how long he'd been quietly thinking things over until she interrupted his thoughts. "They want you to call them to discuss Chinnah having something to do with Trayvon's disappearance."

Shine cocked his head back. "Huh?" His hands began shaking as he puffed furiously on the blunt.

Lola continued, "They are the ones who told me about what happened to Minimart. They believe Chinnah had something to do with it and they know that you own it."

If he hadn't choked on the blunt smoke, the surprised news would have instantly shown on his face. His eyes shot open; his mouth hung agape. "What? How'd they know I own Minimart?"

"Because, Desiree told them."

Shine thought back to his conversation with Desiree in the park. Meeting her demand for sex was the least of his worries. She claimed to know the location of Trayvon's body, as well as the gun. And now she was attempting to blackmail him. Money in exchange for her silence. Ten-thousand dollars to be exact.

After dropping Desiree off at her apartment, he immediately called his partner to find out what he told her. Gorilla Leek swore he never said anything to anyone about the murders. And gauging from his response, he was just as shocked as Shine to find out how much she knew. He was not sleeping with her and he did not have a reason to confide in her. Shine couldn't make sense of it. *We were the only two who knew about what went down. And I know my nigga wouldn't tell that bitch about the bodies we caught.* They both agreed that something had to be done about Desiree.

Now after listening to Lola, his thoughts were not letting him calm down; he started worrying about what her friend would do.

"What else did she tell them?" he asked.

"Nothing."

"You sure?"

"Yes."

"So those pigs don't know what really happened to Trayvon or even suspect that we know where he's at, right?"

"No. They don't know anything," she answered flatly. "It seems like they were more concerned about Chinnah."

Chinnah? Oh shit. Yes! Chinnah! It quickly dawned on him—Lola could see it dawn on him—he could lead the cops to believe that his enemy was responsible for his son's death. He only needed to get the gun back and somehow plant it on Chinnah. *But how? Where? Maybe in his car? Or his store? When? After the party? First thing in the morning?* That way Chinnah would also take the rap for the bodies on it. *Yes,* he thought, *I wouldn't have to worry about those bodies coming back on me or becoming a suspect in Trayvon's disappearance.* The murder he committed was the reason he went to such great lengths to carefully conceal his son's death in the first place. Now he could kill two birds with one stone. They could take Chinnah out of the picture without shedding blood. With the exception of Gorilla Leek's personal grievance, there would be no need to kill Chinnah and start an all-out war with the rest of the Gully Gods.

Lola looked up at Shine and felt a twinge in the pit of her stomach as she thought about the trouble she might be in because of his actions. Why did she fall in love with a thug? Her head shook from side to side as she stared at him. She could see the frustration, laced with worry, on his face as he tried to get his thoughts together. Silently, she wondered how much time he really had left—at most a couple of weeks—before his complete demise. It seemed he had grown oblivious to his own self-destruction, not accepting that he was the reason they were suffering the most savage of all torments.

Suddenly, a muffled ringing sound caught their attention. Shine handed the blunt back to Lola then slowly dug inside his jacket pocket and produced a cell phone. He held his breath and glanced at the caller ID before answering. "What's up?"

He listened into the phone for a few seconds, his faced twisted in concentration. The veins in his neck pulsed furiously, and through his slightly parted lips, his teeth clenched. Finally, he spoke, "What else did they ask?"

Again, he fell silent. Lola could hear a voice coming through the receiver but couldn't make out any words.

"Alright, no doubt. I'll come by and check you in the morning. Just stay in the crib for now," Shine commanded into the smart phone. "Alright? Peace."

He put the cell back in his pocket then leaned his head back against the couch and tilted it toward the ceiling. His voice quivered a little as he spoke without looking at her, "The detectives that came here, was one of them a black dude?"

Lola took a final drag off of the blunt then stubbed it out in the ashtray that sat atop the coffee table. She looked at her man through partially closed lids. "Yeah, one was black. His name was Brown. Buck Brown. The other was Detective Seidman. Why?"

Shine thought back to his previous run-in with Brown at the precinct, and remembered the curious, almost suspicious look the detective gave him, as if he doubted the story about Trayvon's disappearance.

"I'm asking because the cat who we put Minimart's name under, got another visit from the same detective, the Brown dude. And he was asking about me."

Thick lashes lifted, and Lola sat staring at him with fixed intensity. She held his gaze, her eyes begging for the truth. "Shine, that cop said that Badrick and some other guy were murdered inside of Chinnah's house. Just keep it real with me for once. Did you have anything to do with that? Please, I just need to hear it from you. Just be honest."

Guilt gripped his heart as he looked to the ground. She noticed his face flush with concern, and it was then she realized the depth of her man's grief, having known little of his crimes. He stared at her questioningly, the expression on his face filled with confusion and shame.

"Why are you asking me that?" The look he offered was covered with emotions not entirely clear to her.

"Yes or no Shine?" she demanded.

He thought for a moment, his brow furrowing. "No," he answered.

"Shine, you're lying. I know you're lying!" she screamed in nervous anger.

"Look! The less you know, the less you say. Feel me? You don't need to worry yourself with all that right now," he shouted.

The hell I don't, she thought.

He lowered his voice to a soft whisper and continued, "At this moment, we need to focus on keeping those pigs away from finding out what happened to Trayvon."

Listening to him, she knew for certain he was now a murderer who was more concerned about getting arrested than he was about her well-being. He was more concerned about covering up the death of his son than the death itself. All she could think about was Trayvon. But her man didn't seem to be similarly affected, absorbed as he was in his thoughts of avoiding prison.

He didn't carry their son for nine months, breast feed him or wipe his first tears. So, he wasn't afflicted by the same guilt and pain which tormented her. But why did she feel that way. Trayvon's death wasn't her fault. Of course, it wasn't. The pitiful excuses kept rolling through her head like; *it was Shine's gun. He's the criminal not me. I only stayed with him because I thought he would change.* Her mind wouldn't slow down and allow her a moment of peace. And yet suddenly it was very clear, so fucking clear, the danger she was in. She needed to go back home—to Georgia—and be with her family. She would be safe there.

With utter misery in her eyes, she struggled to hold back her emotions. "And what if they do find out what happened? Then what? Huh? What the hell are we going to do then? Huh, Shine?" Lola lifted her head slowly and closed her eyes. After a moment she opened them, then went on more quietly, "Look I know you're worried about the police, but I miss Trayvon too much to act like nothing happened. And I am not going to rot in a goddamn jail for anyone."

He tilted his head to the side and peered sharply at her. "What are you saying?"

She ignored his question. "How long do you think it will be before they find out? They took the baby wipe with them to examine it."

Shine shot her a quizzical look. "Why? What did they say about it?"

"Nothing."

"Nothing?"

"Yeah, nothing."

"Well, if you didn't say anything then they know nothing. You feel me? We're good." The worry etched on his face belied his reassuring words. "They won't find his body or the gun. Soon this will be another cold case."

Cold case? Lola scowled in thought before speaking. "If you say so. The black dude seemed to be more concerned about Chinnah and the murders than Trayvon anyway."

Shine lowered his face into his palms, resting his elbows on his knees. He lifted his head and looked around the apartment until his gaze fell on the living room window. He caught a reflection of himself in the glass. Behind his transparent image was infinite blackness, reminding him of the inevitability of death. Yet even at that moment, even in the darkness beyond his refuge, there was a glimmer of light. The yellow haze of the dim street lights glowed faintly outside, appearing as a halo over the sinfully wicked streets of the Nineties. Maybe there was hope after all. He took in a deep breath. Then, one by one he condensed the thoughts in his head to a single sentence.

They don't have shit on me yet.

The darkness in his mind was bleaker than what awaited him outside of his apartment. And knowing this, he realized he needed to protect himself from himself. He thought back to the murders that took place at Chinnah's house, searching his memory for any mistakes he may have made. Mistakes that could be costly. The way things went down at the house made him uneasy. There were too many windows belonging to too many people who could possibly talk. Maybe the police had witnesses. Maybe they had found his phone and were waiting for him to slip up.

"What else did the cops want to know?" he asked without looking at her.

"Nothing. But when they found blood on the baby wipe, they—"

A wave of nausea suddenly struck her, and she stopped speaking. She stared ahead vacantly and thought back to everything that had happened. When she tried to sit up, she felt a knot build in her stomach and she became dizzy. Clutching her gut, she bent over to take a deep breath. Her eyes sprang open in surprise as vomit erupted from her mouth and splashed off the floor, splattering bits onto Shine's Jordans. He jumped up from the couch.

Lola sank to her knees on the living room floor, gagging on cries. Shine looked down at her silently, with curious apprehension. All of the color had drained from her face. She could feel him standing over her, trying to see her tears through her hair. She started to say something, whatever came in her head to explain her sickness. Instead, she scrambled to her feet and bolted down the hallway to the bathroom. Shine could hear the toilet water splashing and more gagging cries. Reluctantly, he cast his eyes to the floor and took in the mess, blinking several times to remove the image from his mind of his son lying there earlier in blood.

CHAPTER 11

HIDING BEHIND DARK sunglasses, Copper tightly gripped the steering wheel of his GL450 Mercedes Benz. He drove toward Pitkin Avenue peering through the car's deeply tinted windows into the blackness blanketing the desolate street. His brow furrowed in deep concentration, he had remained silent since entering the vehicle with his two friends. A dark-skinned bearded young man, wearing a dusty dark coat and blue denim jeans, stared grimly over Copper's shoulder from the back seat. With a blue bandana clung to the top of his head and holding his braids back, Six sat still, glowering in a menacing manner.

Jigga Blue watched Copper from the passenger seat. He felt uneasy about his friend's recent business decision. "Are you sure that dealing with this slob is straight?"

Copper kept his eyes on the road and nodded, just a slight silent movement of his head.

Jigga Blue acknowledged his gesture. "Yeah, but what if this is a set-up?"

Copper sighed. "Look, I've explained this to you, mad times already. He ain't thinking about setting us up. He has more to lose if he did. Plus, he already got his hands dirty. Killing that nigga was only the beginning."

"Yeah, but that was your cousin," Jigga Blue pointed out.

"Look, there's no love lost for Badrick. I never liked him anyway. Family or no family. He was out to take my seat." Copper turned sharply toward the passenger seat to see if his friend was listening and had understood. He turned his attention back to the road then continued, "My pops filled my head with all those lies when I was young about how I would one day be in control of the Gully Gods. But then he started pushing me to the back as I got older. He be acting like I am incompetent or something. That's why blue is the only blood I bleed now. The only family I know. You understand, right?"

Jigga Blue was reluctant to agree with his comrade, and Copper took notice.

"Jigga, feel me cuz. You and I both know that we have the whole world to gain from this. And we can't turn back now." Copper tilted his chin up. "I mean you know what my pops would do if he found out we were working with that cracker-ass cop to fuck him over?"

Jigga Blue answered, "Yeah, I know what he would do to me and Six. But you? Loc, you ain't the one who got to worry. He's your dad."

"Cuz, he don't give a fuck about me! That dude didn't even love my moms. She was his side piece. And he's the reason why she's dead. He's loves the hell out of my sister because her mother had him pussy-whipped." An angry growl rose from Copper's throat. "But he despises me! He thinks I'm too dumb to run his operation. That's why I agreed to work with that pig. That's why I'm—we're—doing our own thing now! Fuck the Gully Gods. Cuz, this here is about to be Stone Cold Crip City! We bout to rule the Nineties! You understand?"

Jigga Blue was almost afraid to turn and look at him, because he didn't want to show doubt in front of his friend and upset him more. He had, on several occasions, witnessed the violence spawned by his drug-fueled tantrums. And Copper had already sniffed a couple of grams. He was high out of his mind. The young Crip decided he would simply agree and let his boss do the talking.

Copper felt he had to make a point. "Man, this has to be done. And I knew it had to be done ever since I approached them slobs about buying their store. At first, I was only trying to get their property because that real estate company was looking to pay mad doe for it. But them slobs wouldn't do it." He shrugged his shoulders. "Well Shine wouldn't, but Gorilla Leek was with it. Then me and that pig was going over our plans of how we were going to get at Pops when he came up with the idea to bring Gorilla Leek in on our moves. He said we could offer him a sweeter deal than just buying the store. You know? Since he seemed like the more agreeable one, anyway."

Jigga Blue nodded.

Copper continued. "Not to mention, he's also the one who wouldn't be afraid to pull this off. Seeing how pops murdering his parents gave him a reason and all." He glanced into his rearview mirror at Six who sat motionless in the backseat then added, "I knew both of us wanted the same thing—Pops out of the picture—so I made a deal with him. And I told him that we had to make it look like a revenge murder. So, the Gully Gods wouldn't suspect that I had anything to do with it once I took over, and they would roll with me under my command."

"Yeah, but killing Badrick? Was that necessary?" asked Jigga Blue.

"Loc, it's going to eventually happen to everyone in the Gully Gods sooner or later."

"Yeah, but why him first."

"It was the pig's idea to rob my pops. And Badrick was in charge of that spot. For some reason Gorilla Leek wouldn't do it without his boy, so he somehow convinced him that Badrick was messing around with his girl. You know, to get him to run up in Pop's house. When they got there, that slob lost his mind and lit Badrick up," Copper grinned. "All I did was tell them how much work would be up in there and gave them the key. Them slobs did the rest."

"So, you just let them walk in there and steal all of that coke?"

"Don't worry. We're getting some of it back tonight. That's why we're meeting him now. He's bringing me four of the ten bricks they took."

"Them slobs are keeping six bricks?" The disappointment was etched in lines across Jigga Blue's forehead.

"Yeah, well. Gorilla Leek kept one extra for himself, as payment for seeing to it that my pops end up in the dirt. He told his boy it was for White Mike."

Jigga Blue sighed, "And what do you plan to do with the four bricks? I mean, we can't just sell them while your father is still around. He will definitely find out."

"We're not selling them."

"No?"

"No," Copper shook his head. His mind was made up. "With the original plan the pig came up with, I was supposed to act like I found out through the streets who took the bricks and where they were stashing it. I was going to look like a boss nigga by bringing back the four bricks we're getting tonight to my pops and telling him that I ran down on them slobs to get it back for him."

"Yeah, but he's going to ask about the remaining six bricks?" Jigga Blue shrugged his shoulders. "What then?"

"Well, I was going to tell him that, while getting his coke back, we were able to snatch up one of the slobs responsible, and that we had him tied up in White Mike's basement. You know, to question them on the remaining bricks." Copper smirked then rubbed his chin. "That's how we were going to get him outside of the *Free Market*. You know he rarely leaves there. And the security on that entire block is too tight to try and get at him there."

"I was going to ask you about that," mentioned Jigga Blue.

"Yeah, well since pops likes to be hands on when it comes to dealing with someone stealing from him, I was going to talk him into coming down to White Mike's store to question the slob about the location of the rest of the drugs, himself."

"But of course, there wasn't gonna be anyone tied up, right?" added Jigga Blue.

"Right," Copper grinned, confidence swelling. "The plan was to have them slobs there waiting for him. And Gorilla Leek was going to get his revenge. But that whole shit with Shine's phone messed things up."

Jigga Blue tried hard to preserve his stony silence but his curiosity overcame him. "Yeah but if the pig is on our side, why did he tell your father about finding Shine's phone in the first place?"

"Well, that's why I said that was the original plan. We have to make a few tweaks now because of that fool leaving his phone."

Jigga Blue gave a vigorous nod. "Yeah, I mean that kind of changed everything, because your pops ended up sending Cutty and Pauley after them slobs before you could get a chance to look like the hero who got the coke back. Right?"

"Exactly. But the cop had to tell my pops. Shit, my cousin was dead, and he was one of the first pigs on the scene investigating the murder. Them slobs were sloppy. O'Reilly said they had found some other evidence like tire tracks or something. I think they even had a witness who saw them leaving the house." Copper glanced at Jigga Blue to see if he was following. "So, O'Reilly couldn't have the other cops finding out who the suspects were and that information getting back to the Gully Gods before he himself told my father. Pops would've threatened that cop's whole family if he didn't come back with some answers. And valid answers at that. He did what he would usually do in that circumstance, to avoid appearing suspicious."

After listening to Copper, Jigga Blue began to relax, the stress on his face easing. "So, what now?"

Copper rubbed his chin as his smile turned devious. "Well, that's one of the reasons we're meeting Gorilla Leek and O'Reilly—to discuss just that."

Copper brought the car to a stop at a red light. He glanced in his rearview mirror then looked out of the front window. No one was walking on the sidewalk, and no police car. He released his foot from the brake and stepped on the gas, driving through the red light.

"But why are we involving White Mike?" a nervous Jigga Blue inquired. "What if he tells your pops?"

Copper guided the car to the left and turned onto Belmont Avenue. He cut the lights and pulled into an empty parking space behind a black Yukon. After putting the car in park, he took the keys out the ignition and rested his head back against the seat.

Without looking at his friend, he replied, "He won't say anything. He is gaining from all of this."

"How?" inquired a curious Jigga Blue.

"See, after pops mashed up Minimart, I promised to set Gorilla Leek up in another neighborhood if he left the Nineties after Pop's death. And since White Mike had been itching to get out of the game, I talked him into selling off his store to the same real estate company that wanted to buy the Minimart. I brokered the deal and promised the company that I would find them someone else to lease it out to right away, until they figured out what they were going to do with the property. Then I offered it to that slob."

"Yeah, but you're also talking about killing your pops in White Mike's basement. That couldn't be good for their business. Why not catch him somewhere else?"

"First, it's the perfect place because it's a spot that's familiar to my pops," he said so matter-of-factly. "A place where he would let down his guard. Second, by the time the cops find out that my father was killed there, White Mike will be long-gone, and those slobs will be the only ones left to take the blame."

"So, you're ok with helping these dudes set up shop and make doe in the meantime?"

"It won't be for long. We're going to turn the Nineties into World War Nine and the only ones left standing will be niggas in blue. Just us and the law."

Jigga Blue let out a sigh and remained silent.

Copper glanced over his shoulder and caught sight of Six cocking back his Colt Double Eagle. "Yo, Six, stay in the car and keep your eyes open for anything not right. Okay?"

Six's eyes met Copper's. He barely opened his mouth to reply, "Yeah man."

The front doors flew open. Copper and Jigga Blue exited the vehicle and casually strolled down the sidewalk. As they walked, Copper removed his cell phone from his leather jacket. He glanced at it before placing it back into his pocket. "We're about ten minutes early. When I spoke to White Mike, he said that slob was on his way. O'Reilly texted me that he was running late."

Jigga Blue remained silent and followed Copper toward the corner of the block. Cold rain began to dribble, battering the top of their heads. The night was still, the neighborhood quiet. Not a sound but the raindrops on the sidewalk drumming a steady beat as the two pussyfooted over puddles. Copper cursed under his breath. He was wearing his brand-new all-white Air Force 1s.

The rain grew harder until it was pelting down. Six seconds later, the men were hurrying down the block toward the bodega which sat at the corner. There were two teenage males standing under the awning outside the store, one black and the other Latino. They stood huddled into a corner made by the wall and a green dumpster. Rain-splattering footsteps drew them out of their conversation and they turned to face the two Crips.

Sensing trouble, Jigga Blue's pulse raced, and his instincts went on alert. A cold feeling crawled up the back of his neck. Were they walking into a set-up? He caught Copper's arm, bringing him to a halt, and motioned his head toward the two teens. Copper shot daggers at his partner with his eyes. He didn't have time to waste.

"Yo Cuz, let's get this over with. I'm trying to get out of this rain," uttered Copper. He had money on the brain and didn't understand what his friend was trying to point out.

Jigga Blue decided to be blunt. "Them kids at the corner look suspect."

Copper wasn't bothered by the presence of the boys. That wasn't important right now. No. His thoughts were on executing his plans to take control of the Nineties.

"Cuz, calm down. Everyone ain't out to get you." Copper shrugged his friend's grip off. "You need to be more worried about handling this deal."

Suddenly gunshots erupted inside the store. Then in one fluid motion, the teenagers spun around and sprinted across the street. Running in the opposite direction of the two men, they never looked back. Without uttering another word, Copper ran straight for the store.

"It came from White Mike's place," Jigga Blue yelled as he tried to keep up with his friend's pace. "You think that's Gorilla Leek?"

Copper said nothing. He kept running. The first to arrive at the entrance of the store, he pulled out his Smith and Wesson 627, his thumb automatically going to the hammer. Jigga Blue came up behind him, panting slightly to catch his breath. His pistol was already drawn.

Copper gripped the door handle and braced himself. He shoved it open and quickly stepped inside, the door closing behind him. Two gunshots thundered from behind the door, a split second apart, followed by the sound of breaking glass.

Jigga Blue stood frozen in place, his gun pointed forward, unable to move. His frightened eyes flicking from the door to the corner to the street then back again. The uncertainty of what awaited him on the other side made him extremely nervous. The feeling of fear was overwhelming. Unable to see through the clouded glass of the door, he listened intently for a couple of seconds, hoping to hear Copper's voice. The silence was deafening. It was the silence of death. He decided to throw caution to the wind. In one final moment, he opened the door and leaped through the entrance.

The store was completely trashed. He stepped on broken glass as he moved further inside. It made a crackling sound like hard ice crunching beneath his boots. Shelves were overturned, and ruined store goods were everywhere. Amidst all the disarray, it was eerily silent. At first glance, nobody appeared to be around. Then, out the corner of his eye, he caught a flash of movement on the ground. It was Copper.

He was lying on the floor twitching back and forth, a terrible convulsion racking his body. His eyes were rolling back in his head with fright while his chest heaved up and down tremendously. From a ragged, gaping, bloody hole where his jaw and mouth had once been, he uttered a gurgling cry. His skin hanging off his chin like blood-soaked sheets. Then suddenly, he stretched out and stopped moving. Jigga Blue glanced nervously at the ground, shocked as his friend lay on his back motionless.

♠   ♠   ♠

GORILLA LEEK SAT IN HIS SUV, smoking a blunt. A grey cloud dribbled from between his lips, swirling along the ceiling of the vehicle. Reclining back in the driver's seat, he idly flicked a red lighter on and off, watching the flame flare quickly, then die out. Eyes half-closed, he peered through a haze of weed smoke out into the blackness of the night, made blacker still by windows that were obviously tinted much darker than was legal. With its charcoal exterior the car looked like it was meant to prowl the streets after midnight. The engine purred softly, blending with the hiss of the rain while Gorilla Leek waited with the lights off, parked in the most obscure section of the block. Cloaked in the darkness of the neighborhood, his eyes searched the area for movement. Seeing none, he cut the engine off, eased out of the car, and ground out the blunt beneath his Timberland boot.

A few feet away, a homeless woman was sunk down in the recessed doorway of a tattered, broken-down shell of a building. She was busy trying to keep warm for the night, shoving old newspapers in her over-sized worn-out, shaggy blue coat. Gorilla Leek took notice of her and smiled. Her appearance reminded him of the Cookie Monster, even though the neighborhood was a far cry from Sesame Street. As he neared her, he was met by a strong smell of urine. He held his breath. His eyes fell upon the dirty and oily strands of matted hair that stuck out of her cloaking bandage of torn scarfs. Though homeless, she seemed to have everything she needed, the thick neck of a liquor bottle poking partially out of the side pocket of her coat. There was no trace of shame on her brown unwashed face. As he strolled passed, Gorilla Leek removed two one-hundred-dollar bills from his pocket and tossed it to the ground in front of her.

The Cookie Monster tilted her head back behind her scarfs,

revealing a toothless withered mouth hanging open. "Thank you, sir." She quickly scooped up the bills, her dirt caked nails sticking out of a ragged glove, scraping against the concrete.

He didn't respond. Gorilla Leek continued walking until he came upon an old red and yellow Bodega right at the corner of the block. The large sign on the awning read *Alvarez's Grocery* in thick red lettering. For a moment he stood there, his eyes roving searchingly across the dilapidated sign, only half concentrating on his surroundings. He wondered if the people of that neighborhood actually knew the name of the store. Realizing it was almost time for his meeting, he dismissed the thought then pushed the door open and walked inside.

There was only one patron inside the store, an elderly man rummaging through a freezer full of beer. He bit off a curse then breathed a deep, frustrated sigh, seemingly disappointed at not finding what he wanted. Gorilla Leek turned his attention to the Puerto Rican proprietor who stood behind the store counter nursing a hot cup of coffee.

His eyes filling with impatience, the owner watched as the contents of the freezer were scattered by clumsy searching hands. "A yo, pops. I told you we ain't got no more Old E back there!" he yelled out before taking a sip of his coffee and placing his cup down. "The kids don't drink that anymore, so I don't restock it like that."

The elderly man's chest heaved in anger, but he held his tongue. He slammed the freezer door close, then brushed past Gorilla Leek almost rudely before walking out of the store.

The gangbanger shook his head and laughed, his eyes shifting again to the counter. "What's up Mike?"

The store owner smiled. "Hola, Leek! Whaddup with you, bro?"

Gorilla Leek approached the counter. "Nothing much my dude. Is everything good to go for tomorrow?"

A slight grin curved White Mike's lips and his eyes narrowed. "Si, hermano," he said, barely opening his mouth, "todo es bueno. We're about to get that chavos."

The corners of Gorilla Leek's mouth turned down with an expression which was not so much annoyance as perplexity. "You know I don't speak that Puerto Rican language. Speak English like the rest of us niggas."

White Mike kept his smile, but his eyes stared hard at Gorilla Leek.

"Speak that Puerto Rican language? Really B? That's not the proper—"

"Oh, pardon me, my nigga," Gorilla Leek interrupted, "Puerto Rican is not the politically correct word anymore, right? Y'all prefer to be called Latino nowadays, huh?"

White Mike hissed through his teeth, "Latino? Really? Cupa mi bicho! I'm not from Rome, you ignorant cabrón."

They both laughed out loud. Gorilla Leek was the first to cease his chuckles, but a smile lingered on his face. He took a step closer to the Puerto Rican elder.

"What time will Copper and the cop be here? We need to get this done and over with."

White Mike's shoulders stiffened and understanding flickered behind his grin. He was well aware of how important this deal was. And like Gorilla Leek, he was eager to get it started.

"Copper called a few minutes ago," White Mike looked at his watch. "Actually, about fifteen minutes ago. Said he should be here soon. I told him you were on your way here."

"That's what's up." Gorilla Leek turned away from the counter and walked a few feet to the potato chip rack that was behind him. He snatched a big bag of Doritos and yanked at the top with his teeth. Chips spewed everywhere. White Mike watched as he cradled the torn bag against his chest with his arm and stuffed the chips into his mouth with his other hand. His lips parted to speak, revealing an orange and yellow mush of chewed food. "Guess I'm the early-bird."

"Si, I guess so. So, you still haven't told your boy about what's going down?" asked White Mike.

"Na," Gorilla Leek answered, "not fully. After Chinnah's dead, I'll put him on to everything."

"Everything?"

"Ye—"

Suddenly the bell attached to the door jangled loudly, capturing their attention, and four teenage boys burst into the store wearing red hoodies and black gloves. Every nerve in Gorilla Leek's body revved up, his instincts screaming danger as two of the boys made their way toward White Mike with pistols drawn and leveled menacingly.

A huge Hispanic youth with a powerful look about him stood with his back to the door, holding a machete and blocking the entrance. His unarmed companion charged through, knocking over a display of Dill pickles, jars smashing and spilling. White Mike jumped back startled.

Dropping the potato chip bag and moving a few steps back, Gorilla Leek took a deep breath when one of the armed boys turned around and began to approach him brandishing a Lorcin .25 pistol. It was in his mind to reach for his own weapon, but it was too late. The boy had closed the distance between them, pointing his gun at him quite unsteadily. Gorilla Leek took notice of his trembling hand and remained still.

The other armed thug, a black teenager with a thin, angular build in camouflage fatigues approached White Mike, his .44 Magnum looming large. The bulky pockets of his red ski-vest silently boasted of the extra magazines he was carrying. And if his sudden appearance wasn't scary enough, then what he was wearing beneath his red hoodie certainly was. Wrapped around his face was a black bandana and White Mike could see his mouth moving beneath the menacing dark fabric.

"Yo, where's the doe and coke, Poppi?" the teen demanded as he waved his .44 in the Puerto Rican's direction.

White Mike composed himself, his face smoothing into a guarded expression. "You know who you little niggas messing with? You ain't getting jack from me," his voice held no emotion, "so you better turn your young asses around and march the fuck out of here."

The boy had gone perfectly still at White Mike's words, ignoring him then focusing his gaze on the youth guarding the door. "Yo, you and Syko head outside and make sure no one comes up in here. Aight?"

The Latino giant nodded a silent yes and proceeded outside with the unarmed youth on his heels. There was a loud echoing slam of the door as it closed behind them. White Mike jumped slightly at the sound and a smothered gasp of surprise came from his stiff lips. He looked at Gorilla Leek then darted his eyeballs at the armed man in front of him as if to say, *hurry up and shoot him.* And then, without warning, a heavy fist slammed into his temple, dropping White Mike to his knees. Instinctively, he struggled to his feet. He could feel a trickle of blood on his forehead. Just as he thought about reaching for the gun hidden inside the cash drawer, his attacker reached over the counter and grabbed a fistful of his ponytail then wrenched his head to the side.

"Listen Spic-n-Span. I'll mop this store up with your blood. I ain't playing no games!" He slammed White Mike's head on the counter and released his hair with a sneer. "I hope you're hearing me! You're gonna give it up or take two to the head! We know what you got back there!" The boy pressed his pistol against the back of the Puerto Rican's head.

Gorilla Leek knew he would have to make a move—and soon; but he wasn't sure if he would be quick enough to react before the gun that was pointed at him went off. Eyeing the teenager in front of him as much as the teenager was keeping him in focus, he shot a quick glance at the boy's small weapon and smirked. He prayed White Mike would be able to remain calm and do as he was told. This would give him the time he needed to retrieve his gun.

With his face buried in the counter, White Mike had muffled out some words—no one knew what, exactly—but it seemed to be an unforgiveable utterance. The boy bit off a curse. And raising his weapon, he brought it down in a brutal, clubbing blow to the side of the Puerto Rican's head.

"Speak up bitch! I dare you to say it again!" the armed teen commanded.

White Mike saw stars and a loud thump went through his skull as his forehead slammed down against the counter again. Straining to lift his head, and raising it no more than an inch, he mumbled, "I said, motherfucker—you might as well kill me because you and your little homeboys will soon be dead!"

The boy seemed unmoved by his threat. The tense muscles of his lips moving behind the bandana in a horrible grin. He placed the muzzle of his .44 Magnum against the side of his captive's temple once more and turning away his eyes, he pulled the trigger without hesitation. White Mike's head quivered violently with the impact of the bullet, and blood splattered all over the boy; all over his clothes, all over his gun, and all over his hands.

White Mike struggled to raise his wounded head from the counter as if his skull had grown too heavy for his shoulders. Breathing in short ragged gasps, his lips moved convulsively, and blood gathered in his mouth then popped out with each breath like rose-colored bubblegum. He staggered forward slightly and seized the end of the counter to steady his rubbery legs.

The young shooter's eyes glittered with shock. He couldn't believe White Mike had survived the shot. The boy stood completely still, his mouth open in awe, staring at the blood oozing from the swollen lump of flesh that had risen around his victim's wound. A deep shudder coursed his spine. He had never shot anyone before. All he could feel was the stoppage of time as he stepped back, attempting to put distance between himself and the living dead.

White Mike's eyes, now swollen with terror, scanned helplessly about the store. He could only manage a pathetic wheeze before quietly lowering his head and collapsing face-first. He was dead before his limp body hit the counter and thudded to the ground. The sound of his corpse crashing to the floor seemed to last for forever, its echo carrying through the store.

Turning his attention away from his hostage for a shred of an instant, the teen holding the Lorcin .25 nervously glanced at his partner who had just shot the owner of the store. It was the perfect moment for Gorilla Leek. He reached into his waistband, came out with his pistol and with cruel deliberation, he sent a bullet slamming into the neck of the kid with the .25. There was no time for hesitation; no time to be merciful.

An enormous percussion sounded in the boy's ears as the bullet plowed through him. The bang was terribly loud, tearing through the store with a thunderous force. His flesh ripped away in a millisecond and blood exploded from his throat. In the grip of an intense spasm, his fingers contracted uncontrollably, squeezing the trigger of his Lorcin .25 and sending a bullet whizzing toward the ground. It ricocheted off the floor, cutting into Gorilla Leek's leg.

Stifling a pain-filled scream through clenched teeth, Gorilla Leek dropped his weapon, spun around and ducked into the canned food aisle behind a row of shelves. There was a moment of dizziness as he fought to regain the breath that had been knocked from his lungs with the bullet's impact. His shooter staggered back a couple of steps, dropping his gun when he struck a potato chip rack, knocking it over. The boy's last raspy breath escaped his gurgling throat as he crumpled and fell toward White Mike's killer who was just turning around.

The body slammed into the surviving stick-up kid and forced him scuttling backward into a newspaper stand and they fell in a heap. The collision sent magazines and newspapers scattering across the floor. The lifeless corpse slumped onto the teenager and the gaping hole in its neck leaked blood onto him as it drained from the head. The boy shoved it off him with a look of disgust and quickly sprung to his feet.

With his back to the counter and gun in hand, he darted his eyes around the store, looking for his friend's murderer.

Cold horror raced through the remaining robber's blood. Deep inside his chest his heart thumped wildly, each beat echoing in his ears and growing louder with each passing second. He wondered if the person hiding could hear it. His nerves, along with breathing through a black bandana, turned his mouth into the Arabian Desert. The store was deathly quiet and every breath and movement he made was too loud.

Nausea seesawed his gut as he stood on wobbly legs. His damn hands wouldn't stop shaking. This wasn't the way it was supposed to go down. The plan, the way he had laid it out to his partners, was simple; lock down the bodega, put the gun to the Puerto Rican dude's head, and get him to give up the cocaine and the money. The store was usually empty—or almost empty—at that time of night. What he didn't count on was encountering someone else with a gun. He was about to call out for his remaining partners when he noticed the silhouette of a man outside the store looming through the glass door. It didn't appear to be either of his friends. He could see the man was armed and preparing to enter.

The boy raised his gun and, trembling with panic, he took aim at the figure. A matter of only a couple of feet separating them, he waited for the person to enter. The seconds dragged painfully. But the door did not open. He listened intently and could hear the sound of breathing coming from the aisles, like the breathing of a wounded creature threatened by danger.

His friend's killer was still in the store.

His eyes blinked spastically, trying to cover every angle of the bodega at once, expecting to catch someone creeping up on him.

With his head spinning from a bombardment of regretful thoughts, he realized how big a mistake he had made in choosing this store. But he needed the money. His two-month-old son needed clothes, diapers, and formula. And he had just about had enough of his baby mama complaining about his lack of income. Until tonight, the teenager had never committed an armed robbery, believing no one would dare refuse the demands of a person waiving a gun.

Now he wished he had not been so naïve.

He quickly considered his options. He could make a run for the exit in the back of the store and risk running into whoever shot his friend. Or he could shoot through the front door and take out whoever was on the other side of it before escaping through the entrance.

Suddenly, the bell went off as the front door flew open and Copper emerged, transfixed and bewildered by the grisly sight before him.

The boy didn't hesitate.

Just as the rich, metallic odor of blood and the stench of cordite invaded Copper's nostrils, the teenager launched two rounds into his face. The bullets tore off his left cheek, smashing his teeth and his jaw. Blood and chunks of flesh sprayed against the window behind him then slid down the glass. With his ruined mouth hanging open in shock, he dropped his revolver, then staggered back a few steps knocking over a display of salsa and sending several glass jars and himself crashing to the floor. He thrashed about on the ground; his fists flailing, his legs weakly kicking.

Peeking out from behind the shelves, Gorilla Leek suppressed a gasp when he caught sight of Copper. His eyes fell on the pool of blood collecting under his head as he lay on the ground racked with convulsions.

This can't be happening, Gorilla Leek thought, forcing the panic deep down inside himself. This was a bad joke. With White Mike dead and Copper dying, their plan had backfired badly. This was a damaging blow to the relationship he worked so hard to build.

He wondered about the rest of Copper's crew—where were they? Because he never traveled alone. Any minute now the store could be packed with Crips. And they would surely blame him for Copper's death, thinking it was a set-up. He needed to leave the scene immediately.

Leave.

Hell yeah.

That was all he could do right now. He had to make his move soon or he would have no chance whatsoever. The bleeding from his leg wound was increasing, and the police were probably on their way. Pushing all thoughts from his mind except getting out of that store, he crept through the aisle toward the rear, hoping to find an exit.

Copper's shooter stood frozen, straining his ears for more sounds, but he didn't hear anything. Perhaps his friend's killer had left. But he didn't know if anyone else was outside preparing to come in. Taking no chances, the boy scurried into the corner near the door. When it opened, he would be hidden behind it. He kept his eyes focused on the can food aisle, certain he had heard someone panting heavily just a moment ago. After ten seconds or so, the pounding of his heart ceased, and he forced himself to breathe regularly. Then, the door violently swung open and the bell rang once more.

Jigga Blue's brows rose in surprise as he stepped into the store. He winced when he saw Copper's body on the floor shaking frenziedly; his teething knocking in his head, his face turning purple. The struggling suddenly stopped, and the wounded man settled into death. Jigga Blue couldn't believe what he was seeing. His muscles trembled all over his body, and he fought to keep some semblance of control. His attention was so singularly focused on Copper's corpse that he didn't see the boy hiding in the corner behind him.

Just as the teenager raised his pistol, leveling it with the back of Jigga Blue's head, the bell rang again and Six appeared in the entrance holding the door open with his foot. The boy immediately lowered his weapon and withdrew further into the corner behind the door.

"Wah inna di hell just happen?" Six pushed the door open further to survey the carnage, completely blocking the boy from view as Jigga Blue turned to face the entrance.

"No man! Mi cyaa believe mi eyes." Six's gaze fell on Copper's lifeless body that was sprawled across the ground like a marionette without a puppeteer. "Nuh tell mi dat Copper there lying pan di ground dead."

Police sirens could be heard approaching from nearby. There wasn't enough time for the two men to stand around and determine what had happened. In a moment they would be surrounded by NYPD.

Jigga Blue gazed sternly into Six's eyes. "We need to be out. He's dead and the cops are on their way. We don't need to be up in Rikers trying to figure this all out."

He seized Six's arm almost fiercely as he spoke and pulled him out the store. Just before turning the corner, Jigga Blue looked over his shoulder. He stood still for a moment, the blood running cold in his veins, his eyes fixed in horror on the flickering red lights drawing closer. His purple lips parted, and he drew a long trembling breath, "We're fucked." He then sprang forward, heading up the street as fast as he could.

CHAPTER 12

"I DON'T KNOW WHY THE HELL I let you talk me into coming out tonight," Eden complained aloud bitterly, looking at the line of people ahead of her waiting to get into the Tilden Ballroom night club.

Even in the rain and cold, her friend Ayana didn't seem to mind standing in the long line—a line that moved only sporadically—as it snaked around the building. Ayana knew her bestie did not want to be there. Over the years Eden had grown weary of crowded places, of loud noises and groups of men who looked at her lustfully—who looked at all. Whenever they went to the club, Ayana would find her trying to make herself invisible, standing very close to the wall.

Eden listened to the incessant chatter around her, hoping the rain would drown it out. Every few minutes everyone would inch forward as the line made its slow advance. But it wasn't moving fast enough. She sighed her impatience and an exasperated frown crossed her face. "How long is this going to take? We've been out here for mad long."

Ayana shrugged her shoulders, finally taking on her friend's frustration. "Dunno. But I told you we should've gotten here earlier. We probably won't be able to get in now. Ugh, we might be heading back to the crib."

"Hmm. I wouldn't have a problem with that. If you want to bounce, we can be out. Whatever makes you happy girl—I'm with it," Eden replied, facetious and patronizing. "Plus, this line is ridiculous, and it's wet as hell out here. I could be in my warm bed reading *Black Women in Antiquity*. I just bought it and haven't had a chance to open it up yet. The time it's taking to get into this club, I could have been halfway through the book by now."

Rather than comment, Ayana chose to keep her mouth shut and say nothing. The highlight of her weekend being a bottle of cognac and a handsome stranger in her bed, she wouldn't let her friend's attitude ruin the evening. At times, Eden could be much too puritanical, too self-righteous. What she sought after all her life was not to be found in a club but a library. Yet Ayana was only looking for a one-night stand, so the club was exactly where she wanted to be tonight.

Eden knew her company did not care to hear her complaints. Just the other night Ayana had called her, crying hysterically and slurring her words, "He's having another baby." Her baby-daddy had fathered another child with his new and younger girlfriend. And Eden thought it insane that her friend was still madly in love with him. She couldn't understand why Ayana would pledge her loyalty to a deadbeat who wasn't interested in anything more than what was between her legs. Whatever the reason, tonight it wouldn't matter. Eden's best friend was planning on getting her brains fucked out, to push the thoughts of her ex-man out of her head. Going to the club was her way of coping with her jealousy and grief. And Eden, realizing how much being surrounded by strange men and loud music calmed her friend and made her feel more in control of herself, hesitated to undo that. She decided to keep her reservations to herself for the present as she silently bitched about her surroundings.

Eden's gaze darted back and forth, left and right. Around her, the deafening babble overwhelmed her senses; the vast amount of words and sounds bombarding her from the crowd and far beyond. But then, other things started to intrude on her senses. The soft unhurrying rain started to pour down harder in large, heavy drops. And it brought out a dark lingering scent, somewhat like charred newspapers that had been extinguished by urine then doused in motor oil. It was the musty odor of dampness and dirt trapped in the cracks of the concrete sidewalk.

Fuck. She hated Brooklyn.

An environment where rain didn't smell like rain anymore—it smelled like other things; mold, metal, car fumes, and cigarette smoke. On the other hand, when it rained the street sounds, the gunshots, the loud cursing, and the screams, all became muffled echoes. And if she was lucky, the pelting showers would fall so heavily, it would cut away sight. A rain so thick she could see little of the dismal world about her, save for a few ghostly grey structures and the shadowy figures lurking in front of them.

Rarely did she leave her home when the night skies threatened a downpour. Rather, she would sit alone on her window-sill staring blankly outside into the misery of the rain, welcoming the soundtrack of the streets. The harsh shrilling of the wind, the rush of car tires swishing down the rain-slicked pavement, the footsteps splashing against scattered puddles. While looking out into the darkness she would often get lost in the sound of police sirens, trying to gauge the distance between herself and the nearest crime. Yet the gruff, raspy voices of crackheads yelling at each other about absolutely nothing in their drug and drunken stupor would bring her back to the reality right in front of her. The world she loathed. The Brooklyn she despised.

It wasn't the borough that she hated as much as it was the oppressive conditions of its ghettoes; the police brutality, the economic exploitation, the substandard housing, and the discriminatory education. The Brooklyn she knew had been reduced to a garbage dump of financial decay and urban blight. It was run-down, and crime was rampant. Her Brooklyn had fallen into despair, a victim of ignorance and neglect, eventually falling under the control of gangs. This is what confronted her when she ventured out of her home. And this is what she was surrounded by tonight as she stood in the long line on Tilden Avenue with the rain dashing against her face.

In spite of aching calf muscles and drenched clothing, the rainfall started to bring out a more reflective and calmer side of her. However, the moment was short-lived. The downpour also drew out something not so pleasant—a group of about ten teenagers were walking alongside the line, arguing loudly and harassing people, moving toward the front. Vulgar words rippled through the group of boys followed by derisive laughter. Eden watched the teenagers approach her, strutting, shoving each other, trading taunts and jokes. Every one of them were wearing red somewhere on their person. There were red bandanas, red jackets, red hoodies, red sneakers, red shoelaces. One was even wearing a red Moorish fez too small for his head with a red bandana tied around it.

Eden stood for a moment taking in the all too familiar sight. She knew them well. To all intents and purposes, she had grown accustomed to a life lived under siege in the midst of their brutality. Yet they weren't a part of the Brooklyn she remembered and loved—the Brooklyn that raised her. A Brooklyn where the fringe elements of society, even when rejected, took pride in their cultural identities and banded together to protect their communities. A Brooklyn where degenerate behavior promoted social solidarity by fostering an "us-versus-them" mindset among the poor. No, this new group was foreign to her Brooklyn. Invaders who cared only for destruction. A band of teenagers in red bandanas emptying the city of life, committing random acts of violence such as slashing the faces of total strangers with razors. And unfortunately, throughout the worst sections of the borough their presence was now unmistakable.

After the Bloods first appeared in Brooklyn in the mid nineteen nineties, many viewed them as a misguided street organization that could be redirected to fit the expectations and norms of the larger Black political community. Eden, much like those before her, attempted to establish positive relationships with its members to channel them into more pro-social activities. But after years of witnessing an intensifying cycle of bloodshed measured by excess mortality, the young college grad accepted that their world would always be a place of ever-increasing violence and uncertainty. Now she simply wished to avoid them whenever possible. And tonight, it didn't seem as if that was going to be possible.

One of the boys noticed her and he stopped in his tracks. The group's conversation ceased as all eyes fell in her direction. He didn't look too friendly standing there in his red and black lumberjack coat, a half a head taller than the rest of his friends. A Chicago Bulls cap with a red bandana underneath was pulled down low on his head. He seemed to be the oldest of the teenagers, nineteen maybe, while the others appeared to range from sixteen to eighteen.

He approached Eden. "Damn, shorty, you sexy as hell!" His eyes bucked, and he looked like he was salivating. "I'm saying, you got a nigga?"

Ayana started breathing in small shallow gusts, as if agitated. "Can't you see we don't want to be bothered? My girl is damn near thirty. She doesn't have time for little boys. So, go lay out your cheese trap somewhere else and find you a hood rat."

"Ain't no one talking to you, bitch," he shot back.

Ayana rolled her eyes at the boy. "Little boy, what? You think 'cause you Blood someone supposed to be scare of you? Please. My baby daddy's a P-Stone. El Messiah from the Ville."

Whenever she mentioned her baby daddy's name around other Bloods, fear would wash across their faces, and the utmost respect would be shown to her. That was not the case with this young man.

"You talking about the Mo'? That's my dog. I know his shorty. And you ain't her!"

"Then motherfucker, you don't know him. You might know of him," suggested Ayana. "Cause all you little wannabee gangstas stay riding his dick, trying to be like him. But you definitely don't know him if you don't know me!"

Sparks shot from the teen's eyes. "First of all, bitch—"

"First of all, nothing," Eden interrupted. "There aren't any bitches over here. And if you view women as female dogs and you came from a woman, what does that make you?"

"Ha!" Ayana roared out loud.

The boy was not amused. Before he could open his mouth to reply, Eden sucked her teeth then continued, "Running around here claiming to be a dog. Young brother, you're just a little puppy—a four-legged baby beast. Because you damn sure are not a man. Maybe that's why you refuse to wear your pants like one. I guess when you're used to being on all fours, showing off your ass comes naturally. Huh?"

A puzzled look wrinkled the boy's brow. His eyes widened in astonishment, then his expression turned to anger.

She continued, "What? You're one of those homo-thugs or something."

"Bitch watch your mouth," one of his friends yelled out as the group of boys began surrounding the two girls.

Eden smiled, unaffected by the remark. "I asked, because walking around with your pants hanging below your ass means you've probably been to prison before. And likely, you were someone's bitch. If not, then you must want to go to prison or be someone's bitch."

Pausing briefly as if she had an epiphany, she watched his lips tightened, then she again continued, "Oh, Oh, I think I get it. Is it that you and your homeboys call each other dog because y'all be getting it on doggie style?" A light chuckle left her lips. "Now that gives a whole new meaning to gangbanging. I see why you can call a lady out of her name—you don't like pussy! That's why you use that word as a term of disrespect toward other men. And you only respect hard-rocks because that's the way you like to take it."

Ayana burst out into somewhat encouraging, somewhat exaggerated laughter, inviting others around them to laugh at the expense of the humiliated gangsta. The boy ignored her, clamped his jaw tight, and glared at Eden with an unwinking and unforgiving stare. As he moved closer to her to speak, a gust of wind blew past them, wrapping her short black dress around her, and revealing the shape beneath. His eyes followed the movement of fabric against her thighs. She was thick. He contemplated her body with wolfish interest, his eyes traveling the length of her, taking in her shapely frame. He imagined pinning her down firmly to the ground, her dress rucked up and her panties ripped aside. He wanted to spread her thick thighs and plunder her slick folds with his manhood until she screamed and begged him to stop.

His eyes narrowed at the thought and he felt an involuntary stirring between his legs. He considered snatching her by her locks and dragging her around the corner to show her what doggie style was really like. But before he could act on his impulse, the loud rhythmic bassline of a Hip-Hop song vibrating through a vehicle intruded on his mind. The boy turned around to see a Ford Expedition pulling up to the curb across from them, the stereo rattling its speakers. The tinted window on the passenger side came slowly down. A cloud of smoke rushed out and the music exploded onto the street, reverberating off of the surrounding buildings until it seemed to be coming from everywhere:

We fly high, no lie, you know this (ballin'!)
Foreign rides outside, it's like showbiz (we in the building)
We stay fly, no lie, you know this (ballin'!)
Hips and thighs, oh my, stay focused

Shine leaned his head out of the window. The boy was the first to take notice of him and a bright smile lit up his face.

"What's poppin', Blood?" the teen yelled.

He held his right hand to his heart, palm down, forming a *b* by touching the tips of his index finger and thumb, and leaving his remaining three fingers stretched out. Shine returned the gesture with a series of hand signs, fingers dancing too fast for Eden to follow. The teen quickly forgot about Eden and approached the SUV.

From the passenger window Shine offered his right hand. "What that red be like?"

Eden watched as the two exchanged gang-related handshakes, giving each other a bond of brotherhood. Their middle and ring fingers interlocked, allowing the tip of their pinkies and index fingers to touch. They formed a five-pointed star with their hands.

"Five poppin', six droppin', crip killin' til my crucifixion." The boy displayed a fierce pride when he answered. He looked further into the car and saw Kold Fire gripping the steering wheel. "What up, Blood?"

Kold Fire simply nodded, making no effort to look at the boy or speak. Shine stepped out of the vehicle and bopped over to Eden, with the teen following a few steps behind. Eden was relieved to see they knew each other. She could tell the group of teenagers looked up to Shine, and that was no mean feat to achieve. The Bloods were very violent and held little respect or fear for anyone. And maddeningly, this made the man she met earlier that day even more desirable.

"Hey, don't I know you from somewhere?" Shine jokingly asked as he neared her.

The teen following him spoke before Eden could answer, "You know this chick, Blood?"

"Na, I know this woman," Shine stated. "Why? Are you bothering her?"

The boy swallowed hard and became nervous. "Na, not at all. I mean, I ain't know she was with you. I mean, she's waiting on the line and all." He turned to Eden. "Shorty, I'm sorry. I didn't know you belonged to Shine."

Shine looked at Eden with a silent warning to hold her response. He absolutely wished that she had belong to him. She was radiant, even in the gloom of the fiercely pummeling rain. Strands of her long black locks were plastered across her damp face, hiding most of her soft features.

He tried not to stare and brought his attention back to the teen. "She ain't nobody's property. So, she doesn't belong to me, but—she is with me."

Eden brushed her locks aside and tipped her head back to look at

Shine. "Really?"

"Yeah, really. Unless you want to go off with my son, Caesar Red here?"

The boy cast his eyes to the ground in embarrassment.

Suddenly, Shine's demeanor changed from cordiality to coldness. His icy voice rose spitefully as he stared at Caesar Red. "As a matter of fact, why ain't y'all up in the spot yet? Work don't move by itself, son. The money is in there."

The boy nervously tugged on the brim of his Chicago Bulls cap and shrugged his shoulders. "We bout to head in there now," he hesitantly replied.

Shine hissed through his teeth. "But you're still here."

Caesar Red took that comment as a warning and motioned for his friends to follow him. As he started to put one foot in front of the other, Shine grabbed his upper arm and jerked him back. "Have you seen Gorilla Leek? He was supposed to have been on his way up here. And Blood ain't answering his phone."

The teenager nodded. "No."

"Alright. Well, keep it moving," Shine released his arm. "And if you run into son up in there, tell him I'm on my way in. I'll be over in V.I.P. in a sec."

"Aight," replied Caesar Red. Without another word, he marched down the street toward the entrance of the club with his crew following closely behind.

Ayana looked at Shine with increasing curiosity, but a sudden strong instinct told her to remain silent. *How the hell does Eden know this fine ass nigga? And he's a Blood? I thought she stayed away from gangstas.*

She knew her friend well enough to know that she didn't meet new men often, especially not thugs. So where did he come from? Why hadn't Eden told her about him? And why was Eden smiling so hard in his face? Ayana was determined to find out.

After several seconds of silence, Eden spoke, scarcely knowing what she wanted to say, "Well I guess it was meant for us to see each other again. Maybe there was a reason for us meeting."

"I guess so," Shine replied.

"Hopefully your mind has cleared up some since we last spoke?"

"Indeed, it has, now that I have been graced with your presence."

She smiled, then lightly slapped his arm. "Look at you trying to run game on a lady. Sorry, mister, but as you should know from earlier, I don't fall that easily."

Shine's lips formed half a grin, through which she could see that his front tooth was chipped. "Oh yeah, I know. But I am going to still try. And what's wrong with speaking the truth?"

Eden didn't reply. All she could do was blush. He was physically attractive, yet the complete opposite of the men she was drawn to. She was surprised by her own reaction to him. Not that she was immune to handsome men. But she didn't usually go for the hoodlum types. However, the way he carried himself was alluring. He was his own person. She imagined him confined to his own poetic world. A world where he probably stared into the streets often, pondering great things while he studied the plight of his people with his beautiful eyes. Eyes that, at any other time, would have been the very reason she rejected him. Because they reminded her of the devil.

That didn't matter though. Under the tough guy exterior and even deeper beyond his green-eyes there was something more. He had an undying loyalty to something bigger than himself—his gang. It is not that he held exceptionally high ideals. History and politics were likely foreign to him. Rather he had a clear sense of what he valued. Unlike men she was accustomed to, he seemed unapologetic and unafraid. A warrior, but for the wrong reasons. In her mind she contemplated the violence in his eyes and his lone confident attitude. And in that very moment she discovered a new, thrilling, revolutionary pleasure. The desire to understand his world.

Desperate to end the awkward silence, Shine spoke again. "You know, you two don't have to wait on this long ass line. Y'all can walk up in there with me."

Ayana's eyes lit up. Hopeful that her friend would take the man up on his offer, she watched the interaction between the two of them carefully. The line was barely moving, so his suggestion sounded good. In the time they were going to wait there, they could be inside enjoying the music and drying off. Her eyes begged her friend to say yes. Eden opened her mouth but seemed unsure of what to say.

Ayana decided to speak for her. "If that's the case, we'll hang out with you then," She extended her hand to Shine, which he accepted easily. "Forgive Eden for being rude and not introducing us, but my name is Ayana."

He offered a smile. It was meant to be an inviting and calming smile, but it was marred by his aggressive tone. "That's what's up, ma. My peeps call me Shine. And any friend of Eden is most definitely a friend of mine. You feel me?"

Rolling her eyes, Eden stepped in between them as Shine pulled his hand free. "Please excuse my friend. She has been excited about getting inside of there for a while now."

"Na, it's no problem," he said, recognizing her uneasiness.

Ayana grinned with embarrassment. "I was only trying to get out of the rain. Wasn't trying to beg or leech or anything like that. I mean, you offered."

Shine let a light smile ease across his lips. "Don't stress it sweetheart. It's nothing."

Then remembering that he left Kold Fire sitting in his car, he abruptly turned to face the parked Ford Expedition. "Yo, Blood, go ahead and park my whip around the block. Hang out there just in case Leek rolls up 'round back. I'm going to go and wait for him inside."

An arm waved out of the darkness from the half rolled down passenger's window. From the distance Eden couldn't see the driver's face clearly, but she could hear his slurred words. "Gotchoo, my dog."

"Word. If you see him, I'll be in VIP," Shine shouted back.

Kold Fire put the car in drive and inched the SUV forward. Darting another look at Shine before pulling into traffic, he said, "Dog, don't worry. I can see it your face. Your whip is in good hands. I'll park it in a safe place. Aight?"

"Alright," Shine responded, skepticism clear in his voice. "I'll take your word for it, son. Just remember, whatever pops off—it's on you."

"You already know," Kold Fire assured.

The Expedition rolled away into rainy night. Shine brought his attention back to Eden. Her voice had dropped now, and she was whispering in her friend's ear. Noticing that he was looking at them, Ayana gently nudged her companion and the conversation stopped.

"You good? I'm saying, I'm about to head up in there. Y'all rolling or what?" Shine asked, looking to Eden.

"Well," Ayana butted in fast before Eden could say no, "if we accompany you, do we have to still pay to get in?"

"Na, ma," he said, smiling. "You're good. You're with me." He held out his arm for Eden to take.

Ayana turned toward her best friend, silently urging her to grab hold of him. Eden wasn't sure what to do. She just met him, and barely knew him. Letting him escort her into the club without her having to pay might make it appear that she was surrendering her control—her self-control. And that was too important to who she was. She'd be a fool to abandon caution for a man she'd only known for such a short time. Yet, at that moment, she wanted him with such a subtle desire that it frightened her, because she was ready to give in.

"Look," he said, seeing she was having a hard time deciding, "You don't have to take my arm. But, if you don't plan on hanging out with me, it would be best if you at least walk in with me. Unless you want every Tom, Dick, and Harry trying to push up on you. I mean, I didn't take you for the type to wanna be bothered by a bunch of dudes trying to get at you—at least not by the type of crabs that would come here. You feel me?"

Pursing her lips, she smiled without showing her teeth. "Well, you're here, and if I'm not mistaken, you tried to holler at me earlier. Are you saying you are not my type?"

Shine's right eyebrow went up. It was almost impossible not to like her. "First of all. I ain't no crab. Second of all, I don't know your type. But we could head up in there and kick it for a sec. Then we can see if I'm your so-called type. If not, no hard feelings. We'll part ways. Okay, ma?"

Suddenly, thunder boomed, and lightening streaked across the sky, shaking Eden to her core. Taking one jerky step forward, she quickly slipped her hand into the crook of his arm and said, "Whatever mister slick-talker. Let's just get out of this rain. Then we can figure all of that out. I am not about to get struck by lightning out here."

She could feel power in his arm and sensed it in his walk as they strolled alongside the line with Ayana following behind. They could already hear the music from where they stood in the line. But as they came closer, Eden felt the sound all around her. There was a slight vibration rumbling beneath her four-inch heels. A few more steps and she could feel the vibration in her ears as they neared the entrance. Detecting the faint rhythmic pulse of reggae music, she began gently nodding her head. The beat was strong, thumping loud through the walls. There were a group of females pleading with the bouncer at the door, gesturing wildly. Shine took back his arm from Eden and, stepping past the ladies, approached the hefty man. After a brief exchange, the bouncer held the door open and motioned for him to come in.

Ayana's efforts to keep up with her friend brought her almost shoulder to shoulder with Eden as they walked into a narrow, mirrored hall. They made their way to the main area, their eyes adjusting to the low lights. A billowing cloud of grey smoke curled around like ghosts in the red spotlights sweeping over the dark crowded dance floor. The air was thick with the blended smells of marijuana, liquor, tobacco, and musk. An overpowering odor of desperation seeping from the pores of half-dressed girls wafted throughout the club, disturbing Eden's senses. As she watched Shine walk with purpose and confidence through the crowd, she thought back to earlier that day. She was hoping they would meet again. Barely managing to hold back a smile, she seized his hand once more and pulled herself close to him while he led her through the club. She was glad Ayana had talked her into coming out tonight.

CHAPTER 13

CHINNAH SAT SILENTLY in his black wicker chair swelling with rage, staring straight ahead at Detective Brown. Detective Cardillo stood with his back against the front door regarding the Jamaican gravely. He was exceedingly nervous, having never been in the presence of the Gully Gods before. And by the look on his partner's face he could tell that he definitely was not comfortable giving their leader the bad news concerning his son. Before arriving at Chinnah's home, Cardillo had a moment of worry over how things were going to play out. The only thing he had to base his expectations on was the trail of bodies he had been following over the past few days, so he was expecting the worst. He was feeling his heart wrench out of his chest because he was standing in the middle of a drug kingpin's living room, having a conversation that might not go very well. A conversation he chose to stay out of. There was no way to comfort a criminal with words, so he comforted him with silence. Besides, Brown being a black man like Chinnah, was more than capable of doing this on his own. Even though Cardillo like to think that together they were an irresistible force, he knew he needed to stay in his lane.

The young detective cast a stealthy look at the large man standing guard behind the Gully Gods' leader. Gripping his boss' shoulder, Pauley drew a shallow breath and offered several kind words of consolation. Chinnah silenced him by raising a single finger into the air then leaned forward as Brown spoke, the arm of the wicker chair clenched tightly in his strong hands.

"We found shell casings from three separate guns, and my guys discovered blood splatter that doesn't appear to have come from your son or any of the other—umm," the detective cleared his throat before continuing, "victims that we found at the scene. We won't know for sure until we hear from the lab, or the suspect we have in custody decides to talk."

"Suh, who dis man dat yuh ave inna yuh custody?" Chinnah inquired, his gaze beaming with rage.

"He's a boy," replied Brown. "Seventeen years old. And he is not speaking much."

"An dis bowy, him di one who murda mi pickney?" inquired Chinnah, looking up quizzically.

"We are not sure, but we will find out. We have what we believe to be the murder weapon. It's at the lab now."

"Fi wah reason wud anyone wa fi tek di life of mi ongle son?" Chinnah asked, his tone even and calm as always.

"We don't know if he was there to kill Copper. So far it looks like your son just happened to walk in on the kid right after he shot White Mike. He might've panic when Copper showed up and—well—you know."

"An di bowy, him did nuh sey wah issue him might ave had wid White Mike?"

"No, He's not cooperating. But we did speak with White Mike's wife and she said he didn't have any enemies at all. That, he was actually preparing to sell his store off to some local real estate company and move out of Brooklyn to get away from all of the crime." Brown's chest heaved with a soft chuckle. "I guess he was too late."

Chinnah spoke again, his voice a mere whisper, as he stood up facing his unexpected guest. "Well, wen yuh duh find out wah happen to mi son, mi wud like fi yuh to contact mi. Mi saying as soon as possible. Dis here situation fi mi to rectify!"

The Jamaican elder shook his head softly trying to free himself from the bitterness of his grief. He fell silent for a moment and then asked aloud, "Wah dem causing mi dis sufferation?"

For a brief second, Brown felt a twinge of pity for the grieving father, having also lost a son to violence. But then he betrayed his own sympathy, becoming skeptical of Chinnah's claim to be clueless as to what was going on. Perhaps he was feigning ignorance to draw the detective into dialogue to gauge how much the police knew. Either way, something had clearly gone wrong. And Brown planned to get to the bottom of it.

"Yeah, well, giving it to you straight, you can't expect the dirt you dig to not come back around to you," declared Brown.

Chinnah's brow was dark with disdainful anger. And his eyes, shimmering with venom, held the ferocity of a killer. "What yuh saying?" Chinnah hissed through his teeth. "Yuh best mind ow yuh chat, detective."

Brown ignored the man's threatening tone and continued on, "The sins of the father shall be visited on the sons. It's biblical."

Brown's words fell on a quiet, nervous room. The soft ticking of an antique clock hanging above the sofa emphasizing the silence engulfing them. Chinnah grinned then deposited himself in his wicker chair, darting hateful glances at the two detectives. Cardillo could not seem to look away, wondering what was going to happen next. He took in a labored breath as the Jamaican simply sat back and twirled a grey strand of his long locks. Pauley, with his pistol tucked in his front pocket, kept his eyes on his boss, waiting for him to give the word.

The corners of Chinnah's mouth crept up. "An wah did yuh sins, detective? Cuz mi kno dat yuh no stranga to dis here grief," he said, his voice a mere thread of sound in the solemn stillness of his dimly-lit home. He knew he had touched a nerve because something went cold behind the detective's eyes.

Brown decided against addressing the bereaved father's last comment and carried on with making his point. "Look, Chinnah, I need you to help me, if you want me to help you. I didn't come here just to deliver bad news."

Chinnah folded his arms across his chest. "Mi listening."

Brown continued, "Your son was murdered earlier this evening. And a couple of days ago, there were two murders at a house you own. And one of the bodies was your neph—"

Chinnah flashed the detective a smile that was perhaps more practiced than sincere before interrupting, "Mi tell yuh man, mi nuh own dat property. Mi did leasing it from a Jew an den mi rented it out to mi nephew to mek extra funds an gi him a place to stay. Suh, mi neva kno wah did gwaan inna dat yaad. Whateva mi nephew did doing, dat did fi him bizniz. Mi tell di babylon dat already."

Brown gave Chinnah a mischievous smirk and crooked his

eyebrow. "I should have known better than to expect you to help me. The only reason I won't go back and forth over the issue with you right now is because you need some time to grieve. However, I do have one more question before we leave. One thing that you may be able to help me with."

"Sure, Detective," said Chinnah.

"Why Dwight Mannschein?"

Chinnah appeared confused, his blinking indicating that he had no clue as to who the detective was speaking about. "Ah who dat?"

"Dwight Mannschein," answered Brown, "you may know him as Shine. What's he got to do with all of this?"

Still looking baffled, Chinnah started to say something, then he stopped. Realization swept across his face and his mouth fell open. "No. Mi nuh kno him. Wah mek yuh asking bout him? Does him ave sup'm fi duh wid mi son's murda?"

Detective Brown lips moved as if he was about to utter something and then pressed together in frustration. His expression was stony, serious. His eyes hooded, his face tense. He had been indulgent thus far but had now clearly run out of patience. Suddenly, his phone rang in his coat pocket, interrupting his thoughts. He looked at Chinnah scornfully and took out the cell phone.

"This is Brown." He listened for a few seconds. "Really?" he said into the phone. "The same one?" He listened again. "Understood," he said. "Yeah, that's definitely big. Look, let me finish up what I'm doing, and I will be right in to take a look at what you have. Good job." Brown shoved the phone into his coat and stepped closer to the Gully Gods' leader.

"Chinnah, I know you have no intention of helping me. However, the more I know, the more I can find out about your son. Do you understand me?"

Chinnah sucked his teeth in annoyance. "Mi ongle wa fi si mi son's murdera get fi him justice. Til den mi nuh kno nuhting bout wah yuh asking mi bout."

In reply, Brown simply bared his teeth in a grin. "Yeah, I'm sure you know nothing. We will see."

Brown abruptly turned toward the door and proceeded to leave. Cursing his own lack of courage, Cardillo quickly reached for the doorknob. He cracked the door open then stopped when he felt the weight of his partner's hand come to rest on his shoulder.

"Hold on, not so fast," Brown whispered to Cardillo. He looked back at Chinnah, his eyes never leaving his face. "You know that phone call that I just got?" He paused a moment to see if he had the drug lord's attention, knowing full well that he had, as Chinnah sat rapt and silent before the detective, anxiously awaiting his next words.

"It was from the station," continued Brown. "It appears that one of the weapons found at the scene of your son's murder was also one of the guns used on the victims at your house."

Chinnah rose from his chair and stood, feet planted slightly apart, hands still folded across his chest.

"Suh, yuh saying dat di bowy who murda mi son di same person who tek di life of mi nephew?"

"We haven't determined who your son's killer is yet. But if you're asking me if I believe the person responsible for your nephew's death is the same man to blame for your son's murder—then I would say yes. He is," Brown smirked while exhaling a gust of air from his nostrils, "because that man is you. You introduced this lifestyle to both your son and nephew. So, you, and only you, are the reason they are dead."

"Waah dis bullshit yuh chatting?" Chinnah shot back, his eyes ablaze. "Just find mi son's killa an lef mi alone!"

"Yeah well, with a lack of information, right now I can only make guesses. That's why I need your cooperation. But one thing is certain— the killings at your house are connected to your son's demise," Brown glanced down at his wristwatch, and then over at Cardillo. "Now you can get the door."

Cardillo opened the door and stepped back to allow his senior to pass. As Brown walked out the apartment, he made one last comment, "I'll be in touch."

Cardillo followed him out into the night, the door closing softly behind them.

Chinnah turned then paced slowly over to an oak cabinet along the wall and stared at a small wooden frame hanging above it. In it was a picture that perfectly captured a moment and a feeling in his life. It was a photo of his younger smiling self, standing on a beach in Jamaica, holding the hand of a three-year old Copper. He wanted nothing more than to go back to that time in his life, when he promised his son that he would remain by his side and hold his hand through the waking nightmare of the world he created—the world that had devoured everyone he loved.

On the wall opposite the picture was a plain wooden cross. He cast his eyes upon it and thought, *the detective is right—the sins of the father have now visited the son.* Turning from the picture to face Pauley, his eyes closed then opened and he became unsteady. He approached the chair and grabbed hold of it to gain his balance. Opening his mouth slowly, his gaze drifted off before speaking, "Ave yuh hear from Kam yet?"

Pauley quickly replied. "No man. Kam did following Shine di laas time wi speak. Since den mi nuh hear from him."

"Wah bout Cutty? Him did call yuh yet?"

"No man."

"Weh di hell cud him be?" Chinnah shouted, his anger dripping off of his tongue. "Yuh kno what? There ongle one person who cya handle dis fi mi. Mi wa yuh to call him now. Tell him it a waah emergency?"

"Ah who?" Pauley reluctantly asked. "Arab?"

"Yeah man, Arab," Chinnah answered. "Mi ave let dis gwaan fi too lang now."

"Yuh sure yuh wa mi fi get Arab involved?" asked Pauley.

Chinnah's voice was stony and his eyes stabbed at Pauley. "Yea, an tell him dat nuh one of dem love ones to survive. Kill dem all. Kill di men. Kill di women. Kill di pickney. Kill dem all! An afta him ave kill dem all—I sey, tell him to dig up dem graves an kill dem ah bloodclot again cuz dem neva dead haad enuff!"

Pauley rubbed his sweaty palms on his thighs and swallowed hard. He seemed nervous, as if his next words might harm him in some way. "Um—yea. Understand bredren. Mi wi tek care of it."

"Yuh betta tek care of it or mi wi tek care of yuh! Seen?"

"Yea man."

For at least five seconds Pauley didn't say another word. Then he thrust his hand into his pants pocket, pulled out his phone, and began pecking in numbers. The troubled enforcer said a silent prayer as he listened to it ring on the other end. He drew a breath to clear his head, but the breath was so shaky, he almost didn't get any air in. He waited for someone to answer. Finally, on the sixth ring, someone picked up. However, before Pauley could speak, Chinnah raised his index finger, interrupting him and icily uttered, "Tell him mi wa dem to suffa badly. As bad as mi suffering now."

♠   ♠   ♠

THE PALE GLOW OF THE MOONIGHT beamed down on the old 65th Precinct that sat abandoned in the increasingly depressed section of Brownsville Brooklyn. Originally constructed in the beginning of the twentieth century, the gloomy three-story building—faced with brown-orange brick except for the grey rusticated stonework and boarded up arched windows of the first floor—overshadowed the ill-lit corner of East New York and Rockaway Avenues. Dirt and graffiti marred the front of the building—gang symbols, tag-names, words of violence—all spray-painted in crude, quick strokes. The sidewalk leading to the entrance was laced with large heaps of rubbish and cinder blocks, some covered with dried blood. Trash was everywhere. Bottles, syringes, and old newspapers were scattered on the ground.

To one side of the old precinct were the notorious housing projects, Howard Homes. To the other side, vast boarded ruins. A once, neglected and now partially reconstructed apartment building housed a deli on the ground floor. Beside it loomed a vacant dilapidated structure that had been gutted out by a fire, years prior. Only the central wall and several rotten wooden beams remained, as the decapitated lower story was now a hulking wreck of deteriorating masonry. It was a scene of utter desolation—a dwelling just derelict enough that the plastic orange construction fences, the blockade made of graffiti-covered plywood, and the huge steel gate protecting the shattered store windows would have been necessary if the inhabitants of the area had all but ignored its existence.

Between the boarded ruins and the projects, the precinct stood as a solitary sentinel—a fading bastion of the good ole days when law and order was respected by the Jewish criminals who once inhabited and controlled the neighborhood. It was a time when gangsters and police officers shared a mutual interest—community isolation and peace. But those days were long gone. The ark that their Jewish ancestor built had been sunken by a flood of black faces. And the curtains of the land of Brownsville did tremble.

When the lust-filled gazes of the newly-arrived picaninnies fell upon the young Jewish American Princesses, their fathers panicked.

Having migrated their families to America to escape ethnic annihilation, the fast-growing presence of super-predators gave them cause for much concern. So much so, that at one point in their history, Jewish mothers while being swept away in a tide of patriotic fervor, stood side-by-side with the women of the KKK—their praise of Margaret Sanger for having the foresight to open America's first birth control clinic within Brownsville mutely testifying to their unity of purpose.

No longer a hopeful urban destination for hardworking Jews, the neighborhood was now a prison, and the law—an instrument of brutality. The precinct had become a place where the prisoners sought their freedom. A place where they escaped reality, inhaling the poisonous fumes of broken promises and exhaling their misery.

Totally unsuitable for human habitation, the makeshift living quarters set deep within the stony bowels of the shuttered stationhouse was as shadowy as the souls who occupied it. Souls who were once cast into the pit of a raging political fire ignited by the Ocean Hill-Brownsville confrontation of 1968. Souls whose children were born after the flames of fear and jealousy had reduced Black-Jewish relations to ashes, leaving nothing behind in its wake except for a deadly thick cloud of smoke—crack smoke. An oozing smog that now ghost-drifted along the ceiling of the precinct's corridors haunting would-be trespassers.

Visibility could be measured in inches when this fog of cocaine vapor crept through the halls at night. Clouds of smoke would form the shapes of bodies, hovering above fiends like angry spirits trying to break free of their fleshly cage. With every gust of air, the building would squeal as if it were alive and trying to tell the addicts something. Maybe it was telling them to go home. To take care of the children they abandoned. To remember the struggle that they once fought in and the oppressors they once fought against. That is, before their children with their gangs became their oppressors—and crack addiction, their struggle. Now they, like the ruins of the NYPD's past, sat in the basement of the precinct, destroyed and forgotten.

Among the several bewildered men and women who sought shelter within the crumbling temple, one sat silently on a lone folding chair beneath a single broken light bulb, shaking with laughter. His wild grin holding no trace of humor, he passed a trembling hand over his face before suddenly bending over and scrabbling through the remains of a sandwich nested in a wax paper wrapper. Unable to find what he was searching for, he tossed the sandwich next to the broken cell bars that littered the floor. Standing up in frustration, the vagabond sighed aloud, not because he actually expected to find what he was looking for, but because he knew what not finding it meant.

His tight lips parted for a second and his coal black eyes widened as they swept the room canvassing his surroundings. He smiled unsmilingly. This gave his face a cynical, disillusioned look that wasn't pleasant. There was something inhumanely avid about his gaze. From a distance he appeared quite eerie, a thick beard hiding half of his swarthy face. And stark against the backdrop of darkness, his tattered army jacket too, was black, blending perfectly with his skin. The jeans he wore had been blue but were now darkened and stained with urine and feces. His hair was a mess of matted grey dreadlocks flopping on each side of his otherwise bald head. Tall and broad shouldered, the man's unusually large hands could easily squeeze the life out of another human with little effort.

Taking a deep breath to quell the anger that sliced along his raw nerves, he glanced at the ground for one last lingering look. Then suddenly it hit him. He remembered where he'd put it. The man reached down and caught hold of a large black wool stocking cap lying at his feet and turned it around in his hands. He looked at the outside of it, and he looked at it inside. He stuck his hand into it and came out with a small folded piece of aluminum foil, a Ziploc bag halfway-filled with baking soda, a blue butane gas lighter and a large metal spoon. For the moment he was relieved, and he fell back into his folding chair, placing the items on his lap. Satisfaction swept his face.

His muttering was audible, "Yes—yes—Arab knew you wouldn't abandoned him—"

Down by his feet an unopened plastic bottle of spring water stood sentinel-like beside his portable throne. He collected it from the ground, twisted off the top, and poured some of it into the spoon. Placing the bottle to the side without bothering to put the cap back on, he seized the small piece of foil and opened it over the water. When finally, the contents were emptied out, he sprinkled about a half of gram of the baking soda into it then brought the flame of the butane lighter beneath the spoon until the concoction began to bubble.

Slightly disturbed to see that his gun-hand had a slight shake, he
steadied his grip on the spoon as the bubbling slowed down and the
cocaine solidified into a crude yellowish mass. He then tilted the spoon
so that the murky liquid slid out, careful not to let the drug fall from it.
Again, he grabbed hold of the water bottle and ran it over the spoon
before tossing it back to the ground.

The jacket he wore was equipped with a reinforced mesh pocket
designed to hold a weapon. He reached into it, came out with an
unsheathed Ka-Bar knife, and used it to transfer the substance from
the spoon to a small plate on the ground. Cautiously, he ran the tip of
the knife back and forth over the oily clump, smoothing out the
surface until it was white and round.

"She looks just about ready, Arab," he mumbled to himself. "What
do you think?" Before he could answer his own question, a cell phone
rang, muffled in his pocket.

"What in the goddamn!" he cursed out loud, spilling his anger into
the quiet darkness. His mood was broken abruptly by the loud ringing.
The thought that anyone would—could—interrupt this relatively
carefree and soon-to-be blissful moment sent a wave of sharp
frustration rolling through him. He considered answering the phone
and cursing out the caller. But he knew better than that. Only two
people had his number, and one of them was the person who gave him
the phone and paid for its monthly bill. He figured the faster he
answered the call, the faster he could get back to what he was doing.
So, he felt about his pocket and retrieved his Nokia.

"Yo," he said into the receiver, his voice lacking emotion.

"Arab. Wi need fi meet up inna hurry, bredren. Mi ave wuk fi yuh,"
the voice on the other end replied. There was obvious concern, the
caller's Jamaican accent becoming more pronounced as he continued,
"Meet mi at di Sutter-Rutland train station inna one hour. Brownsville
side. One hour."

Arab said nothing. This infuriated the man. He waited for another
few seconds, but he still didn't get a response.

"Yuh listening? Sey something? Wuh yuh did smoking yuh crack an
mi interrupt yuh?"

Arab calmly mumbled half-words, "No crack, freebasing—not the
same."

"Wah?"

"Yeah, Pauley. Yeah. Arab hears you. How much?" Arab uttered coldly.

"Ten fi two."

"Are these two gonna be in the same place at the same time or will they—"

Pauley all but growled his impatience into the phone, muttering a low curse. "Wah di blood! Mind ow yuh chatting pan di phone. Just meet mi at di train station an wi wi chat den. One hour. Seen?"

"Sure." Arab didn't wait to hear his next words before he hung up the phone and dropped it to the floor. He didn't take orders. He only fulfilled jobs.

Like so many of the young black men who migrated north as a teenager in the 1960s, James Eddie Bess, a.k.a. Arab, fell into the life of gangs early in his journey. In search of his own personal healing, Jimmy found his life's calling when his country sent him to Vietnam. A Green Beret who was able to kill freely without repercussions, he volunteered for several tours and always returned home unscathed—physically that is. Mentally, he became one of the walking wounded. He was emotionally gone. And at the time, he wasn't ready to adopt a long-term course of medication to ease that suffering. That, and his habit of blowing off shrink after shrink were the reasons he often chose to self-medicate with the heroin he was hired to smuggle out of Vietnam.

Not too long after he returned to Harlem, Jimmy was found nodding off near the scene of a nightclub shooting. Although he protested his innocence, he was arrested and charged with murder. While in prison he attempted to change his life by converting to Islam. A desire to sober up may have been one factor behind his conversion, but it wasn't the only factor. The racism he had experienced most of his life added fuel to his yearning to join a Black movement. Yet his newfound religion brought little change from the world he had been accustomed to in the streets. His fast-growing reputation as a former Green Beret led him to working as an enforcer for the Black Muslims in prison. And they were no strangers to dishing out violence.

During the early part of the 1970's he moved up in the eyes of his religious peers when he bludgeoned an Aryan Nation leader to death in his cell. It was an effort to impress the Black Muslim leaders, and it paid off—news of the Aryan's death had filtered back to one of Philadelphia's most prominent and feared Muslim ministers, Suleiman

Shabazz.

Suleiman, who also happened to be a major drug trafficker, sent word to Jimmy that he had a job waiting for him in Philly once he was released from the penitentiary. And he did. After serving his time, Jimmy became a devout paper-pushing and bean pie-selling Muslim who exorcised demons by day. But by night, he fed those demons.

No longer a trained killer employed by the American government; he became a hitman for renegade Black Muslims. He was ordered to commit crimes ranging from the decapitation of rival drug dealers to the drowning of a man's newborn baby in a tub of scalding water because he had defected from the religious organization.

Finding the burden of guilt for having murdered a black child intolerable, Jimmy reverted to his old habits and began using drugs again. This time it was cocaine. His addiction came to the attention of Suleiman after it was discovered that the veteran had been skimming his drugs. No one in Philadelphia ever heard from Jimmy again—nor Suleiman. They both disappeared without a trace.

Some fifteen years later, Jimmy's crimes forgotten, a crackhead walked into a Brooklyn bodega just as three men emerged from the back, holding guns to the heads of the owner and his two children. The fiend quickly sprang into action, his blinding speed giving him a massive advantage. Even though he was outnumbered, he disarmed them all in moments, causing a great deal of injuries, broken limbs and gouged eyes, before killing them. Mindful of the skills the crackhead employed to save his family, the store owner naturally expressed gratitude. In an instant he stuck his hand out and with a Jamaican accent quickly identified himself as what sounded like "Mr. China" then offered the fiend a job. The addict started to ask him to repeat the name. But before he could, Mr. China, noticing the man's silver ring with its carved Arabic inscription, blurted out, "An mi just a guh call yuh Aye'rab."

Moments of Arab's past came and went in an endless parade through his memory, each one begging him to smoke the drug waiting for him at his feet as he sat in the precinct. Totally unaware of what was going on around him, he had gone to a place deep inside of himself. But the sound of mice scurrying across the piles of rubbish brought him out of his brooding thoughts. He went back to finishing what he had started before the interruption. Left alone with his grief, it would have been an easy matter for his guilt to overtake him if he didn't have his pipe. And now with another job awaiting him, he could purchase enough rock to ease his suffering for a couple of more weeks.

CHAPTER 14

NERVES ATE AWAY at Eden's control. She didn't remember him to be this handsome. Her pulse picked up. She was uneasy around him, she knew. But should she be? Patiently waiting for him to come back from the bar, she sat upright on the VIP couch, hands knotted on her lap, knees pressed together, crossing and uncrossing them. Peering through the darkness of the room at the several people who filled the club, she noticed Shine walking toward her with two whiskey glasses in his hands. He pushed past people, heedless of who they were. As he threaded his way through the dense crowd, his eyes met Eden's with a mixture of interest and something else; a glimpse of the warmth she had seen when they first met. Warmth, yet more than warmth; desire, sudden anticipation, a recklessness she also recognized in herself. There was no smile on his lips, but she could see a fleeting smile in his gaze. She remained seated and awaited his approach, feet unconsciously tapping the floor.

The bouncer guarding the VIP entrance reached for the velvet rope and unhooked the clasp, allowing him to walk past. The section was just an elevated platform guarded by a Neanderthal making it a permission-only exclusive area. Shine swaggered past admiring females, sure in the belief that he could have anyone he wanted. At least that's the way he tried to appear.

He couldn't remember a time when he was this interested in a woman. It had to be because Eden was different. He wasn't surprised that he'd been so honest with her the past two hours. At the time, it just felt right, and he was glad they had discussed some of his past. He strutted toward his company, his confident strides belying the paranoid dart of his eyes. He knew that Copper and some of the other Crips might be in club tonight. So, he was alert. Once in front of her, he passed her one of the glasses before sitting down beside her.

"Thank you." She eyed the drink he handed her with a second thought then brought it up to her lips.

They both drank. The sting on Eden's tongue made her eyes water. She turned away spluttering. Shine studied her. She was beyond beautiful. Curls of her locks spiraled around her chin as she leaned on the arm of the couch. When she finally sat up and looked at him, there was a broad smile on his face. Gone was the tough, thuggish frown of a moment ago.

"You good?" he asked.

"Yeah. I'm good. It's been a while since I've had a drink." Once again, she looked away.

"I can see."

"So, were you following me from earlier today?" she spoke without turning to face him, directing her gaze out at the dance floor. A spotlight was on Ayana who was grinding on one of the Bloods who approached them earlier.

"Na, not at all. I ain't no stalker. This right here is fate."

"Fate?" she let out a girlish giggle. "Brother, we decide our own fate, regardless of what circumstances we find ourselves in."

"Really? We decide our fate? I'm not sure about that one. I mean, I ain't God."

"If you aren't then who are you?"

Shine adjusted his pants, a puzzling look clouding his face. He wasn't sure what she was asking, so he couldn't give an answer. Instead, she spoke for him.

"Oh, I forgot, you're a Blood," she remarked in a tone that shamed him.

A weak smile ghosted over his lips as he took another sip. Warmth spread throughout his chest while the Crown Royal worked its way into the blood throbbing deep within his veins.

"I don't bang. I hustle," his tone almost breathless, he barely opened his mouth.

She pursed her lips in disbelief. "Really? A gangbanger who doesn't bang? That's a new one. And besides, what do you hustle?"

"Why? Are you going to give me that hurting my own people speech?"

"Na. I won't. It seems you're already familiar with it. However, just know that the wrong you do to others will come around full circle."

"How you figure I'm doing wrong to others? I don't force people to use." A tiny grin flickered at his mouth again. "They do it on their own. They do it to themselves."

"Brother, a man who harms himself may be called a sinner by some. But he who harms others is looked upon as a devil by all. I mean, you are profiting off of their suffering. And you will eventually have to pay for what you take from them."

Another smile, but this time it barely made it off of his lips with a sigh of emotional exhaustion. "Ma—I mean, sister," The first few times she had corrected him politely, but now she just stabbed him with a hard stare when he called her out of her name. He swallowed hard, continuing, "I ain't no devil and I really ain't worried about what happens to me like that. You feel me? We all are going to die one day, anyway."

Eden had heard it all before, too many times to even pretend to accept it. "What if it is not you who dies as a result of your actions—but someone else—someone you love or care about?"

The weed and cigarette smoke blowing through the club froze entirely and all the world around Shine became silent. His surroundings were clouded to him now; nothing but the spotlight which had dimmed perceptibly in its radiance remained in its proper place. Slowly, his heartbeat sounded in his ears. The sudden shame unleashed inside from her words almost suffocated him. He could hear his labored breathing. Confidence dissolved around his consciousness, and terrible regrets assailed him from all angles as he shuffled around in his chair. He tried to swallow but couldn't. Mouth dry, and heart racing, he decided to take another sip of the Crown Royal.

She could sense he was uncomfortable with their conversation, his voice even deepened considerably. "Someone I love?"

"Yes, someone you love. You know, you may not fear death, but everyone fears losing."

"Losing?"

"Yes, imagine losing a loved one like a mother or child over some karma owed to you."

His eyes fell to the ground and his heartbeat sprinted as her words hit him. He tossed back the remaining liquor, grimaced, and stared at the floor a moment longer. Then a rush of guilt, huge guilt, hit him. Only then did he truly realize what he had done. He'd killed another human being. And his son might have paid with his life for that crime. Even before the murder he wasn't an innocent man. Nonetheless, he was a man who had sought to better his world in his own way—a man trying to survive. Now with one single action, he had become a worse monster than he could ever have imagined. His heart was pounding fiercely beneath his chest, tears numbing his eyes as he bit his lip in hopes of preventing them from falling.

"Uh, yeah. But I don't have any children and my mother died some time ago." The truth he uttered seemed torn from him, as though it pained him to admit he was alone in the world. His mouth barely pulled into a grim smirk, knowing he had to change the subject and quickly. "Speaking of children though, do you have any?"

In some confusion but aware of the attempt to redirect the conversation, Eden answered him, "No."

"What about your family?" he asked. "Do they all live out here?"

"Just my sibling and my parents. Everyone else is in Jamaica."

"Have you ever been to Jamaica?"

"Of course. But I haven't been since I was a little girl."

"Any plans to go back again?"

"Hmm—not at the moment. I am solely focused on finishing my degree right now. Maybe after that."

"Oh yeah, that's right. Before I went to the bar, you were saying how you were studying to be a doctor right?" With the change of subject, he'd been spared from having to entertain those emotions that might cause him to lose control.

Eden let out a restrained giggle. "Actually, I am working towards getting my master's degree in nursing education."

"Really? A nurse? What, like the kind that patch up bullet wounds? The way you talk I would've expected you to say you were studying to be a psychologist or something. You know, something where you don't get your hands dirty."

"Well, at first I wanted to become a social worker."

"A social worker?" he cocked his head back in surprise. "Why a social worker? They don't make that much money, do they?"

"It wasn't about the money for me. It was about helping the youth. I wanted to be able to make a difference."

"Have you ever worked with the youth before?" he asked, half-expecting her to say yes.

"Indeed, I have. But then I realized I needed to first focus on solving my own personal problems before I could solve anyone else's." She gave a little grimace with her lips. "I had to make a living. And nursing comes with a decent salary. Pretty much, I had to think about saving myself before I could save others."

"I agree one hundred percent with that. You know, saving self, first. It's like Darwin's survival of the fittest out here," he stated. "That's why I do what I do. Because self-preservation is the first law of nature. Right?"

She would have choked on her drink if she'd taken a sip at that moment. Not only was the man beside her very handsome, but it was evident that he was somewhat well read.

"I didn't think thugs were into Darwin," was her reply.

Shine tilted his head back, his mouth hooking upward to one side as though he was trying to keep from laughing. But he couldn't help himself. He let out a tremendous guffaw.

Eden stared at him and watched his face with extreme fascination. *Goddammit, a man shouldn't be allowed to sound that sexy with just a laugh.*

As the quake of his laughter waned, a smile of self-satisfaction flashed across his lips. "So, a nigga ain't supposed to read?"

Eden blushed. "I am not saying that. I was only—"

"Yeah, I like to count money and yeah, I like to read books. But it makes sense that I focus more on my 1-2-3s before I concern myself as much with my ABDs. I'm saying, that's the order in which I learned them in school anyway. You feel me?"

She nodded. "Well, other than purposefully leaving out a C, it appears you at least paid attention in school."

"Yeah, I did. And the one thing I remember learning in history class especially, is that these white boys gained all their doe and all their power by having their goons roll on the weak and take what they wanted. Just like we be out here fighting over blocks, that's how they came up, fighting over land. They went from being European barbarians to forming street gangs in Five Points New York to becoming Chicago mobsters then legit American businessmen and politicians." He huffed out a small breath. "And now they run the planet. And it ain't because they read some books, sweetheart—I mean—Eden."

She saw those gorgeous green eyes light up with intelligence as she tried to work her way through his identity. "So not only are you familiar with science, but it seems you are fond of history too? Who are you, Mr. Shine? I mean, is that even your real name?"

A slight chuckle escaped his lips. "My name is Dwight. People started calling me Shine because of my last name. It's Mannschein. My pops was a Jew."

"Oh. And your mother?"

"Black. Born and raised in Brooklyn, just like me."

"Are your parents still alive?"

"My pops left before I was born because his family wasn't ready to accept me. So, I never met the nigga and I could give a damn about him. He got his taste of Black pussy but didn't want to stick around to get a taste of Black living."

"You seem to be very upset with him?"

"Na. Not at all. I'm just calling it like I see it. My parents were teens when I was born. And I mean, you can't expect a nigga who ate hummus all his life to settle for chitterlings."

This brother knows what hummus is? He continued to surprise Eden with his comments. Curiosity set in once more.

"So, what made you want to become a Blood?"

"Brotherly Love," he answered.

"Brotherly love? Really?" Sarcasm dripped from her words. "Is it brotherly love that you guys are thinking about when you are harming your own people?"

"If harming someone is going to help me feed my brothers—then, yes."

"Oh. I see. So, your love is really just loyalty to you homeboys. Right?"

"Hell yeah," he uttered with pride.

"Brother, that's not really my idea of brotherly love. What you're talking sounds more like tribalism, which is just a primitive form of nationalism." She tipped her head to the side. "If you were to just broaden your mindset, you could be building a nation instead of destroying your community."

"Nationalism? Building a nation? Destroying my community?" Her point was lost upon Shine. "First of all, ain't no such thing as a black community. We just got neighborhoods with niggas in them." After gazing at her for a moment with a sort of quizzical, mock seriousness, he again broke into laughter. "Look around sister, the only black power out here is white powder."

"And you think that's black power?"

"Keeping it one hundred—it doesn't matter, because I don't see color anyway. I only see come-up."

Her eyebrow shot up. "How can you not see color, when you live in a country where racism is the dominant culture?" she asked.

"Racism? The culture of this country? Na, the culture of America is not racism." He chuckled. "It's capitalism. You know the saying—if it makes dollars then it makes sense. And on the real, the nature of capitalism is competition, so you have to have a thorough team riding with you. You feel me?"

"Yeah but gangbanging ain't a team sport. And it ain't a come-up if it leads to incarceration." Eden let out a sigh as she placed one of her hands on his leg. "I mean, really brother, you seem too intelligent to be living this lifestyle. I can tell you are a good person who has a lot of potential. Why limit yourself? You could go back to school if you wanted to. It's never too late. I mean, don't you want to see more out of life?"

"See more out of life?" He tilted his head and smirked. "Why C-life when I can B-life?"

Eden fought the urge to scream in frustration. She had grown to love her people with a bitter pride, only to be constantly let down by them. As an educated black woman who in recent years had been most sympathetic to the plight of young black men in the ghettoes of America, she was now beginning to lose patience with them. She could no longer speak out against the wrongs done to them by the white race, yet never admonish them for the excessive violence they were committing against their own people. White hoods weren't as much of a threat to her generation as were red and blue bandanas. There wasn't a single white man who scared her those nights when she rode the subway alone. And if a group of white men were walking down the sidewalk toward her, she wouldn't feel the urge to cross the street. Was it that her people were no longer victims? Were they now their own victimizers? She couldn't fully understand why anyone would willingly choose to live in such ignorance. Because—after all—it was a choice. They enjoyed living like savages. They lauded violence—like modern-day Vikings. And the man next to her was no different. Yet still, she was deeply drawn to him and she wasn't sure she could explain how she felt about him even to herself.

Eden shook her head, looked steadfastly at Shine and said, "I guess you are fine with letting another man run game on you and out-hustle you then."

"Huh?" He didn't understand what she meant.

"You are being tricked into thinking that gangbanging makes you a man. It's the way you get to feel some sort of power in a world where you are powerless. But it doesn't make you a man. Gangbanging, sleeping with random women, selling drugs—it's always been referred to as the game. Because games are for children. You know the saying, tricks are for kids, right? Well, you're the kid getting tricked."

"Tricked? Like the rabbit? Yeah, ok." A low chuckle rode the sigh that left his lips.

"Yeah, tricked. Tricked into volunteering yourself for slavery. It's a hustle that they are running on you."

"You talking slavery now? Look, I know you're about to go into that whole Plymouth Rock fell on our head rant, but I ain't a slave, yo."

"Read the constitution of this country, brother. Slavery is legal when used as a punishment for those who commit crimes. And with several major corporations outsourcing their jobs to private prisons, it is in their interest that you commit crimes." Eden let out a long, exaggerated sigh. "Think about it, why would a corporation pay a college grad fifteen-dollars an hour to answer phones, when they can train inmates to be customer service reps and pay them next to nothing? Or why would they even hire illegal immigrants to do manual labor when they have a prison full of slaves who can be forced to work for free?"

Shine hissed through his teeth. "Ain't no nigga working for free. We barely work for pay."

"Free labor is still big business in this country. That's why they promote Rap music that endorses criminal behavior—to make it cool to break the law and go to jail. So, they would have a line of brothers jumping in front of each other trying to be the first to get locked up.

And now they are even using music videos the way the military used Uncle Sam posters as propaganda to get people to join." She paused, shook her head and blew out a frustrated breath before continuing, "But instead of the army, our youth join gangs. And instead of war, they excitedly go off to prison with the idea that they will somehow become tougher and more of a man for doing so. But in reality, they are just volunteering themselves for slavery."

"Well, going to prison doesn't make a nigga a man. And just because a dude's been locked, doesn't mean he's hard-body. You feel me?" He searched her eyes, but she refused to nod.

"No one that's incarcerated can act like they are so-called hard-body because they are letting another man tell them what and when to eat, when to go to bed, when to take a shower, and when to keep quiet. An inmate can't even consider himself a man. So there really isn't much of a difference between a gangster and a baby. It's just that one is innocent and the other is not."

Shine let out a confident chuckle. "Well, I've been lost my innocence and right now I ain't behind bars, and I take care of myself. I don't depend on no one for my food, clothing, and shelter. So, even though I bang, I am still a man. I ain't no baby."

Eden inhaled deeply. "Either way brother, being a gangsta is so yesterday. It's immature and it's time to grow up."

Even though he didn't appear upset, his defensive glare and something in his body language warned her to tread lightly.

"Shine—Dwight—I'm just saying. I can't understand why a man like yourself, with such a beautiful mind would get involved in doing things that could put you behind bars for the rest of your life. Why downplay your intelligence like that just to feel important among people who don't have your best interest at heart?"

Shine let out an exaggerated sigh. "Look, I didn't choose the environment I was born into. I was raised in hell, and I wasn't about to go through this shit by myself. The friends I have are the only ones I could have—the ones who proved they had my back in these streets."

"Yeah, but you don't seem like the average thug from the streets. I mean, all of you guys may have been raised in the same neighborhood and went to the same school, but for whatever reason, you did come out different."

"Well, yeah, we all grew up in the same neighborhood, but we didn't all go to the same school." Shine paused. He swallowed hard, then continued. "I didn't go to the public school in my hood. I went to a private school until I was eleven—"

"Private school?"

"Pilgrim Christian Academy. Went there until my grandmother died. We were living with her in her apartment. And when she passed, my mother had to take care of the rent by herself and couldn't afford to send me back to that school anymore. So, by the time I was twelve, all that private school shit had gone out the window."

"Well then that explains a lot," she said with a smile. "You had a good foundation for your education, which is why you like to read."

"Uh yeah, I read. But who said I like to read?"

"Um, I can tell."

"Yeah, well maybe you're right. Reading was the only way I was able to escape the bullshit around me. But trust, just because a nigga read, don't mean a nigga ain't quick to put in that work."

Eden rolled her eyes then said, "Yeah, but it takes some degree of reasoning to comprehend any kind of literature. And since reasoning entails the prediction of results, you're more likely to consider the consequences of your actions than most of your peers who don't like to read. Which means—you're more likely to make the choice to abandon the reckless lifestyle of gang-banging.

"So, no—I don't believe you are quick to put in that work. And I am not implying that you are not tough. Trust me, I can see that you aren't a punk. I just don't believe you believe one hundred percent in the things you are doing. That is—the negative things. I think you are at a point where you can't justify what you do anymore. You just simply have to make a choice."

Shine's eyes fell to the ground. How did she read him so well? She was right. He was finally ready to bend to the changing circumstances of his life. Maybe the murder he committed had softened him. He wouldn't be the first. Or perhaps the thoughts of his son's death were about to extort from him a confession—a confession as he had never made before. But not a confession to the police. A confession to himself, because the guilt he was feeling was personal not criminal. He couldn't live a lie anymore. No longer was he innocent, but neither was he some heartless thug.

At that very moment, he had decided that there would be no war with Chinnah. At least he wouldn't be involved. And he would have nothing to do with the cocaine they stole. And he would forget about trying to frame the old Jamaican for Trayvon's death. It was over. He was done with that lifestyle.

He glanced at Eden and shrugged, his thoughts very far away. "Well, to some degree you are right. I am tired of all of this."

"Then give it up brother," she replied excitedly. "Walk away from it all tonight."

"Tonight?" For a moment he seemed deathly still, unmoving, but then lowering his head he said, "I'm saying, even if I stop it all tonight, what makes you think God would even forgive me for all the stuff I've done? Because I've done a lot."

"You should be asking yourself that brother. Are you willing to forgive yourself?" Her words came out softly, but sternly.

The question caused him a surge of anxiousness and longing to change his corrupt ways, to pursue and win the final war with himself. Sensing that, Eden turned on the couch and slid over to him. She took his slender jaw between her soft palms and guided his face toward her. The strobe light glinted on the long scar that ran down his cheek. A gentler look had crept into his eyes. She told herself to look away, but she couldn't. His stare was sucking her soul from her body, and she needed all her will to force her gaze from his. Despite his appearance as a hardcore gangbanger, he wasn't the average ignorant hoodlum. But he also wasn't an academic type or anything. He appeared to be well-read and street smart—quite balanced. And this made her wonder what the typical literature of non-cultivated people could possibly be.

Often, she met men who were very intelligent. But they were kind—too kind maybe, for in the end she would come to think of them as weak. Perhaps all intelligent, attentive men were weak. And that was not for her. Then there were the "super-masculine beasts"—Ayana's phrase. Big dick, illiterate, thugged-out, eager to make a woman cum; and little interest in anything but getting high, fighting, and fucking. That was not for her, either. She remembered being told how boys, both the intelligent ones and the ignorant ones, disliked girls who proved to be smarter than them. But she could never pretend to be stupid, at least not long enough to establish a fleeting relationship.

Eden held Shine's stare, measuring the green depths, seeing concern in his eyes. It appeared that the enormity of whatever he was facing had finally hit him. After a moment she decided that she had much more to ask him but was distracted by loud yelling coming from where the bouncer stood guarding the VIP entrance. Though she couldn't hear what was being said exactly, she could tell from the tones that someone was shouting at someone else in fury. One of the voices was pitched high with anger, but still indistinct. It belonged to a woman. The screaming didn't concern her at first, but the young lady was making so much of a commotion, Eden finally turned to glance her way. Shine followed her eyes. He instantly recognized the woman.

It was Desiree.

She was arguing with the bouncer. He could hear bits and pieces of their conversation but could not make anything out, until she pointed right at him and yelled, "I'm with him!"

Eden turned her head swiftly toward her company, uncertain which was worse—to be humiliated by the girlfriend of a man she desired or to feel that she might have no choice but to be rude to another black woman, who in theory, probably had more of a right to be seated in the place she now occupied. Shine didn't utter a word but rose from the couch and inched his way toward the commotion. By the time he reached the two, the bouncer had one of his large arms around Desiree's waist, preventing her from taking a single step.

"Yo, what's going on?" Shine asked, speaking to no one in particular.

Desiree was visibly angry, but the bouncer seemed entirely insensible to her feelings, for he calmly replied, "This chic said she's with you. I told her not tonight 'cause I knew you didn't want to be bothered." He motioned to Eden with his head as if to tell Shine, *I got you.*

Shine looked at the bouncer pointedly and they exchanged a silent communication that Desiree couldn't help but notice. *What the hell is that about?* she wondered. She snuck a glance at Eden who didn't appear to be disturbed by her behavior, but who did seem out of sorts.

Poking a twig-like finger in her direction, Desiree screamed out, "What? You think I care about that chic?" Frantic to loosen the bouncer's grip, she clawed at his arm then snapped her neck around to look at Shine. "Tell her to bounce! I need a drink!"

Shine moved closer to her, icy contempt rising in his eyes. "Look, bitch," He remembered their little encounter with disgust. It was blatant blackmail, but she was who she was, and being he was who he was, he wasn't going to let her get away with it. And he wasn't going to let her presence ruin his evening with Eden. "You're crazy if you think you going to walk up in here giving orders. Ain't no one leaving but you!"

"Muthafucka! Are you forgetting our arrangement?"

"We ain't got no arrangement!" Shine screamed.

She wrenched herself from the grasp of the burly bouncer and demanded, "Either let me up in there and tell that chic to go home, or not only will I let Lola know you're in here with another broad, but I will kindly take my ass over to the precinct and have a nice long chat."

Shine's eyes hardened to slits and a fierce expression marred his face. The twitching muscle in his jaw, the fast throbbing pulse in his throat, his glowing eyes all bore testament to the tension surrounding them. He knew the game she was playing with him, but he had to deal with her without attracting too much attention. He couldn't risk putting any heat on himself by arguing with her in public. Still, the situation was getting out of hand and since he knew the threat of Desiree and what she might do, his lack of control over it started to seriously bother him.

No longer was there a need to kill Chinnah. The need for revenge was gone. Totally gone. But his world was still plagued by a number of internal wars that the need had spawned. The fading look in Badrick's eyes that night continued to haunt him. They kept staring back at him, accusing him. He had always thought he would be able to take a life, since he was no stranger to shooting a man. But what happened with Badrick was different. He should have turned on his heels and left the house. Instead he reacted on instinct and the consequence of his decision was final. It was fear that made him pull the trigger. Fear made him go to the house that night. Shine knew fear well. He feared losing Lola. Before every robbery, before stepping into Minimart each day, he felt fear, nauseating fear. Every move he made in the streets was greased with fear. But the fear he felt now was different. He feared losing his freedom. He feared becoming the slave that Eden spoke about. Since taking another man's life, the sand in his own hour glass of life had begun to descend faster. The time of judgement was coming sooner. This was now very clear to him, and he had convinced himself that if he did go to jail it would only be Desiree's fault.

He fought with himself over what to do with her. At that moment he barely felt anything but the desire to hurt her, kill her, to shoot her in the face over and over again, until she was dead. But this was not the time, nor the place. And the more he told himself he couldn't do anything, the more helpless he felt. So, he narrowed his eyes and looked sternly at the bouncer and commanded, "Kick her ass out of the club!"

An expression of almost painful confusion crept onto Desiree's face. She didn't expect him to jump into her arms, because she knew she didn't mean anything to him—emotionally that is. No. Lola—who he believed to be unfaithful—was the one. But the fact that he had just committed a murder made it less reasonable to expect him to resist her threat. With prison looming as the only possible end to his journey, she calculated that all of her demands would be met by him. She was wrong. And she was going to make sure he paid for proving her wrong.

With an effort that showcased his strength, the bouncer picked Desiree up by the waist and tossed her over his shoulders like a duffel bag, nearly knocking the wind out of her as her chin bounced against his back. The thin fabric of her red dress rode up several inches, revealing the smooth globes of her panty-less ass. Noting her embarrassment, Shine tilted his head back and laughed his anger away. This infuriated her. And this of course also made it easier to tell him the news that she knew would devastate him.

With a deep breath, she yelled for all she was worth, "That's why your wifey been sleeping with another dude! And it wasn't Badrick!"

Shine's eyes blinked owlishly, clearly caught off guard by her words—words she was all too happy to say—and he felt a sliver of hate inside. Those words stung, but he wasn't going to give her the satisfaction of knowing that she had gotten under his skin. Left unsaid but perfectly understood by him was that this was his chance to find out the truth about Lola's unfaithfulness. It was one hell of a spot to be in. Unwilling to give Desiree the upper hand by having to beg for information about his woman; and yet, knowing that if he turned her away he'd regret it for the rest of his life. Either way, he could very well be drawing near to the end of both his sanity and his freedom. It was odd to him that he was standing there thinking over the situation. Instead of doing something he was watching her and letting her make a scene. She had to be dealt with but not right now. Not in a public place. Not tonight.

He shot one final commanding stare at the bouncer and calmly ordered, "Get her out of here now. And don't ever let her back in when I am around."

Frank surprise covered Desiree's face. A deep worry wrinkle appeared at the bridge of her nose as she looked at Shine with the expression of a puppy who had just been scolded for peeing on the kitchen floor. His reaction to her helplessness seemed to confirm the decision she had just made in her head.

As the bouncer prepared to carry her off, she began to struggle and scream. "Tell this black-ass monkey to put me down! And I will tell you who she is seeing behind your back. What! You don't care that it's your boy she's been giving it up to?"

Shine's eyebrows went up in surprise, his gaze swinging to the place where Eden sat waiting for him. He brought his attention back to the bouncer and called out to him to stop, "Yo Sincere, hold on."

The big man stopped dead in his tracks. Desiree clawed at his back in an attempt to lift herself up. "Put me down!" she gasped. "I ain't no—"

"My boy?" Shine wanted her to skip the drama and get straight to the point.

"Yeah, your boy."

"Who?"

She stopped struggling and stared at him. She had no intention of telling him anything without getting something in return. "If he puts me down, we can go over to the couch and discuss it."

Shine gritted his teeth in disgust. "Feel me. You got five seconds to give me a name!"

"Man, fuck you, Shine! Tell him to put me down!"

Shine snapped at her words, baring his teeth, "I ain't telling him a damn thing!" He smirked smugly then gave the bouncer the command once more, "Go on and throw her out."

"Shine!" A sudden crash of anger as she realized the bouncer had taken a few steps. "You're joking right? You can't do this." Before the burly man had a chance to push his way through the crowd, Desiree blurted out, "She's been sleeping with Gorilla Leek!"

"What?" Shine's mouth went wide.

Frustration buried under a wave of nervous anticipation shook

Desiree's thick frame as she yelled out, "Yeah, your main road-dog has been laying up in your bed with your baby mama every Wednesday and Friday morning while you at Minimart counting your doe. They been seeing each other since last year. The dude even got a key to your apartment . . ."

Her voice faded as thoughts flew through his mind. He watched the bouncer disappear with her into the crowd. She was gone before he could gather his words into his throat. His heart sank to his stomach and for a moment he couldn't breathe as anguish viciously coiled around his chest like a python. Rage, helplessness, and fear exploded inside of him. How could he know if she was telling him the truth? Even if it wasn't true, it made sense. The signs were clear. That would explain how she knew where Trayvon's body was. Gorilla Leek could've told Lola, and Lola probably confided in Desiree. Which would also mean that Lola knew about his involvement with Badrick's death all along. If she could betray his trust by sleeping with his best friend, then there was no telling how much he could depend on her not to go to the police.

But, was she really having an affair with Gorilla Leek? Would his longtime friend do that to him? He wasn't ready to accept it. His thoughts bounced back and forth a thousand times between the possibilities. Sucking in his breath, he started to go after Desiree to question her further when he felt a hand on his shoulder.

"Is everything alright? I hope I didn't get you in trouble with your girl."

It took longer than usual, but after several seconds he turned around to find Eden standing quite bewildered, holding her glass out to him.

"Here, I'm done with my drink. Maybe I should go." She waited a moment to see if he would speak.

He reached for her glass. "My girl? Na, ma—I mean, uh—yeah, everything's good. That is definitely not my girl. Just another thirsty, disgruntled chic trying to get into VIP for free. No need to bounce."

"So, do you have a girl?"

"Do I have a girl?" His shoulders moved in a shrug then he glanced around. "Do you want to get out of here?" He decided to change the subject to avoid the uncomfortable experience of confession.

Eden was familiar with that tone of voice and demeanor. He wasn't ready to be completely honest. Yet for some reason, she instinctively dreaded to find out the truth anyway. It was indeed time to change the subject.

"And go where?" she asked.

"I don't know. Maybe we can hit up Brooklyn Diner on Utica Avenue and get some grub."

"That sounds tempting. I mean I am starving. But I came here with my home-girl. She's my ride."

"Look Ma—queen—I'll get you back home safely. And it's my treat. K?"

With eyes narrowed in concentration, Eden caught her lip with her teeth, uncertain how to respond. "I can't leave my girl by herself."

"I'll have my dogs watch after her. My word is my bond, she'll be safe with them," he assured her, pointing in the direction of the Bloods who were taking turns dancing with Ayana.

She thought of asking him again about having a girlfriend. And then she felt upset that she wanted to ask him, wondered why she should ask. She barely knew him. He was a criminal, and yet she had an awkward sense of safety just being around him. She felt confused, and guilty, and pathetic. Just as she was about to respond to his last comment, he abruptly stuffed his hand into his pocket and came back out with his smart phone. Eden immediately noticed the light flashing on it. It was ringing on silent.

Shine put it to his ear and addressed the caller, "Peace." While the other person spoke, he smirked naughtily, seething. "Really? So, you still haven't heard from Leek? You telling me nobody has seen dude? Son, send someone to find his ass asap. There's something I need to ask him."

It was as if Eden was seeing a different person—a person who only surfaced when conflict arose. She listened to his conversation, hoping to either hear warmth or to discover danger before it discovered her.

"Son nevermind that. Are you inside? Alright, I'm coming to get my keys now. And I got somebody with me. I'm going to drop you off and then I'mma be out and grab something to eat."

He lowered his phone without uttering another word then turned to Eden, his eyes apologetic. "Are you ready to go?"

Uncertainty stopped the swift rejection that began to rise to her lips. She shifted from foot to foot. With each movement the uneasy flutter in her stomach increased. She forced a smile and tried her best to appear nonchalant, smoothing her sweaty palms inconspicuously on her dress. What should she do? So much was at risk because she really knew nothing about him. Should she leave with him? At that moment he seemed dangerous and somewhat reckless. But—how could she say no?

CHAPTER 15

"DO YOU THINK HE** will cooperate?" inquired Detective Cardillo.

"Not sure. Doubt it," responded Brown as he guided the Crown Victoria down Livonia Avenue beneath the elevated train tracks. He had little focus on sights and sounds while he drove through the night, only the thoughts that preoccupied him.

"More than likely he'll try to handle it himself. Chinnah lives in his own world where he is the law."

"Hmm. I can tell," Cardillo replied.

"Either way, I would like to know who owns that house."

"What do you mean?"

"Chinnah said that he leases the house where his nephew was murdered. Maybe the actual owner can give us more information—maybe he knows what's going on. He might just be willing to talk." Brown took his eyes off of the road momentarily and searched his partner's face. "While I work other angles, do you think you can handle that?"

"What? Finding out who owns Chinnah's stash house? Of course. I think we both know I would be better at handling the light work."

Brown stifled a laugh. "Yeah, I guess so."

As the car moved through the shabby streets, Cardillo glanced out of the passenger window and saw a depth of shadows; scowling black faces set sternly against the increasing purple of the evening. The trembling bodies of teenage addicts were scattered liberally around the sidewalks and on the stoops of buildings, their hands passing around a 40oz bottle of malt liquor as though it represented some cherished thing. Hostile eyes filled with the seething red glow of intoxication peered back at the young detective as the car passed by. Above their heads hovered the greyish stain of crack, marijuana, and cigarettes; a ghostly halo of diabolic corruption that no layer of blackness seemed to cover for long. Cardillo saw at least a dozen faces scarred as though by razorblade-cuts; contorted, evil faces; dark, menacing faces; faces marked by unrestrained passions; brutal, beastly faces. It was all an ever-moving stream of strange creatures scurrying through narrow blocks hedged by project buildings darkening the sky.

As the car slowed to a stop at a red light and the beam of its headlights cast moving black phantoms along the street, the young Italian detective could not fail to notice a woman, probably in her forties, waving a kitchen knife menacingly in the face of an older gentleman. The man wore a light-colored coat, covered with streams of blood, his head swathe in a turban of dirty bandages. Cardillo stared at him thoughtfully. Perhaps he was just released from the hospital. Between winces of pain the man pleaded, then opened his arms offering the woman a hug. Knife still in hand, she waved away the gesture with a frustrated scowl. It caused the rookie to wonder if the two were lovers. They both appeared to be drunk so it seemed inevitable that they would end up locked in each other's arms before the night was over. He recalled having seen their kind before. He was beginning to know them well. Trying to help people like that sometimes seemed useless. They thrived on dysfunction. It was their whole life.

Cardillo glanced at his partner, frowning slightly in thought. "Well, if this is the world in which Chinnah wants to be the law, he can be it. Unfortunately, these people would probably respect him more than they do us."

Brown cut his eyes to Cardillo, then back to the road. His cell phone rang, and he grabbed it just as he gunned the car through the green light.

"Hello."

"Man, where have you been? I've been trying to reach you for over an hour now," the voice on the other end of the phone said.

"Seidman?" inquired Brown.

"Yep. The one and only."

"Trying to reach me? For what?"

"I have a location on Baby Bye."

"And? That's your case. I just wanted to know how it was connected to my murder case. I mean, don't get me wrong. It's good you might be able to close your—"

"Whether I want you to or not, the chief is asking for you to work this one." Seidman made a meaningful pause. When he realized that Brown wasn't going to encourage him to continue, he cleared his throat. "It looks we have a ten fifty-four. And I have a lead on the body's possible whereabouts. According to the information received, the child was shot in the head, then buried along with the murder weapon."

Brown's voice burst with excitement. "The Bye child might be dead! How credible is your lead? Do they know the father's involvement?"

"Not sure if it's on the money, and they didn't mention the child's father. The tip came from a call in to 9-1-1. It was a lady who claimed to know where the body was hidden."

"Do you have her contact information?"

"She hung up without identifying herself. But we have the number she called from. We're getting info on it now."

Brown steered the car in and out of traffic then yelled into the phone "Look, don't go anywhere! I will be there in twenty minutes!"

He sat the phone between his legs and took the next right, leading the car onto an abandoned block where it seemed the medieval civility of Brownsville abruptly ended and unfolded into a stretch of concrete desolation littered with crack vials and debris.

Curiosity prickled in the back of Cardillo's mind, bringing with it a naïve awareness. He eyed Brown strangely. "Was that about the Chinnah case?" the rookie asked.

"Kind of. It's all connected, just not sure how yet."

"So, I guess we're headed back to the station?"

"You know it, brother."

"Then why are we turning down this street?"

"I have to make a stop first."

"Really?" Cardillo studied him in the dim light, waiting for him to elaborate.

"We are going to speak to my CI," Brown informed his partner.

"Your confidential informant is out here?"

"Yes."

"Let me guess—Arab?"

"Yes."

♠   ♠   ♠

ARAB APPEARED CALM, stoic almost, as he slowly walked down Rutland Road treasuring his lonely thoughts. Trapped in his own world of torment, he pictured the wet street without the rain driving down in silver sheets across the backdrop of oblivion; without the shrilling of the wind on the buildings surrounding him; without the occasional headlights passing across his lids before darkness took over again. It was the emptiness of the ghetto that eased his mind into a more focused state.

Bending his eyes down to escape the drift of rain as he turned the corner, he surveyed the block, weighing the task awaiting him. It was strange how in the brick and concrete desert where there was hardly any greenery, he at all times imagined the noise of Vietcong footsteps trampling over dead leaves and twigs, trying to sneak up on him. There were also the imaginary gulping mud sounds that trailed him. The wind swayed the few trees that were scattered on the sidewalk, the remnants of a once desirable family-friendly neighborhood. And beneath each tree Arab found cover from his invisible enemy.

"The enemy is the inner me. The enemy is the inner me. The enemy is the inner me—" Arab devoutly muttered, in utter absence of mind "—the enemy is the inner me."

He seemed to float effortlessly from shadow to shadow, moving through a treacherous path of broken street lamps, vacant vehicles, and half-filled trash cans. He strained to see ahead and thought he spotted a small guerilla unit.

It was a group of teenagers hanging out on the stoop of a run-down, two-story apartment building. These boys, whose red baseball caps, knotted red bandanas around their heads, and strings of red and black beads stacked up their necks, showed the influence of hip hop's subculture. They were a joke to Arab. Nothing like the gangsters he once knew. No, they were a cultural type created by Hollywood. The new American criminal. A caricature of a gangster who aroused affectionate sympathy rather than terror. They were victims and not victors like his generation. In other words, they were food.

Most of the boys were too busy to notice him, and the one that did, wanted no part of him. He stepped back as Arab neared the group and nudged his friend in the side.

"Yo, Redrum. Look. Who dat?" the boy asked, pointing in the direction of the oncoming stranger.

When he heard his name mentioned, Redrum looked up from his conversation and took notice of the man who now stood a few feet away from him. He inched forward, threatening outright contact, hoping to intimidate the vagabond.

"You need to back up old man. This ain't the place for you to be right now."

Arab stood there in silence staring, just staring at them. Then suddenly, he was seized with a fit of coughing. Stepping back and turning, he fell against a park car and bent over it, his knees buckling, all of his weight on his arms, hacking and hacking. The boys snickered. Looking over his shoulders, he saw their heinous eyes watching him. He stopped coughing and pulled a tattered red bandana out of his pocket, and spat into it, blood spotting the corners of his mouth. The boys' eyes widened, and they became livid at the sight of the man disrespecting their flag. Tossing the cloth to the ground, Arab neared Redrum once more.

"Fi—filthy rag." The crackhead snorted loudly then uttered, "Uh, excuse Arab. Can you help? Um—in need of a friend."

"A friend? You crazy old crackhead," Redrum scoffed. "You 'bout to need a doctor."

"No, no, no. No doctor. Arab is looking for his friend."

"Your friend? Nigga you high?"

"Arab? Shit—Arab always high. But this a job. Arab's friend's name Cutty. The last place he said he was-was here. In that there apartment." He jabbed his long finger toward the building the group was loitering in front of.

"Cutty?" Redrum's hardened stare was loaded with suspicion despite the shiver he felt go through him at the mention of Cutty's name. *This cat knows Cutty*, he thought to himself as he tried to get his courage back in check. *Who is this fiend?*

"Arab needs to know—this where Gorilla Leek lives?" the crackhead asked.

Redrum raised an eyebrow. Now he was anxious to learn who this man was. "Why the hell you asking bout Gorilla Leek?"

All half dozen boys moved closer to Arab, enclosing him in semicircle, his back against a line of parked cars.

"A'yo pops, you might wanna break north. You too old to be playing around over here. I think it's time for your midnight nap," said one of the Bloods.

Arab didn't utter a word. Instead he placed his right foot behind him and distributed his weight.

"Yo, I asked you a question. Why you asking bout Gorilla Leek?" inquired Redrum once more.

"Arab told you. Cutty was here. Now Cutty is not. Arab need to go inside there." Again, he pointed at the apartment building. "Arab needs to look around."

"Why that nigga talking like that?" asked another Blood.

"Arab ain't going a damn place," Redrum furiously asserted as he poked his index finger into crackhead's chest. "You heard?"

He started to poke him once more but before he could, Arab deftly seized his finger and bent it back toward his wrist, breaking it. In one continuous motion, he shifted his weight and sent the side of his other hand crashing into Redrum's Adam's apple.

Had he been able to, the boy would have screamed, releasing the pain he felt inside as he fell. But he was only able to manage a violent hack. Panicking as his air supply was cut off, he rolled over onto the concrete and crawled behind a parked car.

Arab quickly moved between the teenagers, feinting towards one and kicking at the other. He ducked as a haymaker whooshed above his head, then stepped off to the side and punched hard into his attacker's kidney, smashing his lower ribs. As he came back up, he launched a slashing elbow downward at a 45-degree angle across the boy's temple. Stretching the same arm to the rear of the boy's head and around his neck, he applied a Guillotine choke, swiftly pulling up his forearm into the throat. He dropped his shoulder to push the head down, then thrusted his hips forward, instantly blocking the windpipe. His right hand then reached under the chin and his left hand cuffed his victim's head, and in one quick movement he snapped the neck.

He let the body fall to the ground just as a glimmer in his peripheral vision alerted him to another gang member coming in from the left. Sliding forward diagonally with his left foot, he dropped below the line of attack, slipped outside the oncoming hook and seized the wrist of the attacking arm. With his opposite forearm he delivered an upward strike to the boy's elbow, breaking the joint.

Immersed in gripping agony, the teen hollered out a nearly unintelligible plea for mercy. He pulled his broken arm to his chest to protect it from further damage just as Arab reached behind the boy's neck and brought his face crashing down into his filthy raised knee. The teenage gangsta toppled backwards with a broken nose, unconscious before the back of his head slammed against the ground.

The thug who first noticed the crackhead approaching them turned and ran down the street, while the remaining pair hesitated. Arab chuckled then came with a sudden rush, sliding his foot off the ground and angling it so that the bottom of his army boot was facing the closest boy's knee as he drove the ball of his foot through it. Collapsing on the concrete and screaming hysterically, the thug grasped desperately at the bone sticking out the back of his torn jeans. His squealing reminded Arab of the annoying noise the half-starved pigs made in Pennsylvania when he threw the body parts of his victims over the fence. The memories of their feeding frenzy sickened him, so he raised his boot high above the soprano's head and brought his heel down hard on his skull, crushing it like a watermelon. The body shook in a maddening convulsion.

Having just lost two of his friends, the last man standing was somewhat reluctant to move forward. Instead he reassessed his situation and managed to pull a gun from his waist before Arab was able to reach him. He raised the gun toward the killer, his hand shaking. "Stop! Please stop!"

Arab snorted. "You'll shoot an old man?" Arab was sure to move slow and non-threatening, as he inched forward, hesitating then advancing a few feet closer to the gangbanger.

"Yes," the boy's voice quivered as he spoke. "I will. Because you're trying to hurt us." Horror welled into his throat, his face showed a dreadful combination of fear and shame.

"Hurt you?" Arab's eyes expanded with surprise. "No, no, no, no, no. Arab is not trying to—" He suddenly paused.

A muffled chuckle rumbled up from the crackhead's gut. Then a sudden change came over his demeanor. His shoulders stiffened, his eyes rolled ghastly, and the corners of his mouth crept up in a ghoulish grin. The gangbanger looked around for help then back at the man to find his eyes fixed steadily on him. He saw a momentary flash of emotion cross the killer's face and settle in his gaze, as if some old pain had returned to haunt him.

Finally, Arab broke the silence with a calm, steady, and powerful voice, his personality completely changing, "Young man, *I am* not trying to hurt you." His eyes held the boy's gaze, keen, unwavering—definitely sane. "*I'm* trying to kill you."

Arab swiftly seized the gun barrel from the outside while ducking away from it. Pinning the trigger finger against the side of the trigger guard, he twisted the boy's hand, turning the barrel upward and forcing him into a painful wrist lock. This caused the boy to loosen his grip on the weapon. Arab then stepped back from the gangbanger, taking the pistol with him.

The boy never had a chance to chamber a bullet so Arab quickly cocked the gun. The deadly metallic click echoed in the thug's ears, sending terror rushing through him. He tried to pull himself together and stand strong in the face of death but despite his best efforts, panic edged his consciousness.

"Please don't kill me," the boy pleaded.

"Don't kill you? Arab doesn't want to kill you," Insanity had once again taken control. "Arab wants information."

"B-b-but you just said you were going to kill—"

"Arab just need to know where to find Gorilla Leek. That's all. That's all. Then you can go. You can go. You can go . . ." his voice trailed off into a soothing sob, and then continued in a whisper, "and you can do whatever you need to do. Arab will not cremate you. Arab's word is his bond. Just help Arab. Okay then. Or just please help yourself. Don't make Arab do anything to you. Understood?"

The boy nervously nodded.

"Good. Now tell Arab where Gorilla Leek is."

"I don't know," the boy frightfully confessed. "We were just told to keep an eye on his wifey while she came back over here to collect some clothes."

"His wifey?" Arab glanced at the apartment building. "Where? In there?"

Another nervous nod. "Yeah, she's in there now. Packing some things."

"Who else is in there?"

The boy's eyes fell to the ground.

Arab leveled the gun to his head. "Who else?"

"Uh—well," he swallowed, trying to form more words. "Cutty's in there also."

"Cutty? In there?"

"Yeah—but he's dead."

"Dead?"

"Yeah. Leek had us cut up his body and dump it into a barrel of acid."

"Really? And no one else is in there?" Arab asked, with more than a hint of disbelief in his tone.

"No. No one else. I promise. I'm telling you the truth. Look I'll put you on to whatever I know. Ask me anything you want."

When Arab's lips parted to do just that, he felt his phone ring, vibrating in his pocket. With the gun still held on the teen, he wisped it out of his jacket and quickly answered it.

"Who this?"

"Arab," said the person on the other end, "it's Detective Brown. Where are you? We need to meet."

Arab glanced at his hostage and raised his chin, as if he wanted to say something. The teenager just stared at him helplessly.

"The Mighty Buck Brown," Arab announced. "You should know Arab dreads your phone call in the evenings."

"Yeah, yeah, yeah. Spare me the drama Arab," remarked Brown. "I am in your neighborhood and I need your help. Where are you?"

"Arab is everywhere at all times, detective. That's why Arab is nowhere to be found now."

Nerves danced in the boy's eyes upon hearing the word, *detective*.

"Ok. Whatever. Look, I got something for you if you can answer a few questions," Brown said, growing increasingly impatient with his CI.

"Arab's listening."

"I need to know if you know a young man in the streets named Shine, and whether or not he has some connection to Chinnah."

"Yeah, Arab knows Shine. He's a Blood. But Arab knows nothing of him having anything to do with Chinnah. Chinnah don't do business with Bloods."

"Yeah, yeah. I know he doesn't. But does he have any beef with them? Maybe over territory?"

Arab glanced once more at the teen to find him staring at the apartment building.

"Look detective, Arab has to go. Arab has some business to take care of. However, Arab did hear that Chinnah was sending henchmen to take care of a problem he had with a Blood named Gorilla Leek. You should send cars to his house before they get there."

"Gorilla who?"

"Sorry detective. Arab has to go."

"Wait! Gorilla who? How do I find him? Where does he li—"

"Bye, bye Buck Brown," Arab said, hanging up the phone before the detective could say another word. He immediately brought his attention back to his teenage hostage.

Interest flared in the boy's eyes. "Who are you?" the teenager asked, his voice trembling. "You a cop?"

A sinister grin parted Arab's blackened lips.

"What? You a snitch? A government agent or hitman or some shit? Who are you?" The boy tried to sound brave, but his tone betrayed his fear.

As he studied the thug's face, Arab's grin grew distant then faded from his lips, and something fierce crept into his expression. He opened his mouth into a cruel, predatory smirk as if he was preparing to utter a demonic chant.

The boy took notice and his blood ran icy in his veins, causing him to shake uncontrollably. His lips grimaced away from his teeth. But like an old soldier sensing his end, he gathered himself one last time and spoke up valiantly to again ask, "Who the—fuck—are you?"

"God," Arab calmly said as the gun in his hand erupted, sending a flaming bullet into the teenager's abdomen, "damn you." He fired once more, and another slug slammed into the collapsing, smoke-hazed red rag doll.

The boy inhaled a gasp of shock, his eyes widening as he fell onto his back. He looked up weakly at his attacker—his injuries clearly catching up with him—and struggled to speak in a whisper that sounded raw and painful.

"B—b—but you said your—your word was b—bond. You said you w—w—wouldn't kill mmm—"

"Arab gave you his word," said the crackhead as he knelt beside the boy. "But me—" Leaning over, he pressed the gun barrel to his head—"I didn't promise you a damn thing!" He pulled the trigger.

The single crack of the bullet eclipsed the thunder and reverberated through the night, startling Dina who was struggling mightily to tug a suitcase through the unlit hallway of her building. Upon hearing the gunshots, she dropped the luggage, pulled out her keys, and took a large step back. Never taking her eyes off the building's doorway, she inched back toward her apartment, then quickly spun around and unlocked the door. Glancing over her shoulders every few breaths, she squeezed through the opening and slid inside.

The apartment was pitch black and cold. The air was thick with the same stench that filled her nostrils when she first entered to pack. This time it oozed down the back of her throat. She felt the need to inhale deeply but was afraid it would make it impossible to hear if someone was sneaking up on her. A shaky breath escaped her lips as she nudged the door close. Pausing a moment to hear it click shut, Dina stood with her face pressed against the wall, listening intently for voices.

After a few seconds of nervous anticipation, the front door to the building creaked open loudly with a gritty scrape. The sudden sound of footsteps approaching could be heard. She struggled to remain calm as they pounded down closer and closer and closer before stopping right in front of the door to her apartment. Careful to make no sound, she eased backwards to the restroom just as the doorknob to her front door twisted violently. This caused her to pick up her pace.

The entrance to the bathroom was covered by a blood-speckled plastic strip curtain that hung from a shower rod. The door was missing. Barely able to see inside, she was warned by Gorilla Leek to stay clear of it. But with her heart thudding vigorously, instincts urged her to enter. Cautiously stepping through a gap in the plastic cover, she quickly retrieved her phone. It was the only light she had. The vile sickly sweetish odor of acid and burned flesh immediately caught her throat, and for a moment she was convulsed by an uncontrollable fit of coughing. Perhaps it was the sight of the floor tiles glazed black from dried blood. Or the meat-red, long flap of flesh dangling from the hacksaw that lay in between the blue oil drum and the bathtub. She abruptly lowered her phone.

Suddenly, the rattling noise of the doorknob stopped, and Dina could hardly hear anything but the unnervingly close sound of her own breathing. Remembering where to find Gorilla Leek's gun, she ran out of the bathroom and down the hall to the bedroom. With only a moment's hesitation she reached into the closet, found the pistol then pointed it into the darkness.

Slowly she stepped into the hallway, her hands shaking wildly and out of control. She started to continue forward but she heard something. Something loud and awful. It was the scream of metal grinding and wood splintering as the front door burst open, being kicked off its hinges. Panicking, she raked the shadows with random shots. Her whole body jerked at the noise of the discharge, and her finger seemed stuck to the trigger. She pulled it again and again and again and kept squeezing off rounds, the weapon barking in her hands until the gun's slide locked open on an empty chamber.

There was a noise; a half-uttered groan, and then the sound of a body falling. Dina heard nothing else. No movement. No pleads for help, no voice wailing in anguish—nothing. An uncertain silence lingered in the apartment. She took a cautious step forward, trying to feel her way through the dark without making a sound. Broken fragments of plaster and shattered pieces of wood shifted and crunched under her feet. The blackness was so complete she couldn't see more than a few inches in front of her face.

Once again, her phone became a dim flashlight as she raised it and held it in the direction of the front door. A mist of dust specks danced and floated upward in the pale, incandescent glow of her cell phone. The ghostly light revealed the broken rubble of the smashed door on the floor. She also saw bullet holes in the wall near the mangled hinges. Screws were scattered on the ground. There was sawdust everywhere. But no body. Nobody.

Scattered debris clung to her Jordans, and with every inch she moved, the apartment seemed to grow colder. Not sure what she was going to find on the other side, she held her breath and poked her head out the doorway into the darkness of the building's main hallway. Again, no body. Slowly, she eased out of the apartment and crept toward the front entrance of the building. With each step holding her foot firmly on the ground before trying to take another one, she trudged to the door and kept looking behind for the threat of instant death. Adrenaline coursed through her as she neared her escape. She reached out a shaking hand to turn the doorknob but jumped back in alarm when she heard footsteps outside racing up the stairs.

Then, without warning, a terribly loud, banging sound shook the door and overwhelmed her, causing her to drop her phone and the gun. A rush of fear ripped through her body. The banging from the outside continued, pounding. Fists, big ones rattling the door. Then a kick. Then nothing. Quiet. Dina stood still a moment, listening. The sudden silence set her heart beating wildly.

"Dina!" a familiar voice called from the other side of the door. "Dina. Open the door!"

She stood on her tiptoes and pressed her eye against the peephole. *Thank God!* It was Redrum staring back at her through the hole. Forcing down the panic, she took in a deep breath and relaxed. She was safe.

"Dina, open the door right now!"

With her hand on the doorknob, she yelled back, "Okay, okay. Hold on."

"Dina, hurry up! A crazy old crackhead just killed Rumble, Flames and Sinnin Blood. And he's in there with you now. Hurry up and get out!"

His words struck her as a desperate plea, stealing her breath. Time slowed down as the reality of his warning set in. Her mind told her to move forward but her feet wouldn't let her. She was confused. Was Redrum tricking her? Was he the one who kicked in her door? Was he trying to kill her? Her hands fell to the side and her eyes searched the ground for her phone. She needed to call Gorilla Leek right away. Backing away from the door, and shaking her head, she suddenly felt a presence at her back. A black hand reached out from behind her and clamped down hard over her mouth. The powerful grip smothered her scream as it pulled her into the darkness.

CHAPTER 16

BRIGHT WHITE BEAMS OF LIGHT flooded the heavily wooded section of Lincoln Terrace Park. They swayed back and forth, crisscrossing the leafy shadows, hoping to catch a glimpse of a body or a burial site. There were voices chattering and yelling, speaking fast, too fast to hear over the sound of several footsteps rustling through leaves. The faint *swish* of the wind along broad branches blended with whispers crackling weakly from walkie-talkies. Dogs panting with madness, too exhausted to bring in a scent, pulled on their leashes as their masters' coat sleeves bulged with muscles fighting to hold them back. Uniformed and plainclothes police were everywhere—more than fifty, active and alert under the skillful management of Detective Buckminster Brown—searching through the trees, the bushes, and the surrounding grounds of Dead Man's Hill.

While certain parts of New York City parks bore hollow, irrelevant titles, this one was aptly named. Aptly named, because during the 1980s—when the park served as the neighborhood's headquarters for prostitution and drug trafficking—Dead Man's Hill was the area where corpses were discovered nightly among unsightly rubbish heaps. However, during the early 1990s it became a gathering place for the neighborhood youth who would race their bikes down the wide winding slope, daring each other to go faster, further, and harder often with a certain thrilling degree of peril.

Now at four o'clock in the morning with the area flaring to a near blinding yellow, the hill resembled the stage at a Madison Square Garden concert, even though it was covered by an atmosphere of deathly despair. The woods seemed to radiate a sense of bitter suffering; the silent pleads of so many poor and incorrigible souls who had been so horribly murdered and whose ghosts had been unable to claim refuge. Memories of the dead were scattered everywhere along the dirt trails and among the black trash bags found every ten or so feet. The uniformed police searched through the garbage piles and the straggling, untrimmed shrubs with speechless loathing, hoping to discover the body of little Trayvon Bye.

Several plainclothes detectives stood around in various attitudes of interest. Hurried was their conversation—it was but a murmur of jungle sounds—a chaotic melody of heavy breathing, cursing, and grunting. At times the voices would grow faint, then louder again with mounting enthusiasm as someone would discover something of interest only to find out it was nothing. Hundreds of small plastic flags on wire rods marked potential evidence.

Detective Phillip Cardillo stood looking at the spectacle like he was in another dimension, almost forgetting he was in the middle of it. The hill would have been empty were it not for all of the police. His guess was that the crackheads had retreated into the darker reaches of the park—since they were nowhere else in sight. With a recessed scrutiny he observed his colleagues interact, as though he was relieved to play the background on the case.

Seidman and Brown were briefing the crime scene technicians who had been diligently working the area after discovering a gun buried there. So far, the information they received from the anonymous caller was correct. Now, if they could only find the body.

A fluttering line of yellow crime-scene tape ran between metal stakes sticking out of the soil. On the other side of it stood men and women dressed in white jumpsuits and wearing latex gloves. They were hovering over a portable digital field instrument, guiding the probe that was connected to it into the ground.

"What's that for?" Cardillo asked, nudging his chin in the direction of the device as he neared the group. "That chunk of metal there is going to tell us if a body is buried around here?" he added, taking the edge off his naivety.

The sound of his voice caught Brown's attention. The older detective momentarily turned away from his conversation, his eyes narrowing against the searchlights burning brightly in the distance behind his partner. "It's used to check the density of the soil to see if the dirt has been disturbed."

Cardillo's head nodded slightly. "Ohhh."

"If the body was buried around here, then the dirt would have been tampered with and weakened from the digging and refilling. I would be happy to explain to you in detail the process, but now is not the time."

"Okay," the young detective replied, his voice sinking into a whisper. "I guess I'll stay over here. You know—out of the way so as not to interfere with the professionals."

Cardillo's eyes felt heavy, tired, and ready to close. It was clear he had not slept in days. The case was wearing on his nerves and he now longed for his bed, his curtains shut, and his lights off. And he knew his partner could care less what the time was or where he wanted to be. It was going to be a long night even though daylight was right around the corner.

He started to ask Seidman a question when, suddenly, a loud growling noise came from deep within the woods, echoing along the hill. Then came barking. Loud, vicious barking.

The continued barking from the K-9 unit caught Brown's attention. He turned at the sound and began walking toward all the commotion. Seidman and Cardillo followed behind him leisurely, unable to see much beyond the bright lights.

Then someone yelled out, "We have decomp!"

Brown began jogging slowly along the hill with the two detectives at his heels. As they pushed through the bushes, the barking seemed to grow nearer. Within seconds all the dogs in the area became suddenly agitated and broke forth in loud barking as well.

"Wait!" Cardillo called out, in between barks, "Did he say decomp?"

With an instinctive glance over his shoulder, Brown answered, "Yep, looks like we have a body!"

♠ ♠ ♠

"YOUR BODY?"

"Yes, my body," replied Eden, averting her gaze from Shine who sat slumped next to her on the loveseat in the living room of her two-story home.

"I can hardly believe that unless they were blind, deaf, and dumb."

"Well it's true." Eden blushed. "I looked much different back then. And brothers used to clown me because of my body. I used to have the build of a teenage boy."

"Man, please. I bet they would be begging for your forgiveness if they could see you now."

Again, slightly blushing she replied, "Thank you. You're not too bad yourself."

Shine stared at her with interest, seeing out of the corner of his eye a floor-to-ceiling bookshelf packed to overflowing. Turning his head, he eyed some Edgar Allan Poe, Walter Mosley, Yosef Ben Jochannan, dozens of Shakespeare titles, Thomas Sowell, Ayn Rand, Josephus, a Black Law's Dictionary, the Talmud, and several books on spirituality. There were heaps of handwritten notes on legal-sized paper stacked wherever space permitted. Clearly Eden was well-read. To one side of the bookcase was a twenty-four-by-thirty-six-inch poster of a man standing by a window holding an automatic weapon—Malcolm X, Shine guessed.

Besides the bookshelf and poster, there was a traffic jam of Asian and African art holding up every wall. There were wooden masks, some with straw, and some without. Exotic fabrics were everywhere, hanging from the walls and spread out on the floor. One huge African Senufo mud cloth from the Ivory Coast displayed hyenas, snakes, and antelopes. Polished-stone sculptures added to the frenzy, some floor-sized, with the smaller ones competing with picture frames for room on a mahogany coffee table. It appeared she was obsessed with her ancestral roots, filling her living room with items collected from Oriental art peddlers who moved through black neighborhoods like gypsy merchants.

"So, you like African art, heh?" Shine was impressed by what he saw.

"Yeah. I am sort of a collector. We, as a people, have a very rich history. And I like to remind myself of that often."

"Remind yourself of your own history?" He gave her a confused grin.

"Yes. I didn't grow up knowing about how great our history was. And in this society, it is easy to forget what wasn't instilled in you as a child. So, the art serves as a reminder."

"Taking things on face value, I would've guessed that you've been talking like this for your whole life."

"Really?" A giggle tumbled out that sounded like naivety. "Me? No, I actually grew up in a predominately white neighborhood. And went to an all-white private school."

Shine's eyes ricocheted around the room. "Yeah right. With all of this blackness you got going on in this crib, you expect me to believe that?"

"Uh, well. It's the truth. I lived in Brownsville until I was about twelve. But then, my mummy moved us as far away as she could from my father without taking me out of Brooklyn. I ended up growing up in Bensonhurst until I left to go to school."

"Why didn't she want to be around your pops?"

"Well, they were never really together. Not to mention, he was heavily involved in the streets, and she wasn't ready to accept that lifestyle."

"Then why didn't she just leave Brooklyn altogether?"

"Because, my brother still lived here, and she didn't want to separate us."

He pursed his lips and nodded. "Makes sense," Seemingly curious, he tilted his head. "But then how did you get so pro-black growing up in all-white Bensonhurst?"

"I won't say that I am pro-black. I am pro-humanity."

"Ok. Whatever you want to call it. What made you become the person you are now?"

"I started reading up on our history after I went to college. You know, getting out of a familiar environment can sometimes expose you to different things. And for me it did." Her tone was low, her voice laced with pride. "It exposed me to a whole lot. And I started realizing that the country I was living in was built on a lie."

"How so?"

A sort of chaotic happiness covered her face like she'd been waiting years for him to ask that question. "Well, for one. America claims to be a country that supports and fights for freedom, while . . ."

Shine listened in a narcotic stupor as her voice drifted off into a despairing gripe. He could see the protest flaring in her eyes and noticed that her excited grin seemed belied by a deeper anxiety.

Eden realized he wasn't listening to her, so she raised her voice, an uncommon occurrence for her. "Dwight Mannschein," When she had his attention her voice softened again. "I hope you are hearing me. This country not only became wealthy from slavery, but it continues to benefit from it today. Like I was saying earlier in the club, there are private—"

"Hold on now," Hearing her speak with such conviction as if there was really anything she could to do change things made him a bit irritated. "Are you saying we are not living in the land of the free? Yeah right! This is the land of the free market! This country is about getting that money. If slavery didn't bring in doe, it wouldn't have been such a big deal over here." Shine swallowed bitterly, gritted his teeth and took a big breath. "We need to stop getting in our feelings over how these white boys went about feeding their families hundreds of years ago and start worrying about how we are going to feed ours today. When you're seeing profit, you don't have time to focus on losses. You feel me?"

There was something so dangerously passionate about his soapbox speech that it made Eden all the more drawn to him. "You know brother, I am actually hearing everything you're saying. And you're right. This is the land of the free market and it is all about getting money. But the way you, yourself, are going about getting it is all wrong. And someone somewhere is waiting to profit off of your mistakes."

"Yeah. I'm feeling you on all that. Well, at least now I am. But still. Even if I stopped hustling—I mean—I ain't got no college degree like you, and I ain't never worked a day in my life. Hustling's always been my ticket to the American Dream."

Teeth in her lower lip with concentration, Eden let out a deep sigh and played with the dreadlock in front of her ear. "There are more ways of getting doe than just hustling. You did graduate high school, right?"

"No."

"No?"

"No."

She raised an eyebrow. "Hmm. Then that's where we have to start."

"We?"

"Yes, we. I can help you look into getting your G.E.D. Then you can think about attending a community college for a couple of years.

After that, you can decide which route you want to go."

"I don't know if college is for me."

"Well, you say you are a hustler, then you shouldn't have a problem passing a business class. If you can cook crack, you can study chemistry. If you know how to push dope, then you know how to market a product. You could pursue a marketing major." She paused as if contemplating various possibilities. "Shoot, Danilo Blandon—the cocaine broker who was instrumental in introducing crack into the black community—had an MBA in marketing. And he made millions. You just have to put a degree behind your desire, and you can achieve so much more."

"Yeah but that's not going to feed me in the meantime. That stuff takes a minute to do."

"Anything worth anything takes time. You have to take small steps. Who cares if you get a menial job for now. Something small is better than nothing at all," she rambled excitedly. "Just get something by which you can feed, clothe, and shelter yourself. Set a goal and work toward it. Know where you are headed. Because if you can only think about the now, and not see the future then you are already doomed. Look ahead brother."

"Yeah, I guess you might be on to something. I just need some time to figure it out," emotion throbbed in his voice, "and plot my next steps. Because I have a lot on my plate right now."

Eden could see anguish in the violence around his eyes. Pain was there, and a sudden suspicion clutched at her gut. She could sense his uneasiness. His inner war played over his face—nostrils widening, teeth clenching as he stared at her. And she knew the reason for it. He was a killer. She could now see it clearly. But he was a killer with regrets.

"Look. I can tell you have much on your mind. But at your age, you still have time to change it all around. Get out of Brooklyn and become someone different. Do something else with your life," she pleaded.

Shine chuckled. "You're telling me to get out of Brooklyn, but you're here and I just met you. You have a way of making a dude feel wanted, you know."

His words gave an impression of humiliation. But she knew he wasn't being serious. The thought sent a giggle to her lips.

"Whatever," She reached over and tenderly slapped his thigh.

"Now you should know I am not trying to run you away after inviting you into my house for a snack at three o'clock in the morning. But what good is it getting to know each other if you might get locked up or shot up the next day?"

"I guess you're right, but—uh— as far as inviting me over at three in the morn, it seems like you had to. Seeing how I spent my money on you and drove you home." He grinned at the warmth creeping into her eyes. "I'm saying, you had me order all that food, and you didn't eat any of it."

They both laughed.

"Uh, had I known you were taking me to a place where they cooked everything in pork, I would have suggested that you come to my house and let me hook up something for you instead. And yes brother, I did invite you in because I felt bad for having to send all of that grub back. I knew you were hungry, but I could smell that swine grease as soon as they brought out our plates and it ruined my appetite," She narrowed her eyes. "Besides you seemed to like what I cooked for you any ole way."

He licked his lips with exaggeration. "That indeed is the truth. Those eggs with the peppers and onions were banging."

With a chuckle in her voice Eden replied, "Those weren't eggs, king. It was tofu you were eating."

"Tofu? What's that?"

"Good is what it is."

"Huh?"

"You know about hummus but not tofu?"

"Tofu? Is that some type of martial arts? Like Kung Fu?"

"Are you being serious right now?"

"Ooh I see. Is that the stuff that pro-black activists eat?" A laugh rumbled in his chest. "What? Animal blood make you too violent? If we stop eating beef, we will stop all of our beefing? Is that what it is?"

"Ha, ha, ha. You're a comedian I see," her tone was patronizing and tinged with sarcasm. "However, you should be aware of what you put into your temple though. I mean, you do know that you are what you eat, right?"

Shine's eyebrow shot up in mock astonishment and his head jerked back. "Are you telling me that you're a cannibal?"

"What?"

"You're a cannibal!"

"Me? No, I'm—"

"You're a cannibal. You just said you are what you eat. And you're a human. So, you must be a cannibal."

Her face twisted into a bitter smirk. "Really? I see you're on a roll with the jokes tonight. Maybe that can be your alternative to selling drugs. You might have a future in show business."

There was a twitch of amusement teasing at his lips. "Na, I don't think I'll respond well to people laughing at me."

Again, they both chuckled.

The warm inviting melody of his laugh made her feel as if she had known him all her life. Yet, a nagging worry had sunk into the pit of her stomach. He was insanely handsome, but he was dangerous. Something didn't feel right.

Was it her conscious?

It definitely wasn't her body as she could feel the desire churning around inside her. Of course, there was a part of her that wanted it—wanted him. But she was also worried about the trouble he would bring into her world. Having avoided thugs most her life, she was both concerned and curious about the man next to her. During her time of traversing different continents, living in white suburbia, working in the ghettoes of Brooklyn, and attending both Howard University and NYU, curiosity had become an unlikely visitor. This feeling of attraction was new to her.

She hadn't concerned herself with men as much. She had been viciously single-minded and ruthlessly focused on her education and building her career. Dating would have proved a great distraction had she not vowed to stay clear of any romantic entanglements. But the man seated on her loveseat at that moment had the face and body of every bad-boy fantasy she'd ever had. Tonight, she wasn't interested in the good intelligent Dwight, and she wasn't interested in being levelheaded Eden. She had been too well behaved for all of her life.

Suddenly she felt vulnerable, exposed. Without all the little self-imposed rules that stood as protective walls around her, there was nothing to keep her safe. Nothing to thwart his silent charming advances and dismantle his masculine gaze. That thought made her feel skittish. Made her quiver. She lived her life according to such a rigid set of standards that it often frustrated—and at times amazed—those around her. She weighed every option, considered every consequence. Rationalized and nitpicked things to death. And her conservative approach to life was never more evident than in her attitude toward sexual intimacy.

Sex by itself meant little more to her than the satisfying of an appetite. She needed more. She always expected more. But tonight, all that she desired was Shine. In him, at this moment, she saw everything she needed, everything she expected.

As she watched him laugh, she couldn't remove her gaze from him. Her body was ready, and she was about to slide herself closer to him when his phone went off, shoving reality into her face.

Shine reached for the cell phone that sat on the coffee table in front of him and picked it up. When he finally managed to answer it, he heard a voice say, "Dina's dead!" It was Redrum.

Shine listened gravely without a smile or any particular sign of interest. Eden could hear Redrum's voice through the phone—Dina was found with her neck snapped in the hallway of a building. She wondered if Dina was the girl who caused the commotion in the club earlier. But she quickly dismissed the idea after studying Shine's changing expression and realizing that he was very dismayed by the news. This was a person he cared about.

Shine drew a deep, calming breath, then stood up. He chewed the inside of his cheek and tried to think. Turning down the volume on his phone so as to keep Eden from hearing the full conversation, he said, "Ok, ok. Chill out son. And no one has seen or heard from Gorilla Leek?"

"No." Redrum's answer was clipped, but even in that one brief reply, Shine could hear the strain in his voice.

"So, he doesn't even know what happened yet? This doesn't make sense. Where the hell is son?"

"I tried hitting him up mad times. But nothing. No call-back. Nothing," replied Redrum.

"And this cat just came out of nowhere asking questions about Leek before he started taking niggas off?"

"Pretty much. He asked about Gorilla Leek, but he was also looking for Cutty."

"What!" Shine's eyes involuntarily glanced sideways toward Eden. "Does he know what happened to him?" His question was almost whispered, the words uttered quickly, as if he was worried he might not get it out if he didn't hurry. "You think the old man sent him?"

Redrum knew he was referring to Chinnah. "Not sure. But I don't think so," he paused as if considering his next words carefully. His tone grew more serious; his voice suddenly dropping to a low hoarse murmur as he continued, "Yo Shine man, I heard the nigga talking to a pig on the phone right before he shot Rumble."

"Huh?" Shine's eyebrow went up. "How'd you know it was a cop he was talking to?" he sounded intrigued.

"He referred to him as detective and called him Almighty Buck Brown. I think he's the one who sent him there looking for Gorilla Leek and Cutty. He also mentioned your name."

Overwhelmed by surprise and worry, a mass of concerns began bouncing around in Shine's head. With his mind racing in every direction trying to answer all the why, how, and what if questions, he thought back to his interaction with Detective Brown at the precinct. *Maybe he didn't believe me after all and decided to look into me. But how would he know about Cutty?* He knew it didn't make sense, not even to himself, so how could it make sense to Redrum—a cop sending a goon to Gorilla Leek's house. The only person who would have an interest in looking for Cutty and Gorilla Leek would be Chinnah.

Then in a moment his eyes shot open wide, filled with shock as if he just received an epiphany. *What if detective Buck Brown works for Chinnah?*

"Yo, are you sure that dude was talking to a cop named Buck Brown?" Shine asked.

"Positive." Redrum gave another one-word reply.

What was the connection between Detective Brown and the Gully Gods? It wasn't simply a coincidence. There was something more, and Shine couldn't put his finger on it. But he also couldn't, for a second, entertain the notion that the police and his enemy were conspiring against him. Not before he found out whether or not his woman and his best friend had betrayed him. Then there was a flashing thought.

"So, what the hell were you doing when all of this was going down? How did you get to see everything and you're the only on left breathing?" he screamed into the phone.

Redrum took a deep breath, deep enough that Shine could hear it over the phone, then said, "I—I—was trying to—"

"Forget it. I don't want to hear it," Shine interrupted. "I ain't got time to listen to your shook-ass story. All I really give a damn about right now is Gorilla Leek's whereabouts."

"Yeah but Rumble, Sinnin Blood, and—"

"Man save it," Shine interrupted once more. "Niggas die every day. We can get some get-back later. But before we find the cat who did this, we need to find Gorilla Leek. You feel me?"

Redrum refrained from replying.

"Blood, go and look for son. We need to have a 9-1-1," Shine continued. "We got too much going on right now for him to be doing a disappearing act." He paused for a very long time and peered out from under his raised eyebrow at Eden as if carefully weighing his next words, then reluctantly commanded, "Go by my crib and see if he's there. He might be with Lola. Ten-ten."

Without saying anything else, he hung up the phone and placed it back on the table. His head snaked around to Eden, a teasing grin covering his face. It was an effortless grin, somewhat apologetic. Despite the pleasant evening he anticipated having with her and the insane amount of liquor he consumed at the club earlier, he still couldn't shake his thoughts.

Could Desiree be right? Was Lola cheating on him with his best-friend?

"Is everything okay?" Eden's lips pressed together, as if she didn't want to let her next words out. "Do you have to leave?"

His lips parted reluctantly, "Yeah, I should go. I have to handle some business."

"At this time of night?" She stood up. "I thought you agreed to leave that life alone." She moved closer to him and stopped in front of him, staring at him, frowning.

Shine felt her nearness to him, he felt the warmth of her breath against his neck, and he felt her losing her self-control. She placed her hand on his chest, feeling the hardness of his muscle stiffen at her touch. His heart was pounding.

Looking up into his eyes, she demanded, "Stay—please stay—stay with me for the night. It may just save your life."

Her hands framed his face and tilted his mouth down. He started to protest, but she raised her chin up, placing her lips over his in a kiss that compelled him to remain silent. Both of their tongues thirstily searched out each other's while her thumbs feathered over his strong cheekbones. Barely able to breath, she kissed him over and over again, refusing to pull away. The deeper she thrust her tongue, the more he pressed his body against hers, snaking his arms around her waist. Drawing her into his embrace and crushing her against his chest, he held her tightly.

The delicate feel of her body was yielding in his arms. Her weight lay gentle and warm against him. The salt of her skin along with the light floral-sweet scent of her locks was in his nostrils, causing his heartbeat to roar in his ears. Breath mingling with breath, the passion heightened until Eden pulled back, and rested her forehead against his chest to allow her racing heart to slow down. When she felt in control again, she smiled up at him then took his hand in hers and led him into her bedroom without saying a word.

The room was quite dark, yet he could see well enough by the light of the street lamps that filtered in through the curtains. Everything was a jumbled mess, with covers thrown back on the bed, the corners cluttered with books, and clothes strewn across the floor. Underneath Eden's veneer of discipline and control ran a torrent of disorganized, chaotic passion. It made him like her even more.

As they neared her bed, she gave him a shove that sent him sprawling backward across it. Lying flat on his back, he watched while she stripped off her short black dress and the black G-string beneath it, and her black silky bra. There was nothing rushed in her strip tease. She was slow and deliberate in her movement, her eyes never leaving his, acknowledging his hunger for her.

He dragged his eyes from her beautiful face to every delicious curve of her naked body. His gaze slid over her round, full breasts to her narrow waist and flaring hips, then lower still until lust darkened his stare and his breath suddenly quickened—she was smooth and completely shaven. Her vagina looked like a plump, ripe brown peach. Like it had never been touched.

She slowly crawled up on the bed, painstakingly slowly, and crept like a black panther toward him, with her back arched and her heart-shaped ass sticking high up in the air. Desire guided her fingers to trace the hard ridge along the zipper of his pants before working his belt out of the buckle. She pulled at his clothes until buttons and the zipper finally gave—removing his shirt and undergarments. Then clutching his hard, sculpted biceps, she straddled him, her fingers digging into his arms as he kicked his pants off the rest of the way. They were both naked.

Eden looked down and could see his long and veined penis jutting out from his pelvic area. She stretched her arm beneath her thighs and gripped it tightly in one hand, her fingertips failing to meet. She caressed his shaft in slow, rhythmic strokes, watching it swell. Her fingers tightened as it grew even larger in her hand. Sliding along him and making him moan from the sensation, she smiled when his head fell back on the bed and air exploded from his lungs.

"Shit," his words came out in a thin whisper.

Reaching up, he swept her locks back behind one of her ears, then cupped her cheeks with his palms and pulled her down to kiss her. She gasped, but he kept kissing her while sliding his hand along her thigh, dipping it into her wetness. Her breath deepened as thick fingers curled up inside her vagina, caressing her G-spot. She felt his knuckles against her folds. His thumb found her clit and rubbed the little bundle of nerves without mercy while a finger on his other hand slid into her ass. Eden panted and kissed him back. Passionately. Hard.

Soft whimpers fell from her lips and her eyelids fluttered before drifting shut. It felt good. Too damn good.

Then her eyes shot open and she moaned in protest when his fingers left her. With all her longing unleashed in the way she looked at him, she raised her ass up, squeezed his hips with her knees and eased herself down onto his blood-pounding penis. She could feel her delicate channel clenching tightly as his bulbous tip slowly slid inch by inch into her moist depths. Her eyes closed once more as he drove his hips upward, completely filling her. She began to grind, taking her time at first to feel all of him moving in and out of her. Squeezing the muscles of her vagina and grabbing his manhood, she held it and then slowly let it go. The pleasure started to intensify as her contractions gripped him.

He felt her shifting her hips and stirring, so he began pushing harder, faster, until with a groan he rolled her onto her back, moved on top of her and took charge. His hands cupped her firm ass, and he drove and drove his massive, stiff dick into her, feeling her heave and strain upwards to meet his rigorous thrusts. She held onto the bedsheets for dear life as the pressure inside her built with every stroke of his cock.

Hooking her legs over his shoulders, he raised her ass off the bed so only her head and shoulders were touching it. His rapid pace sent her breast wobbling each time his pelvic bone slammed against her clit. Bouts of warm juice squished out of her tight slit. She trembled at the feel of him stretching her—her vaginal walls quivering as an electrifying orgasm hit her in waves. An explosion of colors flashed behind her eyes. Madness seized her, her thighs shaking, her pussy flooding his shaft with hot juices.

Then, suddenly, his penis erupted.

Feeling his manhood exploding and jerking in spasms inside her, she threw her legs tightly around his waist and urged him on with a violent writhing, arching her back to meet his driving penetration. Bursts of semen shot in her so hard she could feel every pulse of his blood-swollen tip. His hot, sticky wetness overflowed her milking cunt and dribbled down the crevice of her ass, as he slowed his pace, moaning and gasping. With a grunt of satisfaction, he rolled off her and onto his back. Side by side, they lay there in silence staring up at the ceiling.

Eden melted into the bed. She'd never felt so much pleasure with a man, never had an orgasm like that—and never had it happened so fast. Her sense of self seemed to belong to her body, while her consciousness was possessed only by her guilt. Her thoughts crossed deep into the mind of the person she once was, before having allowed Shine to enter her home. The bliss she was experiencing had left her feeling ashamed.

As he traced his finger along her jaw, she silently cursed herself for not using protection and giving into him so soon. She shivered slightly when he turned her chin to gaze into her face. It was impossible for her not to lose herself around him, enjoying the feel of him against her skin. Everything about Shine was stern and serious, masculine. But those eyes—they were so piercing—yet soft and beautiful.

"Now I definitely have a reason to change my life," he said, resting his forehead against hers.

"I hope so," she replied sleepily, her voice low and hoarse.

She started to doze off but was woken by the sound of a phone ringing in the other room.

"That's my cell," he said.

He rose from the bed and walked quietly into the living room. She watched his upright and powerful back, taut buttocks and thick thighs—thighs carved with muscle—as he disappeared into the darkness.

The phone vibrated across the coffee table in the middle of the living room, lighting up the ceiling above it. Sweat cascaded down Shine's neck when he picked it up and saw the name. His nervous eyes darted as indecision gripped him. Not daring to believe who it was, he placed the phone back down on the table and stared at it, waiting for it to stop ringing. It felt like minutes before the name disappeared and a black screen appeared, along with the message, *Missed Call*.

Willing his heart to return to a normal beat, he made his way back toward the bedroom. Just as he was about to call out to Eden to see if she was still awake, the phone went off once more. He turned around almost instantly, and marched back to the table. Unnerving curiosity made him reach for it again. *Why would he be calling so late? It must be something bad*, he thought to himself before he took a deep breath and answered.

"Yes?"

"Dwight Mannschein?"

"Yes."

"It's Detective Brown. I need to speak with you in person right away. Can you come down to the station?"

"Uh, for what? It's almost five in the morning. Can this wait a couple of hours?" It made Shine nervous, not knowing what the detective had in store for him. Really nervous. Perhaps Brown was indeed working with Chinnah.

"No, it can't wait," replied Brown. "This is important. I need you to meet me at the station now. There is something we need to discuss regarding Trayvon."

His heart thudded to a dead stop and his stomach tightened at the mention of his son's name.

"Trayvon? What about him?" Fear gripped him. *Could he know? Could he have found out?* Shine thought wildly. "Look detective. Whatever it is—if it's so urgent—why can't we just discuss it now, over the phone? I'm saying, we're talking about my boy here. I really rather not wait until I get down to the precinct to find out what's going on. You feel me?"

There was a long pause.

Shine listened, waiting for a reply. Unsure of what to say, he continued waiting.

Brown didn't utter a single word, but Shine knew he was still on the line. He could hear him breathing. His mind raced, and his heart panicked at the prospect of what the detective would say next.

He was about to ask Brown the same question once again. But then, in a quiet voice, the detective spoke, "Mr. Mannschein. We know what happened to Trayvon."

CHAPTER 17

"**T**HE INNER ME IS THE ENEMY**—the inner me is the enemy—the inner me is the enemy—the inner me . . ." Arab had no idea how long he'd been loitering in Shine's living room, repeating that chant. He was sitting Indian style in the middle of the floor leaning on his hands, waiting numbly. After several minutes, he fell silent and looked at his cell phone. Of course, it could be some time before Shine arrived home from the club. But it was almost seven o'clock in the morning. Tilden Ballroom had been closed for a couple of hours. And who knows if that was where he'd really been all night. There was no reason to believe that Dina had been honest with him. But he did see the truth in her eyes. And she was prepared to tell him all she knew just to save her life.

At first, she had given him cryptic answers concerning the whereabouts of Gorilla Leek. However, sensing his roiling emotion, she quickly told him about the party at Tilden Ballroom—that both he and Shine would be there. Yet it wasn't a place where he could blend in. So, it wasn't the place to commit a murder. Too many people.

Just before Dina took her last breath, Arab was able to strangle Shine's address out of her. That was all that he needed. Now he only had to be patient and wait. The prey would eventually return to its nest.

Once he had Shine, Gorilla Leek wouldn't be too hard to find. With luck, the police would pick him up to grill him with questions about his girlfriend's death and the dead gang-members they found in front of his building. It was as if mentioning his name to Detective Brown was equivalent to conjuring up the man himself. He calculated that once the police got a hold of Gorilla Leek, it wouldn't be long before the detective would reach back out to him for any information he had on the Blood gang leader. Then he would know where to find him. And he would only need to follow his victim from there.

Noticing family photos on the wall, Arab checked his phone again, then got up and crossed the room. He could only imagine the manner of man he was about to encounter. The pictures would offer a hint.

He stopped in front of a framed crayon drawing that Trayvon had made of three crude stick figures seemingly holding hands. There were no dots for eyes, no curves for smiles or frowns. Just empty circles for the heads and staggered lines for the limbs. He felt certain the art was the work of a toddler. It was supposed to be a depiction of the child holding his parents' hands—both of whom he was unfortunately there to kill. For some reason the drawing disturbed him. The idea of leaving a kid without any parental support in a world overrun by maddened beasts seemed to be an awful sacrilege to him. But it wouldn't be his fault. This was the result of the parents' bad decisions. So why should he feel any regret or remorse?

He shook the thought away, disappointed that he'd allowed himself to be so easily distracted, and quickly shifted his gaze to the next pictures. One image drew his interest, and he zeroed in on it.

Now here was a sight worth seeing.

It was Shine and Lola holding hands, laughing as they shared some private joke. In the photo Shine looked normal. He appeared to be so innocent, wearing a sly grin, posing like he was on the cover of an R&B album. He didn't have a worry etched into his face, unlike most of Arab's victims. In the picture, he was not yet a daddy; his son would be born to the lady standing next to him. The couple seemed happy. He wondered if that was still the case.

From outside, the wind wailed like a thing demented and blew a tree branch against the living room window, begging his attention. Cautiously, he turned around and walked over to the window and peered through the curtains. The street below was deserted. There were no signs of life except for the plodding stride of one young lady traveling alone. For a moment, her eyes—perhaps drawn to the motion in the window—looked up. Arab recognized her. The face was a bit older, of course. But he recognized it sure enough. The same face he'd just seen in the photo on the wall. It was Shine's girlfriend. And she was preparing to walk into the building and head upstairs.

Lola had, for just a moment, let her defenses down as she strolled along the sidewalk, swinging her Chanel bag. Earlier that morning, she'd decided to leave the apartment and eat breakfast at *Soldier's Restaurant*, so she could sit down and think things over. Detective Brown's words kept running through her mind—she was in danger. She knew she had to tell someone what was going on or she was going to explode. Protecting Shine wasn't an option any longer, because he was now in no position to protect her. She wondered whether she would see him again. She didn't want to.

As she neared her building, it dawned on her that he might be inside their apartment. Quickly, her eyes shot up from the ground to her second-floor window, expecting to see the light on if he was home. The windows were curtained. And despite the strong morning wind, the sun was shining so brightly that the glare made it difficult to see anything. Even so, she would still follow through on her plans. She calculated it would be the early afternoon before he returned from the club, by which time she would be gone. He never came straight home after a night of partying.

Ice-edged wind whipped her hair around her face as she retrieved her keys and dragged her tired body up the stairs, legs trembling with the effort. The harsh gust of air bit into her skin, and her numb fingers ached from gripping her cold keys. With her hand shaking, she slipped the key into the lock, turned it, and pushed the door open.

Welcoming the warmth of the building, Lola quickly closed the door behind her so as not to let any of the heat escape. Opposite of the entrance she had just come through was another door which creaked as it opened, revealing a badly lit hallway. She walked cautiously into the corridor.

Step by step, and a bit awkwardly, she crept forward and soon reached the bottom of the staircase. Her foot was on the first step, when a flash of light issued suddenly from the second floor. Glancing up, she stood still for an instant, reluctant to move another inch. There was the slam of a door then dimness again, and a quick patter of feet above her head. Her breath caught in her throat. She tensed momentarily as she recalled the detective's words once more.

The footsteps were at the top of the stairs. They came closer. They were on the stairway, descending slowly.

Thump. Click. Thump. Clack.

Closer. Almost on top of her now.

Sensing that there was untold trouble waiting to be dealt with, she blinked, trying to force her eyes to quickly adjust to the dim lighting. At once, her attention was held by the sight of a little girl—all primped and prettied up in pigtails and a puffy pink winter coat—prancing proudly out of the darkness. The small wedge heels of the girl's black patent leather dress shoes tapped their way down the staircase toward her. Her mother was behind her panting, trying to keep up and not having much luck. Lola watched both of them fly past her and out the door. The sight took an edge off of her nerves. They seemed to be prospective tenants checking out a unit. She continued up the stairs.

Without warning, a dread came over her—an unpleasant, sinking feeling. She had to get away from all of this or she would eventually lose her freedom, or at worst—her life. A sharp stab of regret pierced her heart. She thought back to the phone call she made earlier that morning. This was the way it had to be. She knew that, and it troubled her. Her feelings for Shine were the most complicated part of their history, yet this sentence in the story of her life needed a period at the end of it. There was a time when she had loved him, but now she loathed him. Her ties to him had been severed, and the few things she'd possessed when she first arrived in New York were all that she was there to collect.

No more than a few hours ago, she had spoken with her mother, revealing to her everything that had happened—Trayvon's death, the murder Shine committed, the pregnancy—everything. She'd been left with no money and a boyfriend who would've been on his way to prison had she not lied to the police at first.

Her mother quickly purchased an airline ticket for her, insisting she had no choice but to come back to Georgia. The flight was scheduled to depart that evening. However, getting to the airport would prove to be a challenge. If she asked Shine to take her, he would try to stop her from leaving or, worse, kill her. And although she'd left a goodbye message on Desiree's voicemail, involving her was out of the question. Public transportation would have to do.

She felt like she had spent the entire night and every minute of the morning planning her escape. She had to believe it would work, that she would get back to Georgia safely and somehow find her way back to her mother. But now came the risky part. If Shine was in the apartment, she'd have a problem on her hands.

For one brief moment, she considered forgetting about her belongings and turning around. Just as she stopped on the last step to catch her breath, a thought struck her. She recalled the anguish of seeing her son's lifeless body on their living room floor. Guilt gnawed at her then and she still felt it now, the sorrow of knowing that she lost a child because she made a bad decision in men. She really missed her son. He was a vital part of who she was. And the few things she had left in the apartment would only serve as a reminder of what she could have been. Maybe coming back was a mistake.

Imagine that. Her making another mistake.

Maybe it would've been safer to hit the road, put Brooklyn behind her. Maybe—just maybe, if she turned around now, she could board an earlier flight. Why risk running into Shine when she already had what she needed inside her womb? There was nothing left to hold on to, nothing but meaningless belongings to anchor her in the painful memories of the past. A past she'd soon forget once her plane was in the air.

A thousand thoughts rushed through her head. A thousand choices. She glanced over her shoulders at the door she'd just entered, unsure if she should proceed to the apartment. Unsure if she shouldn't. Unsure if she even needed to. Besides, without any luggage it would be easy to navigate through the airport.

Yet, the little pocket-change she had wouldn't last long. And she had plans—big plans. Plans to change her life for good. With the money Shine had stashed in their bedroom, Lola could live a comfortable life in Georgia, get a nice apartment in Atlanta, and maybe find a man who would love her and her unborn child. She leaned against the wall and held her breath, contemplating a life without Shine or even Gorilla Leek. Her thoughts whirled in wild spirals of indecision.

"Girl you need that money," she whispered to herself so quietly it was more of an exhale than a statement. "Get a hold of yourself."

She wasn't going to lose it just yet, she told herself. She hadn't lost it up until this moment, and she wasn't going to start now. She knew what she had to do, and she could not turn around. She'd made the decision the moment she dialed 9-1-1 and told the police where to find

Trayvon's body.

Continuing forward, Lola shuffled through the hallway towards her apartment. Four strides took her to the door. She approached it warily and seized the handle. It was already slightly open, about two or three inches.

Shit! Shine must be home, she thought.

As if uncertain whether to enter or not, she hesitated a moment. Somehow, she was going to have to sneak the money out without him noticing. Icicles ripped through her nerves and scattered out from her spine. Then, flicking her gaze over the darkened hallway behind her, she decided to get it over with—she'd already psyched herself up to do so on her way up the stairs—and she'd planned to waste no more time thinking about it.

"Fuck it," she said aloud to herself. "You have to do this."

Even before she pushed the door open, she knew something wasn't right. Daylight from the living room spilled into hallway. She peered through the slight opening just as the figure of a man passed by. The footsteps stopped behind the door. She caught a faint whiff of something foul and sniffed again, thinking her nose was playing a trick on her. But there was no mistaking the horrible lingering odor of shit.

"Shine?" she called out.

No answer.

Then muffled footsteps across the living room carpet.

Silence again.

"Shine? What's that smell?"

Footsteps again. Light footsteps, not heavy enough to make out how close they were.

"Shine is that you?"

Then heavy footsteps stamped toward her.

The door flew open.

Raw fear for her unborn child's safety churned in her belly as a large black hand reached out and seized her arm, violently yanking her inside. Her panic-stricken scream reverberated down the stairwell, flooding through the door after it slammed shut behind her.

♠ ♠ ♠

INSIDE HER APARTMENT, DESIREE sat alone on her

couch bristling with hostility, her voice hysterically shrill and bitter as she screamed aloud, "Who the hell he thinks he is? Throw me out the club? Yeah, ok. We about to see what's really good. I promise that!"

Lazy ringlets of smoke rose from the card table in front of her. She snorted and leaned forward to snag a smoldering blunt from the ashtray stationed on it. Falling back against the couch, she took a drag, and exhaled a lungful of smoke, fogging her vision. Through heavy lidded eyes, her gaze took in her miserable surroundings—the disheveled couch, the lightbulb hanging from an exposed wire in the ceiling, the ashtray overflowing with marijuana roaches, the card table littered with scraps of torn Yellow Book pages, old lottery tickets, and a couple of TV remotes. It was all too depressing. From the looks of her living conditions, she needed money, badly. That's why she'd been confident enough to blackmail Shine. Not because she was greedy, but because she was poor. She'd been living in that building with her grandmother since her father's death.

After graduating from high school, she applied for Section 8 and used it to get a one-bedroom unit on the same floor. Now, having lived there forever, she'd grown tired of the untidy and ill-ventilated apartment—the clatter of water pipes, the strong smell of sewage fungal slime, the noise of teenagers who passed their days listlessly loitering in the hallway outside of her door. She was ready to leave it all behind.

The mid-morning sun drifted through a tattered curtain and cast dancing shadows on her dirty and paint-chipped walls, bringing a fleeing measure of luster to her otherwise bleak existence. Nature was teasing her. Taking notice of it, she hissed through her teeth.

"To hell with Shine! He needs me more than I need him," she yelled, lacing each word with faint wisps of weed smoke.

She took another drag then laughed out loud at how little she knew herself. Of course, she needed Shine more than he needed her. A long, hazy greyish cloud seeped through her nostrils. Since she first met him, she wanted him for herself, and not just to torment Lola. She just wanted him. That was all. Maybe she really didn't know what she wanted aside from what she thought she couldn't have. Because she always got what she wanted.

From the time she was a teenager, she'd been haunted by a lingering fear that she wasn't pretty enough to keep a man. So, she forever found ways to trap them with everything she did and said. And once she lost interest in them, she would set them free. She expected it would be no different with Shine. How wrong had she been? What he'd said to her in the club hurt her. And the venom in his eyes emphasized exactly what he thought about her.

Whore.

Beneath his sharp words, all she could hear was—*whore.*

Until now—until not too long ago at least—she'd always thought of being a whore as being free. No one could control her—she could come and go as she pleased. Sleeping with other women's men had been her badge of independence. No one loved her, and she loved no one. Only recently did she clearly see how wrong that was. How alone she would end up. But given her life, she believed it was too late to do anything about it. That is, until Trayvon died.

The only thing that tied Shine to Lola was their son. And not only was he no longer alive, but Lola had left her a voicemail saying she was preparing to flee the state. Now Desiree could have what she wanted most—her own nigga, a home with that nigga, and a hustler's lifestyle that would establish her as one of the baddest bitches in the Nineties. Yes, it was her time to shine.

She was so preoccupied with the chaos tumbling through her brain that she scarcely noticed the knob to her front door being slowly turned from the outside. Suddenly, her nerves were shattered by the violent pounding of a fist thudding against the door, rattling its hinges. She nearly rocketed off the couch as the hammering continued, shaking the apartment. The door appeared in danger of being knocked from its frame. Then the banging stopped.

Desiree stood motionless, barely able to breathe. Her throat went dry. She waited, hoping that whoever was on the other side had left. Then the knob turned once more, and an attempt was made to thrust open the door. It did not yield.

A sudden crash. A shotgun sound of boots against the door.

Each kick throbbed in her temples as a murderous pulse, a heartbeat of death.

A loud, imposing voice boomed from the other side, "Open the damn door! You Triple 9 bitch!"

As soon as she heard those words, Desiree knew right away who it was. She ran to the door, unlocking it quickly. Having little choice but to give way, she stood aside and watched the door swing open. Shine shoved his way past her and into the apartment. He pulled the door shut.

There was a great silence, broken only by his footsteps as he scoured the apartment. Desiree watched the lights go on in the rooms, one by one, and he appeared then disappeared for a moment, passing through each entrance and then out again. She stayed out of sight while her eyes followed him around. After searching the entire apartment, he came back into the living room and stood stiffly right in front of her, his eyes wide. She could smell the weed on his breath.

"Bitch, you went to the pigs?"

A storm of emotions raged across her face. Surprise. Confusion. Fear. "Huh?" was all she could say.

"You went to the scramz!" He hissed through his teeth.

"Went to the police? About what?" she asked innocently. Too innocently. He could hear the edge in her voice.

"Look, don't bullshit me!" Spit exploded from his mouth.

"What? You think I snitched bout Trayvon? Na, I didn't go to no one. I promise." The breath that stuttered out of her gaping mouth almost sounded like begging.

He wasn't buying the sudden softness of her tone, his eyebrows snapping down to frame the anger in his stare. "That detective dude who stepped to you and Lola called me. They found Trayvon's body." Feet planted wide, he whipped out his pistol, "You are going to tell me everything you said to the scramz. I'm saying—everything."

Terror stricken at the sight of the gun, her mind saw only one choice. Comply. The ash from her blunt broke and drifted to the floor as her hand trembled uncontrollably.

"I swear, Shine, I ain't said shit to no scramz. You know I'm air tight. Always, forever," she pleaded.

He put the gun to her forehead and demanded, "Tell me what they know or I'm going to blow a hole through your fuckin' skull!"

She started crying, and in between sobs she screeched her pleas. "Listen—listen—I promise Shine. I ain't say nothing. You have to believe me. I came straight home after I left the club. I'm telling you the truth! Please!"

"So how did they know where to look for the body? And the gun?"

Her shoulders convulsed with each pathetic cry—great, gulping sobs that almost choked her when she went to speak. "Shine, you have to believe me. The only person I can think of—I mean—who actually knew—is the person who first told me."

"Really? And who's that?" he asked, disbelief coloring his tone.

Immediately her whimpering stopped, and huge bleak eyes stared up at him in fear. "Lola. Lola is the one who told me everything, and Gorilla Leek's the one who told her."

The edge of his mouth dipped as a pained expression covered his face. "Lola?"

Suddenly, the pistol felt clumsy in his hands, and something deep inside his chest tugged at his heart. He glanced to the ground, perplexed and out of sorts. Lowering his gun to his side, he asked, "You think Lola went to the police?"

Relaxing a bit, she said, "I dunno. I just know I didn't go."

"Why would she go to the police? I mean, we could both get locked." He sounded helpless, broken, at a loss without the loyalty of his woman and his best friend.

Desiree struggled to think of something to say. After a moment, she simply shrugged her shoulders and mumbled, "Maybe because she's pregnant."

Shine looked up, blinking his eyes in surprise. "Pregnant?"

"Yeah, she just found out yesterday," she replied matter-of-factly.

His face relaxed into a mask of tragedy, humiliation.

"By who, me?"

"Well," she hesitated, just long enough to make him think she was contemplating her answer, "she's not sure if it's yours or Leek's. That's why she's getting ready to leave."

Tears pounded against his eyes but couldn't force their way through. Disgust and hatred strong-armed his consciousness, and his throat burned with bitterness. His vision thinned and blurred, he could hardly bear to look into Desiree's face. He raised his chin until he could see the ceiling.

The ceiling was there. The single, naked light bulb and its frayed wire was there.

His eyes felt better. He brought his gaze down and gave her a thin, quizzical smirk. "Leave?"

"Yeah, she's going back to Georgia. That may be why she decided to go to the cops."

Shine went silent, her words piercing his heart like a 9mm slug fired from his own weapon. He couldn't believe what he was hearing. He had been kicked in the gut when she first told him about Lola and Gorilla Leek. And now here she was—with even more devastating news of betrayal—calmly and coolly announcing that his girlfriend might be pregnant by his best friend and getting ready to leave the state.

He wanted to fall to the ground and die. He wanted to wallow in the concrete mud like the filth he was and bury himself beneath all the dirt he'd dug over the years. In less than three days, he'd lost both his son and his woman. Was he now to lose his freedom? His nerves crawled up into his stomach. What did it matter if they locked him up now? If Chinnah killed him? What did he have to live for?

For a second, he felt a fathomless and howling hopelessness at losing the life he'd made for himself. But then he asked himself, *what life?* Life was what he would've had with Trayvon and Lola. This was no life. No. At this point, this was just an existence. Survival.

In truth, he knew before Trayvon was buried. Before the police got involved. Before Desiree threatened him with blackmail. He knew when he squeezed the trigger, and watched Badrick exhale his last breath, that it was over. That he would end up living the rest of his life in the prison of the white man or dying at the hands of a black man. Somehow, somewhere deep inside himself, he'd always known it would end this way. What other way could it possibly end for a nigga in the hood? Especially for a nigga who refused to refuse being a nigga in the hood?

Pride made him lift his chin and lock eyes with her, studying her as if he wasn't sure he should believe her. He needed to know how much the police actually knew, because they didn't seem to be aware of his involvement yet. All the detective told him was that an anonymous caller—a girl—had provided them with the information of Trayvon's whereabouts. That they'd obtained her phone number from the precinct's Caller ID device. And that they would be at his apartment within an hour to discuss possible suspects. But, taking charge of the situation, Shine said he was expecting some family members over. That it wasn't a good time or place. He said he needed a couple of hours and suggested that they meet later in the day at the precinct. Brown, unable to hide the suspicion in his tone, reluctantly agreed.

Shine knew it was only a matter of time before they identified Desiree. That's why he immediately rushed over to her apartment once Eden had fallen asleep. He'd thought for sure she was the one who'd snitched, but now he wasn't certain. And even if she didn't talk yet, it's probably that she still would go through with her plan of blackmailing him. He couldn't dare take any chances. The fewer people who knew, the better.

With the opportunity to rethink the situation in the cold light of day, he wasn't sure he had the stomach to do what he came there to do. But there was no doubt in his mind that a loyalty shoved down Desiree's throat by threats would mean little once the police pressed her for information. He wasn't going to attempt to scare her into obedience, but he damn sure wasn't going to pay for her silence either.

His eyes held hers with a fierce intensity, reflecting frustration and confusion. And though he was silent, she could tell from his gentle grimace that some sort of internal debate was taking place. Slowly, he moved closer to her, reached over and traced a trembling finger across her forehead and down her cheek.

"You know what? I believe you," he uttered softly like a prayer.

A hint of a smile crept over her quivering lips. He caught sight of it and motioned for her to sit on the couch. As she sank into the sofa she noticed his gun hand started to shake slightly.

"I just needed to make sure. I hope we're still good after what happened last night. I was a little gone off of that Crown Royal," he said, walking over to the card table.

He picked up a remote, pushed a button to turn on the TV then tossed it back on the table.

Sitting beside her, he had to shout over the blaring chatter of the morning news. "Look, I didn't mean to wild out on you. I was just a little stressed over her dealing with my dude."

"Yeah I feel you," she said weakly, as wary now of his sudden calm demeanor as she had been of the chaotic outburst he'd unleashed only minutes ago.

He leaned over, rested his hand on her thigh, and caressed her flesh in a slow, circular motion. "How long have they been messing around?"

She relaxed at his touch, and her heart pounded madly. Her words raced out her mouth in a soft, subdued voice, "About ten months now.

He comes over after you leave out for Minimart every Wednesday and Friday morning like clockwork. He even has his own key." She briefly paused. Then making the mistake of assuming she was out of danger, she continued, free of worry, "She started dealing with him 'cause she said y'all always fighting and you never be in the crib. You always out. They hit it off pretty fast and been on the low since."

"Well, where is Leek now?"

"Dunno. She been trying to get up with him too."

"So, you saying every Wednesday and Friday—on the days I'm at the store—he over at my crib?"

She took a drag from the blunt, let out a long billow of smoke, and said, "Yeah. Except for this past Friday. I mean, I saw him go up into the building that day, but he came right back out. Look like he was rushing to get out of there. He couldn't have been in your apartment any longer than a couple of minutes."

For a moment he considered her words which had taken the air out of him as quickly as the bullet he'd spent the past couple of days expecting, and it took him a minute to realize why.

"Last Friday? About what time?" His eyes glittered with hatred as it occurred to him that she was referring to the same day Trayvon died.

"Sometime after eleven."

Shine had been at the apartment all morning, up to the time Trayvon accidently shot himself. Gorilla Leek must have turned around when he saw he was home. Desiree said he had his own key. That would explain why his door was unlocked that day. A million thoughts skidded through his head, muddled by anger, confusion, and the influence of the liquor from last night. He couldn't believe his woman was having an affair with his best friend, while her best friend was blackmailing him.

He stared at Desiree scornfully as she brought the blunt to her lips once more. After a few puffs, she turned her head and started coughing uncontrollably. He gave her an insidious grin and shifted away from her but was stopped by the arm of the sofa. She leaned forward, hacking, while he slowly rolled off the couch and stood up. Rubbing at her eyes with her free hand and gasping, she didn't notice Shine leveling his gun to her head. She saw nothing except a shadow moving along the edge of her vision. By the time she lifted her eyes, his internal debate had ceased. He had no choice. He had to do it. When it had been necessary he'd done it before. This time it would be easier. He inhaled deeply then pulled the trigger.

CHAPTER 18

"ARE YOU SERIOUS?"** Buck Brown spat into the receiver of his cell phone.

Gritting his teeth, his grip on the steering wheel tightened as he sped through red light after red light, doing everything he could not to hit anyone or anything. Cardillo was hanging onto the overhead grab handle, staring wildly at his partner who seemed to be delighting in his own NASCAR performance. Even as he wove in and out of the nervous drivers buzzing around them, Brown kept his composure and continued his conversation.

"The same gun that was used in the murders at the store? You have to be shitting me," Brown did not slow down, but whirled the Crown Victoria around the corner, almost on two wheels.

"That's some goddamn connection! I didn't see that one coming. The father was supposed to meet with us at the station. But we've just discovered that it was the mother who tipped us off. So, we're on our way now to pick her up." The detective paused for a deep breath then continued, "But, what you're telling me now has thrown us for another loop."

Brown spoke a few more words into the phone, hung up, and shook his head.

"What's the news?" asked Cardillo.

Keeping his eyes on the road, Brown replied, "The gun used on the Bye child was also one of the weapons recovered from the Alvarez Grocery scene."

Cardillo's expression went still. "What? The gun we found buried in the park?"

"No. The weapon we found in the park was a nine-millimeter. And the exit wound on the boy's skull was consistent with a forty-four. The crime lab just confirmed it. One of the guns retrieved from the scene of the Alvarez's Grocery shooting is our murder weapon in the Bye case."

Brown glimpsed at his rookie partner and saw his eyes widen with surprise.

"Huh? Are you saying that—"

"Whoever murdered that little boy was also involved in the shooting that took Chinnah son's life," revealed Brown.

"So, what about the gun we found in Lincoln Terrace?"

"Not sure. But it's not the murder weapon. The geeks are examining it now. And one thing is for certain—we need to speak to the mother to find out what she knows about all of this. I mean, she sat there and lied to my face. She knew where her son was all along."

Suddenly, the police radio crackled, and a voice shouted over the static, "I need a unit to proceed to 950 Rutland Road. Be advised, caller reported they heard gunshots coming from apartment 609."

Brown immediately recognized the address. Desiree grew up in that building, and for years he'd sit outside in his car, watching it—watching her. But that was years ago. Tonight, he had a case to crack. He glanced at Cardillo and could see that his partner wanted to respond to the call, since they were in the area.

"If no one actually witnessed a gun being fired, and no illegal activity has been reported, it's not our problem. Dispatch will get a number and handle it as a call back," Brown calmly said. "A patrol unit can check it out. We have actual murders to solve."

"Understood," Cardillo replied, concealing his disappointment.

With his eyes fixed on a point somewhere off in the distance, Brown uttered in a somewhat eager and agitated tone, "We have a string of deaths that are somehow all connected—the incidents occurring at Chinnah's stash house and Alvarez's Grocery. Plus, the Bye child's murder, and the massacre that went down at Minimart," He paused to let out a weary sigh. "Now if we can only get the mother to tell us what she knows, we may be able to close every last one of these cases within the next twenty-four hours."

"What about the father?" Cardillo asked.

"We'll find out what he knows as well. He said he was having family over at the house this morning, so he should be there too. If he is, we'll take them both down to the station without causing too much of a commotion in front of their loved ones."

"And if neither one of them are there?"

"Well, let's hope they are. Because now that Chinnah's son is dead, more bodies will be dropping very soon. And I wouldn't be surprised if one of them are next."

Cardillo felt the car slowing down and stopping. He looked out the passenger window and saw the stone steps leading to the entry way of Shine's building. He turned to his partner and looked him up and down, his eyes wide. "What if the father is the killer?"

"Of who? The boy?" Brown caught a glimpse of himself in the rearview mirror as he turned off the car engine. "I'm not sure about that one. However, one thing is for certain and nothing is for sure— I've been doing this for too long."

The two men got out of the car and walked up the steps to the building. Cardillo proceeded halfway up the stairs then turned to Brown and asked, "Do you think your CI, Arab, would know anything about what's going on? Maybe he knows what happened to the Bye child."

Brown, noticing that the front door was unlocked, pushed it open and replied without looking back at his younger companion, "Not sure. But my guess is that I will be seeing him very soon. And when I do, you better believe I will find out what he knows." He held the door open as Cardillo walked past him and then closed it behind them.

♠ ♠ ♠

LOLA THOUGHT SHE WAS DREAMING—or that she was already dead. Darkness was everywhere. Her own grandmother, Velma Mae, who'd been deceased for a decade, was calling her name in a low, strange voice. She was calling Lola to "Wake up." Trayvon was also calling her to wake up. Yet, she had no feeling in her body. She wondered if she was dead. And if she was still alive, why could she not see or feel anything. She was trapped and unable to move.

Then it dawned on her.

Open your eyes.

Almost forgetting where she was, she slowly blinked open her eyes.

The lids were so very heavy. There was nothing to see. Her vision was fuzzy, and she'd realized why. Her left eye was almost completely swollen shut. How long she had been unconscious, she didn't know. Was it the same day or the next day? She was unsure. But she doubted much time had passed since she had let herself into the apartment, only to be bullied, beaten, and bound. She knew full well why the stranger had tortured her as she lay on her stomach, naked and tied to her bed with a rag stuffed in her mouth—to learn the whereabouts of Shine, so Chinnah might finish what her man had started. The detective had tried to warn her. It was too late to take heed.

Hard plastic zip-ties cinched her wrists to the bed posts, digging into her flesh. Another tie bound her ankles and she used what little strength she had left to spread them apart and stretch the plastic. It bit into her skin, and she gritted her teeth to keep from crying out as a scorching hot river of urine dribbled down the inside of her thigh. She stopped struggling and turned her head to see that the large unsightly black man who sat wordlessly beside her on the bed had produced a large knife from inside his black coat. He appeared happy that she'd awoken.

What more could he possibly do to her? He need not press her for information, for she'd long ago told all she could, which didn't amount to much. He'd already whipped and scarred her with a coat hanger that had been heated and burned into her skin. She'd suffered much. Yet she had no idea where Shine was.

Her agony was undeniable. Arab could see that. He had done much to her in the short time he'd been there. But his frame of mind prevented him from doubting the moral rightness of what he was doing. He saw gangsters and their women as war mongers and whores who roamed the battle-torn ghetto searching out atrocities to commit against innocent youth. And it was his job to see to it that they suffered the same fate—though worse perhaps—as those who, in their weakness were too powerless to protect themselves. Yes, that was his job—to save the babies.

Of course, it was.

And Lola was also a job to him. She was merely one of hundreds of such jobs which were handled as routine matters by him. This morning however, he wasn't planning on working overtime. In preparation for this moment, anticipating his tight schedule, he'd planned to do the most horrendous things to her. Sooner and not later the quietness of her ambiguous responses to his questions would be shattered by a seemingly never-ending cry for mercy. Sooner and not later she was going to tell him everything she knew.

He reached over and passed the cold Ka-Bar steel along her buttocks until the tip of the blade was against her anus. "Please don't play games with Arab." Hostility bled into his voice. He reached over and pulled the rag out of her mouth.

Uncontrollable sobs shook Lola's small frame. Fear sent her thoughts racing. Perhaps the stranger was there to torture and kill her regardless of how much she told him. Her heart pounded as she mustered courage to speak.

"I'm not playing games. I promise. I don't know where Shine is right now," she whimpered, clenching her teeth when she heard the fear in her own voice.

There was a sign of annoyance on Arab's face at her response. He removed the blade pressing against her buttocks, but she assumed it remained just inches away. She lay still for a moment, waiting for him to resume abusing her. She drew in a deep breath and let it out slowly. The sound of her sigh filled the quiet darkness of the room, and then she realized what had terrified her the most at the moment. The silence.

A few seconds later, she heard him rustling through his jacket pocket. *This can't be happening* she thought. *I'm not ready to die. I can't let my child die.* It was now or never, she decided. She couldn't just lay there and allow another child to be taken away from her. But, there wasn't anything she could do, no way she could get free and get to the old rusted .38 revolver that Shine had stuffed under the pillow.

The bed springs squeaked as Arab moved closer to her. The smell of old sweat dried into his dark, scarred skin, the pungent smell of his body—infected flesh, feces—burned their elements into her nostrils as he leaned over her. Turning her head to meet his eyes, she shivered at the coldness she saw there. A hellish blackness stared back at her.

Taking rapid deep breaths, she blurted out, "I'm pregnant!" Then she squeezed her eyes shut as tears sprung to life, pouring down her cheeks.

Arab's eyes went wide at the mention of a baby—it was one thing to kill a woman, quite another to murder an innocent child. "There's a baby inside of you?" His voice was solemn and serious.

"Yes," she said, eyes still closed.

He thought back to his former days as a soldier for Islam and remembered the baby boy he had drowned. The baby boy that had gone quiet after one peculiar wail—the slight tremors of the child's body and the spasmodic sobs still rankling in Arab's memory. He didn't want to be responsible for bringing innocent blood upon himself again.

He set the knife on the bed then reached into his pocket and pulled out his cell phone. He held it out, so she could see it. "Tell Arab his number. You're going to call him and get him to come home. Then Arab will let you leave. Arab's word is his bond. Do you understand?"

Her head shook up and down, and she mumbled something incoherent.

"Good," said Arab. "What's his number?"

"3-4-7-7-5-6-1-1-4-7" The faint words stuttered out of her.

He punched the numbers into the phone, then placed the receiver to her ear.

She lifted her chin a fraction of an inch, waited for a moment then spoke, "Baby, I need you to come to the apartment."

Arab could hear her boyfriend's muffled voice coming from the other end of the phone line.

"What? Like right now?" asked Shine.

"Yeah, now. It's important," begged Lola.

Curiosity gripped Shine and a strange anticipation filled him as he uttered his next words. "What is this about?"

For a moment he thought she might actually confess to having an affair with Gorilla Leek and to being pregnant, until she'd said, "It's about Trayvon."

His thoughts immediately went back to Buck Brown, and how he had said it was a female who called in the location of his son's body. The fact that the detective mentioned he wanted to meet back at his apartment, and now here was Lola trying to lure him home. Desiree's words also came to him, and it crossed his mind that she had hit the nail on the head.

Lola was the one who'd betrayed him.

She was the one who went to the police. But he also wanted to see it for his own eyes—to know for sure that she'd been talking to them.

If she was setting him up, NYPD would be waiting for him at his apartment. Maybe, to get a better handle on things, he could drive over there and take up a position where he could scope out the building. If he spotted a vehicle on his block that even remotely resembled an unmarked police car, he would abandon his rendezvous with her in a heartbeat. And then he would know the truth.

Sensing she was nervous, he kept his voice low, doing his best to make her feel at ease. "Alright, I'll be there. Are you at home now?"

"Yes."

"Are you for dolo?"

After some hesitation, she said, "Yes. I'm alone."

"Okay, give me a sec and I'll head toward you. I'll be there in about thirty minutes."

Before she said goodbye, she had a passing thought. What if the stranger was lying? What if he had no plans to let her go? He no longer needed her—was way past needing her—since Shine had already agreed to come home. Now, there was nothing to prevent the man from killing her.

"Please Shine," she pleaded, "please hurry home."

There was a pause as Arab pulled the phone away from her ear. He hung up, grinned, then stabbed a few more buttons on it and waited.

It only rang twice before Arab heard Pauley's strong, thick Jamaican accent. "Waah gwaan?"

Arab dipped his chin, bringing his mouth closer to the phone. "Arab has Shine's old lady. She just called him, and he is on his way back to the apartment now. You said you wanted to question him before Arab expired him. Well you have about twenty minutes to get here before he does."

"Eff him get fi yuh before mi, nuh kill him. Kip him there," Pauley commanded. "Mi wa fi find out wah him did wid di cocaine. Seen?"

"Copy," is all Arab uttered before he clicked the off button and ended the call. He shoved the phone back into his pocket. Without warning he unclipped a smaller knife from his belt and quickly cut the zip ties, freeing Lola's hands. She dropped her face into the mattress— her sweat-covered nakedness now chilled, her head throbbing with a dull ache that turned her stomach—dreading what was to come next.

Arab stood up and glanced around the bedroom. He chewed on his lower lip thoughtfully for a moment when he caught sight of a white ceramic plate, a razor blade, and a cut-off straw sitting on the dresser across from the bed. He narrowed his eyes and made off toward it. Wordlessly he examined the items, picking up the plate, and inspecting it closely from every angle.

"Y'all have coke here?" he asked in a low voice, with his back to her.

To answer his question, Lola raised her chin and looked over her shoulder. "Yes, somewhere in one of those dresser drawers."

"How much?"

"About an ounce or so."

She was lying. There was no cocaine in the apartment. Shine had taken it with him when he left for the club the evening before.

Arab started ripping at the drawers trying to find the drugs. He ripped out the top drawer, and there was nothing. He threw it to the ground and it splintered. He ripped out the next drawer. Nothing! While he was distracted, Lola took the opportunity to stick her hand under the pillow. Moving faster than she thought possible, she groped blindly, expecting to find a gun, but it was bare underneath. She lifted the pillow. Her heart sunk. Nothing lay beneath.

"Were you looking for this?" Arab called out.

She turned her head toward his voice to see him standing beside the bed with Shine's .38 pointed directly at her.

"Arab was going to let you live. Let your baby live. But no. No. You want to kill Arab."

Her chocolate face went manila-paper pale, and terror screamed from her eyes. "I'm sorry. I was scared. I am scared. Please."

He thrust the gun barrel against the back of her head. "Where would the world be without justice? Without law? There is always the law. After all else fails. Just law. Eh?" A hiccup escaped his lips. "All law. That's what's greater than you, than Arab, than me. All law. And one such law is an eye for an eye. You know that one?"

"Please mister!" The sobbing began again.

"Ain't no please. You were trying to kill Arab. Trying to kill me! There's no mercy for Arab's enemies."

Lola sobs were so morbid, so weak.

"But my baby!" she cried out suddenly. "Please! My baby!"

She turned her face into the mattress and squeezed her eyes shut as Arab moved closer, the barrel still pressing against her head.

"That there is your fault, not Arab's. Your actions just killed your child. Not Arab. This here is justice! An eye for an eye and—"

There was the abrupt nerve-rattling noise of a door crashing in and something shattering and breaking, getting crushed. Then the loud crack of a gunshot exploded in Lola's ears and echoed through the apartment. She braced herself expecting that more were coming. And they did.

Three more gunshots.

Then heavy footsteps stamped across the room.

Suddenly, there was the sound of breaking glass—the window shattering as though it had been struck by one of the bullets.

More footsteps pounded in the distance, coming closer.

Lola had no feeling in her body. She had no feeling at all. Again, she heard Trayvon calling her name and telling her to get up. She wondered if the first gunshot had paralyzed her and that was why she'd felt nothing. With her eyes closed tightly, she reached up and twisted her shaky fingers through her hair. She couldn't feel the wound. No bullet had touched her.

Then out of nowhere she heard a familiar voice yell, "My first shot hit him, but he got away. The bastard jumped through the window! Call it in! Now!"

The footsteps moved closer.

A gentle hand was laid on her bare shoulder, and gentle words were spoken into her ear, "Lola Bye. Ma'am. I heard you screaming. Open your eyes. You're safe now."

She looked up to find another pair of dark eyes fastened on her, but these were eyes filled with puzzlement and whirlwinds—of what? Reassurance? Compassion? Suspicion? These were eyes that belonged to Detective Buck Brown, and though he'd just saved her life, he did not appear too thrilled about it. He uttered something else, but it didn't register. She only heard the drone of his deep, strong voice when he yelled, "Get her some clothes now!"

CHAPTER 19

SHINE'S CAR CRAWLED PAST the unmarked Crown Victoria parked next to his home. He drove by the building slowly, stealing glances at the top window, hoping to catch a glimpse of the peril that awaited him. When he saw the shattered glass and the shadows of people moving inside, he accelerated and went around the block. Steering the car down the street for a second pass, his heart rate increased when he noticed a storm of red and blue lights flashing in his rearview mirror. Wiping his perspiring face with the cleaner side of his red bandana, he came to the end of the block and saw the police behind him double-parking their car in front of his building. He turned left, gunned his motor, and made his way back around the block for a third time.

Just once more, he told himself. *I need to know for sure. Need to see it for myself.* He knew he was putting himself at risk. A car rolling down the same block more than twice would surely be noticed. Didn't matter. He needed to know how far Lola had gone with her betrayal. When he turned into his street again, he immediately saw more flashing lights— three city police cars, two unmarked detective cars, and an ambulance.

He nosed the SUV into a parking space near the corner, only a half block from his building entrance. Through the windshield, he watched the flood of uniforms enter the apartment. Two minutes later, three more police cars screeched to a halt on the street. There were the dull thuds of car doors being closed, and the spectacle of twirling red lights spinning in colorful strobes across the buildings.

He wondered, if somehow, Gorilla Leek had convinced Lola to go to the cops. Maybe his friend wanted him out of the picture, so he could have both his woman and his half of their business. Then he thought back to his conversation with Redrum. Was Detective Brown working with Chinnah? Should he be worried?

The sharks were circling, and he could do little at the moment to protect himself, except remain hidden. He felt his eyes go wide as he imagined storming into the apartment and shooting everyone inside. After all, he was now a killer. And he surmised that some of the police officers on the scene had likely never seen a dead body before, let alone the body of a person dead by gun violence. If he could surprise them and get the drop on them, he might stand a good chance of getting them all, including Lola. The plan could just work—why had this not occurred to him earlier? But then he had another thought.

Leave.

There were too many cops.

He didn't need to see Lola with the police anymore. They were at his front door. That told him all he needed to know. Just as he was about to start his car and drive off, she came out of the building and down the steps, escorted on each side by an officer. Detective Brown brought up the rear and ushered her toward his Crown Victoria, waving away the EMS crew. He passed her a cell phone then unlocked the car door for her. A battered Lola climbed in and closed the door behind her while the detective stood outside talking to the uniformed officers.

Shine watched them all, obviously growing more agitated and nervous by the moment. Suddenly his cell phone rang. Slightly startled, he fumbled with the pocket of his jacket, then almost dropped the phone in his haste to answer it.

"Peace!"

There was silence on the other end.

"Peace," he said once more.

No answer.

He looked down at his phone and saw the name *Buck Brown.*

"Yo, I'm about to hang up if you don't say anything," Shine threatened into the phone.

"It's me," Lola said in a soft beseeching tone. "Wh—where are y—y—you?"

"Not in jail yet. No thanks to you," he answered in a voice that did not waver.

"What does that mean?"

"You know what that means. You called me to come to the crib to have me arrested? I know that the scramz is up in there with you."

"No. No. That's not true. The police actually saved my life. Chinnah sent someone here to—"

"Saved your life?" he interrupted. "I'm supposed to believe that?"

"I swear to God Shine. I came home and—"

"Bullshit," he interrupted again. "I can't believe you actually went to the pigs and told them about Trayvon."

Silence.

"You told them where to find Trayvon's body! And now you're trying to get me hemmed up," he screamed into the phone.

More silence.

"And you told them where to find the gun! So that I would be the one to get locked up! So, you could go on sleeping with Leek!"

"Sleeping with Leek?" she echoed his words in disbelief. "What are you talking about?"

"Yo, my word!" he yelled, anger rising in his tone. "Now is not the time to be playing with me. You feel me? I know all about everything that's been going on with you two. You think you are going to just snitch on me then go and live happily ever after with your new baby? Really?"

Lola was caught off guard at his surprising accusation, and she knew instantaneously that Desiree had told him everything. She wasn't sure how to respond. An awkward silence stretched between them, as she didn't expect the conversation to take such a turn. The cowardly part of her told her to hang up the phone, but instead she sat in the back seat of the unmarked police car staring blindly out the window.

"What? You ain't got nothing to say?" he asked, anger dripping from every syllable. "I guess not. My life is over, because they got all the evidence they need—thanks to you. I mean, what? They had you call me down here to arrest me? Telling them where to find the body and the murder weapon wasn't enough?"

"The murder weapon?" Lola could hardly breathe as she gasped to form her words. "No Shine. It—it—w—wasn't—your gun."

"Huh? What the hell are you talking about?" he asked in a far more commanding, take charge tone.

She decided to be blunt. "The police said that it wasn't your gun that—that—killed Trayvon."

His teeth began to chatter as he stammered the words, "What are you—what—what are you saying? My—my gun—"

"No," Lola uttered calmly and coldly, "the detective who saved me said that the gun they found buried in the park wasn't the murder weapon." She paused, hearing a surprised little intake of breath coming from the other end of the phone. Her next words, words she wasn't willing to say, were stuck in her mouth. But in the back of her mind, when she cast the dull ache in her heart aside, she knew she had to tell him. "Shine, Copper is dead, and the same gun that was involved in his murder," Again she paused. "The gun they found at the scene of his murder was the same gun that took our boy's life. They said he was killed with a forty-four, and not the nine they found buried in Lincoln Terrace."

It was happening—her words were about to crush him.

Lola swallowed hard. "It was never your fault. Someone else killed our boy."

Silence

"Shine?" she whispered into the cell just before she pulled it away from her ear and looked at it. She listened into the phone for a few seconds then uttered once again, "Shine?"

Dark thoughts weighed down inside Shine's skull like a dead black stone, his vision seemed to be down a murky tunnel, his hearing distant, his senses nearly divorced from reality. The inside of his stomach became a bottomless pit and felt as if it were filling with ice-water. He opened his mouth to speak and struggled to draw breath—each gasp sucking down dry, thick air that scorched his lungs.

"Copper's dead?" was all he could utter. "Like dead, dead?"

"Shine did you hear me? Trayvon's death is not your fault."

Ignoring her last comment, he asked again, "Copper got lit up? When? Where?"

"Someone took his life yesterday in a shootout at Alvarez's Grocery."

"What the fuck!" He immediately thought back to his last conversation with Gorilla Leek in the park. "Leek was supposed to be there last night. He had to handle some business with White Mike."

"Yeah, well the detective said White Mike was also killed. And some other people—"

"Wait!" He couldn't believe what he was hearing. "Both White Mike and Copper are dead? What about Leek? Did they mention if he was there?"

"No, they didn't say anything about him," A ragged sigh escaped her. "But, did you not just hear what I said? It's not your f—"

"Did you not just hear what I said?" he interrupted, repeating her question back to her with a tone that suggested she was naïve for even asking. "I just told you that your little lover was supposed to be there last night to do business with White Mike. And now your saying that the scramz just told you that our enemy and the man Leek went there to see are both dead?"

Lola said nothing.

"And to top it off—fuck—this is a good one," A sarcastic chuckle rumbled from his belly upward. "You're also telling me that the same gun used at the scene of White Mike and Copper's murder is the same gun that was used on our son. And it was a .44? Which is what Leek be holding."

"What are you saying Shine?" Terror strangled the trace of curiosity that was seeping into her tone.

"I know he has a key to our apartment. Which is why our front door was unlocked on the day Shine died."

"Shine!" Her voice was almost a shriek. "What are you saying?"

"Leek was in our apartment that day."

"No—no—no he wasn't. He—"

"Someone already told me he was there. That he went into the building then quickly turned right back around. And it was around the same time Trayvon was shot."

"What are you really getting at Shine?" she asked, her voice scratchy and shrill.

"If it wasn't my gun that took Trayvon off of here," he swallowed, trying to collect himself, "then it was Leek who murdered our son."

Lola's breath hitched in her throat, and her heart beat a deafening rhythm. It couldn't be true. Her thoughts scattered like dust in the wind.

"I've been running around this whole time with that nigga thinking that it was my gun that sent Trayvon back!" screamed Shine. "But it was him! He did it! And I went to the cops! I've killed someone else behind this! And now you're saying the pigs are saying it wasn't me?

Then it had to be Leek!"

"Did you say you killed someone el—"

"Look," Shine continued "It makes sense now. That's why Dina's dead."

Lola gasped then tightened her grip around the phone. "What? Who told you that?"

"Someone who was there when it happened. And they also pulled my coat to who killed her. Some dude named Arab that works with that detective dude you just walked out of our building with."

She gasped again, and stole a glance through the car window, frowning when she saw Buck Brown looking back at her. "Huh?"

"Yeah, and yesterday Leek told me that he had a connect with a cop. It's probably Brown Buck! And that pig probably had someone take Dina off for Leek, so he could be with you."

"That seems a bit extreme. I don't think—"

"Extreme is the way niggas think when it comes to pussy and money! Now, son only has to get me out of the picture, and what better way than to have my ass go to jail for the death of Trayvon. I'm saying, I don't think he was looking to set me up to get locked at first. Son ain't that bright." A somewhat half-chuckle, half-grunt burst from his lips. "It just worked out that way. But I do believe he killed Trayvon to be with you and your new baby, knowing you wouldn't leave me because we had a child together. So, in all, our son didn't die because of me. He died because of you!"

A sharp pang of guilt hit low in Lola's belly and a chill whispered through her as she gripped the phone tightly and listened in horror to Shine's words. She started to reply when the car door suddenly opened with a screeching *whoosh*, interrupting anything she might've said. Buck Brown stuck his head inside.

"Is that him?" the detective yelled, reaching his hand out to her. "Give me that phone!"

Shine sat inside his car, watching Brown intently and listening into the receiver. He could hear some scuffling and the phone being snatched from Lola's grip.

"Dwight Mannschein?" Brown spoke into the receiver as he remained hunched over with his head in the car.

Shine said nothing.

Without warning, the lonely wail of a siren blared in the distance, blending in with the outpouring of rhythms echoing from the commotion in front of his building. Another emergency vehicle was on its way to the scene. As Shine listened, it came closer. Detective Brown heard it also—through the phone and approaching him.

Then it hit him.

Shine was in the area. And he was likely watching them.

Brown began walking slowly into the street, his eyes darting left and right, his senses alive. He immediately recognized the black Ford Expedition. His slow saunter became a fast strut as he neared Shine's vehicle.

"Cardillo!" he called out to his partner, pointing at the Ford that was now pulling out of its parking space. "That's him! The father's in that car right there!"

Shine eased his car into the street before throwing it into reverse and speeding backwards away from his building. He swerved the SUV around the corner, spinning the wheel so the rear of his vehicle swung out into the cross street. Without looking down his block, he jammed it into drive and slammed on the gas, surging up Rutland Road.

Brown turned on his heels and ran down the street back toward his car. Out of breath, he swung open the door of the Crown Victoria and vaulted his tall frame into the driver's seat. With his head over his shoulder turned, he eyed Lola in a moment of curiosity. His dark eyes narrowing with instant suspicion as he asked her, "What did you say to him?"

♠   ♠   ♠

SHINE'S VEHICLE SPED DOWN the FDR Expressway, weaving through traffic. If a car didn't move out of the way, he leaned on his horn. It hadn't taken him long to get to Harlem. He had been going ninety miles an hour, occasionally pushing the speed up to one hundred. Flying by several cars, he tailgated a few before he passed them, honking as he passed, and after he passed. With both hands on the wheel, he glanced at the gas needle then flicked his eyes toward the digital clock on the dashboard. There wasn't much time left.

In the hour since leaving his neighborhood, he'd managed to get a hold of Gorilla Leek on the phone. He was at Daffney's apartment recovering from a gunshot wound he received after stumbling into a bungled robbery at *Alvarez's Grocery*. In response to Shine's questions, he confirmed that Copper was dead, and that he'd witnessed the murder. He didn't admit or deny his involvement. It was a read-between-the-lines conversation because Gorilla Leek was very paranoid, thinking the cops were looking for him. But the things he did say recalled all Shine's suspicions. His friend, he concluded, had taken the life of his son. And as long as Shine sounded perfectly normal, acted perfectly normal, his son's killer would not suspect that he'd put two and two together, and he would likely let his guard down.

At the moment, Gorilla Leek wanted nothing more than to put as much distance between himself and Brooklyn. He had asked Shine to come to the apartment where he was laying low. He told him that he wanted to discuss his new plans for the cocaine they'd taken from Chinnah, to see if he was interested. It could be a trap, of course. But Shine cared not. He knew then, as he now knew, what had to be done. The want, the need to kill his betrayer, was at odds with his better judgement. Lola was in police custody, and he'd narrowly escaped being caught himself. There was no reason he should have still been in New York. But then again, the cocaine was also at the apartment with the man he sought. And he could almost taste the money coming his way once he had his hands on the drugs. Money that would set him up in another state for a good, long while. Money that would ensure his freedom.

Even so, a terrible rage burned in his heart. And in his hatred, his anger, he was suddenly more beast than man. He wanted the flames from gun barrels to turn upon all the Lolas and the Gorilla Leeks of his wretched world. The more vague his conviction became—that he should not commit murder—the less guilt he felt when planning how he would do it. Fueled by revenge and filled with despair, his mind went adrift, and he never noticed the black sedan that had been following him since he'd left his neighborhood.

After receiving the phone call from Arab, Pauley had arrived near the corner of Shine's block just in time to see his SUV skidding backwards in reverse before turning and barely missing a metal dumpster. He immediately recognized the vehicle, and as it sped off, he followed several feet behind, wondering what happened to Arab. The Jamaican enforcer was, however, more concerned with finding the kilos that had been stolen from his boss. Maybe Shine would lead him to it.

Maybe he could kill two birds with one grenade.

Pauley kept a discreet distance from the Ford and followed when it exited the expressway. Remaining two car-lengths behind, he idled his vehicle at a red light while Shine pulled into a gas station. He drove past once, then he drove past again, going the other way. The second time he saw the Ford parked at a gas pump, but he didn't see anyone inside it. So, he made a quick U-turn at the end of the block then pulled into the gas station behind the SUV.

He put his car in park, rolled his front windows down, and craned his head around to search for the person he was following. For a moment, he saw no one. Then dimly, at the edge of his peripheral vision, his eye picked up an unexpected motion outside the passenger side window. Before he could turn toward it to look, thunder exploded with a deafening report, filling with his car with a loud boom as flames leaped out and a bullet slammed into his face. It sent his skull crashing into driver's side window. The glass cracked into a frosty spider web, but the window held in place. His head jerked forward and blossomed crimson. He was dead before he slumped over the steering wheel.

♠   ♠   ♠

SHINE CAREFULLY NOSED his SUV around the narrow corner coming off the expressway ramp and drove into a gas station. His hands were gripping the steering wheel so tight his knuckles were red. He was homicidally angry. There were a few cars in the gas station but lots of foot traffic along the sidewalk. Several churches had barely let out and already the bars were open, loud music blaring from their yawning doorways and disrupting what could have been a blissful Sunday afternoon.

He parked alongside a gas pump and got out of his vehicle. Out of habit, he scanned the area looking for anything out of place. Something was not right. Something began to bother him. His eyes narrowed on a black sedan with tinted windows just as his senses told him that danger was close. Real close. As the car made a U-turn, he caught a glimpse of the license plate—*SHOTTA*.

He knew who it was right away. Every instinct demanded that he duck behind his SUV, so he wasted no time doing so. He popped his head over the hood and took a quick glance, watching every movement of the sedan until it pulled into the gas station. At that moment, he crouched out of sight and eased around the front of his car as the vehicle pulled up to his bumper. Taking a deep breath, he drew his gun and moved alongside the Ford toward the passenger side of the sedan.

He quickly stood up and pointed his pistol through the partially open window. Now, in full view of his enemy, and without hesitation, he fired one thunderous burst. The weapon's horrific blast caught Pauley by surprise. There was no chance to react. It was over in seconds.

Shine turned on his heels and calmly walked back to his SUV. There was a scream. Then someone began shouting obscenities. Another scream, then the loud terrible wail of a woman or a child. As the voices carried on, he heard the cry, "Police! Police! Someone call the police!"

He slid into the driver's seat, turned the key in the ignition, and the Ford roared to life. He drove off watching in the rearview mirror for any movement from Pauley's car. Just before he pulled out of the gas station he looked again and saw people scrambling for cover—voices pitched in frenzied screams—and one of the gas attendants running across the parking lot waving his arms frantically. Having taken a mental note of Shine's license plate, the young Middle Easterner stumbled and fell trying to reach the landline inside of the station. He remained frozen on the ground for fear of being shot, not moving until he heard the whining of the Ford's motor and the screeching sound of the tires peeling out.

The monstrous, hulking mass of metal blasted its way through every red light between the gas station and Daffney's block. Doing a normal drive-by, Shine barely glanced at her building. All he wanted to do was run inside and find Gorilla Leek, but he had to take precautions. So, without stopping, he circled back and scanned the area in every direction.

Nervous tension building, he found himself breaking out in a sweat as his car came to a slow, effortless stop in front of Daffney's home. He placed the vehicle in park, grabbed his gun from beneath the seat, and stepped out onto the sidewalk. Jamming the Springfield XD9 into his pants, he walked briskly up the stairs leading to entrance of the building.

The frigid, biting air rushed past him, lashing his army fatigue jacket with raging slaps. It howled warnings to unsuspecting wanderers who ventured unwittingly into the territories of concrete predators.

The chill of nervous anticipation settled upon Shine's mind and became an undesirable companion just as the rain began to beat a dismal *tit-a-tat-tat-a-tit* onto the concrete beneath his feet. Though the weather was unforgiving, it sheltered the neighborhood from the flames that usually ballooned out of gun muzzles each day. Being one of the coldest mornings in weeks, not one ghetto animal could be found roaming the street.

He hesitated at the top of the stairs, remembering all that Desiree had said, and gave the three-story building a cold look. As he raised his hand to ring the doorbell, he caught a light tremor, and realized that he had to calm his nerves. For just a moment he could hear the wind whispering doubts, and his heartbeat gurgling a deep gut groan. Even so, it didn't deter him from pressing the buzzer and summoning what could possibly be his own death.

After the first ring, the intercom crackled once, and a voice answered, "Is that you my dog?"

It was Gorilla Leek.

"Yeah. Buzz me in," Shine replied back.

"Aight. Cool. Come upstairs to 2B."

The buzzer went off. Shine pushed open the door and went through. He climbed the stairs and was only three steps away from the second floor when he heard the door to the apartment open. Furrowing his brow and squinting, he kept moving, his eyes scanning the end of the hallway watching, waiting. After a nervous glance over his shoulders, he put himself against the wall and eased a few feet down the hall. The floor creaked beneath his feet. Noticing that the door to Daffney's apartment was slightly ajar, he froze.

Prepare for the worst.

In one fluid motion, he pulled his gun out and tiptoed over to the entrance. He peeked through the slit then walked into the apartment. He didn't spot Gorilla Leek at first, but what he saw startled him, causing him to lower his weapon. A tall, pale-skinned bearded gentleman with dull grey hair was standing in the middle of the living room. There was an NYPD badge dangling from a silver chain around his neck. It appeared that he'd been waiting for Shine to arrive.

"What the hell is this?" Shine yelled the moment the door closed behind him.

♠ ♠ ♠

"SO, WHAT DO WE HAVE SO FAR?" asked the uniformed young female rookie who was standing in the hallway of the 67th precinct talking with Detective Cardillo.

"Well, right now, Brown is in there interviewing the vic's mother. Not sure what to make of it so far," answered Cardillo. "All I know is that this has been the longest weekend."

The officer gave Cardillo a questioning look. "Do you think the father had something to do with it?"

"Not sure. I don't think so, but my money is on him knowing who did."

"Really?" she asked.

Cardillo started to reply when, from the end of the corridor, he heard the door to the interrogation room opening. Brown walked out with Lola behind him, and they made their way toward the officers.

"Grayson," said Brown as he approached.

"Yes, sir," the uniformed rookie quickly answered her superior officer.

"Do you mind showing the young lady to the bathroom?"

"No, not at all." With a jerk of her head, Grayson motioned for Lola to follow and immediately, without saying any more, the two went quietly down the hall.

Cardillo kept his eyes fixed on his partner with a slight frown. "So, what's the deal? Is the case cracked? Are we going home?"

Brown let out a deep and slow sigh. "No. It doesn't appear that she knows anything. She was under the impression that the boy had accidently shot himself with the father's gun."

"Which is the weapon we found buried in the park near the body," added Cardillo.

"Correct. And the lab has determined that-that firearm was one of the murder weapons used during the robbery at Chinnah's stash house. Which, if it belongs to Mr. Mannschein, would explain why the incident at Minimart happened. And maybe even why Chinnah's son is now lying in a morgue." Brown's eyebrow shot up. "Speaking of Chinnah, did you ever speak with the actual owner of his stash house?"

"No, not yet. That's what I was waiting out here to talk to you about."

"What do you mean?"

Cardillo's throat tightened. He inhaled deeply through his nose, before saying, "Well, while I wasn't able to speak with anyone, I did find out who the place belongs to."

"Ok. Who is it?"

"It's a company. The same company that Mike Alvarez's wife told us about. The company that was looking to buy his bodega from him. *Bern and Seed Capital Real Estate and Loan.* They also own Chinnah's grocery store."

"The *Free Market?*"

"Yeah, he leases it from them. I tried reaching out to them, but they're closed on the weekend. So, I wasn't able to reach anyone. I'm going to call them first thing tomorrow morning."

"So, wait, are you saying that Chinnah doesn't own any of his property?"

"Nope. I'm thinking that the company probably finds it easier leasing their buildings out to criminals. For the quick under-the-table cash."

"Or," Brown calmly added, "it's possible that Chinnah may just be a front man for someone else. Someone bigger."

"Hmm, maybe that's what it is."

"Well, we need to speak to whoever runs that company to be certain. I don't think that can wait until tomorrow. I need you to find out who that is and reach out to them asap. Understood?" Brown squinted his eyes and slightly shook his head. "It can't be a coincidence that White Mike and Chinnah—both being well-known drug dealers—are connected to the same real estate company. There's something else going on here."

"You are right, Brown. Chinnah's son was murdered at Mike Alvarez's store, and the same gun used in that incident was used to kill the Bye child. All of this has to be connected it seems," Cardillo scrunched up his face in confusion. "But how?"

Brown's confidence had faded, and his expression had slightly changed. He bit his lip, and a modest look of perplexity crossed his face. "Not sure. Maybe we are dealing with a third party. An outsider who's calling all of the shots."

"A new player moving in on the Nineties?"

"Don't know. Who's to say they're new. Maybe they've always been around, and our guys were just never aware of them."

"So then, what's our next step?"

"We really need to find out who owns that real estate company. Our answers may lie there."

"And what about Dwight Mannschein? Where does he fit in to all of this?"

"I don't know. That is what I was hoping the mother would help us figure out. But she is playing stupid right now." Brown sighed. "We need to get a hold of Mr. Mannschein ourselves."

"What happened when she called him? Didn't she speak with him?"

Another sigh escaped Brown's lips. "Yeah, but she said he became frightened when he heard what happened and hung up the phone. He has not answered since."

"You think he has any connection to the perp I have in room 2?" inquired Cardillo.

"Who? The kid we caught at the scene of the Alvarez's Grocery killings? Not sure. He still isn't speaking yet?"

"No, not yet. The young punk thinks he's tough. But he'll break once we send him to the Island overnight. It doesn't take long for Rikers to do that," asserted Cardillo as he pulled his shoulders back and swung his head to the side to relieve the tight muscles in his neck. "Seidman is in there now questioning him about his involvement in the Baby Bye murder." He let out a yawn.

Suddenly there was a nagging question in Brown's mind, one he doubted he would have asked himself if Cardillo hadn't mentioned the young thug they arrested at the scene of Copper's murder. The words were out his mouth before he could think another thought. "Does the mother know him?"

Cardillo moved his lips to answer but before any words could form, he heard the lock to interrogation room 2 turn. Doors opened, and a young black teenage male was dragged out by Seidman and a uniformed officer. They pulled him down the hall toward Brown and Cardillo so fast that he stumbled. They paid no mind to his lost footing and hauled him on past the men.

Brown turned his head slowly to follow them as they moved out of reach. "Where are you guys taking him?" he shouted at Seidman.

"He has to drain his pipe. So, we will probably be hanging out at the restroom for the next hour or so," Seidman chuckled. "You know you brothers' irrigation systems can stretch for miles."

All the way down the hall, Seidman kept laughing over and over until, turning the corner, he almost ran into Lola going in the opposite direction. She immediately recognized the teenager being escorted in handcuffs by the detective. It was Anthony, the kid who was hanging out with Lil' John John in the hallway of her building the night before Trayvon's death. Anthony didn't appear to recognize her. At least he didn't have time to, as Seidman shoved him around the corner and along the corridor.

Brown took notice of the young woman's reaction when she ran into the teenager. He could tell that she knew him from somewhere. Glancing in the direction of the detective, Lola found him watching her silently. She wasn't sure what to expect, or what lay ahead, but she wasn't in handcuffs like Anthony and that was a good thing. And truth be told, Detective Brown was not sufficiently prepared for an arrest. Even if she had something to do with her son's death, he had no evidence, and no way to charge her. But he was not going to advise her that she was free to leave.

At her approach, he opened his mouth ready to direct her back into the interrogation room for further questioning, when his cell phone vibrated in his pocket. He pulled it out, answered, and his face fell. Lola paid him no mind and kept moving, with the rookie officer by her side.

"What? Where? In the wall? I'll be there in fifteen minutes. Don't have anyone touch anything! How many did you find?" Brown paused, giving the person on the other end time to reply. "Okay, I'll be there!"

Slowly he lowered the phone to his side and looked at Cardillo. Then jerking his head in the direction of Lola, who had just past them on her way back to the interrogation room, he said, "I need to get back over to her apartment to check out some additional evidence that the uniforms found."

"Additional evidence?" Cardillo asked seemingly confused.

"Yeah, the mother just may be telling the truth. She may really not know who's responsible for her son's death. While I am gone I'm going to need for you to reach out to the owner of that real estate company. Find out if they have any connection to these murders."

The expression on Cardillo's face carried just a hint of naivety. "What? You think they might have something to do with what happened to the Bye child?"

"Dunno. But it seems the child's death might be somehow connected to the killings that occurred on their properties." Brown shrugged his shoulders. "Either way, from the call I just received, I think we're getting closer to the truth."

CHAPTER 20

"**H**ELLO, DWIGHT,"
As the door closed behind Shine, he was greeted by a tall, hefty detective who didn't fit the normal profile of a New York City police officer. His grey hair was parted to the right side and slicked down. He wore blue jeans, an open black leather jacket, and a blue and orange jersey that celebrated the New York Mets' 1986 World Series Championship. He smelled brut and musky like whiskey and cigars.

Smiling, he offered his hand. "My name is Detective O'Reilly."

Shine didn't return his smile. Instead he just stared at the middle-aged officer. Wonderingly he said, "I don't know you or who you might be looking for. I came here to meet someone. And you're not that person."

"Calm down, dog. Ain't nobody out to getcha," a familiar voice screamed out from the back room, the other end of the apartment's hallway. "The detective wanted to meet you in person," said Gorilla Leek as he limped into the living room.

"What the hell son?" Shine had been more surprised by the presence of the detective than he'd been by Gorilla Leek's torn pants leg and the bandage tinged with blood that was covering his thigh. He shoved his pistol back into his waist.

"Be easy my dude. O'Reilly ain't hear to lock no one up," Gorilla Leek assured him, his tone blithe.

His words didn't seem to dull his friend's edginess. "Son, you got the scramz all up in our stash spot when you should be having a doctor up in this piece. You over here looking like a war victim," Shine said in a cruel chuckle.

"I'm good. Just a little bullet wound. Nothing too major. O'Reilly was the one who got me up out of White Mike's store. He got there right after everything went down. I was sneaking out the back right when he was coming—"

"Yeah," interrupted O'Reilly, "I heard the gunshots and decided to enter in from the rear, and that's when I ran into Malik, bleeding like a pig."

Gorilla Leek nodded. "The detective drove me up here, and had a shorty come by and patch me up on the low. She's a nurse and—"

"The detective?" Shine snapped him short, remembering that the man was a police officer.

"Yeah, the detective," Gorilla Leek replied diplomatically. "He's the connect I was telling you about."

As Gorilla Leek spoke, Shine remained silent on the outside but a screaming, murderous rage was welling inside that made his throat burn. He held himself right at the threshold of that staggering fury while a voice inside his head hissed, drowning out his friend's words. His mind drifted far away from their conversation. He thought about his son, his woman, and even his freedom. All was lost.

He thought about his life up to that point. It was not until he could pinpoint the emotion plaguing his thoughts that he finally relaxed. It was empathy. Maybe he couldn't hate his best friend, but he wanted to. He always knew that Gorilla Leek felt a swelling surge of envy for the life he'd led since they were kids. And though at times he felt sorry for him, he encouraged the sour thoughts by showing off the toys he received from his family when they were children, bragging about the grades he earned in middle school, parading his teenage girlfriends around the neighborhood, and simply just being himself. It was at the moment when he became other than himself that he found acceptance—that he found friendship. But Gorilla Leek was no more a friend. No, he'd proved himself to be an enemy. So, Shine could now finally be himself. And though he was no longer certain as to who that was, he knew one thing for sure—he was a killer.

Suddenly, Shine's mind went blank. He could do nothing but stare as his friend continued to yammer away. A million questions began forming in his head at once. He wasn't sure which to ask first. A sickly smile parted his lips before his mouth opened to interrupt, "So why is this Mr. Otis ass cracker trying to link with us? And how did y'all meet?"

"We met through—" Gorilla Leek started to answer but Detective O'Reilly cut him off.

"Copper," O'Reilly said with icy barbarity, "was supposed to introduce us at White Mike's store, last night."

"Huh?" The detective's words were lost on Shine.

"Copper stepped to me one night after he tried to buy our store and said he had a way for us to make mad doe together," Gorilla Leek added.

"Make doe together? That's some bullshit. What about Chinnah?" Shine asked.

The detective decided to add his two cents. "The boy wanted to go for himself. He wanted to take over his father's operation. He couldn't stand the fucker."

Shine glanced at Gorilla Leek. "So why get you involved?"

"Because—" O'Reilly tried to answer for Gorilla Leek but Shine boldly interrupted him.

"I wasn't asking you pig!" Shine's green eyes practically shot lasers through the apartment as they bore into O'Reilly's blue ones. They stared at each other for what seemed like eternity.

"Feel me Blood, O'Reilly and Copper had a good plan," Gorilla Leek assured. "And they wanted to bring me in on it. You just need to hear the detective out."

With a cold stiffness in his tone Shine glanced at O'Reilly and said, "So, you and Copper were working together and now Copper's dead. How do I know that you're not the one who set him up to get killed? Or maybe both of you guys did it yourselves." His eyes darted back and forth from O'Reilly to Gorilla Leek.

"That's a bit of a horse's hoof I think," the detective stated roughly. "We needed Copper for all of this to work. And now that he is dead, we have to make a drastic change of plans. We have to find a way to keep everything moving, because none of us wants to miss out on the money that can come from this."

"Speak for yourself pig. I already got doe," Shine wryly responded.

"Don't be such a dryshite." The Irishman was becoming agitated. "I don't have to be here. I can find another group of nig—uh— gangsters who would be more than happy to get their hands on the kind of stuff I've been getting from the station."

"The station?" Shine was confused. Very confused.

"Yeah. The drugs we take off the street gets placed into lockup as evidence. If the case never goes to trial, then it all just sits there in storage. And guess who has access to that area of the building?" O'Reilly tucked his chin into his chest and belched.

"Yeah," Gorilla Leek added, "and that's why he's going to give it to us for so cheap."

"How cheap is so cheap?" Shine stared at him unimpressed.

Gorilla Leek steadfastly fixed his eyes on O'Reilly.

"Ten per key," said the detective.

"Ten per key?" Shine's face flared with interest. Greed leaped in his eyes, and a sudden, sharp intelligence that faded as quickly as it appeared, replaced his hollow stare. Faintly flushed with excitement, he began figuring how much profit could be made from a partnership with the officer. Gorilla Leek watched his friend, lips moving, silently counting. He knew he was weighing his options.

"Yeah, but we have one issue," O'Reilly pointed out. "That's why I asked Gorilla Leek to have you meet us here. We needed to speak to you in person."

"Oh yeah? Well, I'm here. What's the issue?" asked Shine.

Gorilla Leek tensed and his back stiffened. His lips tightened as his mouth crept open to say, "You."

"Me? Huh?" Shine's eyes darted back and forth between the men.

O'Reilly spoke first, "Yeah, according to my guys at the station, someone called in the whereabouts of your son's corpse. They also reported to our officer that a weapon was buried near the same location. And when our guys dug up the pistol, they found partial prints on them." The Irishman tilted his chin and grinned as he said, "Needless to say, I don't think any of us would be surprised if those prints come back as belonging to you, right? According to Malik, that's the weapon you used to kill Chinnah's nephew. So, my guys will soon have a warrant out for your arrest."

Shine's face became a portrait of ruin, pregnant with concern. Suddenly, his thoughts were far away from the money they could make with the cop. He remembered what he'd came there to do.

The detective continued. "They haven't mentioned Malik yet, but word is, they believe that all of the murders we have been recently investigating in the Nineties are connected to you somehow. So, trying to move the kind of weight we're talking, with you having all of this heat on you, will prove to be a problem."

Shine's lips parted to sigh with disbelief of what his ears had just heard. He wanted to shout at the top of his lungs. It wasn't fair! Gorilla Leek had pushed him into this war with Chinnah against his better judgment. His best friend had thrown him in headfirst, all under the guise of getting revenge against the man who'd slept with his woman. And yet his friend was the culprit all along.

It crossed his mind at that moment to mention Dina's fate, but he decided against it. He was there for only one reason. He needed to know if his partner had orchestrated it all, that he had somehow planned the death of both Trayvon and Copper.

"So, now you're in bed with this pig?" Shine directed his question to his friend.

"Yeah dog," Guilt thudded through Gorilla Leek's words and his voice cracked on a deep breath.

"And you didn't think to let me know about any of this from the jump? That you were working with Copper?"

"Dog, all of this just went down, and I knew you wouldn't be onboard right away. But I couldn't pass up this opportunity. Copper showed me how our unity could be more profitable than our beef. So, I had to make the move. I was going to bring you up to speed slowly."

"And I guess this is how you got the key to Chinnah's spot that night?" asked Shine.

"Yeah. Copper gave it to me. When I told him about what happened with Lola and Badrick, he—"

"What happened with Lola and Badrick?" Shine knew Gorilla Leek was lying and knowing there was no hope for the truth, he uttered quietly, "So, he set his cousin up to get killed to help me get revenge on him for sleeping with my woman?"

Gorilla Leek had a queasy feeling in his gut knowing that he had been keeping something very awful from his friend. "He didn't expect Badrick to get popped. And he also had a personal interest in us running up in that spot."

Shine cocked his eyebrow. "What kind of interest?"

"Blood look, the detective and Copper had something good going. They came up with a plan that could get cats mad paid. And they wanted to bring us in on it. It's not about red or blue anymore. There's no black or white in this. It's about that green now. It's always been about the green. Open your eyes!"

Shine blinked at the switch in conversation. "But, what's going to happen, now that Copper is gone?"

"That's what we're here to discuss," Gorilla Leek answered.

"Discuss with who? This pig? Keep it real son. You two already have a plan. I don't have any say so on this, do I?"

Gorilla Leek could hardly tell him no, but anything else was a lie or a truth he wasn't prepared to utter. Again, he took a deep breath, then with all he could muster, his voice calm, he said, "That's up to you, and the choice you make."

"The choice I make?" Shine's lip curled into a harsh snarl. "How can I make a choice when I don't know anything?"

"What do you want to know, dog?" asked Gorilla Leek.

"Well first, did you have something to do with Copper's death?"

The obvious distrust in his question came at Gorilla Leek like a sharp blade, piercing through the cover of lies he had wrapped around himself. Although he had nothing to do with Copper's murder, he felt a great need to lie a little about his involvement, a small lie to keep him from admitting the total truth.

"No," O'Reilly said, speaking up for his new partner. "The kid who shot both White Mike and Copper is in police custody. He—"

"Again, I wasn't talking to you!" snapped Shine. He darted his eyes to his friend.

Gorilla Leek frowned then stuttered, "Uh—na. No. Copper was meeting me there to introduce me to O'Reilly and uh—well—to pick up the bricks, but—"

"Pick up the bricks? What bricks?" His thoughts ran back to the night of Badrick's murder. "The bricks we stole?"

"Kind of. That's what I meant by him having an interest in us running up in Chinnah's spot. He's the one who told me how many bricks would be up in there. Not White Mike. White Mike had nothing to do with any of it. Copper told me where the work would be. That's why I sent you upstairs. I went down into the basement and bagged up all ten while you were checking out the top floor."

"There were ten?"

"Yeah," Gorilla Leek took a big, nervous swallow, "but the plan was to meet Copper at White Mike's to give him four of them. He was going to take them back to his father, to act like he ran down on us and got some of the drugs back."

"Why? For what?" Suspicion and concern faded beneath Shine's curiosity.

"Well, that's another reason we asked you come here. To discuss just that," said Gorilla Leek.

"Speak for yourself. That's why you wanted him to come here," O'Reilly interjected. "I have a different reason for meeting him today."

Gorilla Leek rubbed his chin. "Look Shine, I asked you to come up here, so I could be straight up with you. I'm gonna put you on to everything that's been going down and everything that's about to go down. I'm not gonna keep any more secrets from you. Ya heard?"

"Yeah. Sure," Shine said with a shrug, but he didn't entirely believe them. If they were lying for some reason, then what would be that reason? Perhaps they were planning to murder him as well. He considered the fact that if his friend could take the life of his son, he would likely not hesitate to kill him also. Feeling his anger begin to prickle at the back of his eyes, he cut their conversation short, "Yo, Leek, being straight up, all of this sounds shaky. I have to give it some thought. But first, you and I need to discuss something in private."

"Private?" For a second Gorilla Leek seemed confused.

"Yeah, private. You know?" Shine glanced in the direction of the detective. "Without the extra ears. Seeing how you just met dude."

O'Reilly opened his mouth to respond, but Gorilla Leek held up a silencing hand before he could say the words forming in his mind.

"Aight dog," Gorilla Leek's eyes flickered to his friend, "let's head downstairs. We can talk in your whip."

The wounded thug limped past the two men, opened the front door and stepped back so his partner could go outside. The friends walked silently into the hallway, the door slamming shut behind them. Once they were outside of the apartment, Shine let the injured man take the lead. As he followed him, he seized the opportunity to draw his weapon, raising it to the back of the traitor's head.

Gorilla Leek took no notice and kept moving until he reached the staircase. He put one foot on the first step. It creaked, causing him to momentarily glance over his shoulders.

"Yo, dog, can you imagine how straight we'll be once we—" The gun in his face set off shockwaves through his nerves. With both feet now on the first step, he turned completely around. "Dog! What the fuck!"

The gun shook uncontrollably in Shine's grip. "You shot my son!"

Gorilla Leek's face went lax with confusion. "Huh? Shot Trayvon? Are you joking?"

"Son, stop the games! The pigs told Lola that the same gun used in Copper's murder was used to kill Trayvon. It wasn't my gun. It was your gun!"

Gorilla Leek tilted his head as his palms went up in the air. He could see that Shine was serious. "Blood, I don't know what you're talking about. I ain't kill no Trayvon or no Copper. You heard what that detective just said—that the police had the person in custody who shot Copper. Maybe, he had something to do with Trayvon's death. I thought Tray died by your gun, just like you told me."

Shine hissed through teeth barely open, "How you just happen to be around both Copper and Trayvon when they got lit? Huh? I thought you were my dude. My road-dog? How could you do this to me?" The gun swayed in front of him, gleams of silver catching in the dim light.

"Blood, I don't know what you're getting at, but you need to slow down. I ain't kill Tray and I wasn't there when it happened," declared Gorilla Leek.

Shine edged toward him and pressed the muzzle to his head. The cold, stiff jolt against his forehead sent him back hard across the wall of the stairway.

"Leek, I know you was smashing Lo! So, keep lying to me, and I will not only put a slug in you, but I will put one in each of your children!"

Gorilla Leek dropped his hands, and his eyes went wide. He glanced at the door to Daffney's apartment, hoping that someone, anyone would come out. He'd no idea what to say to calm his friend down.

Venomous saliva flooded Shine's mouth. "Desiree said she saw you leaving the apartment the day Trayvon was murdered. Said you be over at my crib every Wednesday and Friday banging out my shorty."

Gorilla Leek took in a deep breath. "Look, Shine, I—"

"Save it, son! Lo already admitted it. I just want to know—why my son? You could've done whatever you wanted with my girl. But my boy?"

With his back still against the wall, Gorilla Leek pleaded for forgiveness. He began speaking of his affair with Lola, about how he was drunk when it first happened, and that it was a mistake. "Look, Shine, I'm sorry about Lo. What happened with me and Lo wasn't supposed to go that far."

"But you made me think that Badrick was the one she was dealing with. Why?"

"Son, I needed you down with what we were planning. I couldn't do it without you. That's why I lied about seeing him coming out of your crib, after you found the condom wrapper. Well that, and I was afraid to let you find out the truth about me and Lo. So yeah, I lied about that, but I swear I could never hurt Tray—"

"So, what happened when you came to my crib last Friday, the day Trayvon was murdered? You were there!"

Inwardly Shine was fuming at himself. Why did he trust people so quickly? It was at his insistence that Lola got to know his best friend when they first met, his naivety that allowed the two of them to be constantly around each other when he wasn't present, his passiveness and perhaps his fear of retribution that kept him from seeing the truth all along. But he now knew that friends could betray, and the ones you love could inflict pain beyond belief. There was nothing so bitter as that discovery. Perhaps it hurt worse than the death of his son.

Gorilla Leek swallowed, then swallowed again. He was trembling slightly. His eyes swept over the hallway then fell on Daffney's door once more. He looked back at Shine, his expression unreadable. His mouth slowly crept open.

"I heard it happen."

Shine sucked his teeth and sighed. "Heard what happen?" he snorted with impatience.

"When I unlocked the door, I saw Trayvon in the living room pulling some toys out from beneath your couch cushions. I peeped your coat on the floor and figured you were home. Usually you would be gone by that time, checking on Minimart, and Tray would be sleep. So, I closed the door back and bounced. I heard the shot go off while I was walking down the stairs. It didn't sound like it came from your crib, so I thought nothing of it and got up out of there before any pigs came."

The story didn't make sense to Shine. "So, if you turned and bounced, how did he get shot with your gun?"

The sweat that covered Gorilla Leek's forehead was not the sweat of fear; more than that, it was a sweat of guilt. "My gun?" He cocked his head back and spread his hands in feigned innocence.

With his frustration mounting, with his stomach in knots over his best friend's betrayal, Shine huffed loudly, impatience creasing his brow. Pistol gripped tightly in his hand, he lowered it until its menacing barrel was pointing toward his captive's groin.

"Since that dick of yours is what led you to fucking me over, how about I blow it off and then maybe you'll get your head together and start telling me the truth. Heh?" Shine's eyelids lowered a fraction and he studied Gorilla Leek intently. "Or, better yet," he leveled the gun at his forehead, "to hell with all the games. Maybe I just send you back to the essence altogether. Put one in your head and be done with it."

Seconds passed. Gorilla Leek saw vengeance and death in his friend's eyes. Movement seemed impossible. He swallowed the nervous lump that threatened to suffocate him. His mind racing, he knew he had it coming to him since the first night he'd laid in bed with Lola and was prepared for whatever was going to happen. But he didn't expect for it to happen like this. The wide terror of his eyes fell upon the barrel of the gun, and he noticed Shine's finger twitching lightly against the trigger. Just as he braced himself for the impending impact of the bullet, the deafening crack of a nearby gunshot made his nerves leap from his flesh.

A loud gasp escaped Shine's lips. His mouth gaped wide and his eyes rolled downward as he began to fall forward. He made a vain effort to catch his balance but his feet, beating at the edge of the steps, and the second shot that exploded from behind him thrust him down the staircase. Gorilla Leek watched in shock as his friend went tumbling below into the darkness.

♠   ♠   ♠

SEVERAL SMALL CLUSTERS of people milled about Shine's apartment, performing various tasks. One of the men wore a plain suit, while the others wore uniforms, police uniforms. Some had a painful look of fatigue as if they were slaves being forced to carry sunbaked bricks for Pharaoh, wishing they were somewhere—anywhere—else. Others watched Detective Buck Brown closely, hoping to get some meaning out of the pieces of the puzzle he was uncovering.

Except for a few simple rules for the officers, he paid them no mind. None of them were concerned enough about the case to ask him what they should be looking for, so they searched aimlessly. They cut out much of the carpeting from the living room. They bagged and tagged several items that they had gathered for evidence. They photographed the area and measured it. But nothing they did seemed to catch Brown's attention like the wall he'd been standing in front of for the past three minutes.

Brown stood motionless, eyes wide open, rapt in distant concentration. At his side was a uniformed female officer in her mid-twenties, her eyes blinking the cold and well-lit room around her. She turned to Brown and studied his absorbed face.

"So, was I right?" she asked.

Silence answered her as Brown moved closer to the wall, his eyes fixed on a single spot. With his head to one side, he pointed with one finger, then two, toward the area of interest. Slowly—very slowly—he traced his fingers along the surface searching for an answer to the young woman's question. He looked over his shoulder to the couch—where Trayvon had died—before searching the floor beneath him. Fragments of paint chips and drywall dust were scattered over the carpet in front of his feet. His gaze once again fell upon the wall. There were lines of cracked plaster streaking across it, toward the floor and onto the ceiling. As he ran his palms over the damaged stucco, he felt a hole. He stuck his latex covered index-finger through it then sighed aloud. Gradually, he started moving backwards until he was by the couch. Keeping his eyes on the wall, he kneeled and placed his hand in the spot where Trayvon bled out.

Without looking at anyone in particular, Brown said aloud, "It appears that you are indeed correct, Smith." He threw a glance at the female officer. "Looks like we don't need to find Mr. Mannschein to solve this after all. Thanks for the call."

A ghostly smile lifted the corner of Officer Smith's lips. She gave Brown a nod and whispered, "Just trying to do my job sir. I have more than twelve career points, which is why I put in for a detective track assignment. But—what would be better than a thank you would be to have someone in my corner who could recommend me for an appointment to Detective Third Grade."

Brown cut his eyes up at the young lady, and she didn't shy away from direct eye contact.

"Keep up the good work, and you will have nothing to worry about," he said as he stood straight up and swept his frosty gaze once more across the living room. "But right now, I need for you to lay hold of another officer, so the two of you can accompany me."

"Accompany you?" she asked, baffled.

"Go grab another officer." His eyes became stern as his chin sunk to his chest. "We don't have leisure time to waste on discussing your career goals. Go. Now."

His gaze strayed past her to the nothingness of space. "And whoever you find, please make sure they are not as ambitious as you. Understood?" He turned away from her and walked toward the door to exit the apartment.

"Yes sir," she quickly replied. She rubbernecked the living room and seized the arm of a male officer who was passing.

He gave her a slightly aloof, reproving look. "What the—"

"The detective needs us to walk with him," she uttered with authority. "Now."

Trying to soften the frustration he knew was all over his face, he replied, "Okay," then followed her out of the apartment.

When the two officers stepped into the hallway, they found Detective Brown waiting for them by the door of the adjacent apartment. He stood still and silent for a moment before retrieving his badge from his belt clip and knocking loudly. At first there was no answer. Then he heard someone on the other side of the door, inches from him.

"Hold on. Hold on. I'm coming," the person said in a frantic, thin voice that was partly a whisper and partly a raspy whine.

Detective Brown stood with the doorknob in his hand, impatient to open it. He turned it, but it would not budge, so he listened at the door. He could hear locks being undone on the other side.

The two uniformed officers looked at each. One of them made a joke and they both laughed heartily. They seemed to be amused at the number of locks they heard turning, but quickly straightened as the door opened.

"This thing always gets jammed," an elderly lady complained as she peered out from behind the door.

Brown and the officers backed off a few steps to allow her to come out.

"Yes?" The woman's thick bifocals magnified her sleepy, red-rimmed eyes. Her brilliant white hair was matted and unkempt. She shuffled out into the hallway in a tattered, terry-clothed lemon-colored bathrobe with support hose and worn pink slippers. Placing her palm on her breast, she looked Brown up and down then frowned at the uniformed officers.

"Listen, no need to bring the police here again," she said with contempt in her voice. "I told that other guy from your company that I would sign the papers first thing Monday morning. I'm through fighting with you all."

The two uniformed officers glanced surreptitiously at Brown and then away, not knowing what to say.

"I just spoke to him this past Thursday. So why did he send you all here?" the lady asked. "No need trying to intimidate me with cops anymore. I said I would sell. For the price you're now offering me, I'll sell the building and leave as soon as the check clears."

Brown held up his badge and decided to speak. "Um, ma'am. You may have me mistaken with someone else."

Confusion rose from the lady's face. "You're not with that real estate company? By the way you were dressed—you know—with your fancy get-up and all, I thought—"

"No ma'am," Brown interrupted. "I'm not with any real estate company. My name is Buckminster Brown. I'm a detective with the NYPD. Do you reside here?"

"Well, I am answering the door, young man. Ain't I?" The look of irritation accompanied by the lady's words was sharp enough to sting.

Brown did his best not to react, but she intimidated him. No matter how he'd planned the dialogue with her, she'd already gotten the upper-hand because she reminded him of his mother. His words stumbled clumsily out of his mouth. "Yes, I know, but—um—ma'am—well—I'm sorry, but—what did you say your name was?"

"I didn't say my name, honey. However, if you would like to know, it's Ms. Martha Wellington. I own this building." She pulled her robe closed at the top then crossed her arms over her chest. "So, why are you knocking at my door?"

Brown opened his mouth and sucked in air to say, "Well ma'am, we are working a murder that took place in the apartment next door." He hesitated a second before adding, "And we think you may be able to help us with our investigation."

"Murder investigation?" She appeared not to understand the question at first. "Oh my god, who? When did this happen?"

"A couple of days ago. The victim was a three-year-old boy."

The lady's eyes widened in shock, and she clamped a hand over her mouth. "Oh no! Not that handsome little boy? Sweet Jesus. That poor girl must be devastated. God knows she loved him something fierce." Her gaze fell to the hideous elephant-grey, brown-flecked hallway floor, and without looking up, she asked, "That's really a shame, but how can I help your investigation mister?"

"Well, ma'am, before answering that, I need to know if there is anyone else inside the apartment with you."

"No, my grandson is outside somewhere." Her eyes darted between the curious faces of the two uniformed officers. "You know how hard it is keeping up with that boy? Especially since he started hanging with all of these new friends."

Brown stared at Ms. Wellington, eyebrow raised in response. "Grandson? Is he friends with the people next door?" he asked.

"Oh no. No, no. My grandson didn't hang out with anyone next door. They are much older than he. Although I wish he did, because that Dwight is such a good young man. Known him since he was a little boy, before his mama died. I would have preferred for John John to have made friends with Dwight and his wife rather than that damn Anthony."

"Anthony?" Brown went still. Just the mention of the name of the boy they had in custody was enough to get his mind working again. "And this Anthony—does he spend time with your grandson in your apartment?"

"He does." She shook her head mournfully. "Ever since John John started hanging out with that boy, he has completely changed."

"Changed? Like what?"

"Like trying to be some sort of tough guy now. You know—trying to act like those gangster rappers he sees on TV."

Brown opened his mouth to ask another question, but Officer

Smith interrupted. "Ma'am, I hate to ask this, but do you know if your grandson or his friend carries a gun?"

Ms. Wellington seemed in no hurry to answer the officer's question, appearing to consider it from every angle, wondering what kind of trouble her grandson could be in. She did not want to see him end up in anyone's jail cell. He was too smart for that. An honor roll student for most of his life, he had started going down the wrong path after his father's incarceration. And in her own protective way, she tried to warn him about the dangers of gangs and crime, with the same warning she offered to her own son.

"Gun?" was all she could utter as she fought to find the right words, staring into the mocking face of the detective. The nervousness behind her eyes was almost ready to spill over, and Brown took notice. He could see her reluctance to trust him, and he didn't suppose he could blame her.

"Yes ma'am. A gun," replied Brown. "I hope you don't mind but could we step inside your apartment to talk? And possibly, take a look around?"

"Take a look around?" A sudden wave of worry washed over her face. "My apartment? For what?"

"Because," Brown flatly stated with his eyes drained of emotion, "the bullet that took the life of the young boy came from your apartment."

Ms. Wellington didn't know what to say. She shifted her eyes away as soon as the words left Brown's mouth. Holding the door open and not realizing how long she had been staring at the ground, she finally managed to step aside and let the police officers in.

Brown could see her confusion, her curiosity—yet, she was a bit more than curious. She was frightened. But, why? Then suddenly the wheels of his mind started turning. He was a cop and he couldn't ignore certain things. Her earlier words came to him. He placed his hand on her shoulder as he entered the apartment and looked sharply into her eyes.

Just as the door closed behind him, he asked, "Ma'am, did you just say that a real estate company has been using people from our police department to threaten you?"

CHAPTER 21

"**Y**O! WHAT THE HELL WAS THAT?"

"It's called saving your life."

"Did you have to shoot him?"

"What was I supposed to do? I come out into the hallway to tell you about the call that just came in, and I see your so-called best buddy holding a gun to your head. You should be happy I'm such a good shot."

Panicked voices intruded, bringing an unconscious Shine back from the darkness into the dim light of the hallway. Opening his eyes to a sideway view of the first floor, he could hear Gorilla Leek and Detective O'Reilly talking but could hardly see them. It took a minute to remember he had been shot. Listening, he lay still with his head at the base of the stairs, not wanting to let them know that he was alive until he could get his bearing and figure out what to do. He tried to look to the exit, but his vision would not go that far. Everything more than a couple of feet away was a greyish cloud. Everything was blurry. There was a burning sting slicing through his shoulder as sweat rolled into his bullet wound. But he ignored it. How long had he lay unconscious? He glanced about, bewildered. How could he still be alive? Frankly, he wasn't quite thrilled about it.

A cold hallway draft wafted toward where he lay, carrying the stink of burned cloth and the metallic stench of blood into his nostrils. With his heart hammering against his chest, he slowly reached his hand into his hair. Blood ran red between his quivering fingers. The first bullet only grazed his head. But the second one took a clean path through his shoulder. Somehow the hole clotted up and stopped bleeding before he regained consciousness. The pressure of lying there on his back must have slowed down the blood loss.

Suddenly the voices went silent. Footsteps made their way down the stairs. Struggling against the ground, Shine attempted to lift himself up before they reached him, using the staircase banister to brace himself. With one knee on the ground, his vision came into focus and he could see the two men approaching him.

"That there fella is one tough son of a bitch. He's still breathing," yelled O'Reilly. "Hopefully no one heard the shot. You are sure there are no other tenants in this building, right?"

"What? He's alive?" asked Gorilla Leek as he reached the bottom of the stairs, not wanting to believe what was happening. "Yeah, no one else lives here. I doubt anyone heard anything." He put his shoulder under Shine's arm and helped him up.

O'Reilly watched his victim regain his feet shakily before leaning back against the wall. "We have to finish this," he demanded.

Sparks shot from Gorilla Leek's dark eyes as he turned to face the detective. "You didn't have to shoot him. It was a misunderstanding. I could have handled it," he thundered.

O'Reilly laughed, a deep, throaty sound that sent a warning prickling all over Shine's body. "Ha! Handle it? Listen, you plank—you were about to be where he's at right now. This ape came here to wack you—not discuss business."

Gorilla Leek's eyebrow went up and he gave the detective a pointed look. "Ape?"

"Chill the beans fella. It's not a racist thing we're I'm from. It means a dumb ass. That all," O'Reilly assured. "What you should be more concerned with is why your friend here wants you dead. Because that is not good for business. Trying to set all this up was murder to begin with. And we don't need any more monkey wrenches getting thrown into our plans."

Gorilla Leek's eyes went back to Shine. "Dog, why? What, for ole girl? Or do you really think I had something to do with Trayvon?"

With his hand covering his injured shoulder, Shine rocked silently against the wall, gritting his teeth. His eyes searched the ground until he spotted his pistol at the feet of the Irishman. He considered reaching for it but thought better of it. It was too far away.

Shards of pain swept through his arm as he shifted his body to get a better look of his friend. His shoulder started feeling hot, feverish. Then a heavy numbness mercifully set in. Pain now posed no significant threat to his plans, and real hatred became his driving force. Betrayal had left him an emotional wreck; still angry, still suicidal, yet still determined, still with the will and ability to finish what he came to do—despite the setback.

"You picked the wrong day to start a beef with your partner, boy," O'Reilly calmly warned as he raised his gun to Shine's head. "See, the truth is, I didn't ask Malik to have you meet us here so we could discuss a change of plans. You are the change of plans."

For a moment Shine's gaze remained fixed on Gorilla Leek, and the kicking of his heart against his rib cage alone indicated the dreadful war of emotion in his head. He knew the detective was threatening death. He could care less.

"Hold on, hold on!" Gorilla Leek stood between O'Reilly's barrel and his friend. "You didn't say anything to me about killing my boy."

Rage and hatred warred in the green of Shine's eyes as he felt his bruised forehead, his fingertips coming away wet and crimson. His lip curled, and he said in a sly voice, "I ain't your boy! You murdered my son and slept with my woman. So, you of all people," he yelled, "should be the last person to yap about being my boy!"

O'Reilly smiled. "You people turn on each other in a heartbeat. The boy said he's not your boy. So, get out of my way or there will be two dead apes lying in this hallway. He's too much of a goddamn liability."

Seeking answers in the midst of his troubling thoughts, Gorilla Leek shook his head and stepped aside. O'Reilly moved toward Shine, keeping the gun pointed at his face. With his free hand, he gave the injured man's throat a taunting squeeze before hurling him to the other side of the hallway and onto the floor.

The Irishman's palm shook violently as he shoved Gorilla Leek to the side and leaped across the hallway. Within seconds he had Shine by the throat again. He lifted the gangster by his neck.

"I'm tired of babysitting you," O'Reilly spat as he crushed him against the wall, his massive pale hand clamping around Shine's throat. "We've been trying to keep your ass out of jail. Been trying to work around this situation with your kid—trying to give you time to handle everything. We've been trying to help you all this time." He released his grip and leveled his weapon to Shine's head once more.

Shine stared, stared into the detective's eyes. "Help me? All this time? None of you have helped me at all. Not you or Leek! If anything, Leek has made my life worse than it's ever been!" he screamed.

"I am not talking about Malik. I'm talking about my partner. We've been keeping our department off of your trail, so that we could—"

"Your partner?" Gorilla Leek's eyebrows rose in confusion, and his voice cracked. "Who the fuck is your partner? Copper said this was just between me, you, and him? I'm not trying to have another person come in on this with us."

"Well, you don't have a choice," O'Reilly said without hesitation. "If it wasn't for my partner being involved, your boy would've brought unnecessary attention down on us when he showed up at the station to report his son missing."

Confusion was all over Shine's face, and the detective took notice.

"Yeah," O'Reilly stated, "My partner noticed you when you first walked into the precinct."

"You went to the cops about Trayvon?" Gorilla Leek nervously asked.

Shine ignored his friend's question and glared at the detective. "You've been watching me?"

"Ever since Copper told us you were Malik's business associate," the detective said with a chuckle. "We needed to know you a little better. Copper said Malik didn't think you would agree with what we were trying to accomplish, so we kept an eye on you to see if you would be a liability or not. Truth is—we never wanted to involve you.

"Our business was with Malik, but he swore up and down to Copper that he needed you by his side. That he wouldn't do anything without you. So, we gave it a chance, and then that incident happened with your son. And we knew we had a problem." O'Reilly took a pause and sighed. "You see, we couldn't have the department trace the weapon thought to be used in your son's death back to the murders at Chinnah's house. That would've led back to Malik which would've ruined our plans, and not to mention, probably could have brought the department's scrutiny down on my partner and I."

O'Reilly's eyes swept the length of the hallway then landed on Gorilla Leek. "Because there's no telling how much either of you two would've talked once arrested."

"Partner? You ain't tell me 'bout no partner, man!" Gorilla Leek growled. "How could I snitch on your partner when I ain't even know you had a partner?"

"Well now you know," the detective replied.

"You could've told me you were bringing another pig in on this," Gorilla Leek shot back.

"I didn't bring him in on this. He brought me in."

"Huh?" The bewilderment was clear in Gorilla Leek's eyes.

The Irishman noticed the frown creeping into the corner of Gorilla Leek's lips, and it only encouraged him to say what he'd eventually intended to tell him once Chinnah was out of the way. "Yeah. My partner's the one who actually got Chinnah established when he first came to this country, way before I joined the ranks."

"What are you saying? You guys made Chinnah into who he is?" Shine asked, his curiosity momentarily distracting him from his thoughts of murder.

"Yeah, he's kind of like our black Frankenstein you could say. Our own little Jamaican Saddam Hussain. How do you think he thrived all of these years without being investigated whatsoever?" O'Reilly smiled. "We've always provided him with his cocaine, his guns, and sometimes, even his men. In return, he would cut us a percent of the profits to look the other way. And he would also help us to meet our arrest quotas."

"Meet your arrest quotas? What are you talking? Chinnah be getting people locked up or something? What? Like an informant?" Shine asked, holding his injured arm against his body.

Again, a smile covered O'Reilly's face. "He's a little more than an informant, boy. He knows where his drugs go—what dealers they get distributed to. So, every so often he gives us some names and the inside track to the operation of those lower down on the totem pole, so we can move in on their crew and make some arrests. Then once we clean house, we recycle the narcotics back into the streets through his organization." O'Reilly winked at Shine, a symbolic pat on the back. "NYPD looks like their winning the war on drugs, he gets to keep his business going, and my partner and I make enough money to put our children in good homes and private schools—you know—to keep them away from the reaches of your kind."

Gorilla Leek started to open his mouth to reply to the detective's last comment, but Shine was too fast with his curiosity, immediately cutting him off. "So why make a deal with Copper and get Leek involved if you are already making money with Chinnah?"

"Because," the detective's eyelids lowered, and through the cracks between his lashes he stared grimly at Shine, "the old Jamaican fool is losing control of his territory. His time is up. Rudeboys and Shottas are a thing of the past. No one respects them anymore. You know who gets the respect now?"

"Who?" Shine asked.

"The gangs. The Bloods, the Crips, the Latin Kings. You're kind. That's who." The detective tucked his wrist under his chin and made slight scratching motions. "Chinnah's an old man. Plus, he started getting a conscious about working with us and setting his people up to get arrested. Apparently, someone in his crew had convinced him that he was selling them off into slavery or some bullshit. At least that's what he told us when we asked him to find a way to ramp up the crime in the Nineties. The poor fool couldn't see the future. But his son could. So, we decided to work with him."

"What do you mean ramp up crime in the Nineties? You're trying to create crime?" Shine's eyes darted between O'Reilly and Gorilla Leek.

"Not necessarily. We can't create what's already there. We just need it to escalate," answered O'Reilly.

"B—but you guys are the police. Why would you want to make things worse? Wouldn't it be smarter to keep things from getting hot, so the work could get moved without—urgh, shit—" His face screwed in a grimace, and his body stiffened against the wall. He squeezed his arm and continued, "—without anyone noticing?"

O'Reilly could see the pain etched into the lines of Shine's eyes and lips. He knew the gansta's time was limited so he smiled before answering, "First of all, what do you think I get paid to do? If there is no crime, I have no job. So, we don't want to stop crime, we only need to control it. Besides boy, this is bigger than drugs. If crime goes up, then the value of the property in the Nineties goes down. And my partner has a real estate company looking to swoop in and buy up all of that cheap-ass land that will be readily available over the next few years. They're looking to put some condos up, to develop the area and get new businesses, like Old Navy, the Disney Store, Best Buy—you name it—to move in, so we all can make one helluva profit."

Shine hissed through clench teeth before saying, "So, you're going to p—put a Disney Store right up in the hood around a bunch of b—broke and thirsty-ass niggas? And you think you're going to make helluva profit? Psst! Yeah right!"

"There won't be any broke and thirsty-ass niggers left in the hood," O'Reilly said with a smirk. "Most of them will either be locked up for the rest of their natural lives or dead. See, what your friend here hasn't told you yet is that, before Copper's death, they had planned to orchestrate a gang war together and—"

"Wait," Shine's mouth twisted in an awkward way. Then it bunched up toward his nose. "What do you mean they were going to orchestrate a gang war together? Copper and Leek? What—like a fake beef?"

"Just fake enough to warrant a spike in police recruitment—which would provide employment for some in my community—and fake enough to destabilize your neighborhood. Your people will eventually beg us to come in and lock up all of the gangsters and drug dealers."

"Our community would never rally behind the police," Shine shot back.

A chuckle escaped O'Reilly's lip. "Your community? There's no community in the Nineties. The place is a jungle. As for the poor, hardworking families brave enough to live in the mist of that savagery and terror—well, let's just say that even if they don't beg us to come in, we won't have to beg them to come out." The Irishman threw Shine a pitying look and shook his head at the gangsta's naivety. "After we clean up the area, rebuild the neighborhood, and those new businesses start popping up, they will eventually move out on their own, because the cost of living will be too high."

"And what about all of the mom and pop shops on Rutland Road? You think they are going to just sell off their businesses or close down and make way for a bunch of big corporate stores?" Shine asked.

"Well, I can guarantee you this; they will find it difficult keeping their doors open with a bunch of Bloods and Crips killing each other in front of their shops. They too will ultimately leave and be willing to take whatever offer we give them once business slows down, the cost of insurance increases, and the value of their property goes out the window due to the gang war," answered O'Reilly.

"Fucking devils!" shouted Shine. "That's all you are! Both of you!"

"Yeah maybe," snickered the detective. "But just look around boy. New York has always thrived off of gang violence and drug wars. That is nothing new. It's survival of the fittest out here and you have to be viciously shrewd to stay on top. See, your fear stopped you from winning. You could've been right there with Gorilla Leek at the head of all of this directing your soldiers as we saw fit, like pawns on a chessboard." O'Reilly grimaced and shrugged. "Devil or not, you would've been on the winning team. The plan was for you to start the war and end it on our command. And it all was to begin with Chinnah's death."

Shine hissed through his teeth. "You were planning on killing Chinnah? And Copper was down with that?"

"Not only was he with it, but he helped planned the way it was going to happen," O'Reilly answered.

"Yeah, but Copper's dead," Shine pointed out. "So, what are you going to do now?"

"Don't worry. We're still moving forward with our plans to get rid of the old man," the detective stated flatly. "See, after your son's body was found along with the weapon that killed Badrick, my partner figured we could kill two birds with one stone."

"Huh? What are you talking about?" Confusion leaped from Shine's eyes.

"Well, the new plan is to call Chinnah—to inform him that you're dead. And to tell him that I captured Gorilla Leek, while also retrieving the four kilos. I'm going to lure him here to Harlem—to the apartment—to question Malik about the rest of the drugs, and we are going to finish the old man off for good."

"That's not why you told me we needed to meet Shine here," Gorilla Leek blurted out.

O'Reilly ignored him and continued speaking, "Once the police find both of your bodies, it will look like it all had something to do with Chinnah's nephew getting killed. Since I have your cell phone, I can use it to place you at the scene of his murder which will give the police a motive for why your son was found dead—to revenge Badrick's death. We only need to tie it to Chinnah, which won't be hard. Not only will my partner and I look like heroes for solving all of these murders at once, but your death, as well as Chinnah's would be the starting point of this war. You will be like a little ghetto martyr. Bloods will kill in your name and the city will hire more police to storm the Nineties to stop it all."

"Wait," interrupted Gorilla Leek. "I told you, I'm not about to let you kill my boy."

"Don't be foolish. You have everything to gain from this. You will be the only one left to run the Nineties. We will help you take out the Gully Gods and the Crips. Think about the money and power you will have. The Nineties will be all yours."

"Money? Power?" Shine glanced at his ex-friend. "You really think you're going to get rich doing this? What happens when they have no more need for a war—no more need for you? What happens to your hustle when the police come in and they rid the neighborhood of all the drugs?"

There was an air of danger about his friend that entered Gorilla Leek's lungs like a sliver of ice when he sighed. His shoulders raised, and he took in another breath before uttering, "My hustle?" He screwed his face with the frustration of being misunderstood. "This ain't my hustle. This ain't our hustle. This is their hustle!" He shook his finger in O'Reilly's direction.

"No, it's—" Shine tried to butt in, but Gorilla Leek wouldn't let him get a word in.

"It's never been our hustle. It's never been our neighborhood. It's always been theirs. So, I'm gonna do what they say and make as much doe as they let me make until I can't make no more. Then I'm moving my seeds and my woman down south away from all of this. Dog, all I care about is the getting that doe and killing Chinnah! I don't care about this neighborhood or the niggas in it. Just me and my family. Word!"

It suddenly dawned on Shine that Gorilla Leek definitely had no idea that Dina was dead. Trembling in his anger and pain he sucked a deep breath into his lungs. He tried to speak but couldn't get the words out fast enough.

"Now you're suckin' diesel my friend!" shouted Detective O'Reilly as he glanced over his shoulders at Gorilla Leek. "I knew you were a smart fella. We've always known it, ever since you were a boy,"

"Whatchoo mean, ever since I was boy?" Gorilla Leek stared at the back of O'Reilly's head with a fixed, naïve curiosity.

"Yes, boy. We've been watching you since your folks passed away." The detective's eyes went alarmingly wide. "We knew you would grow into beast one day. You had too much anger and rage in you. And no guidance. You were bred for this!"

"You've been watching us?" Another question jumped from Gorilla Leek's lips.

Without taking his eyes off of Shine, O'Reilly answered, "We watch everyone in the neighborhood. We're the police. It's our job! You guys grow up right before our eyes. From the playground to the corner. All the same faces. We can tell who is going to make it out of here and go off to college, and we know very well, the many who we will eventually have in the back seat of our squad cars."

"What, so now the scramz are fortune tellers?" Shine asked.

"We don't need to be prophets or fortune tellers," O'Reilly replied with a childlike giggle. "It's all about the family structure, and most of you guys have none. You have no fathers in the home. You have no guidance. So, you're easy to pick out. From the time we notice you hanging out in the streets, we start snapping photos of you from our vehicles when we patrol the neighborhood. Hell boy, we have pictures of most of y'all growing up—some of them going back donkey's years—like our own little family photo album." Another chuckle escaped his mouth, more sinister than the first. "Don't you see? Policing is the new parenting. You're our children. We watch over you and prepare you for entry into a private or state institution—but instead of college, prison is where you will get your higher learning."

"I can't believe this shit," Shine uttered, his anguish and pain barely overshadowing his rage. In the depths of his hate-filled eyes, something stirred, and O'Reilly felt a strong need to hurry up and get rid of him.

"Who cares what you believe," the detective said almost heatedly, impatience in his voice. "It doesn't matter now anyhow. And all of this talking is getting us nowhere. My partner wants you dead, whether Malik agrees or not. We're just wasting time."

"Your partner," Shine's voice vibrated with a strange chuckle. "Or do you mean, your boss?"

O'Reilly's head cocked to the side and his eyes squinted. "Aye, mind your mouth boy. No one is my boss."

Shine laughed, and with it came a rainstorm of saliva and blood, painting his lips crimson. He spat it at the detective's feet. "Yeah, ok.

The way you've been talking about him, he sure sounds like the one calling the shots," Shine said, sarcasm dripping from his tone.

"Is that true?" Gorilla Leek asked. "This dude—whoever he is, your partner—is he the one running things?"

"No one is running me or running anything. We make all of our decisions together," O'Reilly assured.

Shine grinned faintly, drew a short breath then uttered, "So was it was both you and your partner's decision to kill Dina?"

Gorilla Leek's eyes wasted no time dancing between Shine and the detective before flickering contemptuously down the length of the Irishman.

"What are you talking about dog?" he asked Shine, his gaze remaining steady on O'Reilly.

His ex-friend was more than happy to break the news to him about his woman. "You don't know son?" Shine quizzed, fully aware of the answer.

With a worrisome look on his face, Gorilla Leek inquired, "Know what? What are you talking? You just said Dina was dead?"

"I thought you knew, and that was one of the reasons you disappeared and—"

"Dog! Get to the point," interrupted Gorilla Leek. "Are you telling me that my baby-mama is dead?" A small frown pulled at the corners of his mouth.

"Yeah son. Redrum called me and told me that they took her over to your place to do some packing, and some crackhead-looking cat showed up. Red said he was looking for you, and he ended up merkin' a couple of our homies before going after Dina. Police found her dead inside of your building."

"What! Na. No." Gorilla Leek dropped his chin, further confused, and was giving slight shakes of his head—no—like he didn't want to believe what he was hearing.

"Yeah son," Shine continued, "you took my woman and the scramz took yours."

"Stop acting the maggot," O'Reilly shouted, his pistol waving in the face of Shine. "You're making up foolishness to buy yourself some time."

"Really," Shine's stare went through the detective, he shuddered. For a few heartbeats, his eyes remained focused on O'Reilly, then he brought his attention back to Gorilla Leek. "My word is my bond son on Trayvon's grave, Redrum heard the dude who killed Dina reporting back to a cat named Buck Brown—a cop! A detective to be more precise! Ask Red if you don't believe me. So, he must be the partner this pig is talking about. Why else would the police send a cat to your home to kill your woman and look for you?"

O'Reilly's brow wrinkled as confusion washed over his freckled face. He was stunned to hear Buck Brown's name.

"He wouldn't be trying to kill me or Dina. We're doing business together," Gorilla Leek stated, almost like he was trying to convince himself.

"Wasn't Copper doing business with this pig and didn't he just get killed!" Shine yelled.

Breath hissed through O'Reilly's clenched teeth. "Don't listen to this boy. He is making shit up! I came out into this hallway originally to tell you that a call had just come in from my partner saying that the lab had determined that the pistol found on the boy who murdered Copper was the same weapon used to kill his son." He motioned his head toward Shine. "You know I had nothing to do with Copper's murder. You were there and saw it with your own eyes. And I sure as hell had nothing to do with anything that happened to your misses."

Gorilla Leek's eyes were on the Irishman, worry lines etched into his forehead. O'Reilly could feel the gangster watching him, so he glanced over his shoulder at him.

"Listen, this guy is lying because he is scared, and he is trying to confuse you. He is in panic mode right now. I know, because my partner told me something else when he called." The old man paused for a moment then continued, "Apparently, your friend's car was identified as the vehicle involved in a shooting that just occurred here in Harlem at a gas station. They're searching for him now. You see, your friend here is out for blood, and you were his next victim. That's why my partner wants him dead right now and not a minute later. He's become too much of a liability. Your boy is done for regardless of how you look at it. Don't let him bring you down as well."

Disregarding the Irishman's comments, Gorilla Leek asked, "Are you sure Dina's dead?" He appeared baffled.

Shine looked over O'Reilly's shoulder and made eye contact with the man who betrayed him. "Yeah, she is. And he's right—I caught

Pauley slipping and I returned him," he said nonchalantly.

Gorilla Leek half opened his mouth to speak, but the effort was too much. Mostly because his thoughts were heavy under the burden of the news his ex-friend had just dropped on him. The only words that came out was, "But, Dina?" Seemingly oblivious to what Shine just said regarding Pauley, he shook his head and turned to stare past the ash wood glass-paneled door at the street outside.

The detective cocked his head and rolled a skeptical eye towards Shine—giving him one of those really? looks—then said, "It was Pauley who was murdered at the gas station? When did you—"

"Oh shit!" Gorilla Leek cut the Irishman short. With his eyes still on the door, he yelled, "Po-Po!"

"What?" asked O'Reilly.

"Police. They're walking out there around Shine's whip," he said with his finger pointed toward the door. "They're looking through his window and all that."

O'Reilly lowered his weapon then turned to face the entrance. He immediately noticed two uniformed officers looking inside the driver's side window of the Ford Expedition. The taller of the two turned toward the building and began approaching the steps to the entrance.

"Fook!" O'Reilly cursed. "Someone must've called 9-1-1 after I shot your boy here."

"You said they identified Shine's whip during the shooting. You think they recognized it out there?" Gorilla Leek inquired.

"Not sure, but it doesn't help that it's sitting right outside of this building. Especially if someone reported hearing shots coming from inside here," O'Reilly answered, eyes steadily fixed on the officer nearing them.

Uneasily now, the Irishman watched as the cop closest to the Ford suddenly froze and lifted his walkie-talkie to his mouth. He spoke into it for a few seconds, then placed it back on his belt and yelled out to the other officer. Almost immediately upon hearing what his partner said, the policeman—calm yet determined—drew his weapon and cautiously advanced up the stairs.

"Something is going on. They're coming up here," O'Reilly warned. "Is there another way out of here?"

"Yeah. The entrance to the basement is at the other end of the hall. There's an exit down there that leads to the backyard," answered

Gorilla Leek.

"All right, well, another change of plans. Get ready to run," the detective commanded as he leveled his pistol on Shine. "When the uniforms get in here, I'll tell them I was investigating a lead when I ran into your boy here who—when seeing my badge—thought I was here for him and decided to draw that there weapon on me." O'Reilly motioned with his head towards Shine's gun on the ground.

A sinister chuckle crept through the flickering, tight-lipped smirk that appeared on Shine's face. Slowly shaking his head from side to side, he licked the corner of his mouth with sadistic delight, sighed deeply and said, "Go ahead and kill me. It doesn't matter anymore. I ain't got nothing left, anyways. But know this—" his eyes fell on Gorilla Leek, "—this cracker's been playing you all along. If he's been watching you from day one, and he's been in business with Chinnah this whole time then what makes you think he didn't have anything to do with Chinnah killing your folks over their property? Huh?"

Gorilla Leek squinted his suspicious eyes as he examined the back of the detective's head. He said nothing, which said everything.

Shine saw the doubt forming in his ex-friend's gaze. "Yeah, don't be surprised if this dude betrays you like you betrayed me. Just like he betrayed Chin—"

"Look boy," O'Reilly interrupted. "You're making a holy show of yourself with all of this foolish talk. Your time is up. Time to say your good byes."

The Irishman's chest heaved. Inhaling deeply, he held his finger against the trigger. Shine watched with unwavering attention as the detective went to empty his lungs. Then suddenly, a halo of light erupted behind O'Reilly's head followed by a thunderous boom that echoed all around. For just a moment he resembled a Catholic Saint. For only a moment. Then a sudden bright splash of blood sprayed across Shine's cheeks and the detective's eyes shot open, his head violently lunging forward as if it was about to leap off his neck. Off-balance the cop stumbled toward the wall, just missing Shine who—after hearing the gunshot—instinctively ducked.

Splinters from the rugged wood paneling punctured the tips of the detective's fingers as he released his weapon and scratched with his hand along the wall in order not to fall. He tried to brace himself, but his weight dragged him to the floor and he fell, landing on his knees.

The officer twisted around to see Gorilla Leek pointing his gun at him. His eyes widened from shock and fear. Mustering what little strength remained in his body, O'Reilly slowly raised his hands to the back of his head and threaded his trembling fingers through his wet hair. He pulled his hand away and inspected it.

Blood. Lots of it.

Another kind of shock passed over his face then without warning, the Irishman's gaping mouth blew a cloud of crimson mist as his eyes rolled back and his body went limp. He folded to the floor with a boneless ease, and blood erupted in great throbbing gouts from under his greasy hair into a spreading pool.

Relief warred with confusion as Shine glared down at the detective's unconscious form. He felt something warm and wet dripping down his cheeks—O'Reilly's blood. Without hesitation he reached down and snatched the dead man's pistol off the ground and aimed it at his betrayer.

A compassionate flash of disbelief froze Gorilla Leek in his tracks. He stood still, staring at O'Reilly's body, gun shaking in his outstretched hand, oblivious to the weapon Shine was holding on him.

The moment the gangster shot the detective, the unexpected sound of gunfire reverberated off the hallway walls and broke the stillness outside. And that put the officers on immediate alert. The cop nearest to Shine's car rushed forward, grabbed his partner by the arm, and pulled him to the side, forcing him to take cover behind the cement staircase.

"Shots fired! I repeat, shots fired!" the officer screamed into his walkie-talkie. "Central, we need back up! 10-13! We received a call of multiple gunshots fired at 130 W 128th Street. When we arrived at the scene, we spotted a vehicle believed to be involved in the recent shooting death of a man at a nearby gas station. While we were investigating the area, someone started firing a weapon. We need back up quick!"

Gorilla Leek could hear the officer shouting outside. But he paid no attention. Instead he looked at Shine, a smile on his face—a smile which collapsed when he saw his ex-friend pointing the Irishman's pistol at his head.

"Whatchoo gonna do, shoot me?" Gorilla Leek excitedly asked, his voice rising with unexpected frustration. "That pig just told you that I didn't kill Trayvon. C'mon dog."

Shine said nothing.

Gorilla Leek stared into his eyes and saw the monstrous thirst for death carved deep into his former partner's face. "Blood, I just saved your life. I could've let that pig return you."

Still no words.

"Don't do this my dude," Gorilla Leek pleaded. "C'mon."

"Don't do this? Really? You should've told yourself that when you slept with my girl," Shine blinked repeatedly, then twisted his mouth into bitter disgust. "Even if you didn't kill Trayvon, you still caused all of this. You're the one who told me that Badrick was banging out Lola. That's why I went along with your plan to stick him up!" Blood-speckled saliva shot from his mouth.

"Look son—"

"Look nothing! Because of you I caught a body!"

The intensity of Shine's stare made Gorilla Leek's breath freeze in his lungs. His stomach clenched as he forced his mouth to open. "Shine, dog, I didn't mean for this shit with Lola to happen, it just did. One day you guys were beefing, and well—I'm sorry my dude. I was just being a nigga." Malik swallowed and cleared his throat before continuing, "The last time I was over there, the condom wrapper must've fell out of my pocket after me and Lo finished—you know—handling our business. When you came to me heated, saying that you knew she was messing around on you—how you had found the wrapper—I saw an opportunity to—"

"Man, you ruined my life!" It was all too much for Shine. He had no defense against the emotions tearing at his insides. He felt his face beginning to crumple. Not with misery, but with a rage too intense to contain. He stared at his betrayer stonily, his eyes working with anger so strong they were almost more than Gorilla Leek could bear to look at.

"Shine, dog, we can handle this some other time," Gorilla Leek begged. "Right now, we have to get out of here. Those pigs will be in here soon and then we will—"

A cell phone suddenly chimed among the dead cop's body. The two men eyed the lifeless form silently, then looked at each other. Shine sucked in a breath, slowly reached down and shoved his hand inside O'Reilly's pocket. He fished around until his fingers grasped the phone, then jerked it free. It rang on, shrill and unrelenting.

The number that appeared on the screen brought a scowl to Shine's face. "I know this number."

Then the ringing stopped. And before the two men could say anything to each other, the screen lit up with a text message alert. Anxiety built in Shine's throat when he glanced at the screen and saw the message. It read: *Call me when you conclude your meeting with Malik. We have another issue concerning the Bye child.*

"Oh shit. This must be his partner. And I know who it is," Shine said, his eyes darting back and forth from the phone to Gorilla Leek. "I know him. He's a cop. He's the one who—"

The distant sound of emergency vehicle sirens made him pause. In silence he listened. Within seconds they became louder and louder. Then they stopped. Shine spun on his heels to face the door. Flashing red and blue lights played across the windows, and he heard the sound of tires screeching and police officers screaming commands.

"We gotta go now Blood!" Gorilla Leek demanded.

Stunned by the urgency in his ex-friend's voice, Shine turned to respond to him, "But what about the coke—" His jaw went slack with surprise when he saw Gorilla Leek raising his weapon to shoot.

It is what it is, Shine told himself as he took aim, his hand tightening around the butt of the pistol, his fingers already squeezing back on his trigger. He wasn't going to let Gorilla Leek get off the first shot. Once that happened it would be too late. But it was already too late. Gorilla Leek's gun barked a fury of flames—through the front door.

The woodwork shook and rattled as bullets shattered the window and a shower of glass shards cascaded down to the floor. The sound of the first shot roared through Shine's head, stopping his breath. Before he could realize what was happening—that Gorilla Leek was firing on the police—his finger pulled the trigger, sending a bullet into his betrayer's left shoulder.

"Argh!" Gorilla Leek gritted between his teeth. "Shit!"

The impact of the shot was like a sudden cramp deep in his muscles. But it did little less than stagger him, and he opened fire on the police once more. But this time they returned fire. The gunshots battered the staircase, sprinkling slivers inches from Shine's face as he plastered himself flat against the wall. A volley of bullets hammered Gorilla Leek's chest, one after another, making him jerk as though he was being electrocuted. Projectiles screeched around him, thudding into the hallway walls on each side of him, one slicing a scorching line across his neck just below his ear. Another shot blasted through his arm causing him to trigger his pistol into the floor around his feet.

He kept triggering the gun again, and again, and again—and each time it bucked in his hand—until the magazine was empty. Still, he squeezed the trigger reflexively, laughing hysterically while attempting to raise the weapon toward the door.

"Run nigga, run," he screamed at Shine over the wail of police gunfire. "I got this! I—I—I'll take the heat while you—you—skate through the basement!"

Gorilla Leek continued squeezing down on the trigger, struggling to level his empty gun at the door until the bullets from outside stopped. With blood pumping from the holes in his chest, he winced at the pain throbbing through his body, then held out his hand to Shine, "Give me that gun Blood—and you get outta here!"

Gorilla Leek gave his former friend one long look that told him he was sorry then uttered with a grunt of pain, "W—w—we'll be brothers again—one day—even if it's in hell!"

Before Shine could hand him the weapon, the hallway erupted once more. More booms, more flashes, and more blood. He stood helplessly and watched Gorilla Leek drop his gun and stumble back a step. It was true that Shine wished his friend dead, but it was also true that he'd not yet found the courage to do it himself. What he desired most, what he longed for the past couple of hours had been the demise of his betrayer. And yet, there he stood, saddened by the thought of him dying.

A few days ago, he would have given his life to save this man, the same as he would've done for Trayvon. Had he not been betrayed, he would have cried out, "Shoot me instead!"—or at best, shouted some trite, dramatic phrase taken from one of his favorite action movies. Yet he said nothing. He watched as his friend, with a calm strength, made his decision to die as if dying had always been a part of his life. He'd been dying a long time—ever since his parents were taken away from him. And now here he was, allowing himself to be taken from his children—to save the life of a brother.

The father of three let out a deafening bellow of rage—a harsh, guttural howl of pain and anger all at once. Then the gunfire ceased.

With hard-earned breaths, Gorilla Leek's chest worked violently fast as runnels of crimson snot dangled from his nose and lips. He stood, wobbling on shaky feet, his shredded clothes bright red with blood. Taking a few deep and painful breaths, his chin dropped to his chest and he slumped to the ground like the duffel bag of a soldier returning home from a long-fought war. For him, it was all over. He would never see the inside of another prison. Malik was finally free.

Tears burned in Shine's eyes. The only friend he'd ever known was dead. And he watched him die, and the worst part was he died trying to save him. His thoughts returned to the cocaine that was in the apartment. It was too late to go back upstairs and look for it. The police would be inside the building soon. Not only was he wanted for murder, but his means of making money once he left the state was now gone. He needed to leave before he lost his freedom as well. He turned quickly toward the bullet-ridden front door, leveled the pistol in his hand, and fired four shots. Outside a yowl went up and he knew one of his bullets had hit a cop. By the time they returned fire, he was already pounding down the stairs to the basement.

CHAPTER 22

"**N**OOOOO! AAH, SHIT!** Mmm—eh –Pu—pu—
please, Chinnah!" Thick wet crimson ringed Jigga
Blue's bruised mouth and smeared his face. Stark
naked and handcuffed to a metal chair with icy eyes
screaming out of his head, he began whimpering—a chilling stutter of
short breaths. It had only been a few minutes since he'd awakened,
gasping for air as cold water splashed hard against his battered and
bleeding face. His whole body was filled with pain, pounding in his
head, his chest, his arms, and his feet. He tried to muscle himself
upright, but with each attempt the handcuffs cut deeper into his raw
and bloody skin. It felt like metal teeth were gnawing at his wrists. He
cried aloud as his splintered bones failed him. No matter how hard he
struggled, he couldn't break free.

A horrific sound welled up from his gut and a ragged moan
escaped his lips. "Mmm—Pleeease . . ."

It was almost completely dark inside the basement where he was
bound. Everything was dark. Inky dark. He could see nothing, feel
nothing—except pain, excruciating pain. This is what hell must be like.
A sheet of sweat covered his exposed dark skin, running down his legs
in rivulets as the ache in his feet throbbed with the beat of his heart.
Someone had nailed each foot flat to the floor. He closed his eyes to
soothe himself. His muscles were cramping horribly. He was sitting
directly under an air vent, and it was showering his soggy flesh with
cold air.

"P-p-please Chinnah. Please—"

Jigga Blue had defecated all over himself just hours before and the smell made him want to retch. It was bad enough he had to suffer so much—the violent blows that rain down from the hammer smashing his toes, the burning razor edge of the box-cutter slicing a deep furrow through his eyelids, the sickening thud of the baseball bat crashing against his shins—but why did he have to endure the horrendous odor of his own waste? It made him wish he could fade away into unconsciousness again.

The last thing he remembered before waking up naked and bound in a basement was the pain—an explosion of brutal, awful pain. He had a vague recollection of being attacked from behind after walking into his apartment, but he couldn't remember much more. The last thought to cross his mind was that someone had just hit him over the head. His world had gone black shortly thereafter.

Now here he was, unable to lift a finger—his hands hanging in emptiness over the edge of the armrests, his legs limp and helpless—the mangled bones twisted in hideous angles, his pulverized feet resembling ground beef—the muscles and meat a mess, leaving the metatarsals exposed. He was a swollen, trembling lump of shredded flesh and matted blood. Tears had cut sharp lines through the crimson staining his cheeks, showing signs of life. But his face held nothing recognizable as human eyes. He was the living dead.

His ghastly mouth gaped, and he slowly groaned out another cowardly plea, "Please, Chinnah. Please don't–"

"Please?" Chinnah's leering face suddenly loomed out of the darkness and swam in front of Jigga Blue like a mirage. "Yuh expect fi mi to please yuh?"

A stiff grunt escaped Jigga Blue's nostrils as he slowly raised his head and squinted into the void. "I—argh—didn't have any—thing to do with set—setting the—the meeting up. I knew nothing about it. He—he—told mmm—me about it for the first time when we w—w—were going there."

Yellowman came around from behind Chinnah hefting a three-pound hammer. Without warning, he slammed it into the suffering gangsta's knee, hearing a satisfying crunch as it planted itself in shattered bone.

"Aaarrgghh!" Jigga Blue howled out in agony. His cries seemed never-ending.

"Now yuh really a Crip," Yellowman said with a dark chuckle. He laid the hammer between the boy's legs. "Next wi be yuh balls. Suh, chat—an chat quickly."

"He was d—d—doing a deal with that cop, O'Reilly," Jigga Blue stuttered between sobs. "He was going to start c—c—copping coke from him just like you. Copper worked something out with them slobs, where they all would work together to move the work. That's all I know."

"O'Reilly? Di Irishman?" Chinnah asked, his voice lacking emotion. "Suh, wah mek yuh did at di store wid mi son—Di place weh him get murda? Di store dat belong to White Mike? Eh?"

"The reason I was there or—the reason we were there was to discuss," fear took shape deep in Jigga Blue's chest and he swallowed it back, knowing full well that what he was about to say would jolt Chinnah's world, "to discuss moving the work through White Mike's spot. He was preparing to get out of the game and sell his store to O'Reilly's partner. And the partner was going to lease it to them slobs."

"Really? An yuh sey yuh nuh kno a ting." Chinnah's devilish eyes were glowing bright red in the dark, and he appeared to be smiling at the tortured young man. "It seems yuh kno much. Suh, den tell mi. Who murda mi pickney?"

"I'm not sure. I wasn't in the store when it happened. I swear to you." Tears spilled from his eyes once more and raced down his cheeks in a snot-laden dribble. "But I think it was Gorilla Leek. Because, before we got to the store, Copper called White Mike, and he said that slob was on his way there. He should've gotten there before us. But when I went inside the store after hearing the shots go off—I didn't see him. Just Copper—laying on the ground."

Chinnah paced back and forth like a lion in a cage, his shadow alternately casting darkness then dim light over Jigga Blue's crimson-soaked face. Suddenly, the Jamaican elder stopped in front of the chair and faced his captive. "Did O'Reilly ave nuhting fi duh wid di murda of mi son?

"I—I—I don't know. B—b—but I don't think he had anything to do with it, because he wanted them to work together."

"Suh, weh di coke?" Chinnah asked, staring up into the darkness above Jigga Blue's head.

"The coke?" The young man's forehead creased, and a look of sudden shocked comprehension washed over his face.

"Listen, mi nu ave any time fi games," Chinnah blurted out. "Weh di cocaine di did stolen from mi? Di cocaine dat yuh had dem deh thieves tek from mi yaad! Di cocaine dat mi pay Babylon fi!"

"I—I—don't know. I really don't."

"An di plan to kill me—wah? Yuh nuh kno nuhting bout dat eitha? Whetha dis dida mi son's idea or O'Reilly's?" Chinnah said sarcastically.

Jigga Blue cleared his throat to hide his surprise, his eyebrows and lips motionless.

"Yuh, me kno," Chinnah said slyly. "Mi kno bout it all."

Out of nowhere, an adjacent door creaked open and the squeaking noise of metal wheels sliced through the darkness. It sounded like a child clumsily dragging a rusty tricycle. The air became heavy with a pungent odor. Jigga Blue's nostrils flared. It reminded him of when he was a boy—the smell of his palm after counting the pennies his aunt gave him for rubbing her feet. He knew that odor well. He had smelled blood too many times to mistake it. The squealing wheels seemed to be devouring the ground, getting closer, and closer, and closer. They seemed to have a terrible appetite. It frightened him. His body jerked. He lifted his head in the direction of the sound. Then he saw it—a wheelchair. And he saw Six strapped to it. One of Chinnah's henchmen rolled it directly in front of him.

The light coming from the open doorway washed over the wheelchair and Jigga Blue's heart stuttered for a spilt second at the sight of his friend. He watched as Six's chest rose and fell pitifully. He too was naked. There were marks on his puffy and peeled flesh, egg-shaped bruises that appeared to be bites of some kind. The skin around his neck was chafed, as if by rope. His right eye was badly swollen and had a raw gash that appeared to have been almost gouged. He had been beaten, almost to death by the looks of it. A moan escaped his cracked lips, letting Jigga Blue know he was still alive.

"Yuh should kno by now dat mi kno everyting," Chinnah uttered with a sinister scowl. "Suh, yuh wa fi continue lying to mi? Mi ave all di time inna di world to watch yuh suffa."

"Uh, Chinnah—look, it was all the pig's plan. Not Copper—or me," Jigga Blue swallowed hard and gasped before continuing. "The pig said he wanted you out of the picture. He felt like you didn't have the neighborhood on lock anymore and he wanted to work with Copper and them slob niggas. They were going to get rid of you, take over the Nineties and start a gang war—to make the hood hot. He promised Copper and Gorilla Leek that they would make mad doe and wouldn't have to worry about getting locked up. They just needed to control the gang war . . ." He spoke so quickly he had to stop to take in air occasionally in mid-thought.

Soon after Jigga Blue began spilling his guts, a sudden surge of muffled shouting came from the floor above, interrupting him. Doors were being slammed open and someone started shouting orders to someone else. "Chinnah! Chinnah! Go get Chinnah! Mi need to speak to him now!"

"Man, mind yuh voice. Him nuh up here. Dem having a meeting inna di basement. Him tell wi to stay up here," another voice said.

Then there was the sound of feet running like a frantic stampede overhead. The basement door cracked lightly and gave a faint squeak as a sliver of light came racing down the stairs.

Footsteps followed.

"Chinnah? Yuh dung here?" The voice asked.

Chinnah slowly turned toward the voice and squinted his eyes tightly against the piercing glare coming from upstairs. It took but a second for him to make out the person's face. It was Kam.

"Wah happen to yuh? Weh ave yuh been?" Chinnah asked.

"Mi try fi reach yuh yesterday pan di phone." Kam, said, panting like a bloodhound.

"Pauley say him call yuh several times an yuh nuh ansah. Suh, wi call Arab to tek care of it."

"Mi cud nuh ansah cuz mi phone dead while mi did following di yankee bowy," replied Kam. "Mi call yuh dat night as soon as mi reach mi yaad."

Chinnah's eyes went to the floor and he sighed heavily. "Mi did nuh taking any calls laas night cuz mi had just been inform of sum troubling news. Babylon come to mi yaad an tell mi dat mi pickney did taken from mi."

Kam's head jerked backward, and his eyes grew wide. "Wah yuh mean? Nuh, man. Did sup'm happen to yuh dawta? Mi did just coming here to tell yuh dat—"

"No, nuh mi dawta," Chinnah answered. "Copper. Mi son did shot an kill yesterday evening."

"Copper?" Kam's face lit up in shock, then he became confused and worried. "Nuh, boss. Dat cyan nuh be."

"Yeah man, sum'ady tek di life of mi ongle son," Chinnah responded. Then he paused as if he lost his thought. It was a long pause—an uneasy pause—marred by a probing question. "Wait. Wah mek yuh aks bout mi dawta?"

Kam glanced around—wondering why his boss was in the basement—and immediately noticed Jigga Blue and Six. His eyes roamed across their naked bodies. Looking at the frightened men he felt pity stir. But it was quickly replaced by fear. Blood-curling fear. Fear that bounced around the inside of his gut like echoes in a cavern. He had bad news for Chinnah, and he didn't want to end up like the men before him.

Kam's lips slowly crept open, his heart lunging out of his mouth as he said, "Bout yuh dawta . . ."

♠ ♠ ♠

THE 4 LEXINGTON AVENUE EXPRESS train rushed with a furious roar through a dark Brooklyn tunnel, the noise of its metal wheels rattling over steel tracks as it pounded through station after station without stopping. It went through so fast, the passengers onboard couldn't even read the stations' names. Not that they cared. Their attention was caught by something else. There was a man sitting at the far end of the train near the conductor's booth, head sunken between his shoulders, holding his arm. His fingers were wet and sticky and closed tightly over his blood-soaked jacket sleeve. There was a lot of blood, so much blood, all over his clothes. All over the right side of his face. Blood stained his hair. Blood covered his ear. Blood dripping down his cheek, drying into the collar of his beige fatigue jacket. He was a mess.

One toddler kept tugging on his mother's dress, begging for attention, as she stood holding the overhead hook, but she was distracted by the sight of the man. He appeared to be wounded. He appeared to be dying. She'd never seen anything like it. She scanned the handful of passengers to see if anyone else noticed. They did. She watched him as he watched them, and then his eyes landed on her. Quickly, the mother turned away and pretended to search for someone in the subway car, twisting her head left then right. She was embarrassed to be caught staring.

Shine noticed her looking at his injured arm, and when he felt she was no longer looking, he looked at it too. His shoulder was bleeding again, blood spilling through his fingers and running down his wrist. Throbbing Blood. Throbbing Pain. And it hurt like hell. He felt weaker with each passing moment. Every muscle and bone beneath his scarred flesh was shouting at him. He was going to need a doctor a lot sooner than he'd thought. Lights flickered up and down the car as the brakes on the train howled out a warning of its approach, and the Franklin Avenue station slid into view. He searched intently for signs of police and thought about getting off to avoid further scrutiny.

The passengers watched the wounded young man struggle to get up from his seat, using the railing next to him as leverage. His eyes darted up and down the aisle, checking each person for signs of anything out of the ordinary. The police were after him and someone had just tried to kill him. He needed medical attention immediately, but somehow his injuries seemed insignificant compared to the mental pain and anguish he was enduring. He needed someone he could talk to and someone who could heal his wounds. But he couldn't go to a hospital—the police would arrest him right away. And he no longer had anyone he could trust. Then an abrupt thought struck him. Eden was studying to become a nurse. Perhaps she could help him to remove the bullet or at least stop the bleeding. Perhaps he could trust her. After all, she did seem somewhat concerned for his well-being.

The train rolled to a stop, the doors opened, and Shine stumbled out. On the platform, he moved with the crowd, and dazedly clambered his way up the stairs leading to the street. Cold air bit down into his wound like icy, razor-edged steel fangs. A huge gust of wind slammed into his face, blurring his vision and leaving behind an aching dryness of skin. His quivering lips cracked like a frozen lake once he reached the top of the stairs and stepped out into the glowering cloak of fog and pollution.

The sky seemed a shade darker that late afternoon as it hung over Brooklyn. There was no real color at that moment. The day was grey as if nothing of consequence had just occurred. The streets were silent for the first time in Shine's life.

It was all over.

His troubles were done. He needed only to visit Eden to ask for help then leave New York. Money or no money, family or no family—it was time for a change.

Small groups of people moved along the sidewalk, but he paid more attention to the cars that crawled down the street, expecting plainclothes detectives to jump out of one. As he staggered across cracked concrete and debris, he plucked his cell phone from his pocket. Holding it in his palm, he used his thumb to dial a number. It didn't ring long before someone answered.

"Peace and blessings," greeted Eden.

There was a long, slow moment and Shine gave no response.

"Yes?" Eden's voice came heavily through the receiver. "Is someone there?"

"Um. Yeah. What's going on?" he asked, finally opening his mouth.

The sound of Shine's voice excited Eden. She had been thinking about him all day. She'd never fallen for anyone so quickly. It was as much out of her character as it was intoxicating. "Hey! I'm not doing anything but laying down in my bed and thinking about you."

"Really?" His voice was hoarse, little over a whisper, his discomfort thickening.

Eden took notice. "Is something wrong?"

"Kind of. I—uh—I need your help with something?"

"Are you ok?" Eden asked.

"I'm fine. Well, I'll be fine. I just got into a little situation and got injured and was thinking maybe you could help me."

"What happened? How bad are you hurt?"

"It's not that bad. It's probably better that I show you when I get there."

"What? Did you get into a fight or something?" She was clearly worried for his safety. "Maybe you should go to the hospital."

"Na, it's not that serious. I just need some help and someone to talk to."

An uneasy feeling tugged at Eden. She could hear the stress in his voice. But she ignored it. "That's fine. How soon before you get here? I was about to get up and go out for some groceries."

"I'm on Franklin Ave right now. About to catch a cab. Should take like twenty minutes or so."

"Okay, well, I'll leave the door open, in case I am not here. I shouldn't be long at all. Do you remember how to get to my place?"

"Kind of. I'll know the crib once I see it. What's the cross streets again?" he asked.

"Avenue D and Forty-second Street."

"Alright, I'll be there soon. Peace."

"Ok. See you then," Eden happily uttered before she hung up the phone and sat up on the edge of her bed.

It hadn't even been 24 hours since they were last together and he was already looking forward to seeing her again. She could only assume that Shine had managed to fall for her harder than she imagined, and the thought excited her. She was thrilled that he was coming to see her, but also concerned at the thought of him being in some kind of trouble. Mostly she was thrilled.

Eden stood up, catching a glimpse of herself in the mirror on her dresser. She bit off a curse, and a sigh blew from her lips. The glass was dusty, and it gave her body additional curves. She needed to fix herself up before he arrived. She dragged herself out the room and lunged for the bathroom.

After showering she felt slightly more attractive, if no slimmer. Midway through buttoning the black skinny jeans that were hugging her ankles, she heard a knock at her front door. She paused and listened intently, the noise becoming terrifying as the knocking sounded louder and more desperate. Then the knocking became faint. Almost a murmur. And she wasn't certain if it was a knock or a deep voice. It sounded like both. Was someone muttering her name? No, it was a knock. Slowly she crept out of the bathroom and walked toward her front door.

"Hello? Who is it?"

There was nothing but stillness now. Silence. Not even a knock.

"Is someone still out there?"

Then it came again. A knock? A voice?

"I'm coming," she whispered.

Knock. Knock. Knock.

She reached the door, looked through the peephole and gasped. Her fingers slid around the doorknob, and she forced a grin as she began turning the lock. The door creaked open and Chinnah's face, more hostile than ever, appeared before her.

The smile that wreath Eden's lips disappeared when she opened her mouth and uttered, "Daddy? What are you doing here?"

7

CHAPTER 23

"**U**NDERSTAND THIS ANTHONY**, we don't have time to play games with you. You need to tell us what happened now. You've already admitted to why you killed Mike Alvarez and Copper Lee-Chin. You're going to prison—one way or another—for a very long time. So, make this easy for us. Just tell us why you chose to kill the Bye child." Detective Seidman paused to allow his words to sink in, and he fixed the puzzled young man with a challenging gaze. "Look boy," he continued after a moment, "what the hell do you think the judge is going to do with you when he finds out you showed no remorse for killing that innocent little child? Consider the time he is going to give you if you blow trial."

Uncomfortable with the detective's words, Anthony frowned then closed his eyes and imagined being outside of the interrogation room. A second later, eyes still closed, he said, "I ain't kill no kid." He opened his eyes and sat upright in the uncomfortable metal chair, fighting back tears. "I know what you're trying to do. They did the same thing to my uncle. You got me on a couple of charges that's gonna sit me down for a long time. So, you like, fuck it, let's put some cases we can't solve on him. Won't matter 'cause I'm gonna spend the rest of my life in the bing anyway. Right?"

Seidman let out a sigh of frustration, knowing the boy was right. It was one thing to say he was the child's killer. It was quite another to prove it. Although ballistics had already confirmed that the pistol recovered from him was the one used to kill Trayvon, Seidman wanted a confession. He was working to ensure that the boy—someone—took the blame for the crime.

"Look, Ant. That's what they call you, right?" smirked Seidman. "Give the parents some peace. Admit to the boy's murder. Your life is done with already. It's over for you anyhow."

"Give his parents some peace?" Anthony's face was blank of all emotion except anger. He stood up from his chair. The harsh *clink-clank-clink* of the metal chain that secured his handcuffs to the table rattled—each link—as it took up slack. "I don't even know his parents. I don't even know him!"

"You don't know him? Really? Well, his name was Trayvon Bye. His mother's name is Lola. She's in the next room right now, waiting for us to bring in the boy's father—who you may actually know," a mild frown tugged at Seidman's lips, "because he's from your neighborhood. His name is Dwight, but he is known in the Nineties as Shine."

Some of the anger had drained from Anthony's face, and his eyebrows pulled together. He was taken aback by the detective's words—that he was the suspect in the death of Shine's son. He knew what it would mean if the Bloods thought he had something to do with that little boy's murder. He wouldn't last a month inside Rikers, let alone upstate. Killing two grown-ass men made him a gangster but killing a toddler—that made him a monster.

"Shine? I know Shine. You think I killed Shine's son? I ain't even know he was dead."

"How could you not know he was dead? He was killed with your gun." Seidman cocked his head to the side, a faint, almost insulting sneer playing around his lips. "What? You mean to tell me you're gun has a mind of its own? That it kills people without you knowing?"

A sudden downpour of thoughts overtook Anthony, and he sat back down shaking his head. Between attempting to make sense of what he just heard and deciding what he was going to do, he muttered casually under his breath, as if in an afterthought, "My gun? Did this happen sometime between Thursday night and Friday morning?" His eyes dropped to the ground.

Seidman's gaze went wide, surprised at the teenager's question. He looked at the boy, so close, his eyes were so huge, pleading. *Just admit it already, please.*

"Well it seems like you know something," Seidman replied smiling.

"According to the mother, the child died on Friday morning."

Anthony took in a sharp breath, then swallowed, trying to gather some words that made sense. Something. Anything. Why weren't his lips moving fast enough? "Look, I can tell you what may have hap—"

Suddenly, the door to the interrogation room flew open, and Detective Cardillo hurried into the room, slamming and securing the door behind him.

He seemed breathless and puzzled. "I thought Brown was in here," he said, holding a thick file folder under his arm.

"Nope, just me and the perp from the Trayvon Bye case," Seidman answered. "It seems you're confused. This is room 2. Brown was using room 1 to question the child's mother."

"Oh—oh—ok," Cardillo stammered, clearly nervous, as a puzzled, half-defiant grin slowly began to spread over his face. "You're right. I must've mixed up the rooms."

"Uh, yeah you did. But even so, didn't Brown run out of the building some time ago?" inquired Seidman.

"He did. He left to check on some additional evidence. I thought he had returned already. He left me a voicemail saying he was on his way back to the station."

"Additional evidence for the Bye case?"

"Uh, yes."

The folder in Cardillo's arms attracted his colleague's attention. "Is that what you got there in your arms?" Seidman asked, pointing to the files. "Additional evidence?"

"Uh, um. Yeah sort of," Cardillo replied, his tone flat, a note of distrust in his voice.

"Sort of? C'mon rookie. Stop holding out. I am involved with this case as well. What's in that folder you have there?" There was an unmistakable hint of suspicion behind his question.

Anthony felt the tension straining between the two men and didn't want to be in the room with them anymore. "Can I go back to my cell now?" he asked.

The detectives ignored him, their eyes firmly planted on each other. The soft notes of an uncomfortable silence filled the room.

"It's nothing really," Cardillo remarked, breaking the stillness. "Nothing that can help either way. I'll just get out of your hair and let you finish questioning your suspect."

Seidman cocked his eyebrow and shrugged his shoulders. "Ok," he said, a slightly displeasing grin surfacing from his face. "But you sure seemed quite excited when you came in here looking for Brown. Like you had found out something important. Like maybe you knew something no one else in the department knew."

"Nope. Was just looking for Brown to let him know that I checked out what he asked me to look into. And that I didn't find anything. That's all. I'll go ahead and see if he's down there in room 1."

"If you say so."

Cardillo turned around and headed out of the room, letting the door close behind him without looking back. He pulled his cell phone out and with the folder tucked between his arm and chest, he dialed Brown's number. He was put through to the voicemail on the first ring. Looking around he decided he should put some distance between himself and the interrogation room.

As he made his way down the precinct corridor he whispered into the phone, "Brown I need you to call me back asap. I was able to get a hold of some info on the owners of that real estate firm. It appears it was founded by two men—Eli Bernstein and," he paused for about three seconds then said, "Albert Seidman—Detective Seidman's father. It seems . . ."

♠   ♠   ♠

THE CAB CAME TO AN ABRUPT, whiplash stop at 917 Forty Second Street in the bustling, Flatbush neighborhood of Brooklyn. Without a word, a wounded Shine managed to open the door and get out of the vehicle. He offered a nod to the driver then limped toward Eden's house. About a quarter of the way up the stairs, one of the corner bricks moved a little under his foot. He stopped and looked at the ground. The stones of the staircase were old and some of them had crumbled a bit with the years. Apparently, everything falls apart. He glanced around and wondered why things had to change. Why people or places he was so familiar with had to go away or become other things. He stood there, momentarily forgetting his pain, remembering what it was to be a boy growing up in Brooklyn. As he turned around to take in the rest of the neighborhood, he saw a familiar car, an all-black Range Rover parked in the shade of the building, almost at the steps, its tinted windows half-cracked. Shine stared at the license plate. He'd seen it hundreds of times before. It read *SOL-JAH*. The car belonged to Chinnah.

He peered into the driver's seat. There was no one in the vehicle. He checked both ends of the block. Nothing. Pulling his handgun from his belt underneath his jacket, he continued up the stairs. Pauley must've been following him since last night. Perhaps he'd seen the two of them enter the house together and reported it back to Chinnah. He may have just led his enemies to the only person left who he cared about. As he stared at the entrance he played over in his mind the worst-case scenario, imaging what was happening inside the two-story home. He knew that if Chinnah was there, he was not alone. At least one of his henchmen—excluding Pauley—would likely be rolling with him. Mostly troubling, anyone inside the house could easily be hiding upstairs or in one of the several rooms. The place was so huge his enemies could be anywhere. Even so, regardless of the danger, it certainly appeared as if Eden needed his help. And he was determined to help her.

The screen door was set into a rusty, bent frame that was curiously dreary for such a large and ornate house. Behind it was a front door that was only partially closed. Shine took a deep breath—the only sound on the entire block until he pulled on the screen and it creaked on its old hinges. He gently pushed the front door open with his foot and stuck his head in a little way. It was quiet inside, so he slipped in and shut the door behind him.

The sound of muttering voices and a throat clearing could be heard not too far off. He stood stiffly, straining his ears to identify the voices, then tiptoed across the living room toward the kitchen. He recognized the speakers as he drew close. Chinnah and Yellowman. The clipped pace of Chinnah's voice told Shine he was angry about something, and that Yellowman was on the receiving end of his rage. Shine only managed to catch every third or fourth word, but he got enough to piece together an idea of what they were discussing. Not only did Chinnah lose his son, but someone had taken out his other child and now he was looking for revenge.

Without warning, a sharp violent ache stabbed through Shine's shoulder and a surge of warmth poured down his arm. The unexpected pain from his reopened wound reminded him of his condition. He staggered back with a soundless grumble of rage and bit down hard, trying to pull himself together. *Got to keep moving*, he thought to himself.

As he slowly crept into the kitchen, he heard Chinnah snap an order. Upon entering, he instantly recognized his enemy even though the elderly Jamaican had his back to him. Yellowman was facing his boss and was the first to notice the injured man's approach.

"Wah di blood!" Yellowman yelled as Shine hovered behind Chinnah.

Realizing something was wrong and reacting as quickly as he could, Chinnah turned to look over his shoulder. He stiffened at the sight of the young man, then slowly spun around to face the barrel of a 9mm as its muzzle planted a frigid steel kiss against his forehead.

"You better not reach for anything or I will throw a slug right into your boss' face," Shine ordered Yellowman, keeping his weapon on the elderly Jamaican standing before him.

Chinnah immediately noticed the bullet wound in Shine's shoulder and wondered if it was Pauley who had done it to him. The injury was clearly serious. He smiled a little then said, "Mi hope it did one of mi soldias who did dat to yuh. Did it Pauley? Cuz mi—"

"Pauley's dead," Shine declared, interrupting him, "And the bullet in my shoulder is the least of my worries. I only came here for one thing. Where is she?"

"Weh shi? Weh shi?" asked Chinnah, a low chuckle escaping his slightly parted lips. "Yuh just say mi bredren did dead an yuh tink mi a guh be more concern wid answering yuh questions dan bout wah happen to him? Yuh mad?"

"Na, I ain't crazy. I'm just more worried about the person who lives here than I am about you."

Still as stone, head tilting slightly to the right as if he were straining to see something behind him, Chinnah uttered, "Yellow, yuh cya believe dis foolishness? Him sneaks inna mi yaad, puts a gun to mi head, tell mi mi bredren dead, an den ave di nerves to sey him interest inna di welfare of mi dawta. Dat ow di youth aks fi a father's blessing nowadays?"

"Your daughter?" Shine narrowed his eyes, great confusion evident in his voice and facial expression. "What are you talking about old man?"

Chinnah's hoarse laughter almost drowned out his reply. "Yuh nuh kno yuh. An here mi tink yuh did smart enuff to try fi harm mi by getting to mi dawta. Yuh mean to tell mi dat dis a ongle a coincidence?"

Shine's eyes misted with a cloud of confusion. He thought of Eden—his Eden—and at the same moment realized what Chinnah was saying.

"Your daughter?" Waves of fire swept through the young thug's chest, setting his heart ablaze as his thoughts erupted into a rage. "What the hell do you mean your daughter?"

Chinnah laughed once more but offered no words.

"Wait! Are you serious? Your daughter?" Shine's anger was mounting quickly. "Is this a joke? Was this all a part of some set up?"

Chinnah hissed through his teeth. "A set up? Wah, mi dawta? Shi nuh set yuh up. Yuh set yuhself up wen yuh decide to court har an den murda har bredda."

"Murder her brother? Copper? I didn't have anything to do with Copper's death."

"But I bet," another voice came from behind him, utterly unlike Eden's, yet unmistakably hers—a voice rough with hate, "like daddy said, you do know who killed my brother—because it was one of your Blood niggas!"

Shine glanced behind him. It was Eden. And she was leveling a .357 revolver at his back. His mind raced as he turned back around to face the hostile stares of Chinnah and Yellowman. Shock leaped from his eyes and he shivered slightly at the revelation of Eden's identity. No less of a surprise, though, was the language that left her mouth. From the short time he had known her, he'd never heard her use that word. *Nigga.*

Eden's hand trembled as she fought to hold the gun steady. Tears were in her eyes. "Remove yuh gun from mi fada!" she shouted in a thick Jamaican accent. "Now!"

"You can't be serious, Eden," Shine uttered without looking back, his weapon still trained on Chinnah.

Her hand continued shaking. "I'm not playing," she warned, again speaking in an American accent. "Get your gun off my father!"

"What are you doing? I came here for you," he pleaded.

"You came here to do me harm like your people did to my brother."

"Again," Shine turned sideways so he could keep his eyes on Eden while pointing his pistol toward her father, "I didn't touch your brother. I had nothing to do with that. I wasn't even around when it happened. I am telling you the—"

"So, what, you're here to kill me too—because of my father?"

"No, no. I didn't know Chinnah was your father. I saw his car outside and I came in her to—"

"To what? Kill him? Kill my daddy?" she screamed, her eyes near frantic.

Shine's gaze pleaded, but she shook her head. She shook and shook. "I can't believe this. This is why I stayed away from your types. Niggas like you—and my daddy."

There goes that word again. *Nigga*.

"Look, Eden—" Shine could barely get out a word.

"Look nothing. Put your pistol down or I will pull this trigger," Eden demanded, her gun hand shaking and her voice raising a pitch.

Shine's eyes swept the cramp space between himself and Chinnah then fell on Yellowman.

"Chinnah, tell your daughter to drop her burner," he snarled, "and tell your boy there to keep his hands steady."

Yellowman bit off a silent curse and balled his fists at his sides. He was seconds away from drawing his pistol when Shine had noticed his eyes growing anxious. For now, he would have to wait for just the right moment to retrieve his weapon. It seemed as if everyone in the kitchen was prepared for murder. Prepared for war. The air was saturated with mixed feelings. Confusion, anger, grief. And there was a hint of regret.

Tears rose flaming from Shine's throat, but he swallowed them down and narrowed his eyes to slits. "Look Chinnah. I know about the business you had going with O'Reilly. I also know that cracker cop had plans to send you back to the essence. He's the one who did this to me." He nodded to his wound. "My closest homie and your son were working with that pig to betray both of us. He's the one responsible for both of our sons' deaths, whether he pulled the trigger or not. And because of that—he's now taking a dirt nap."

Chinnah eyes went wide.

"That's right," Shine explained, "he's dead. And I watched him die. Now, all I care about is getting out of Brooklyn, and away from the cops. You won't have to see my face anymore or worry about me messing with your daughter. My word is bond. Just let me leave here with no problem."

"Let yuh lef wid no problem? Yuh di one holding a gun to mi head," Chinnah replied, his tone calm, even, and cold. "Bowy, yuh di problem—but yuh just nuh kno it."

"Tell Eden to lower her joint, and I'll walk out of here without causing any more trouble," Shine demanded in the same icy tone.

Chinnah's gaze fell on his daughter and his blackened lips curled back over his crooked yellow teeth. "Eden baby," his mouth twisted into devilish grin, "kill him—kill him before him kills one of wi. Now!"

A scowl passed like a shadow over Shine's brow. He was in panic—a sweaty panic—a beseeching panic. "Don't, Eden! You are not a murderer. Please don't. Let him do his own dirty work. Don't let him corrupt you."

Chinnah's head snapped back, surprised. "Mi corrupt her? Or yuh? Dis a mi dawta an shi knows mi wud neva hurt har. Mi asking har to save haarself—" his eyes grew frosty and darted a violent reproach, "to save haarself from yuh!"

"Please Dwight, I don't want to do this. Just put the gun down and leave now," begged Eden through her choked-back tears.

She was scared and confused. Shine could see it in her eyes. "Eden, don't. You're not built like that. This is not something you want on your conscious."

"This is your last chance," she warned, her finger throbbing over the trigger in readiness to squeeze off a round.

She inhaled deeply and tried to gather her thoughts, willing herself to stay strong. *Squeeze, Eden. Squeeze the damn trigger. Squeeze it now. For daddy. For Copper.*

Her hands were still trembling. Trembling fiercely. Trembling more and more as she kept her eye on her target and began to put pressure on the trigger. But the look in Shine's eyes held her. It was a look of pathetic fear. The look of a lost toddler searching for his mother in a crowded marketplace. What she saw in his eyes was nothing less than utter surrender. She watched as his aim slowly sagged and his eyelids fluttered. He seemed lost in thought for a moment.

Yellowman, taking notice of the man's drifting eyes and seeing his opportunity, casually slipped his hand into his waist to retrieve his gun. But Shine, having snapped back into reality just in time to catch sight of the albino's movement, quickly pointed his arm straight toward Chinnah's lieutenant, and holding a steadier grip he squeezed the trigger. The bullets tore into Yellowman's chest as he was pulling out his pistol. His gun slipped from his fingers and he stumbled backward into the kitchen table. He placed his hand to the oozing wound near his heart and slumped to the floor. He didn't really have a chance.

The roaring sound of the 9mm barking flames startled Eden, and moving on instinct alone, she jerked the revolver suddenly, firing several nervous shots. Shine would've continued sending a stream of lead into the dread's pale flesh had not the stampede of monstrous firepower from the frightened young lady's revolver crashed into him, chewing chunks out of his arm and torso. The impact knocked the gun loose from his grip and dropped him to one knee. But almost as soon as he hit the floor he staggered back up to his footing then wobbled crazily toward her with his arms outstretched flapping helplessly.

For an instant Eden thought he was trying to attack her. But then she realized his steps were merely reflexive. There was no fight left in the young warrior. She would have no trouble with him.

A wheeze slid through Shine's lips as he stumbled sideways and jabbed his fingers against the air, scrambling for balance. He fell into the wall, hitting it with the side of his head before sliding down like a groaning, crimson land slug. Folding his hands across his chest, his head fell back against the cold linoleum.

As Eden stood over him, he drank in the sight of her face. And at that very moment, his eyes found a glimpse of heaven in the blankness of her gaze. Strangely, a smile appeared on his face. It was more a smile of relief than happiness. He was finally able to see beauty in such an ugly world and find peace within his pain. As his eyes grew heavy, he heard a sudden howl rip out of Eden's lungs and cut into the air.

"Noooo! Daddy! Noooo! Please daddy! No!" she screamed.

Shine tried desperately to focus, struggling to turn his head in the direction of Eden who had abruptly shuffled past his failing body.

"Daddy, Please Daddy. This is not happening!"

Using his last bit of strength, he lifted his chin just in time to see Chinnah take his final breath. One of the bullets meant for Shine had ripped open the old man's throat and sent him sprawling to the floor onto his back. Eden was standing over him crying hysterically.

"Oh my god! This is my fault. Daddy, I'm—I'm sorry. I didn't mean to shoot you," Her voice broke around her words. "I wasn't trying—I was only . . ."

Eden's words trailed off as Shine's gaze became fixed on the blood-stained, flowered wallpaper that lined the kitchen. For a second, he imagined himself lying in a heavenly garden beneath an apple tree. There was a faint electric hum in his ears, not quite sound, but not quite silence either. It was like a subtle shifting of air. The chaos went quiet and it appeared that all motion had stopped—the dying, the death, and the dead were all suspended in time. Flecks of blood bubbled around his lips and his ragged breath pounded the air harder than the beat of his heart. Sweat and blood had cooled down his burning rage. His fire was fading. He lay still thinking about his life, his son, his girlfriend, his best friend, and—Eden. Her words stood true. The violence, the drug dealing, the indiscriminate sex—it was all a game. And games were for children. With death at his door he would never have the chance to live as a man. And unfortunately, he would never live to find out who murdered his boy. But then it dawned on him—as if a final revelation—he was the only one responsible for what happened to his first born. Him alone. No one else. And as he took in his last gulp of air he thought, *in the ghetto, men are only born after death.* Then he exhaled, his breath a serene lullaby as his soul drifted to sleep in a cradle of eternal darkness.

CHAPTER 24

INSIDE THE TEN BY TEN mess of an interrogation room Lola sat, skinny fingers threaded together, staring in quiet contemplation at Detective Cardillo who was sitting opposite of her with his elbows on the table and his chin propped on his fist. There was a loose-leaf notebook and a pen on the table surface in front of her. In between the questions, as she wrote down her statement, she glanced about, wondering how much the police actually knew before she opened her mouth. Papers and folders were stacked in disheveled piles all around them. Some on the table and some on the grey metal folding chair next to the detective.

"And this Anthony fella we have in the next room—you know him from the neighborhood?" asked Cardillo.

"Like I said," Lola cleared her throat, trying to fight the exhaustion clouding her eyes, "I don't know him personally. I just know the boy he usually hangs out with in my building. He lives next door to me. His name is John John. Anthony comes to see him every now and then. I'm not even sure how long they've known each other. Think they just started hanging out a couple of months ago."

"Has your boyfriend ever had any dealings with him?"

"Who? John John?"

"No."

"Anthony?"

"Yes."

"No."

"Are you sure?"

"Uh. Well one time they got into it when Shine went off on him about not being a real gangsta. But that's it."

"So, they had an altercation?"

"Not really?"

"Then what?"

"It wasn't physical. More like an older dude putting a younger dude up on game."

"And you think it worked?"

"Worked?"

"Yeah. Putting Anthony up on game. Did it work?"

"I guess not. I mean, I just saw him up in here in cuffs?" Lola's eyes suddenly flew up to Cardillo's face. "Wait, why is Anthony up in here anyway? And why are you asking me questions about him?"

"You all live in the same neighborhood, don't you?"

"Yeah, but I am supposed to be here helping you to find out what happened to my son?" Her eyes widened in astonishment. "Hold up. You don't think Anthony had something to do with what happened to Trayvon, do you? What? Because of the argument between him and Shine?"

The detective sighed. "We are not sure what exactly happened to Trayvon and why. But Anthony was found at the scene of another murder, and the weapon he used during that incident was the same weapon used to—" at Lola's anguished look, Cardillo's throat rose and fell as he swallowed tightly, "—to kill your son."

"Wait, I've written down everything I know about what happened for you. I didn't hold anything back. And you're just now telling me this?" Lola snatched the pen from the table and rose from her chair, speaking almost harshly to hide her emotion while furtively swiping tears away with her free hand, "Are you saying that Anthony is the one who shot up Alvarez's grocery? That he's the one who murdered Copper? That he killed my baby?"

"Anthony hasn't confessed to the murder of Trayvon."

Her hand was tightly gripped around the pen as if she was imagining crushing Anthony's throat. "Why would you expect him to confess? Are you kidding me? You can't be that stupid!"

Cardillo's eyes went to the pen in her hand. "You know, you should probably put that down and take a deep breath. You're getting a little too worked up." He coughed to clear his throat and then asked, almost as if he were thinking aloud, "I mean, why would this kid lie about his involvement with the murder of your son? He confessed to everything else; the murders of White Mike and Copper."

Lola shoved the pen into her pocket and turned her back on the detective to stare at the wall. Then with a curious and gentle dignity, she explained, "Because that was a Spic and a Crip. Anthony was false flagging as a Blood. He'll get respect in prison for killing them. He's not going to admit to taking off the child of a Blood. He won't have anyone to back him up once he gets to Rikers. And forget about up north." She swung around to face the detective, the sturdy Georgia Peach face framed by her inky curls. "Yeah he did it. He definitely did it. Didn't he?"

Detective Cardillo studied the young lady, wondering at the truth of what she had just said. He thought it as roguish, as childish, as naively poetic as anything he'd heard before. But it didn't surprise him. Anthony probably wouldn't care to brag about shooting the child of a Blood, since he was trying to be one. But he would be more than happy to receive a reputation for Crip-killing. Cardillo opened his mouth, carefully weighing the thoughts dancing on the edge of his lips, the words he was about to speak.

"If you were to ask me—yes—he is Trayvon's killer. And you're probably right, he is not going to admit to it. Maybe it did have something to do with what Shine said to him during their confrontation. Who knows? It doesn't matter anyway. They found the murder weapon on him when they took him into custody. He'll be charged for this crime," Cardillo insisted with a casual shrug.

"Yeah, but he won't suffer. Unless he confesses to killing Trayvon, no one up in prison will believe he killed the child of another Blood. He idolizes Bloods. So, he will live like some gangsta-hero up in prison. And that's what he wants."

"What more would you have us do?" asked Cardillo, glancing with mock-helplessness at the ceiling.

"The death penalty."

"That's not up to you or me."

"Well it should be. He took my son's life!" She fought against the tears, but they came uncontrollably as she screamed out, "You hear me! He took away the family I was supposed to have! The family I loved! The child I loved!"

"I understand, but you—" Cardillo felt awkward and his words were clumsy, "—did hide the death of your son. So, if you loved—"

"Look, I've told you why already. It wasn't my own decision."

"It's always your own decision."

"You just don't understand. Shine came home scared the night before. I knew something was up. I knew he had did something to—" She couldn't finish her sentence. And just before fatigue lay claim to her thoughts she granted herself a couple of seconds to remember the nearness she felt with her son when he was alive.

"What? Did something to Livingston Badrick?" inquired Cardillo.

"Yes. Just like I told Detective Seidman already. Shine thought we were having an affair."

"Why did he think you were having an affair with Mr. Badrick?"

"Because his friend told him that."

"Gorilla Leek?"

"Again, yes."

"And he was also involved in the murders that took place at that house?"

"I don't know anything about that. You're asking the same questions over and over again." Lola let out a long, exaggerated sigh.

"Because," Cardillo raked his fingers up the side of the stacks of folders on the table until swiftly he yanked out one that said *Bern and Seed Capital Real Estate and Loan* on the file tab. He set it on top of the other papers spread out before him. "Your son is dead. Chinnah's son is dead. And the same company that Chinnah was—"

Just then there was a hard knock at the door. Before Cardillo could turn around, it was opened by a uniformed officer, who stood to the side to allow Detective Seidman to enter.

He didn't waste any time and went straight for Lola. "Ms. Bye, how well did you know Malik Moore aka Gorilla Leek?" He walked up behind Cardillo, stopping short of the grey metal folding chair, and glanced at the folders scattered everywhere.

"Are we really going to keep going over this?" Lola asked, irritation setting her jaw. "I was just talking to Detective Cardillo about all of this."

"Yeah, Seidman. We were just wrapping up our little discussion," added Cardillo.

Seidman looked uncomfortably across the table before continuing, his eyes scanning the papers. "I am asking because he and O'Reilly just turned up dead together. And her boyfriend's vehicle was parked in front of the same Harlem building where their bodies were found."

"Leek is dead?" Lola's eyes wavered and sunk beneath their sorrowful nervousness.

"O'Reilly? Dead?" asked a curious Cardillo who was still facing Lola, searching her face for answers. "Are you sure it was her boyfriend's car?"

"Yeah," Seidman confirmed, disregarding Lola's question and speaking directly to Cardillo, "they put out an APB on Dwight Mannschein's vehicle after a witness had reported seeing him shoot an unarmed man at a gas station. The officers at the scene identified the victim as Pauley Dawkins, Chinnah's enforcer. Shortly after that Mr. Mannschein's car was spotted by a patrol unit." He raised one contemptuous eyebrow in Lola's direction. "While they were investigating the area, someone shot at them. They returned fire, and later found O'Reilly and Mr. Moore DOA. The fatal wounds on O'Reilly didn't come from either of the officers' guns."

Cardillo slowly turned around in his seat and fixed Seidman with round, shocked eyes. "Huh? Are you seriously saying that Dwight Mannschein murdered O'Reilly? How? Why?"

"We don't have all of the information yet."

"But what was O'Reilly doing in Harlem?"

"He was investigating a lead."

"In Harlem?" challenged Cardillo.

"Yeah, in—" A battered, dog-eared folder caught Seidman's attention and he immediately recognized the name on the tab. His tongue moved very slowly as if he was collecting words like fallen snowflakes "—Haaarlem."

Seidman suddenly turned his attention to Lola, and her watery eyes braved his with a scornful bitterness. "Um, ma'am. You look like you may need some tissue. I can have Officer Johns walk you to the bathroom to get some if you like." He nodded in the direction of the uniformed cop.

"I just want to go home," replied Lola.

"I understand. I'll tell you what. Give Cardillo and myself a few moments to discuss a couple of things privately while you go tidy yourself up, and by the time you get back we can speak about getting you out of here. Ok?"

"Yeah. Well, ok. I do need to pee anyway." Lola sighed, and her shoulders sagged down.

"Good, Johns will show you the way." Seidman held his hand out, motioning for her to follow the uniformed officer.

Officer Johns held the door open, letting Lola pass. Seidman's eyes followed the two of them until the door was pulled closed and their footsteps sounded on the tile floor of the precinct hallway. Frowning, he turned his head slowly toward Cardillo, trying to decide how best to ask the question on his mind.

The Jewish detective's scowl curved into a smirk as he opened his mouth, "So, I take it that-that's the additional evidence you were trying to keep me from seeing?"

Cardillo eyes darted from Seidman to the *Bern and Seed, Capital Real Estate and Loan* folder.

"Yeah. That," said the senior detective, walking around the table and staring at Cardillo. "So, what do you have there, rookie?"

Seidman pulled a chair out from the table and sat down—upright—as he thought a Civil War general might have straddled his horse during battle.

Cardillo stared at the folder and then with uneasiness written all over him, he glanced in every direction but toward where Seidman was sitting. A look of anxiety appeared on his face as he finally locked eyes with the detective.

"Chinnah told us that he was leasing his property from a local company. Brown wanted me to look into it and I did," responded Cardillo.

"And what did you find out about the company?"

"Well, it was started up by two men." Cardillo swallowed heavily. "One of whom I later found out—after doing some digging—was your father, Albert Seidman."

"And?"

Cardillo looked away. "Why would your father agree to do business with the likes of Chinnah?"

"He never did," Seidman asserted. "My father died some time ago, and he never had any idea of what Chinnah was into. I'm the one who set the Jamaican up with the leases. Chinnah's actually been working for me—for over twenty years—as an informant."

"An informant?" the rookie detective's face was filled with

bafflement. "But he's the main person behind most of the crime that goes on in the Nineties. What is he informing on? Shouldn't we be locking him up instead of allowing him to thrive, regardless of whatever information he could possibly be providing us? Unless— wait,"

Only then did Cardillo realize what was going on. And Seidman watched him realize it. He could see it on the rookie's face and in the curl of his hands against the table.

"I think you're getting it now, rookie," Seidman said smiling.

"Wait," there was a pitiful look of naivety on Cardillo's face, "you're making money off of what Chinnah is doing. Off of the drugs he's selling in the Nineties. Aren't you?"

"I guess you're not as dumb as you look, kid. Sure as hell a lot smarter than that Brown I tell you."

"But why?"

"Because," it was the sternest tone Seidman had used since they met, "the city doesn't pay me enough to be a zoo keeper to these animals. Especially not when these criminals are out there making more money than me, and I'm risking my life to keep their streets safe for them."

"Yeah, but we're the police. We're supposed to be keeping the neighborhood safe."

"Safe? You think these people care whether their neighborhood is safe or not? They barely take care of it. That's why it's gone to shit now."

"Yeah, but if we can make the city a better place for them then maybe they will take care of it."

"Listen, you'll be forever trying to climb Mount Improbable," Seidman chuckled at the rookie's naivety. "Adults take responsibility for the conditions of their surroundings. Those people are like children. They're too emotionally immature to be that responsible. Just look at them. That's why they are so loud. Children have a hard time lowering their voices to a whisper. And all they like is sport and play."

"That's an unfair assessment," suggested Cardillo.

"Just listen to them. They refer to each other as son or kid. They call their homes, cribs and their women, ma. Their everyday acts of violence are the equivalent of tantrums—not being able to control their emotions. Hell, Cardillo," snickered Seidman, "listen to their music.

Have you ever seen a sixty-year-old successful Rap artist—No! Because the content promotes immature behavior. It's a lullaby for children. So—no, I can't see them being mature nonetheless intelligent enough to control and take care of their own communities," Seidman uttered his words so ruthlessly, with such a severe conviction that it seemed somewhat like madness.

"Yeah, but it is still their community. We only pol—"

"Not really!" screamed Seidman. "Not really! They don't have a community. They're invaders!"

"What are you talking about?" How are they invaders? It's a Black neighborhood."

"I grew up in that neighborhood and before me, my father lived there and before that, his father. There was a time when there weren't any niggers in that area!"

A grimace of disgust washed over Cardillo's face at the mention of the word, *nigger*. Rather than say something, he allowed Seidman to continue.

"And when they did show up, all hell broke loose. The very thing we worked so hard to build became worthless because of their presence. Our family's investments went down the toilet. Insurance and the price of goods skyrocketed because of their criminal acts. I watched as my father's business started to decline, and I knew that I wasn't going to let it happen. So, while most of my people took a loss and moved out of the area, our company started purchasing as much of the property as we could. And we leased it out to the savages . . ." The Jewish officer rambled on, half-angrily and half-excitedly.

Cardillo could tell his senior was convincing himself of something as he spoke. "And then you just stood by and watched while they destroyed the property?" the rookie asked.

"As long as I made money, I couldn't give a damn at the time," replied Seidman.

"So, what? You get some kind of cut off of the drugs Chinnah sells? To look the other way? Is the money really that good? I mean, what do you tell yourself to sleep at night?" challenged Cardillo. "That this is some kind of career opportunity?"

"That's exactly what it is. And now there's a bigger opportunity in front of us. We can get the neighborhood back and change it for the better," declared the Jewish detective.

"How?"

"Just look at it out there. The appearance of the gangs has driven the value of the property down in that neighborhood. It's damn near worthless. So, our company can now buy up the rest of the area for nigger-pennies. And guess what?" Seidman raised his chin, his eyes brimful of greed. "An even larger firm has made us an offer. They want to build it out over the next coming years. You know, bring value to the neighborhood, and make it worth something again. Something that will ultimately make my bank account look a lot better and bigger. Something that could do the same for you. We're going to make the ghetto great again."

Seidman peered into Cardillo's eyes. Suspicion and curiosity created a nervous greed that prevented the young rookie from looking away.

"But how can you make the ghetto great again, with people like Chinnah and gangs like the Bloods and Crips running around?" asked Cardillo.

"Well, once we ignite a gang war," Seidman snickered, "we will finally be able to get the city to invest in hiring and training more officers that will hopefully look like you and me. More cops on the streets means less gangs on the corners. They will either kill each other or we will lock them up. One way or another we will being saying our final goodbyes to all those little childlike and feeble-minded criminals."

"Hold up. Now, you're talking about starting a gang war? Are you serious? I mean, you don't possibly think you can pull that off?"

Seidman's eyes raked across the room, making the space between them thick with suspicion. He smiled. "Can I trust you rookie?"

Cardillo gave a hesitant nod in answer.

The senior detective didn't break his grin. "Good. Good. Because you could very well be right there with me when the money starts rolling in. You need it don't you? For that new wife? That new baby? Right?"

Another nod.

"I'm sure you do. And this is how we can make it happen . . ."

Cardillo tilted his head to catch his colleague's lowered voice.

The detective spoke like an intimate and close companion. "All we have to do is spark the fire, then sit back and let it burn."

"Yeah, but what happens when the fire gets out of control," asked Cardillo. "Fires are unpredictable. The same fire we set just may end up burning us."

"Not if you contain it and keep it confined to a specific area—you know, like an oven." Suddenly his grin broadened then faded abruptly. "Then you can turn the heat up or down when you want to."

"You're talking about controlling crime?"

"Exactamundo my friend!" exclaimed Seidman.

"But how?"

"Well, O'Reilly and I had set up a meeting between a well-respected Blood and Crip in that area."

"Gorilla Leek and Copper?"

"God damn, you're so smart, it's giving me a hard-on!" Seidman's chubby cheeks broke into a wide sinister grin. "Yes, they both agreed to move their little minions against each other to create a war. A war that we all would profit from."

"But now, they're both dead. And so is O'Reilly." Cardillo looked awkward, as if unsure of his next words. "So how do you plan to start this war now?"

A rather hollow-sounding, snorting of laughter exploded through Seidman's pursed lips, shaking his belly up and down. "Do you know how many little wannabe thugs are out there looking to make a name for themselves off of gangbanging? They're a dime a dozen. There's no shortage of niggers looking to take Gorilla Leek or Copper's place. We just have to find a good nigger. You know, a nigger we could control. A nigger that wants to be a big nigger."

Cardillo scrunched up his face and glared at his senior. "Can you not use that word?"

"What? Nigger?" Confusion widened Seidman's eyebrows. "Hell Cardillo, they use it more than I do. Do you know what they use to call my people when we first came to this country? Or even what they used to call your people?"

"Yes, I am aware," Cardillo screwed his face up, not impressed by what he heard.

Seidman continued, "Back then, we suffered discrimination. We were denied jobs. Your people and my people. We were behind in the race toward the American Dream, while others were ahead. And look at our people now! We have worked hard to earn our respect over here. We didn't beg or hold our hands out for clothing, and shelter. We did not need affirmative action to get us jobs or welfare to feed our families. We made a way for ourselves. Because that's what men do! They make a way, not an excuse."

A rather tense look came over Cardillo's face. "Yeah, but given the opportunity, they could one day make a way for themselves. Because that's what this country is about. Isn't it? It's not about trying to set another people back. If we were able to do it, then we should be helping them to do it. That's equality. That's what life is about, right?"

"No! It's about liberty! And they don't want the freedom to be responsible for their own conditions because they don't want to think for themselves. As a people they have been in this country longer than you and me, but they blame us for their suffering. Not their deadbeat daddies nor their angry mothers. There just like the 19th century lazy-ass rednecks who destroyed the south due to their love of rude and uncultivated behavior." Seidman paused to take a breath then continued, "That's why we must contain and control them. Think about it. What is going to happen once the crimes they commit seeps out of the ghetto and into your pretty little suburbs? Once they surround your beautiful wife and daughter? Huh?"

"Well, that's even more of a reason to stop the crime!" Passion danced in Cardillo's eyes.

"Don't be naïve." The Jewish detective let out a cruel laugh. "The only way to stop it would be to eradicate their population. And take it from me—I know from my people's history—when you try to destroy another people, they become stronger. It's the nature of life. Survival of the fittest. No, instead you control them—to ensure they remain weak and forever do you no harm."

From the look on the young detective's face, Seidman could tell he was deep in thought, weighing the situation, trying to make up his mind. Cardillo couldn't deny the need for the extra income. And he sure as hell knew he would never be a force of change within that community. This became apparent over the last couple of days. Seidman was a thirty-plus year veteran of the police department and knew the streets better than most. If the Jewish detective could get away with it for all of these years, then so could he. Not to mention, Seidman would probably be more instrumental in helping his career than Brown, because of his seniority—and the color of his skin. Besides, what was he going to do? Go to bat for a people who cared nothing for him or his family? No.

"I suppose you're right," Cardillo finally uttered.

"I am right. And I can use your help," Seidman said as matter-of-factly as he could manage under the rookie's uncertain gaze.

Cardillo began shaking his head yes. "Alright. Alright. I have your back on this. What do I need to do?"

A diabolical grin leaped off of Seidman's lips. "First, we need to find out the whereabouts of Dwight Mannschein. Unfortunately for us, he has put himself in a bad predicament. We won't be able to have any further dealings with him, and it would be best if we could get to him before anyone else does. With him killing O'Reilly, he may know more than he needs to know now. And we can't risk letting him talk to another officer." Seidman shook his head. "It's a shame. He could've proven to have been a perfect fit for us. I even knew his father. We grew up together."

"So, now you're talking about killing Dwight? Committing murder?" Cardillo couldn't mask the surprise on his face. "He came to us looking for help with finding his missing son—his son who is now dead. We were supposed to be helping him. Not killing him."

"And we did help him. We have his son's killer in the next room. We did our job."

"But isn't it our job to protect, not kill," Cardillo said with naïve concern.

"Yeah, protect property, not criminals." Seidman paused and studied Cardillo. "Are you sure you're onboard with this? You don't seem certain."

Cardillo thought over his colleague's words. "Yeah. Yeah. I'm onboard. Just a little nervous I guess."

"Good, because now that O'Reilly is no longer with us, I'm going to need someone in this precinct who I can trust. Someone to back me up. It has to be you."

"Sure," the rookie swallowed audibly, then reluctantly said, "but what's the plan now that your star players are dead, and we have no idea where Dwight Mannshcein is?"

"I'm currently working on that. That's why I'm keeping that young boy in Room 2 under my close supervision."

"Who Anthony? Why? I mean, how? How are you going to use him? He's a nobody."

"Yeah but now," Seidman said rubbing his chin as if to wipe away the grin that had just appeared on his face, "after killing a Crip and a former Latin King, he'll be a somebody."

"Yeah, a somebody who also killed the child of a Blood," Cardillo pointed out. "Who is going to side with him? Everyone will be looking to wack him."

"The Bloods in that neighborhood will side with him, once they find out he only murdered that boy because he caught wind of the father's dealings with Copper and his Crips. He was going after a traitor."

"But that's not true." A shade of anxiety crept over Cardillo's face.

"We will make it true. Niggers spread gossip like it's the gospel."

"But how can Anthony be of any use to us? He will be in prison."

"Even better," Seidman grinned the grin of a mad scientist. "Now he will have the credentials to pull this off. And he is just weak enough to do what we say. To go in every direction that we point him in. Besides, who said you can't start a war from prison? That's how it usually goes down in their world."

"So, you have all of this covered?"

"Yes," The blackness of Seidman's thoughts was evident in his gaze. "Though I was hoping to get a confession out of Anthony before he gets shipped out."

"They're shipping him out now?"

The Jewish detective nodded. "The uniforms are preparing him for transfer. We're going to book him on all the murders, including Trayvon Bye. They were putting the handcuffs on him when I got the call that O'Reilly was found murdered. Which is why I rushed in here to find out what the girl knew. I am almost certain her boyfriend had something to do with it."

"Maybe Anthony knows where Dwight is," added Cardillo with a puzzled wonder.

"Not sure." Seidman sighed. "Actually, would you mind finding out if he does? You could oversee his transfer just in case he wants to confess or has anything additional to tell us. You know, also to get him to understand how valuable he will be to us in the near future and vice versa. Since you said you are willing to help."

Cardillo raised an eyebrow while taking that as his cue that their conversation was over. "Sure, I can do that."

The young rookie wasn't confident that he was doing the right thing, but he was certain he was choosing the right side. After all, he was a team player, and they were all born wearing the same uniform. Maybe one day, after he has secured a position of authority, he will be able to change the system. But as of now, he realized that it was designed for only the strong to prosper. And with a wife and a daughter who depended on him, he had not the time to be weak. The gangbangers had their hustle, and now he had his. They didn't think twice about the crimes they committed to feed their families. Nor would he. Without saying another word, he got up from his seat and stalked out the door.

His pulse raced as soon as he stepped into the hallway and saw Anthony handcuffed and restrained by two uniformed men right outside of Room 2. He wasn't sure what he would say or how he would go about getting any additional information out of him. The boy seemed hardened to his predicament—not just his current predicament, but the predicament that he had found himself in his entire life. He wasn't going to talk more than he had already. And by the uncomfortable look on his face, it didn't appear he was in the mood for dealing with any more cops.

Upon noticing Detective Cardillo, one of the officers pulled the teen forward, then shoved him back against the hallway wall. Hard.

"Sit down there until the detectives give the okay to drag your ass out of here," the officer commanded, pointing to a long wooden bench that lined the wall between the doors of both interrogation rooms.

Anthony sat compliantly, not saying a word. He was docile. As the rookie detective neared the officers and the teen, he heard a female voice call his name, "Detective Cardillo! Detective Cardillo!"

He looked behind as a uniformed officer came running toward him.

"Detective Cardillo!" she yelled once more.

Cardillo and both of the officers turned to face her. She stopped in front of them, panting, struggling to catch her breath.

"Yes," answered Cardillo.

"Sir, roughly an hour ago, calls began pouring into the station. There were reports of shots fired in the Forty-Second Street block of Flatbush. One of the callers was a nearly frantic, unidentified woman claiming to be the owner of the home from where the gunshots originated," she paused, inhaling deeply. "She reported that three men were dead inside her house. When our units arrived at the scene they identified the men. Two of them were suspects in your investigation—Orville Lee-Chin and Dwight Mannschein."

Cardillo took a step back and his face went pale, "What?"

"Did she just say that Shine was dead?" screamed another woman's voice from behind the Italian. "Did I just hear that? Huh?"

The rookie detective turned to find Lola a foot away from him, covering her mouth. She'd just returned from the bathroom, escorted by Officer Johns. Her eyes were wide. Shock filled her face.

"Tell me I didn't lose him too. Please. Tell me Shine's not dead. Please!" she pleaded, panic in her voice.

Cardillo opened his mouth, but no words had come. Lola's shoulders heaved, and tears poured furiously down her cheeks. She stood there sobbing uncontrollably. She had lost a son. And now, both of the men she loved were dead. She felt all the horror, heartbreak, and hopelessness of the past couple of days slam into her like one great big eighteen-wheeler of misery.

"I'm sorry ma'am," said the female officer who broke the news. There was a hint of sorrow in her voice, something like compassion. Sympathy. It strangled Lola, black, sharp, and dreadful.

"Please, are you sure it was Shine?" Lola begged.

"Unfortunately, yes. He was I.D.'d by the female who shot him," the female officer replied.

"What? A female? At her house?" Lola's eyes pleaded for understanding. "Why is this happening to me? Why did this happen to Shine?"

"I told that nigga that he would be dead soon," Anthony whispered from the bench, that bludgeoning voice of his so lethal. "I warned him."

Lola really, really didn't want to think about him, and everything his words implied. About her son. About all that he took from her. About what needed to happen now—between them—if she could somehow find a way.

"How was he going to protect his own self, when he couldn't even protect his own son?" Anthony asked, his tone a ragged little bit of a whisper, hardly there at all with the sound of Cardillo and the other officers around them chatting about the details of Shine's murder.

His sinister voice matched the almost-grin he shot Lola's way. It sent a thunderbolt of something terrible like hate arrowing through her. It was as if she'd not only lost the ones she loved but had now lost herself. With one hand in her pocket, she clenched the pen she took from the interrogation room into the palm of her fist, trying to squeeze out the yearning to reach for the animal who hurt not just her boy— but her boys. All of them. From the moment her son's killer pulled the trigger, he had set in motion a chain of events that ruined the lives of everyone she loved. Even herself, the person she had never learned to love. She eyed Anthony, a thin, angular build dressed in a pair of camouflage fatigues, Timberland boots, and a red hoodie. He wasn't that big of a kid.

"You murdered my baby," she said as she neared him. "And now Shine is dead." She continued moving sluggishly toward him. "My baby will be born without a father because of you."

She slid next to Anthony so unobtrusively shadow-like that Cardillo scarcely noticed her movement. What she had said to the teen, the officers did not hear, for her short-lived words were uttered in a low, murmuring voice. Instinctively she removed her hand from her pocket and it went flying up into the air. Her limbs felt numb from the rising adrenaline, then forgetting for a moment that she was in a precinct and with her mouth contorted in fury, she brought the pen down into Anthony's neck. Violently, throwing all of her body weight into it.

Hell blazed across the boy's throat. The realization that it was a fatal blow leaped from his wide eyes. Panic tore through every nerve ending. He tried to scream for help, but she was too swift. Stabbing and stabbing. Hacking away at his throat. There was crimson covering the pen. Splashing onto the bench. Splashing against the wall. Red against her dark, cherry-oak face. The pen came down again and again and again.

"No! Stop!" Cardillo's command came out in a huff of hysteria.

Lola hesitated momentarily. And then the pen came down again. The sound, much the same as the wet scraping noise of a spoon scooping pulp off a watermelon rind.

Cardillo snatched her arm and jerked her to him. But it was too late. Anthony's ghost had been freed from his earthly prison as his body slumped down into the bench before tumbling over onto the hard ground like a felled tree.

"Because of him, I lost everything! My baby is gone! Please let me go! I have to find my baby! I have to find my baby!" she screamed, eyes wild with rage and impulse.

The other officers raced in, moving around her, and dragging her away from Anthony's corpse. Screaming hysterically, with spit caked around her lips, she kicked and struggled to break free of their grasp. Officer Johns yanked her arm from Cardillo's grip and twisted it behind her back. He then guided her down the hallway toward the holding cells, walking swiftly.

"It's not my fault!" Lola's imperceptible rant echoed through the corridor, momentarily bouncing off the walls just before she disappeared around the corner.

Cardillo glanced at the teen's lifeless body. His eyes widened, and his blood ran cold.

Detective Seidman came storming out of the interrogation room. "What's going on out here?"

Without waiting for one of the officers to answer, Cardillo started to reply, but Detective Brown's voice sounded out of nowhere, stopping him, "Jesus Christ! What in the hell just happened?"

Everyone turned to find Buck Brown standing at the entrance of the precinct with a young boy in handcuffs. A strange look of disbelief crossed Cardillo's face, a look of curiosity shredded by horror, a look that demanded soundlessly to know one thing—who was the boy standing next to his partner. Although he'd never seen the teen, he somehow knew that he had something to do with the Baby Bye case.

"Is that the suspect from the Copper Lee-Chin murder?" Brown asked with an anxious and urgent tone, pointing at the fresh corpse.

"Uh, yeah. Well, it was," Cardillo was still trying to come to grips with what just happened.

"I take it, you guys never got a confession out him for the Trayvon Bye murder," Brown said, making light of the crimson mess before him.

"Actually, he confessed right before we brought him out into the hallway—well," Seidman shrugged his shoulders and sighed before continuing, "well, right before this happened."

"He confessed?" asked Brown.

"Yes. Didn't he?" Seidman fixed Cardillo with pleading eyes.

"Uh, he said he—" Cardillo couldn't get the words out quickly enough.

"Bullshit! This is Trayvon Bye's killer," Brown motioned his head to the young boy next to him. "His name is Jonah Jonathan Wellington aka Lil John John."

"Huh?" Cardillo was thoroughly confused, but even more so, curious.

"According to what this young man just told me, Mr. Anthony Crooks had asked him to hold his gun for him last Thursday because of the heavy police presence in the neighborhood that night. He didn't want to risk getting arrested walking the streets with an illegal firearm," revealed Brown. "Curious as to how it felt to handle a weapon, Lil John John here picked it up and started posing in the mirror with it. You know, trying to mimic his favorite rappers. Unfortunately, he didn't know it was loaded and it accidently went off."

"That doesn't make sense," declared a nervous Seidman. "Trayvon didn't die in that boy's apartment. He was shot inside of the parent's home."

"John John lives right next door," added Brown. "And the walls in that neighborhood were built in such thin layers, the bullet penetrated with no problem."

"Are you serious?" Cardillo's eyes blinked rapidly.

"Yes. He confessed in his grandmother's presence. He is our shooter," Brown took in a gulping breath. "And he never had any idea of what he had done. He never even knew he had killed Trayvon."

"This is crazy. How can we be sure that he is not saying this to take the rap for his friend? You know, some kind of gang loyalty he's trying to prove?" inquired Seidman.

Then suddenly—abruptly—out of nowhere—it occurred to the Jewish detective that his plan was not in danger of failing. That this was a situation he could take advantage of. He saw the brighter side of it all.

Seidman stared hard at Brown. "Uh, actually, Brown. Do you mind if I speak with you for a moment?"

"What? Now?" The Black detective's eyes quickly scanned the bloody scene and the shocked officers around him, officers struggling to make sense of what just happened. "I don't think this is the right time for us to have a sidebar conversation."

"The uniforms can take care of this. The person who did this is already in custody. Let them clean this up. We need to speak now. This is important," snapped Seidman, keeping his demanding eyes fixed on

Brown.

"But I have the kid and I need to book him."

"Bring him into Room 1, we can speak there," Seidman replied, holding open the door to the interrogation room.

"In front of him?"

"It concerns him. So, yeah."

Brown shrugged his shoulders and walked through the door that his colleague held open. As it closed behind the three of them, Brown checked his watch for the time.

"I hope this won't take long. Things are going to hell out there." Brown motioned for John John to sit at the table, and he obeyed. "And I need to get this kid booked."

"Not so fast super sleuth," scoffed Seidman. "Are you sure you want to throw this kid to the wolves? I mean, look at him. He won't survive one day behind bars."

"Huh? What are you talking about? He's our perp."

"Yeah, but you said it was an accident. Right?"

"It was," assured Brown.

"Then why should he suffer when we have real criminals out there that we could be chasing?" asked the Jewish detective, authority dripping in each word. "Look, that Anthony boy already confessed to me. Whether he was lying or not—we got a confession out of him. And if he wasn't guilty of committing that specific crime, he sure as hell was guilty of something."

"Are you seriously—"

"Brown, C'mon," interrupted Seidman. "You and I both know that you do not want to see this kid go to prison. Prison, Brown! Prison! Where he will get corrupted and become just like Anthony and every other thug out there. Right now, he's just simply a victim."

Brown glanced at the kid, his sunken eyes seeming to widen and bulge out of his head. The homicide detective shrugged his shoulders and innocently reasoned, "Yeah, but he is guilty."

"Guilty of what? Being misled by savages? He's just a boy. He has the mind of a child."

"So, what? We just let him get away with committing murder? And blame it on a dead gangbanger?"

"Yes!" Seidman stated with excitement. "You always talk about helping your people. Well now's your chance. Let the real fuck-up take the blame for this. He's already a stiff."

"But what? We just teach this kid that he can break the law and get away with it? This may give him the balls to think he can do this again."

"Yeah, well then we will be there to lock him up when he does." Seidman looked overly happy standing there staring at the boy, which seemed hard for Brown to grasp. He had a grin on his face that the detective had never seen.

"I don't get it," Brown muttered.

"What's there to get? Release him. And if it makes you feel better, you can keep an eye on him to make sure he doesn't fall into a life of crime," Seidman paused, still smiling. "But if he does, we'll be there waiting for him."

Brown had well considered letting the boy go when he first arrested him. He didn't want to see another fatherless youth get lost in the system. He knew that to charge the kid with murder would not do much except ensure that he'd become a monster. Or at worst, he would become prey for the real monsters.

He felt the burden then, heavier than he ever had before. All that he desired was the safety and success of his people, his city, and his country. But the existence of the gangs threatened all of that, whether they were murdering each other or influencing young impressionable minds like Lil' John John. They were a danger that would probably always be around to some degree. Much as he wanted to arrest the guilty, he knew that the more misguided children he sent to prison the better chance the gangs had of recruiting them and ruining their lives forever. There would be no salvation awaiting John John behind bars. The correctional facilities never corrected anyone. The ghosts of countless dead youth, the incarcerated souls of poverty, demons upon demons in that city, counting off years until John John would become one of them—until another child is denied adulthood. Until the innocent everywhere is devoured.

Brown nodded, and his forehead furrowed. His jaw was tight, and he appeared uncertain of his own thoughts. "Ok, let's charge the Anthony kid with the murder." He swallowed hard. "I'll speak to John John's grandmother and let her know."

"Good," replied Seidman. "Good. You're doing the right thing and that's what's important. Won't you go ahead and reach out to the grandmother, and I'll talk to the young man here to make sure he understands how lucky he is."

"Sure," Brown said quietly, and hesitantly, his gaze avoiding John John.

Seidman watched as the detective slowly spun on his heels and went out into the hallway. The loud bang of the door slamming shut jolted the boy to alertness. He sat up groggily and met Seidman's eyes for what seemed like a long, silent moment.

"I'm not going to jail?" John John reluctantly asked.

"No, at least not today," said a smiling Seidman. "And you have me to thank for that."

"For real? I get to go home?" The boy seemed fearfully excited.

"Sure, but you will be repaying me back my kindness. I'm going to need you to help me with a couple of things. Things that could make you a very powerful young man in the hood one day," suggested the detective.

"Me? Are you sure?"

"Yeah, I am quite certain you are the right person to assist me," Seidman's grin faded into a devilish scowl, and his unwavering eyes sparkled with wickedness. "After all—you do owe me your life now."

Beyond the door to the interrogation room, the footsteps and chaotic rumbling of several police officers could be heard as they scurried through the hallway hauling Anthony's corpse. While others were busily running up and down the corridor, screaming out for assistance from the appropriate personnel and trying to secure the area, Detective Brown weaved through them, frantically searching his pockets for his phone which kept vibrating.

He didn't notice Cardillo leaning against the door to Room 2, watching him as he walked by. The young rookie could tell his partner hadn't yet listened to his voicemail, because he hadn't mentioned it. He was nervous and unsure of how Brown would react once he heard the message and found out about Seidman's connection to Chinnah. Would this ruin his newfound relationship with the Jewish detective? Will everything that Seidman promised him fade into forgotten words? He wouldn't have much in the way of money to look forward to if the voicemail opened Brown's eyes to what was actually going on in that neighborhood. Maybe the message would be hard to hear. Maybe it was erased. Cardillo bit off a curse then sighed aloud. Then, as if a whiff of the Italian's warm breath had blown across the back of his neck, Brown suddenly stopped and looked over his shoulders to catch the rookie staring at him with a worrisome look on his face.

The senior detective started to say something but was cut short when his phone began vibrating again. He turned back, dug in his pocket and then finding his cell phone, he pulled it out. Noticing there were three missed calls from his partner and a voicemail, he tapped the screen, lifted it to his ear, and listened.

Anxiety rose in Cardillo's throat and the hallway became a hundred degrees warmer. For the moment Brown was quiet as he listened, his thick lips tight together. Then his eyes went wide, and his mouth shot open with surprise. He spun on his heels to look at his partner who was standing with his back rigid, jaw clenched and apologetic eyes fixed back on him. Brown wasn't sure what to do or what to say. It all made sense now. Suddenly all the broken pieces came together in his mind to form a clear picture. A cry of frailty and rage echoed up through his regrets and drove itself into his brain. With everything that had taken place over the last few days, he knew he wasn't left with much of a choice.

Just as he made his decision of what to do, the door to Room 1 flew open, and Seidman walked out. His attention was immediately drawn to his two colleagues who were standing idle in the corridor staring aimlessly at him. All three men were still for several moments as waves of blue uniforms swept pass them. There was a silent promise in Detective Seidman's eyes that wasn't lost on Cardillo, a confidential gesture of the position the rookie longed for in his career and in life. A covenant to always place his people—their people—above all others from now until their families were safe and financially secure or until the savages were either dead or in jail.

Without warning, Cardillo turned away from Brown and made his way down the hallway in the opposite direction, saying not a word. The Italian disappeared among the scampering crowd of officers, his identity being washed away by the sea of white faces.

Certain that no problems would come from Cardillo, and that he had the Italian on his side, Seidman removed his attention from him then cast a stern, questioning gaze toward Buck Brown. "Brown. Buck. Is everything ok—brother? We're still good with not charging our little friend in there? Right?"

Brown stood staring, motionless, and rigid. His mouth slowly crept open, and his lips began to move, forming words. Words he knew he would one day regret. Almost soundless words—cowardly words—words that burned with each breath as he uttered, "Yep. We are all square—brother. No need for throwing out the baby with the bath water."

50624529R00214

Made in the USA
Columbia, SC
15 February 2019